RISE OF THE THRALL LORD
RAIDERS OF THE DARK COAST

BOOK THREE

F.P. SPIRIT

Thanks to Tim for creating the world of Thac, and to Daniel, Eric, Jeff, John, Mark, and Matt for their roles in bringing the characters to life. Also, thanks to the rest of my friends and family who gave their time and support in the creation of this book.

BOOKS BY F.P. SPIRIT

The Heroes of Ravenford

Ruins on Stone Hill

Serpent Cult

Dark Monolith

Princess of Lanfor

The Baron's Heart

Rise of the Thrall Lord

City of Tears

Protectors of Penwick

Raiders of the Dark Coast

TABLE OF CONTENTS

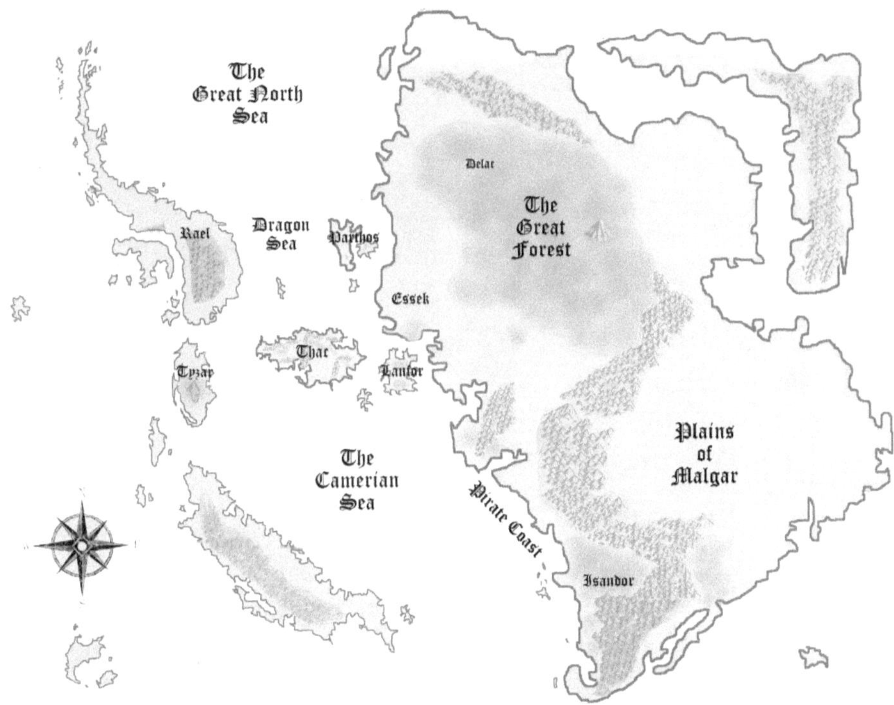

The Shin Tauri blade is perhaps one of the most powerful weapons ever crafted. Forged from cold iron by the master blacksmith, Tauriyama, numerous great runes of power had been painstakingly etched along its length. The legendary hero, Tibarn, wielded the weapon in the most decisive battle of the Thrall Wars. With it he drove the mightiest of all demons, along with its armies, back into the Abyss from whence it came. For ages it was thought the blade resided in the shrine at Tibarn's ancestral home. Only recently the truth surfaced, that the blade had gone missing along with its master over a century ago…

- Lady Lara Stealle, High Wizard of Penwick

1
ACROSS THE SEA

*I don't mind the longer trip. I'm in no hurry to see
her royal highness.*

The mid-morning sun shone brightly in the sky ahead as the *Cloud Hammer* sailed across the open seas. Golden fingers of sunlight glistened across the blue waters far below as if beckoning the ship toward the eastern horizon.

One of the newest additions to the Penwick Royal Navy, the *Cloud Hammer* appeared similar to a seafaring vessel, yet no masts or sails stood upon its wide wooden decks. Instead, a pulsing ring of bright blue energy encircled the three fins that jutted from the stern of the vessel. The magic of a great air elemental powered the ring, but that alone could not keep the large ship aloft. The hull itself made that possible. Constructed from a sacred grove of Arcarion trees, the special wood was laced with mana and made the ship lighter than air.

Captain Pallas Stealle leaned against the rail at the prow of the *Cloud Hammer*, staring out absently at the seas ahead. He knew he should be focused on the mission before them. A lot more rode on it than just an alliance between Penwick and Lanfor. The fate of their entire world might in fact lay in the balance. However, try as he might, his mind kept wandering back to the same image—a dazzling smile and deep green eyes framed by silken tresses of coppery-colored hair.

Alys Dunamal had been traipsing around Pallas ever since she was a gangly young girl. Though shallow and flighty in her youth, Alys had grown in many ways since then. Now a vivacious and driven young woman, she proved to be capable in battle as well. In fact, she had even saved Pallas when his own carelessness nearly got him killed.

Just before Pallas left on this journey, the two of them kissed for the very first time. Enamored with the fiery young lady, he promised to resume their relationship upon his return. Due to the critical nature of their mission, he had thought to push all else aside for the time being. However, that was proving to be far more difficult than he imagined.

"A copper piece for your thoughts," a familiar voice sounded behind him.

Pallas nearly jumped out of his skin. A glance over his shoulder confirmed that the voice belonged to his sister Thea. She met his gaze evenly, her pale blue eyes dancing with amusement.

Thea Stealle exuded an almost angelic presence between the pristine white robes she wore and her porcelain skin with just a hint of freckles. Regardless, at just three years her senior, Pallas had spent a good portion of his life at the receiving end of her sharp tongue and quick wit.

The corner of Pallas' mouth lifted ever so slightly. "Is it me, or were you practicing some sort of stealth technique?"

As a spiritblade, Pallas could typically sense the aura of someone as they drew near. Yet his sister had also studied those arts, one of them being the masking of one's own aura.

Thea drew up next to him at the rail and pushed back a lock of long brown hair that swept down well past her shoulders. "It wasn't anything I did. You appeared lost in thought." The amusement in her eyes traveled to her lips. "Perhaps it had something to do with a certain mutual redheaded friend?"

Pallas' cheeks grew hot as the blood rushed to them. Alys and Thea had been close friends since their early teens. They had been nearly inseparable before the fatal incident at Thorn Isle. Afterwards, Alys had been sent away, not to return into their lives until just recently.

Apparently satisfied with the response she elicited, Thea chose not to press the subject any further. "Mutual friends aside, I must admit I'm surprised that you left Penwick at all—especially with everything going on back there."

Pallas grimaced. Ever since the death and destruction of the pirate raids, he had sworn to protect their city. He had pushed himself to his limits and beyond learning the art of the spiritblade and climbing the ranks of the Penwick navy. Yet, none of that had quite prepared him for the invasion of their city by a pack of vampires. If it hadn't been for Lloyd and his newfound friends, Penwick might have been overrun before they could stop the fiends. Much as Pallas hated to admit it, his kid brother had been better prepared to handle the situation than he himself.

Pallas cocked his head to one side and shrugged. "I wasn't exactly given much choice. Alburg suggested I act as courier to Lanfor and Caverinus agreed. It's kind of hard to say no to both the Master of Coin and the Baron of Penwick."

Thea wore a wicked grin as she elbowed him in the side. "You wouldn't want to upset your future father-in-law, either."

"Hmph," Pallas snorted. "Alburg being Alys' father had nothing to do with my decision. It was my duty, nothing more." A sly look crossed his face as he reached around her shoulders and gave her a rough squeeze. "You on the other hand, sis, chose to come of your own free will."

Thea peered out over the seas ahead, a closemouthed laugh emanating from inside her throat. "Not exactly. A good part of me thought it my duty to stay in Penwick, but the High Priestess convinced me that I was being *shortsighted*." She turned her head to meet his gaze, her expression darkening. "This business with the demons and those towers—if someone doesn't do something about it soon, our entire world could go up in flames."

"That's why we need those rune scrolls," another voice said from not too far behind them.

This time Pallas had sensed someone approaching—two some-ones in fact. He and Thea turned about to find Donnie and Elladan walking across the foredeck towards them.

The two elves were like night and day. Donatello, or Donnie as his friends called him, was a wiry fellow with sandy blonde hair, pale blue eyes, and boyish good looks. Yet the baby-faced elf was far from innocent. He looked the part of a pirate with his puffy white shirt, brown vest, pants, and long boots. He also seemed to know far more about the Dark Coast than any outsider should.

In stark contrast to Donnie, Elladan was of a medium build with tightly-combed jet black hair and dark soulful eyes. Dressed almost exclusively in white, the elven bard was a talented performer. His smooth mannerisms and velvet voice were perfect for the stage, but he was far too handsome for Pallas' taste—a fact exacerbated by his sister's apparent interest in the elf.

"With demon slaying weapons we'd stand half a chance," Donnie continued his point.

"Donnie's right," Elladan added with a dramatic wave of his hands. "The Shin Tauri blade was a powerful rune sword. In the hands of the legendary warrior Tibarn, it proved a match for even the Lord of All Demons."

Pallas folded his arms across his chest and fixed the elf with a cynical stare. "While I agree that rune weapons are of the utmost importance, I don't think anyone short of my father could live up to the legend of Tibarn."

Elladan pursed his lips together and bobbed his head from side to side. "I wouldn't be too sure about that. I've seen Cyclone bury that overgrown hatchet of his in the hide of more than one dragon."

"And I wouldn't go selling your brother short either," Donnie said with a toothy grin. "He's felled everything from giant snakes to golems and dragons ever since I met him."

"Gentlemen, let's not get ahead of ourselves," Thea chided the three of them. She stepped into their midst and swept her gaze around them all. "First we need to find those scrolls. After that we can talk about making weapons and who will wield them."

Pallas unfolded his arms, a thin laugh escaping his lips. "You're right as usual, sis."

A sudden deep rumbling sound disrupted their conversation. Pallas arched an eyebrow at Thea, then led the way as the four of them crossed to the opposite rail. Down below on the main deck, the dragon Calipherous appeared to be having a discussion with two of the three Greymantle sisters.

Sprawled across the deck of the *Cloud Hammer* like some impossibly large cat, warm coppery scales covered most of the dragon's body. Small spots of teal blue accented those scales here and there, while its great bat-like wings lay folded down close to its torso. The dragon's large horned head rose up on its serpentine neck as it conversed with Ves and Ruka.

"It would have been much faster if we flew to Lanfor on our own," Cal rumbled in his deep voice.

Ruka leaned back on one foot and smirked up at the stodgy dragon. "I don't mind the longer trip. I'm in no hurry to see her *royal highness*." The sandy haired, emerald-eyed teen was the middle child of the Greymantles sisters. True to form, Ruka had the same temperament as Thea, right down to her acerbic tongue and stubborn nature.

Seemingly disquieted, Ves wrapped her arms around herself. "So how long will it take this ship to get to Lanfor?" The eldest of the three sisters, the golden-haired, green-blue eyed young lady seemed far more sensible and even-tempered than Ruka. In fact, in that respect she reminded Pallas much of himself.

"The Captain told me it will take about two days to cross the Merchant's Channel," Pallas called down to them.

The Queen herself had requested the Greymantles presence in Lanfor. The others had chosen to accompany them in hopes of pinpointing the location of the rune scrolls. According to Ruka, the Queen of Lanfor had a vast spy network up and down the coast. If anyone could point them in the right direction it would be her.

Cal, Ves, and Ruka turned their gaze towards Pallas and the others as they descended the stairs to the main deck. Ves pursed her lips together as she cast an eye up at Cal. "That's not really that much longer to wait."

"I suppose you're right," Cal rumbled with only a mild hint of irritation.

Ves moved closer to the dragon and rubbed her hand across the smaller scales along the bottom side of his neck. Cal purred like a kitten in response. Thea strode up next to Ves and joined her in soothing the stuffy copper dragon.

"So what's Lanfor like?" Thea asked as she rubbed the dragon's scales.

Cal made a deep rumbling noise as he cleared his enormous throat. "Haroom, hum—well, the isle of Lanfor itself is about a quarter of the size of Thac, but it has been one nation since Flandril Farbican the First reunited the splintered kingdom in AF-726…"

Ruka stretched her arms wide and interrupted the dragon with a loud yawn. "Cal, she didn't ask for a history lesson."

Cal swiveled his head toward her and tilted it to one side. "But how does one truly know a place without knowing its history?"

Ruka's face contorted into a rueful grimace. "Well if you're going to bore everyone to death, count me out." With that the teen spun on her heel and marched off toward the other end of the ship.

Cal sighed as he watched her go. "Alas, some folks have no appreciation for knowledge."

Ves gently patted the dragon's neck, her voice filled with sympathy. "It's alright Cal. We understand." She took a breath, her tone growing tentative. "Still, in fairness, they probably don't need to know everything that happened in Lanfor since Farbican the First."

Cal peered down at her with a hurt look. "Not you too?"

Pallas had no idea that dragons could be so expressive. He genuinely felt sorry for Cal. After all, he was only trying to help. The young man cleared his throat and attempted to mollify the dragon's feelings. "Ahem, I do know a little bit about Lanfor history. For instance, their war with Parthos predated the one in Thac. That altercation ended with the death of both King Flandril and the Parthian's 'God-Emperor'."

Cal shifted his gaze to Pallas, the dragon's eyes widening. "That is correct, young man." He sounded both surprised and pleased. "Afterwards, since no heir could pass the trials of the Amber Mount, Queen Amerelis ascended to the throne."

"I'm not well versed in Lanfor lore." Elladan admitted. "What exactly is this Amber Mount?"

Pallas was surprised by the bard's admission. In the short time he had known him, Elladan had interjected his thoughts on just about everything. Pallas found it refreshing to find something the bard did not profess to know about.

"Ah," Cal rumbled with apparent relish, "that's the mountain temple that holds the tombs of all the Farbican ancestors. Any heir that seeks the throne must enter the temple complex and pass the ancestral trial. Yet, none has to this day and thus Queen Amerelis still holds the throne."

Pallas let out a low whistle. "That's over three hundred years. Is the Queen immortal?"

"Hmm," Cal murmured. "Not that I am aware of. She does, however, have access to powerful magic. I assume she has used that to prolong her life while waiting for a worthy heir."

"Fair enough." Pallas shrugged.

Thea, not to be outdone by her brother, expounded on what she knew of Lanfor history. "If memory serves me right, not everyone is happy with the Queen. In fact, there have been at least a couple of rebellions since the beginning of her reign."

"Yes, um, that is true," Cal responded in a measured tone. The dragon's eyes strayed to Ves who had visibly paled at Thea's comments.

Thea followed the dragon's gaze and immediately bit her tongue. "Did I say something wrong?"

Ves gave her a wan smile and slowly shook her head. "No, it's nothing you did. It's just—a friend of mine died in the last rebellion."

The deck grew quiet at her dire pronouncement. An awful feeling of déjà vu swept over Pallas. His vision clouded as vivid images flashed through his mind from six years ago.

Four youths lay still on the rocky ground beneath his feet. A slim figure with long brown hair and vacant blue eyes stared up at him. Next to her lay a gangly armed youth with copper tresses and a freckled face bereft of its dazzling smile.

Pallas' heart hammered in his chest. It was all he could do to keep himself from shaking.

While Pallas wrestled with his inner demons, Thea appeared mortified. "I'm so sorry," she said in a soft voice. She went over to Ves and wrapped her arms around the sullen young woman. When she pulled back, Pallas could see tears in both women's eyes.

"Were you very close?" Thea asked in a hushed voice.

"Shandi sacrificed herself to save my life," Ves responded with a deep sigh.

Pallas understood that all too well. He would easily have sacrificed his own life to save his sister and her friends from their untimely deaths. Though they had been resurrected, not every soul came back. Even when they did, they were never the same as evidenced by his sister's sudden decision to join the clergy.

Thea pulled Ves into a close embrace. She held onto her as silent tears dripped down the young woman's face.

"Haroom," Cal cleared his throat once more. When the dragon spoke, his tone was surprisingly low. "That is how we came to know the Farbicans. After Shandillis' sacrifice, Ves' parents flew to Lanfor and helped the Queen crush the rebellion."

Thea grasped Ves by the shoulders and looked her directly in the eye. "You cannot blame yourself for what happened. You were young and what this Shandillis did was truly selfless."

"Yeah, it's hard to believe she was related to Anya," Donnie interjected glibly.

"Donnie!" Elladan smacked his fellow elf in the arm.

Though obviously trying to lighten the mood, Donnie's comment was ill timed at best. For once Pallas agreed with Elladan.

The slight elf drew back and winced. "What? It's true."

Ves pulled away from Thea and gave Donnie the thinnest of smiles. "It's quite alright. Donatello is not wrong. Though she is of the royal line, Princess Anya's behavior has been quite inexcusable."

Her statement left Pallas feeling bewildered. He had heard rumors of the Princess Anya of Lanfor cruising about Thac in her royal airship, but little else. "Pardon me for asking, but how so?"

"You mean besides nearly burying us beneath the Golem Master's monolith?" Elladan answered for Ves, sounding quite agitated.

Pallas' jaw dropped open. "The princess did that?"

"Even worse," Elladan went on, his agitation growing as he spoke. "She kidnapped Ves and tried to turn her into one of her dragon zombies."

Pallas stared at him in stark disbelief. He and his siblings had been raised to believe in *noblesse oblige*, that their responsibilities to the people far outweighed the privileges of rank. While not naïve to the fact that many nobles abused their power, it went against every fiber of his being.

A slight grin spread across Donnie's face as he elbowed his friend in the side. "Come on, Elladan. We know that's not the real reason you're still mad at Anya."

The bard turned and glared at his fellow elf causing Donnie to break out into fits of laughter.

Pallas eyed the two curiously. There was obviously some sort of inside joke going on between them. Mirroring his thoughts, Thea placed her hands on her hips and swept her gaze from one to the other. "Are we missing something?"

Still chuckling, Donnie explained his reaction to her. "When we first met Anya, she turned Elladan into a little fluffy bunny. She walked around with him in her arms for almost an hour before turning him back."

Elladan continued to glare at his friend until Thea placed a hand on his arm. "I bet you were a handsome rabbit."

Elladan's angry demeanor swiftly melted off his face. Pallas, on the other hand, felt the sudden urge to vomit. Stifling the feeling, he swiftly changed the subject. "Ahem, so Ves, if you don't mind my asking, what were you doing in Lanfor at the time?"

Her previous pallor all but gone, Ves returned his gaze with an earnest stare. "I was studying ecclesiastics at the temple in the Greystone Halls."

Once again, Cal expanded on Ves' answer. "Palt is a vast center of culture, knowledge, and magic. Nothing exemplifies that more than the Greystone Halls. Not only do they house the largest library this side of the world, but the temple complex provides ecclesiastical studies of all the gods, and its deep vaults house magic artifacts of unimaginable power."

Pallas had to admit that did sound quite impressive. The others seemed to think so as well.

Donnie glanced at Elladan and whistled. "Glo is going to really regret not coming with us."

Elladan chuckled. "You're probably right."

Donnie's eyes widened as if struck with a sudden idea. He wagged a finger at his friend. "You know, maybe you should consider dropping off the contents of your portal bag there."

Elladan pressed his lips together and nodded. "There are a few things in there that would be better off not seeing the light of day ever again."

Thea frowned at him. "Just what do you have in there?"

Elladan and Donnie exchange a guilty glance. "Just a few evil artifacts we collected along the way," Elladan admitted in a soft voice.

Thea's hands went back to her hips, her tone accusatory. "Why would you hold onto something like that?"

Pallas had been the brunt of his sister's temper more times than he could count. If it were anyone else but the bard, he would feel sorry for them.

"Well," Elladan stammered, "there never seemed like a good time—or good place—to get rid of any of it."

Bad choice of words there, friend, Pallas thought to himself. Knowing what was coming next, he now did feel sorry for the elf.

Thea took in a sharp breath, her face darkening. Yet she didn't immediately lash out at the bard. When she did speak, however, there was a dangerous edge to her voice. "You do know I'm a Priestess of Arenor—you know, the God of *Light?*"

Elladan's face had gone completely ashen. He opened his mouth to speak, but no words came out.

The sudden turn of events should have filled Pallas with glee.

Though, much as he disliked Elladan, even he did not deserve the full extent of his sister's wrath.

Pallas nearly stepped in at that point, but Ves beat him to it. She laced her arm through Thea's and gave her a gentle tug. "Well then, you're just going to love the Greystone Halls. People come from all over the world to study and worship there." Thea's anger swiftly faded as Ves described the temple within the Halls. Engrossed in their conversation, the young lady led the priestess away across the deck.

"Whew." Elladan sighed once the two were out of earshot.

Donnie nudged him in the arm. "Dodged a bullet there my friend."

Elladan glowered back at the slight elf. "Yeah, no thanks to you."

Donnie shrugged and grinned. "What are friends for?"

"You're incorrigible," Elladan groaned at first then finally laughed.

Donnie shrugged and flashed his friend a bright smile. "I do my best."

Pallas could see he was going to have his hands full on this trip with these two. He gazed at the dragon with a plaintive stare. Cal locked eyes with him for a few moments, then tilted his head to one side and let out a deep rumbling laugh.

2
HEIR TO THE BLADE

Aldurin charged me with finding the Shin Tauri blade. It will be sorely needed in the days to come.

Morning had broken two days later when a large land mass appeared on the eastern horizon. At the same time, storm clouds emerged to the south. Frequent bolts of lightning flashed amidst those dark clouds, revealing the storm to be massive. Elladan Narmolanya had traveled far and wide across eastern Thac, visiting most of its cities and ports. Nevertheless, in all his one hundred and fifteen years, he had never seen anything like it.

Donnie leaned nonchalantly on the rail beside him. Nearly as old as Elladan himself, the slim elf had alluded to having spent time along this coast. Elladan decided to put his friend's knowledge to the test. Nudging the elf in the shoulder, Elladan pointed out the strange phenomena. "What in Arinthar is that thing?"

Donnie winked and gave him a sparkling grin. "That, my friend, is what 'coasters' refer to as the Vortex."

As a bard, Elladan was well versed in not just music, but many diverse subjects. Geography and history in particular were two of his favorite areas of study. Yet despite all that, he had never heard or read of this 'Vortex'.

Elladan stared with keen interest at the tall clouds massed along the southern horizon. "Is it some kind of local phenomena?"

Never one to miss the chance to tell a good story, Donnie stood and launched into a colorful tale. "There's nothing else quite like it in the rest of the world. Legend has it two identical storms formed after the fall of the Baleful Moon." Donnie made two fists and held them apart. "Their great winds drew the storms side by side"—he brought his hands within an inch of each other— "and they have been locked in a perpetual dance ever since." The slim elf finished his narrative by spinning each of his fists around the other.

"That's some story," Elladan acknowledged, admiring it almost as much as his friend's presentation. "Any truth to it?"

Donnie shrugged and went back to leaning against the rail. "Who knows—but the storms are real, I can tell you that."

"So that's the infamous vortex," a male voice sounded behind them.

Elladan glanced over his shoulder to see both Pallas and Thea approaching. The bard immediately spun about and executed a formal bow.

"Good morning, Thea." Her name rolled off his tongue with a sensation that warmed his insides.

Elladan had been smitten with the young lady ever since they first met. It was not some kind of schoolboy crush though. Elladan had known far too many women to be that naïve. No, aside from her obvious beauty, Thea had a razor sharp wit, and a strong personality to match. She was also extremely knowledgeable. Elladan found all those qualities in one person quite hard to resist.

"Good morning, Elladan," Thea responded, her serious expression tempered by the glint of mirth in her eyes.

"Elladan," Pallas echoed his name flatly along with a curt nod.

The eldest of the Stealle siblings, Pallas walked about with a distinct chip on his shoulder. Try as he might, Elladan just couldn't seem to break the ice with him. Alys Dunamal appeared to be the only one to have broken through his defenses. Somehow, the fiery redhead had managed to melt Pallas' stone cold heart.

Once their morning greetings were done, Thea peered past them toward the storms on the horizon. "Just how far away is that?"

Donnie placed a hand on his chin as he mulled over her question. "I'd have to say about two hundred to two hundred and fifty miles."

Elladan let out a low whistle. "If we can see them at this distance, they must be huge!"

Pallas strode past them and planted his hands on the rail, his eyes fixed on the giant storms. "I hear it's a thousand mile trip just to circumvent the whole thing."

Elladan followed his gaze with a begrudging smile. "That's one heck of a detour. It must wreak havoc on shipping."

Donnie strode up beside Pallas and pointed a finger toward the center of the Vortex. "There's a tight channel between the two storms. Experienced navigators have been known to 'thread the needle' of the Vortex, so to speak."

"You mean crazy navigators," Elladan snorted, certain no one in their right mind would make such a journey.

Pallas, on the other hand, disagreed with his assessment. "I could see it—with a fast ship and a good navigator."

Thea strode up beside her brother and punched him lightly in the arm. "Just don't go getting any ideas."

Pallas fixed her with an incredulous stare. "Me? You know me better than that. Plus, what would be the point? After all, we have an airship."

A few hours later, the land mass before them had spread across the eastern horizon. A long peninsula jutted out from it with a lighthouse standing at the cliffs on its very edge. The four of them gathered at the starboard rail to gaze at the tall structure as they flew past. Judging from the size of the lighthouse, the lantern inside must have been as large as a person.

"That's Phobas Light," Cal informed them as they drew within a few hundred yards of the towering structure.

"After the original God of Light," Thea murmured, her tone one of awe.

Elladan had to admit, it was a rather impressive sight. The four of them continued to admire Phobas Light as the *Cloud Hammer* crossed from the open seas to the wide bay beyond. Even so, despite the remarkable nature of the structure, it did not adequately prepare them for their first glimpse of the city of Palt.

With the lighthouse receding behind them, the foursome moved up to the foredeck. The silhouette of a jagged skyline towered over the shore at the other end of the bay. At first, Elladan mistook it for a range of mountains, but as they drew closer, he realized those lines were far too smooth to be natural. Dozens of tall shapes marked that skyline, some squared, some rounded, and others rising to a single point.

His jaw dropped as the realization struck him. "That's a city!"

In Elladan's travels, he had visited his share of large cities. He'd even been to Lymerdia, the capital of Thac. Yet the cityscape that lay before them dwarfed all those in comparison.

Shading her eyes, Thea let out a stifled gasp. "It must be at least twice the size of Penwick!"

Pallas nudged his sister in the arm. "If you think that's huge, check out the seaport."

Dozens of docks jutted out from the base of the city where the shore met the bay. Ships of all sizes and shapes sat moored at those piers. Many others approached from the bay waters below, but appeared to be stopped at a line of vessels displaying the gold and purple of Lanfor.

"I wonder what all that's about?" Elladan said, pointing at the queue of waiting ships.

Pallas raised an eyebrow as he followed Elladan's gaze. "It appears to be some sort of blockade."

Donnie leaned over the rail and squinted at the blockade below. "They look to be boarding and searching each ship."

"I wonder what they do about airships?" Elladan mused aloud.

"I think your answer is headed this way," Thea said, motioning toward the city.

A group of dots had appeared in the sky between them and Palt. As Elladan watched, the dots grew in size. Whatever they were, the entire group was headed this way.

Donnie strode over to the back rail and called down to the main deck, "We've got company!"

In response to his cry, Cal's large head rose up over the rail. "Where?" the dragon rumbled.

Donnie pointed in the direction of the city. Cal lifted his head even further, his great eyes narrowing as he peered past the slight elf. "Hmm, they appear to be riders."

"What are they riding?" Ves asked as she and Ruka ascended the stairs to the foredeck.

Cal narrowed his eyes even more. "I believe they are those long boards the Queen had magically outfitted for flight."

"Oh, that sounds like fun," a young voice gushed. A little girl with long golden-blonde hair, bright blue eyes, and big dimples accompanied Ves and Ruka. Maya was the youngest of the Greymantle sisters, her appearance that of an eight year old human child. She twirled out in front of her sisters, her little pinafore swishing about as she spun in circles.

"Not as much fun as flying on your own power," a gruff voice said from behind the three sisters. A muscular young man with short brown hair and intense blue eyes appeared at the top stairs. Once a fierce dragon hunter, Cyclone had turned into something more—a powerful ally and slayer of any creature that worshipped the dark.

"I hear that," Ruka acknowledged, the corner of her mouth lifting upward.

The group gathered at the bow of the foredeck as the longboard riders approached. Elladan counted thirty in all, each balancing in a low crouch across an orange textured wooden board. Affixed to the center of each board sat a brilliantly glowing blue orb. An aura of energy emanated from it, encircling the board in a manner similar to the great ring that propelled the *Cloud Hammer* through the air.

The riders fanned out as they reached the ship, circling about like bees around a nest. Elladan noted the purple helmets and uniforms with golden shoulder pads, buttons, and stripes—once again the colors of Lanfor.

A flier wearing captain's stripes drew up to the railing and hovered there. Interestingly, the rider appeared no more than three feet tall with a black shortsword strapped to his back. Beneath his helmet Elladan spied a youthful face that reminded him of Aksel.

"State your name and business," the captain said with an obvious edge to his voice.

Ves stepped forward and spoke for the group. "I am Vestiralanna Greymantle and these are my friends and family. We wish an audience with the Queen."

The captain peered around the group, his eyes momentarily resting on Cal. His gaze then returned to Ves, his small shoulders visibly relaxing. "Greymantle? Alright. We have standing orders to bring you to the Queen."

Ves responded with a polite smile. "Very good."

The captain hesitated a moment as he swept his eyes around the ship. "Unfortunately, foreign airships aren't allowed over the city at this time, but we can fly you to the palace."

Ruka folded her arms across her chest and snorted. "That's an interesting way to treat your guests."

The captain met her gaze and shrugged. "Sorry. It's the Queen's orders."

Elladan had to agree with Ruka. Something wasn't quite right here in Lanfor. In spite of that, he didn't think it wise to start an argument with thirty armed airborne troops.

Thankfully Ves had more tact than her sister. "There will be no need, Captain. We can fly ourselves without this airship. You may escort us, however, if you wish."

The captain shrugged again. "Suit yourself."

Pallas went to instruct the crew to park the ship back at the lighthouse while Ves, Ruka, and Maya shifted into their dragon forms. The rest of the group then climbed atop the dragons, all except for Cyclone who sprouted wings of his own. The hunter had only recently discovered this strange new ability. At first it only happened when he was enraged, but since then he seemed to have mastered the talent.

They all then took off in the direction of Palt flanked on either side by half the longboard riders. The other half escorted the *Cloud Hammer* back toward Phobas Light. Seated on Ves' back behind

Donnie, Elladan got a better view of the harbor as it passed beneath them. Nearly half of the ships moored at the docks appeared to be warships. It looked as if Lanfor was readying for war. Though it explained their cold reception to foreigners, it still didn't answer the question of whom they expected to war against.

Once the fliers reached the city proper, Elladan got a better look at Palt. Tall buildings stretched out as far as the eye could see, some rectangular, others domed, and still others with lofty spires. Their style denoted classical architecture with smooth flowing lines and a polished elegance. Interspersed between the buildings grew lush parks and gardens full of flowers, adding a touch of nature and color to the vast metropolis.

As they swung southward, Elladan's gaze came to rest on a tall mountain. As they drew nearer, his eyes settled on the great palace that stood on its flat summit. Long battlements and wide towers comprised its thick outer wall. Multiple structures rose inside, each as large, or larger than, the keep in Penwick. Yet one structure in particular stood out from the rest.

Donnie seemed to recognize it as well. He peered at Elladan over his shoulder. "Is that what I think it is?"

Elladan pressed his lips together and nodded. "I believe so."

A tall tower rose behind the building in the very center of the palace grounds. It appeared to be identical to the one they had wrested from the Empress in the City of Tears.

"That is the Amber Tower of the Queen," Ves confirmed for them.

Elladan looked intently at the tower. It was one of the six the demons sought. Despite the midday sun, he noticed a golden glow at the very top. In contrast, the tower in the marshes had shone with a dark purple.

The dragons and their entourage flew over the tall battlements and landed in a wide area in the center of the palace grounds. The riders disembarked, all save the captain who landed with them. Numerous stone dragon statues encircled the area. As the sisters shifted back to human form, Elladan examined the inscription at the base of the largest statue. It said *Welcome* in Draconic, the native language of dragons.

The captain removed his helmet to reveal a head of copper-red hair, the pointed tips of his gnomish ears peeking out from beneath those locks. He spoke a single word to his board and it rose by itself to hover behind him. He then motioned for the rest of them to follow. "This way."

Everyone fell in behind the captain except for Cal who chose to remain outside. Per his previous command, the rider's board floated along a few feet behind him. Once again, Elladan's eyes strayed to the black shortsword on the gnome's back. "That's a very beautiful sword you have there."

The captain glanced over his shoulder at the sword, then peered at Elladan. "Ragnarök says *thank you.*"

The statement caught Elladan by surprise. "Your sword's sentient?"

The captain shrugged once more. "When it wants to be."

Not far behind them, Ruka snickered. "Sounds just like Inazuma."

Ruka also possessed a sentient sword, one that could shoot bolts of lightning at will. Though Elladan had never actually seen the spirit of the sword, they had all heard its voice at one time or another.

The captain led them across the well-manicured lawn up to the main palace. Though not much taller than the keep in Penwick, this building appeared to be twice its size. Made of a similar alabaster stone, it stood four stories in most places, though some sections rose a few stories higher. For all that, no area of the palace stood taller than the Amber Tower.

As they reached the top of the stairs, the large double doors opened before them. Strangely, no one stood behind either door. It was as if they opened of their own volition.

Donnie leaned over and whispered in Elladan's ear. "That's not creepy at all."

Elladan fixed his friend with a sour look. "You just had to say that."

"This way," the captain said, ushering them inside.

Elladan exchanged one last irritated glance with Donnie, then followed the captain into the palace.

Seishin sat quietly in the hall outside the Queen's audience chamber. The room itself was lavish to a fault. A plush gold and purple carpet lay across the center of the floor. Tall lancet-shaped windows lined one wall opposite a rather large hearth. Elegant chandeliers hung from the ceiling, the brilliant rays of the midday sun reflecting off their crystalline prisms.

Floor length tapestries hung between the windows, each inscribed with the heraldic of Lanfor, a rearing gold dragon on a background of royal purple. Various portraits decorated the walls. One in particular was a large mural that depicted a knight in pure golden armor. The knight sat astride a golden dragon facing off against an entire host of enemies.

Seishin had spent these last few days seated on a bench opposite that mural, waiting for his turn at an audience with the Queen. A variety of folks waited there with him, along with two soldiers that guarded her chamber, and a secretary seated at the desk beside them. To date, none of those waiting there had been allowed in to see the Queen.

This unexpected delay had taken its toll on Seishin's nerves. He just had to meet with her. He had traveled too far and given up too much only to fail now. If he did, everyone he ever loved would be lost in the terror that was about to descend upon their world.

In the midst of his exasperation, the words of his uncle came to him unbidden. *Patience is a gift. Do not fight it. Only then will you see what it has to offer.*

Seishin took in a deep breath and let it out slowly. As usual, his uncle's words were cryptic. Despite That, he resolved to be more patient, though he was beginning to doubt it would gain him his audience.

Not five minutes later, the outside doors to the hall swung open. A curious group of strangers strode through them led by one of the sky riders that he had seen patrolling the city. Behind the rider came three blonde ladies. Garbed in a shimmering bronze dress, the first carried herself quite regally, despite the fact that she looked to be no older than Seishin himself. The second appeared to be a young teen in black leathers wearing a decided smirk on her lips. The last was a little girl in a cute white pinafore with the biggest dimples he had ever seen.

A grim-faced, muscular young man with short brown hair and a sleeveless blue longcoat followed the three ladies. After him came a slightly older gentleman dressed in a bright red officer's uniform. His long brown hair did little to hide the man's stoic expression. A brunette priestess in pristine white robes accompanied the officer. She had an almost angelic air about her that put Seishin oddly at ease.

A pair of elves were the last to enter. The first was an extremely handsome fellow with jet black hair dressed almost exclusively in white. His sandy-haired companion had a boyish face and wore an outfit strikingly similar to the pirates from down the coast.

The Queen's secretary rose from his desk, and came forth to greet these strange newcomers. The sky rider gestured to three blonde ladies. "The Greymantle sisters are here to see the Queen as requested."

The regal young lady cleared her throat and addressed the secretary. "And our friends as well."

A pained expression crossed the secretary's face. "I'm sorry, but I was only told to present the Greymantle sisters to the Queen."

The young lady folded her arms across her chest, her tone adamant. "Tell her majesty it is either all of us, or none of us."

"None sounds good to me," the teen in black leathers commented, her smirk widening ever so slightly.

The secretary hesitated, his eyes flickering from the regal young lady to the sarcastic teen and back again. Finally, he gave them a curt nod. "Very well, I will ask."

He turned his attention to the sky rider. "Captain Cloud, accompany me if you please. I'm sure the Queen would like to hear your report."

Cloud frowned for a moment, then shrugged. "Alright, but there's not much to tell." He followed the Queen's secretary to the doors to the audience chamber. The soldiers let the two of them pass, then closed the doors after them, and resumed their guard positions.

A number of folks rose from their seats and went to complain to the soldiers. Seishin knew at that moment they were wasting their breath. None of them were ever going to get in to see the Queen. Despair threatened to overtake him, but once again his uncle's words came unbidden to his mind. *The river always finds a way. If it cannot flow in one direction, it will seek another.*

A closemouthed laugh reverberated in the back of Seishin's throat. Most of his uncle's metaphors involved rivers. Yet, the thought gave him an idea. Unfortunately, it meant he would have to divulge the purpose of his mission to outsiders. After a moment's deliberation, Seishin decided he had little choice. He rose from his seat and approached the lady at the head of the strange entourage.

Seishin clasped his hands together in front of him and spoke to her in a soft voice. "Excuse me, miss."

The young lady's attention had been focused on the leather-clad teen. She now turned to face Seishin. "Yes?" she said, her expression somewhat guarded.

Seishin executed a low bow. "I am Seishin Kazari of the Kingdom of Isandor."

The young lady eyed him for a moment or two, then curtseyed in return. "Vestiralana Greymantle of the Glittering Isles." She motioned toward the teen and little girl. "These are my sisters, Rukastana and Mayattari."

Rukastana gave him a curt nod, her green eyes filled with distrust as they bore into him. Mayattari, on the other hand, curtsied as well, a dimpled smile across her cherub face. "Pleased to meet you, Mr. Kazari."

The little girl's smile was infectious. Seishin found himself kneeling down and grinning back at her. "Just Seishin, please."

"Say-shin." Mayattari repeated his name slowly. She locked eyes with him, her tone suddenly quite serious. "I like the way that sounds."

The little girl was positively delightful. "Thank you," Seishin responded, keeping his tone equally serious.

"Ahem," Vestiralana cleared her throat. "What can we do for you, Seishin?"

Seishin cast a quick glance around the room, but almost everyone else was still busy hassling the guards. Keeping his voice low, he explained his mission as succinctly as he could. "I was sent here by the Wizard Aldurin to see the Queen on a matter of great importance. The fate of the world may hang in the balance."

The elf in white eyed him dubiously. "Aldurin, the wizard from the Thrall Wars?"

"Would he even still be alive?" The officer in red added, his arms folded and his expression even more skeptical than his elven companion.

"Yes, and yes," Seishin answered both questions.

The officer still looked skeptical, but the elf in white pressed his lips together and nodded. "It is possible. Aldurin was an elf after all."

The priestess moved up next to Vestiralana, her pale blue eyes fixed on his. Seishin could feel her reaching out with her aura to probe his own. It felt almost as if she had Shin Tauri training, much like himself. He forced himself not to resist. If he were to gain their help, he needed to earn their trust first.

The priestess probed him for a few moments. It was not an unpleasant feeling. Interestingly, she did not guard herself in turn. Seishin got the distinct impression of a good and kind soul, though also one marked by adversity and hardship. Once she was finished, the priestess placed a hand on Vestiralana's arm. The two women exchanged a glance, the priestess giving the young lady a simple nod.

Vestiralana's shoulders visibly relaxed as she returned her gaze to Seishin. "You said the fate of the world might hang in the balance. Can you elucidate further?"

Seishin took another quick glance around the room. The guards were still arguing with some of the more irate folks. They seemed to be getting nowhere. Gulping down any residual misgivings, he answered her question. "According to Aldurin, demons from the Abyss are staging another invasion into our world."

Seishin paused, sweeping his eyes across the group to gauge their reaction. Strangely, none of them seemed surprised in the slightest. Though not the reaction he expected, he pressed on, nonetheless. "Aldurin charged me with finding the Shin Tauri blade. It will be sorely needed in the days to come."

"Why you?" the officer in red asked, his arms still folded across his chest.

Seishin met the man's gaze evenly, but hesitated before answering. He had asked himself that very same question when Aldurin laid the task upon him. He felt ill-qualified to handle such an important quest, but Aldurin had insisted. In the end, Seishin gave in, but it had cost him dearly.

Seishin drew his shoulders back and swept his eyes around the group. "It is because I am a direct descendant of Tibarn Kazari, the last known wielder of the Shin Tauri blade."

The sandy-haired elf elbowed his fellow elf in the shoulder. "Like I said before, the Shin Tauri blade would come in handy."

The elf in white fixed his friend with a hard look. "Shh, Donnie." He then spun his gaze to Seishin. "If that's the case, what are you doing here in Lanfor? Isn't the blade back in Isandor?"

Seishin grimaced. "I only wish that were true, but that is a falsehood propagated by the leaders of my clan. In truth, the blade disappeared with Tibarn not long after the Thrall Wars."

A few gasps escaped the group. "Well that doesn't bode well," Donnie exclaimed.

"That still doesn't answer the question why you are here in Lanfor," the officer in red pressed.

Unexpectedly, the priestess turned about and punched the officer in the arm. "Let him speak, Pallas," she said angrily.

"Fine," Pallas spat back at her without flinching.

Seishin felt somewhat heartened to have this total stranger stand up for him. He gave her a grateful nod before going on. "Aldurin received a message from the Queen saying she might have a way to find the blade. Unfortunately, I've been waiting here for days, and am no closer to getting in to see her."

Seishin ended his speech with a heavy sigh. It felt good to vent his frustrations to someone. The real question now was would it do him any good.

A number of side conversations erupted within the group. The elf in white argued with his friend, Donnie. The priestess and Pallas exchanged words with each other. At the same time, Vestiralana and Rukastana seemed to be locked in some sort of silent exchange.

It all suddenly stopped, however, when the door to the Queen's chamber suddenly swung open. The entire room fell silent as the Queen's secretary stepped out into the hall. His eyes fell on Vestiralana and he called out to her. "Her imperial majesty has agreed to see the lot of you."

Shocked expressions spread across the faces of those gathered around the guards. Seishin knew it wouldn't last long.

Seizing the moment, Vestiralana ushered her friends forward. After the last filed past her, she grabbed Seishin by the arm. Her grip was surprisingly strong. "Come along if you wish to see the Queen," she told him simply. Seishin didn't have to be told twice.

The guards pushed the rest of the folks back as the group of travelers filed though the double doors. The secretary held up a hand, however, as Vestiralana approached with Seishin.

Vestiralana met the secretary's gaze evenly. "This one too," she told him in a no nonsense tone.

The secretary opened his mouth to object, then apparently thought better of it. "Fine," he said with a simple shake of his head.

Seishin breathed a sigh of relief as he followed the strange group in to see the Queen of Lanfor.

3
QUEEN OF LANFOR

And so there it is. The end times may indeed be upon us.

Althea Kitren Stealle had been enamored with pirates as far back as she could remember. Her fascination might have stemmed from the strange circumstances surrounding her birth. During the last invasion of Penwick, the pirate warlord, Eboneye, had kidnapped her pregnant mother. Thea had been born later that day aboard his ship—the very same day the pirate clans had been driven from Penwick.

As Thea grew, she became obsessed with stories of the lost treasures of Eboneye. She and her friends spent all their free time searching around the city for clues to its whereabouts. Things came to a disastrous head when they ran afoul of pirates off the coast. They all lost their lives in that confrontation.

Though she and her friends were successfully resurrected, something drastically changed for Thea. During her brief stay in the worlds between, she met Arenor, the current God of Light. Arenor set her on the path of the divine, and four short but demanding years later, Thea became an Auric Priestess. Yet now, once again, she found herself on a quest involving pirates.

"This way, please." The Queen's secretary ushered Ves ahead of the others.

As Ves moved to the front of the group, a female voice rang out from across the Queen's chamber. "Welcome gentle souls and dragon friends. To what do I owe the honor of a visit from the Greymantles?"

The room they had entered was huge. The colors of Lanfor stood out everywhere: on the plush carpet that stretched across the white marble floor of the chamber, the intricate wall tapestries, and even the tall columns that rose to meet the cathedral ceiling. At the other end of the long carpet, a set of alabaster stairs rose to a solitary throne.

A regal figure sat upon that throne peering down at them. Queen Amerelis Farbican looked to be not much older than Ves. Garbed in a shimmering ankle-length golden gown, long, wavy flaxen locks flowed down from beneath her jewel-encrusted crown to well below her bare shoulders. Flawless porcelain skin and a slim figure added to that illusion. Yet there was a depth to her crystal blue eyes that belied the image, a deepness that spoke of pain and anguish far beyond her apparent years.

Thea's heart went out to this woman. She had seen that look before, in the eyes of those who had lost someone dear to them. Part of her job as an Auric Priestess was to counsel folks with all sorts of problems. She'd seen everything from small domestic issues to people dealing with terrible tragedies. It was not an easy task by any means, but Thea found it quite rewarding when she could truly help someone.

The brilliant rays of the midday sun streamed through the half dozen arched windows that lined their path to the throne. An equal number of elegant chandeliers hung from the ceiling far above. Leading the way across the room, Ves answered the Queen's question with a question of her own. "Calipherous said you were asking for us. Was he mistaken?"

Amerelis pursed her lips together as she considered Ves' response. "Oh yes, that's right. Dear Cal. Is he here with you?"

"He chose to wait at the landing area with the stone statues," Ves informed her as they reached the base of the steps.

Captain Cloud stood there looking somewhat uncomfortable. His strange board hovered behind him, the bluish glow from the orb in its center lighting up the marble floor.

Another officer stood next to the captain. Nearly double his height, he towered over the gnome sky rider. This new officer cut a rather striking figure with neatly combed-back light-ash hair, a strong set jaw, and broad shoulders that nicely filled out his royal gold and purple uniform.

A whimsical smile crossed Amerelis' lips. "Cal was always a lover of the arts."

A great alcove spread back behind the throne where the Queen sat. Thea's eyes were drawn to a soft light hovering near the top of that alcove. Her eyes went wide as they fell on the small sphere that hung suspended there in mid-air. It radiated a power that felt like many dozens of souls. *That must be a cruex crystal!*

The crystal appeared almost identical to the one her brother and his friends had wrested from the Empress. Yet, where Lloyd had described that one as the color of night, this one shone a deep amber. As if the crystal weren't impressive enough, curled behind the throne at the back end of the great alcove, Thea spied the head and tail of a colossal gold dragon. Her eyes went even wider. With the array of power at her fingertips, this Queen Amerelis was not someone to be trifled with.

Amerelis sat forward in her chair, her whimsical expression fading as she did so. "Well then, down to business. I felt a sudden change at the Tower of Night a few days ago. I assume the Empress has finally fallen?"

Ever the diplomat, Elladan stepped forward and executed a deep bow. "Elladan Narmolanya of Kai-Arborous at your service, your majesty."

Thea had been initially wary of the far too handsome elf. People that good looking tended to be rather shallow. Yet, as she got to know him she discovered all that flash to be a façade. Elladan was surprisingly humble and cared deeply for those closest to him.

Queen Amerelis dipped her chin toward Elladan. "The throne recognizes our elven friend."

Elladan met her gaze with that charming half-smile of his. "Thank you, your highness. We defeated the Empress and took both the tower and crystal from her about eight days ago."

"It is as I thought then," Amerelis said, her brow furrowing. She waited a moment, then sat forward and narrowed her gaze. "Who holds the crystal now?"

"We left our friend Elistra there," Elladan explained. "She's a psychic and has had some success controlling it to date."

"Some?" Amerelis asked, her expression a mixture of surprise and concern.

Elladan shrugged and gave her another half-smile. "Enough to resurrect the protective fields around the chamber and teleport the rest of us to Penwick."

Thea had never met this Elistra, but from the way Lloyd described her, she seemed quite the interesting character. Though she originally introduced herself as a mere fortune teller, she turned out to be an immortal. Her well-honed psychic abilities had helped Lloyd and his friends defeat the Serpent Cult, ruin Princess Anya's plans to dominate dragons, and wrest the tower crystal away from the Empress. What Thea found the most curious, however, was that this powerful immortal had fallen in love with the elven wizard, Glolindir.

Amerelis sat back, absently tapping her chin as she mulled over Elladan's words. "That is a start. Perhaps she would indeed master it given time. However, time is a luxury we may not have much longer."

"We were wondering about that ourselves," Elladan admitted frankly. "Does your majesty have any idea how much time we have?"

The Queen's brow knit into an uncertain frown. "I do not," she answered slowly. "I felt it when the guardian at the Tower of Amethyst fell a few months ago. Though normally I don't give much credence to prophecy, one would be foolish to ignore the signs."

Amerelis had previously referred to the tower in the marshes as the Tower of Night. Now she mentioned the Tower of Amethyst.

Thea could only imagine that to be the tower that had been overrun by demons.

Apparently, Donnie agreed. The slim elf stepped up next to Elladan with a courtly bow. "Donatello, at your service, your majesty."

The frown on Amerelis' face faded, replaced instead with an amused smile. "Donatello? Like the artist of old?"

Donnie flashed her one of those sparkling smiles he somehow managed. Not that his teeth actually sparkled, but it definitely appeared as if they did. "A name given to me as an aspiration, your highness."

A slight laugh escaped Amerelis' lips. "Very well, Donatello. Do you have news for us?"

Donnie's grin faded. "Yes, your majesty. I'm afraid the tower of which you speak is infested with demons. I was transported there myself and barely escaped with my life."

The entire room seemed to darken at his pronouncement. Amerelis' face fell, her expression becoming quite pensive. It was then that Thea noticed the Queen's aura interacting with the crystal floating above her head. Remarkably, its glow had dimmed.

Is it somehow linked to her emotions? Thea wondered.

Amerelis steepled her hands in front of her and stared at them for a few moments. When she did speak, her voice sounded hollow. "And so there it is. The end times may indeed be upon us."

With all the power at her disposal, Thea had not expected such a defeatist attitude from the Queen. Neither had Donnie, she imagined.

That did not stop Elladan, however, from casting a disparaging look at his friend before once again addressing Amerelis. "Your majesty, I'm not sure of these signs, but the towers are the reason we have come to this coast. We intend to take back the Tower of Amethyst from the demons."

Amerelis did not immediately look at him. Instead she seemed lost in her own thoughts. When she finally did focus on Elladan, her tone was rather ominous. "You will not find them to be as easy a foe as the Empress. Undead could never completely master the crystal."

Well that got dark awfully fast, Thea thought dryly.

Still, the sudden grim turn Amerelis had taken only gave Elladan momentary pause. "That is why we seek weapons that would help us against such powerful enemies."

Elladan fell into his storyteller voice as he further explained their mission to her. It had a lyrical style to it that drew the listener into the tale. "We are looking for the great runes of old—the very same scrolls that Tauriyama himself used to forge the Shin Tauri blade. Unfortunately, those scrolls were stolen in the dead of night from the descendants of the long gone master smith. Still, it did not take long for the scrolls to resurface."

Aside from his vocal style, Elladan had a penchant for colorful embellishments. They did not change any of the facts, but instead filled in gaps and made the overall tale easier to envision.

"Word spread far and wide that the pirate clans had a great prize to offer to those with the necessary coin. Such a prize garnered the attention of many, but one group in particular outbid all the rest. And thus a meet was set. It is to take place within the week between the clans and their buyer somewhere along the dark coast."

The chamber fell silent after Elladan finished his colorful narrative. Queen Amerelis sat on her throne, her brow deeply furrowed as she deliberated on the bard's tale.

Nearly half a minute went by before Amerelis broke the silence. When she finally spoke, her words were measured. "You have indeed brought us evil tidings—but with them you bring hope as well."

She turned her gaze upon the officer next to Captain Cloud. "Lieutenant Balthazar, go at once and check with Lord Commander Amaia. We need any and all information she may have on the location of these scrolls or atypical movements of the clans within these last few weeks."

Lieutenant Balthazar gave her a curt bow, his expression grave. "Yes, your majesty." He then spun on his heel and strode across the chamber at a rapid pace.

Amerelis breathed a heavy sigh and returned her attention to her guests. "We have a fairly extensive intelligence gathering network along the coast. If an exchange is to take place as you say, we should be able to tell you where and when."

Ruka gazed at Donnie with a satisfied smirk. "Told ya."

Donnie in turn fixed her with a withering stare.

It had in fact been Ruka who suggested asking the Queen's help in finding the scrolls. However, there was far more behind her teasing of the slight elf.

Thea had noted the tension between these two since they first arrived in Penwick. From what she could glean, Ruka had a crush on the boyishly handsome elf. Having known Ruka in the past, Thea found that fascinating. When they first met, the girl had slim knowledge of social cues. Of course, being a dragon in human form made that all the harder for her. Nonetheless, Donnie was the last person Ruka should have set her sights on.

Donnie exhibited a charm not unlike Elladan's. However, he seemed to treat affairs of the heart as casual things at best. Thea could only imagine that he had been hurt by someone in the past. Unfortunately, those sorts of people tended to hurt anyone else who tried to get close to them.

Amerelis interrupted the two before Donnie could retort. "Ah, Rukastana, as impertinent as ever."

Not batting an eye, Ruka turned to face the Queen. "Good to see you too, *Amerelis*."

"Ruka! That's the Queen you are talking to," Ves chided her sister.

Queen Amerelis raised her hand and made a staying motion. "It's quite alright, Vestiralana. I am quite used to your sister's little—quirks."

Ruka had always been sharp witted, but in the time since Thea last saw her, she had developed a caustic sense of humor. Yet underneath it all, Thea knew her to be an extremely caring individual. After all, it was she who brought the bodies of Thea and her friends back to Penwick after they died. If it had not been for the dragon girl, none of them would be alive today.

All of sudden, Maya danced out onto the steps, a dimpled grin upon her face. "What about me, your majesty? I've learned a song or two from our new friends. Would you like to hear one?"

Elladan gulped, his face turning decidedly pale. Thea had to wonder at just what songs she had picked up from him. Thankfully, Ves intervened before Maya could sing any. "Maya, get down from there. Can't you see the Queen is busy at the moment?"

Maya turned to face her sister with her arms folded and a decided pout. "You never let me have any fun."

Thea found the girl to be absolutely adorable—precocious, but adorable. Perhaps Ves was a bit hard on her. At the same time, having raised Lloyd practically by herself, Thea intrinsically understood the pressure Ves must feel as the responsible older sibling.

Once again, Amerelis interrupted them before anyone else could speak. "You sister is right, Mayattari, but I would love to hear one when this is all over."

Maya spun about and grinned at the Queen. "Oh you can bet on it!"

The little girl's effervescence lifted everyone's spirits.

When Amerelis resumed their conversation, her mood had markedly brightened, as did the crystal over her head. "So once you have these weapons crafted, what do you intend to do next?"

Donnie responded without thinking. "Well, as Anya discovered, a frontal assault on the tower doesn't work so well."

Amerelis shot out of her seat. "Anyabarithia? Is she alright?"

Elladan elbowed Donnie in the side as he tried to quell the Queen's fears. "Yes, your majesty. She made it back to Vermoorden where she is recovering under the care of the Lady Gracelynn."

Amerelis eyed him hesitantly. "You mean the Lady Gracelynn Avernos? I hear she is quite the accomplished healer."

"I've seen her abilities first hand and they are, indeed, your majesty," Ves assured her.

Amerelis let out a deep breath, then sat back down, and dipped her chin to Ves. "Very good then. I will send my regards to Lady Gracelynn and offer whatever assistance she needs in caring for the Princess."

"I'm sure she would appreciate that, your highness," Ves responded with a wan smile. Though she would never admit it aloud, Ves had little love for the Princess.

Thea counseled Ves after she'd been violated by Theramon. What he'd done was the equivalent of mental rape, but Thea learned during those sessions that Anya had previously abused her as well. When she kidnapped Ves, she also inflicted her with a mind altering crystal. Though what Theramon did was far worse, neither attack was forgivable.

Now settled from her momentary outburst, Amerelis returned her attention to the group at large. "Well, since my petulant granddaughter stirred the proverbial hornet's nest, what will you do next?"

Again it was Elladan who answered her query. "We intend to approach the tower from underneath—through the tunnels, your majesty."

Amerelis' eyes widened with astonishment. "Really? You intend to face the purple worm?"

"I'm looking forward to it," a gruff voice responded.

The group parted to reveal Cyclone standing behind them all, his bare, muscular arms folded across his chest. He wore an insolent sneer as he stared back at the Queen.

Thea hadn't spent much time getting to know Cyclone. The young man spoke very little and kept mostly to himself. Though he came across quite arrogant, he was indeed an excellent fighter, something Thea had witnessed firsthand.

"And just who are you?" Amerelis asked warily.

"Cyclone," he answered rather abruptly.

Amerelis raised an eyebrow at the rude young man. "Just Cyclone?"

"Cyclone, the dragon hunter," he responded in a brusque tone.

The tension in the air grew suddenly palpable. Amerelis arched both eyebrows. Behind her, the golden dragon's eyelid lifted just a sliver. Amerelis fixed Ves with a hard stare. "You brought a dragon hunter into my throne room?"

Before Ves could respond, Ruka stepped in front of her sister. "Don't get your panties all in a bunch, Amerelis. He's helped us out of quite a few tight jams. He even saved Ves from an undead red."

The Queen narrowed both eyes at Ruka before switching her gaze back to Ves. "Is this true, Vestiralana?"

Ves met the Queen's gaze evenly. "Yes, your majesty."

Though somewhat mollified, Amerelis did not appear completely convinced. Yet again Elladan tried to smooth things over. "What they're trying to say, your majesty, is that Cyclone has been our valiant ally for quite some time. As for his title, he only hunts *evil* dragons."

Amerelis turned a wary eye back toward Cyclone. "Is what they are telling me true, dragon hunter?"

Cyclone met her gaze unflinchingly. "Can't say I've ever killed a good dragon—yet."

Everyone glared at the dragon hunter. It was as if he were purposely trying to goad the Queen. Behind Amerelis, the golden dragon lifted its head. It spun its gaze straight at Cyclone and said something to the Queen in what Thea could only assume to be Draconic.

Thankfully, Amerelis was not that easy to provoke. She shook her head at the dragon. "No, not right now, Lisirianna. You can go back to resting."

The golden dragon stared at Cyclone for a moment more, then laid its head back down and closed its eyes.

With a confrontation between the Queen and Cyclone averted, everyone breathed a sigh of relief. Elladan wisely brought the conversation back on track before anything else could be said. "So, your majesty—as you surmised, we will in fact have to face the purple worm. Unfortunately, we have found little information on the creature to date."

Having regained her composure, Amerelis fixed him with a pleasant smile. "Well then, you have come to the right place. The great library here in Palt has a number of volumes on the towers. Some of them, in fact, have information about the worm." She sat forward on her throne, her voice taking on a conspiratorial tone. "Though I can tell you, it is not actually a living creature. It is a construct, originally designed to facilitate transportation between the towers."

"Pardon, your highness," Donnie interrupted, "but if that's the case, then why is everyone so afraid of it?"

Amerelis got up and began to pace back and forth in front of her throne. "That is because it was made with a magic unlike any other— not arcane, not divine, not even psychic. It is an alien magic, from the time of the dark moon."

"The Moon of Madness," Thea murmured aloud. Two thousand years ago, the Mad God caused a second moon to appear in the sky.

That moon rained down a plague of madness on the world that lasted nearly a thousand years. It only ended when the baleful moon fell from the sky and crashed into their world. Yet the fall itself caused its own brand of devastation.

"And who is this good priestess?"

Thea peered up to see Queen Amerelis had stopped pacing and was staring at her.

"Forgive me," Thea responded with a graceful curtsey. "Althea Kitren Stealle, of the Penwick House of Stealle and Auric Priestess of Arenor, at your service, your majesty."

Amerelis pressed her lips together, her eyes widening. "A noble and a Priestess of Arenor?" She shifted her gaze to Ves. "It appears you have made some interesting and prestigious friends, my dear."

"A few," Ves responded with a polite smile.

Amerelis returned her gaze to Thea. "Yes, as you said Althea, the Moon of Madness. That magic is what makes the worm so extremely unpredictable and dangerous."

"So you know of no way past it?" Thea pressed.

Amerelis slowly shook her head. "I do not, but again, you might find some clues in the great library."

Having shared all she knew, Queen Amerelis swept her eyes across their group, then abruptly stopped. "And who might this be?" she said, tapping her chin with a single finger. "A Shin Tauri warrior from our good friend Isandor to the south, perhaps?"

Thea followed the Queen's gaze to see it firmly fixed on Seishin.

Though not much taller than Donnie and Elladan, there was an intensity about him that drew one in. Perhaps it could be attributed to his stoic countenance or those strangely compelling amber eyes. His golden tan skin and thick, matted deep brown hair most likely distinguished him as an Isandorian. The curious part, however, was how Amerelis identified him as a Shin Tauri.

Donnie had alluded to the fact that Shin Tauri could channel energy similar to spiritblades. That was a practice Thea was all too familiar with. She had been on the path to becoming a blade before the fateful incident on Thorn Isle. To this day, she practiced the art whenever time allowed, though it never quite felt like enough.

From what Thea could see of Seishin's aura, the energy flowed powerfully through his first chakra. His third and sixth chakras were also quite well developed. That told her two things. One, Seishin was indeed a student of a martial art similar to the spiritblade. Two, Amerelis could read and understand auras as well as Thea, or perhaps better.

Seishin executed a deep bow. "Seishin Kazari, of the Kazari Clan of Isandor at your service, your highness."

Amerelis eyed him thoughtfully. "The Kazari Clan? The premier clan in all of Isandor?"

Seishin took in a sharp breath, a grimace crossing his normally impassive features. "Perhaps once, your majesty, but as of late we have fallen from grace."

A look of keen sympathy spread across the Queen's face. "What can we do for you, young Shin Tauri? I'm afraid we have no sway with the current politics of your land."

Seishin responded with a single shake of his head. "No, it's not that your highness. I have come seeking your aid in another matter." He took a step forward and placed a hand on his chest. "I am of the line of Tibarn and seek the Shin Tauri blade. According to the Wizard Aldurin, you may know a way to find it."

A gleam of recognition lit up the Queen's eyes. "Ah, yes. We were expecting Aldurin himself—but one of the line of Tibarn will certainly do."

Amerelis held out her hands in front of her, her brow knit in concentration. Thea felt a surge of power flow from the crystal above down to the Queen. A moment later, an ornate scabbard appeared within those outstretched hands.

Amerelis peered down the steps at Seishin. "This is the sheath that carried your ancestor's blade. It still resonates with the blade's signature. If you can attune your mind to it, young Shin Tauri, then you will know as you draw closer to the blade."

Seishin fell to one knee, his face flush with gratitude. "Thank you, your majesty. You have given us hope beyond hope."

Amerelis descended the stairs and handed the scabbard to Captain Cloud. Thea noted with keen interest the momentary appearance of a shimmering in the air between them.

That must be a force field, Thea realized. *This Amerelis is certainly taking no chances.*

Cloud walked the scabbard over to Seishin and proffered it to him. Seishin marveled over it for a few moments, then once again bowed to the Queen.

Amerelis beamed at him, then turned her gaze upon Pallas. "And who is this last of your party to whom I've yet to be introduced?"

Pallas took a few steps forward and performed a courtly bow. "Captain Pallas Stealle, of the Penwick House of Stealle and the Penwick Royal Navy, your majesty."

Amerelis swept her eyes from Pallas to Thea and then back again. "Ah, yes. I see the resemblance. So what is it we can do for you, young Lord Stealle?"

Pallas' normally serious expression grew even more grave, if possible. "I come bearing a packet from my government requesting an alliance between my city and your nation."

Amerelis held his gaze and frowned. "Please hand the packet over to Captain Cloud here. I will look it over, but be advised that there is already an emissary here from your sister city of Dunwynn. They are basically asking for the same thing."

The corner of Pallas' mouth upturned ever so slightly. "Dunwynn. I should have known."

The Queen's expression turned sympathetic. "Do not worry, young Captain Stealle. I have no intention of choosing one city over the other. With all that we will be facing in the near future, it would be best if we all could align with one another."

Still new at the art of diplomacy, Pallas seemed unsure of how to respond. Seeing his plight, Elladan stepped in for him. "With all due respect, your majesty, that may be happening as we speak. The brother of our good Captain and Priestess here is engaged to be married to Lady Andrella Avernos, the Duke of Dunwynn's niece and sole heir."

Amerelis raised an eyebrow. "That may indeed be fortuitous. Perhaps they can talk some sense into their respective rulers."

Thea was impressed. Queen Amerelis seemed quite well informed about the pig-headedness of both the Duke of Dunwynn and the

Baron of Penwick. Unable to quite contain herself, Thea just had to comment. "From your mouth to the ears of the gods."

Amerelis unexpectedly burst out into laughter, her entire face lighting up as she did so. She covered her mouth with the back of her hand, obviously having difficulty suppressing her mirth. Once she finally regained her composure, she gave Thea a warm smile. "As you say, good Priestess. As you say."

4
LET SLEEPING DRAGONS LIE

Yes, you traitor! You tricked us.

Donnie was cursed. There was no doubt about it. Any woman he had ever cared about met an inexplicable demise. Alana had been the last of those casualties, a grim reminder not to allow any woman into his heart. Thus he pushed Ruka away. He couldn't abide it if something were to happen to her because of him.

Despite that, Donnie did his best to protect her and her sisters. It was the least he could do with all those undead running around Penwick. When they learned about the rune scrolls, however, he knew he had to join in the search for them.

The itinerant elf had a long history on the dark coast. Not one he necessarily wanted to dredge up, mind you. Even so, with the fate of the world hanging in the balance, Donnie felt he had little choice. His intimate knowledge of the coast and the pirate clans might mean the difference between failure and success. It was just his luck that

Ruka and her sisters had decided to join them. Trouble tended to follow him wherever he went.

Case in point, with all their business with the Queen concluded, Ves chose to broach a decidedly delicate topic. "Your majesty, there is one last matter I would like to discuss."

The seriousness of her tone quelled any last vestiges of humor from the Queen's face. "Ahem, very well. Go ahead, Vestiralana."

Ves shifted uncomfortably from one foot to the other, her face paling as she did so. "This Theramon makes me very uneasy. He kidnapped both Maya and I, and"—she hesitated a moment before going on—"implanted me with a dark seed. If not for our friends, I'm not quite sure I would be standing here this day."

The Queen's face darkened measurably, the crystal above her once again following suit. She responded to Ves in a hardened tone. "We are quite aware of Theramon and his machinations. He is the one who filled the Princess' head with the wild notions of ruling the world. That is why I had him kicked out of this kingdom."

"It's nice to know that someone besides us sees him for what he is," Elladan drawled.

Donnie had to agree. The Duke of Dunwynn and the Penwick Council still seemed enamored with the errant immortal.

"I could say the same," Amerelis responded to the bard with a brief smile. It was quickly followed by a short sigh. "Nonetheless, we have been keeping tabs on him. The last we heard was he was headed to the far west with some sort of fool's notion to release the remaining Titans. Though now that I know about this demon invasion, I am beginning to understand his mad quest."

Donnie's eyes went wide. He glanced at Elladan, but the bard appeared as surprised as he.

"Excuse me, your majesty," Elladan stammered. "I thought all the Titans were slain after the Second Demon War. Are you telling us that some might still be alive?"

A pained expression crossed the Queen's face. "It is not something we like to talk about, but—yes."

"And Theramon has set out to free them?" Elladan asked with clear astonishment.

Amerelis dipped her chin. "According to our sources."

Still incredulous, Elladan glanced Donnie's way once more. Not knowing what to say, Donnie merely shrugged in response. The Queen seemed to have her finger on the pulse of the world, and he certainly wasn't going to question the source of her information.

Even so, despite the Queen's assurances, Ves pressed on with her concerns. "Be that as it may, he is a danger to all dragon kind, and thus I would like to ask a boon of you."

Amerelis narrowed her eyes at the young lady. "Very well. Go ahead, Vestiralana."

Ves took a step forward, the words spilling out of her mouth before anyone could stop her. "Please place my sisters under your protection."

Ruka's face turned flush with anger. She practically screamed at her sister. "What? Ves, you traitor! You tricked us." She grabbed Maya by the hand and began to drag her away from the throne. "Come on, Maya. We're getting out of here."

Maya appeared confused. She struggled against her sister's grip. "Wait! Ruka, what's going on?"

Amerelis held Ves' stare for a few moments, then finally nodded. "Very well."

Ruka and Maya stopped struggling and turned to face the Queen, the former in terror and the latter still confused. Amerelis stood and raised her hands, pointing to each girl simultaneously. The crystal above her head flared for a brief moment, and then both girls fell to the floor.

Donnie's heart nearly leapt into his throat. Despite his better judgement, he confronted Amerelis. "What did you do to them?"

A firm hand on his shoulder gave Donnie pause. He turned to see Elladan staring at him, the concern in his eyes quite clear. In the meantime, Thea had knelt down next to the girls and ran her hands over their bodies. After a moment or two, she breathed a gentle sigh. "It's alright. They're just asleep."

Now Donnie felt foolish—and a little bit scared. He grimaced at Elladan, then turned back to the Queen with a sheepish smile. "Sorry, your majesty."

Amerelis, however, gazed at him with a look of keen sympathy. "It's completely alright, Donatello. Your concern for the Greymantles is duly noted." She hesitated a moment, then climbed down a step and gave him a warm smile. "Understand that this kingdom, and myself personally, owe a great debt to the Greymantles. Thus, it is our desire to protect all of them."

Before anyone could react, Amerelis raised her arm once more and pointed at Ves. The crystal flared again, and the third Greymantle sister fell to the floor.

Thea checked on her as well, but this time with less urgency. "She's fast asleep as well."

Elladan chuckled softly. "She should have been more careful what she wished for."

Donnie peered back up at the Queen as she in turn surveyed the sleeping sisters. It was obvious that she cared for them deeply, perhaps as much as he himself. That's when it dawned on him he no longer had to worry about the girls. They would be staying here with the Queen under her protection. He should have been relieved, but for some reason, that thought nagged at him.

Donnie couldn't imagine why. He was free—he should be happy. Why would leaving the sisters behind worry him? He wracked his brain until the realization hit him. *That must be it!* he convinced himself.

"Your majesty?" he addressed Amerelis.

The Queen tore her gaze away from the sleeping sisters and peered curiously down at him. "Yes, Donatello?"

"May I have a word—in private?" He stumbled over those last words, realizing at the last moment that his request might be construed as inappropriate. Before he could move a muscle though, the world around him suddenly faded.

Donnie found himself in a lovely field of bright flowers, the same field he had been in when he had his last vision of Miranda. Amerelis stood there with him, yet no longer wore a crown and finery. Instead she was dressed like a commoner in a simple peasant dress.

For all that, there was nothing common about her. She was possibly the most beautiful woman he had ever seen. Realizing where his thoughts were going, Donnie chided himself. *This is not the time to be thinking of that, Donatello.*

Amerelis laughed. It was a light, airy sound, like chimes playing in the wind. Her eyes continued to dance with amusement as she addressed him. "You do realize this is your mind and I can hear everything you are thinking."

Donnie's cheeks turned hot. He stared at her with a wan smile. "Sorry, old habits die hard, I guess."

Amerelis chuckled once more. "Do not worry. I am not offended. It has been a long time since anyone has thought of me as something other than the Queen."

She held his gaze, her voice dropping low and throaty. "I find it refreshing."

Donnie gulped. Tempting as it was, a tryst with the Queen of Lanfor might not end so well for him. It took all his willpower to change the subject. "I—do appreciate that, your majesty, but I asked you here to talk about Ruka."

"Oh?" Amerelis replied, her expression a mixture of surprise and amusement.

"Y-yes," Donnie stammered.

"Very well." Amerelis made a gesture and a blanket appeared on the grass in front of them. "Please sit down," she said, motioning toward the blanket.

Donnie hesitated a moment, then sat down cross-legged. Amerelis then seated herself next to him. Donnie forced himself to look away as she demurely adjusted her dress.

"So what's this all about?" Amerelis asked once she was done.

Donnie peered back at her. She was sitting a bit too close for his comfort. Trying his best to ignore that, he launched into his concerns about Ruka. "She's been having problems controlling her powers as of late." He briefly described how she inadvertently let off a few static discharges and blew up some things at dinner a few nights ago.

Amerelis' expression grew quite serious. "I can protect her from herself as long as she doesn't invoke the power of the storm god. If she does that, however, then I will not be able to hold her."

"That's concerning," Donnie said. He had thought the Queen of all people would be able to keep her powers restrained.

Amerelis smiled and gently touched his arm. "Do not worry. Of all the Greymantles, Rukastana is most like her mother, and is thus under the protection of Mad God."

"And that's a good thing?" Donnie responded, trying to ignore the feel of her hand upon his arm.

Amerelis nodded. "In many ways, yes. Neither Theramon nor Urekor, were he still alive, would thus be able to enslave her mind."

Donnie felt both relieved and terrified at the same time. Urekor was the Dragon Thrall Master. If Ruka could stand up to his control, then Theramon had no chance against her. Despite that, there was cause for concern. Disciples of the Mad God had a tendency to go crazy.

"So is that all?" Amerelis asked, gazing at him unabashedly.

Donnie found himself hard pressed not to think about the loveliness of the Queen. Instead he forced himself to concentrate on Ruka, and something else popped into mind. He swung around on the blanket to face Amerelis. "I do have one more confession."

"Oh, and what's that?" Amerelis asked, her eyes dancing with amusement.

Donnie began by explaining how they knew about the girl's missing father, the great wizard, Rodric Greymantle. He also added how the girls set out to search for him without their mother's consent.

"I am aware," Amerelis said, still staring him directly in the eye.

"So"—Donnie hesitated, somewhat intimidated and ashamed at the same time—"while escaping from the Tower of Night, we came across a huge cell. The covering was quite thin and through it I saw the shadow of a dragon." His guilt overcoming him, Donnie hung his head. "I've been afraid to tell the sisters for fear they would rush off in hopes of rescuing their father."

When Amerelis did not immediately reply, Donnie peered up at her. She sat there with her head tilted upward, her eyes glazed over with a faraway look. Assuming she was doing some kind of magic, Donnie sat quietly and waited.

A minute or so later, her eyes refocused and she returned her attention to him. "Your eyes did not deceive you, Donatello. It is indeed the girl's father in that tower." Her face took on a worried expression. "Unfortunately, I can no longer locate the girl's mother anywhere on this plane."

Donnie gulped, fearing the worst. "Is she dead?"

A trace of moisture appeared in the corner of Amerelis' eye. "I cannot say for certain, but I do agree with your discretion in this matter." She reached out and grasped his hand, holding onto it with surprising strength. "Let us continue to share this secret until a time comes when we can safely rescue Rodric from the tower."

A wave of compassion welled up inside him for this brave woman. He could not even begin to imagine how difficult life had been for her, ruling Lanfor for all these years. Over that time, she must have made countless decisions like this one—carefully safeguarding secrets to protect her subjects and allies.

Donnie grasped her hand between both of his and gave her a genuine smile. "As you wish."

Amerelis gave him a warm smile, then abruptly the scene around them faded. Donnie found himself back in the throne room. Neither he nor Amerelis had moved from where they had been standing.

Sweeping his eyes around, he noted that Ves, Ruka, and Maya now rested comfortably next to the gold dragon behind the throne. Donnie peered back up at Amerelis. She met his gaze with a knowing smile.

Pallas had felt like a fish out of water ever since they first caught sight of Palt. Though he intrinsically knew Penwick not to be the largest city in the world, seeing a metropolis this size was quite the humbling experience. The palace itself dwarfed Avernos Keep, easily covering three times the land area.

The Queen also turned out to be nothing like what he expected. Foremost, she appeared to be incredibly young, though he knew that to be a magical façade. More surprising was her obvious intelligence and the fearless way with which she made tough decisions. From his experience, those were rare commodities in a ruler.

Of course, the power at her disposal outshone anything he had ever seen. His rough count of warships in the harbor alone doubled the Penwick Navy. And for good measure, the number of soldiers just on the palace grounds easily rivaled the size of both the Penwick castle and town guards. Yet the Queen appeared to be formidable in her own right. With a mere way of her hand, she put all three of the dragon sisters to sleep. After seeing them in battle, Pallas knew that to be no mean feat.

Not long after the Greymantle sisters were neatly tucked away, the doors to the Queen's throne room opened again. Lieutenant Balthazar came striding through and across the chamber floor. After briefly kneeling in front of the Queen, he reported on the information they sought. "As we were told, your majesty, the rune scrolls have indeed reappeared. However, they are not in the possession of the pirate clans."

Pallas found that quite surprising. He would have bet a platinum piece that the pirates had been behind the theft of the scrolls in the first place. The Queen seemed equally shocked by this strange turn of events.

"Oh?" Amerelis raised an eyebrow. "Then who has them?"

"The priesthood in Kaniron, your majesty," Balthazar informed her. "Apparently, they purchased them from one of the clans."

Now that makes more sense, Pallas thought wryly.

"Word has it the priesthood were the ones who put the scrolls up for auction," Balthazar continued. "It seems that the Parthians were the highest bidders and have sent out an envoy to seal the deal."

The Parthians? Pallas thought angrily. They were actually worse than the pirates. Parthos had been trying to extend its rule by force across the globe since the fall of the Naradon Empire. The Parthians had even invaded Penwick for a short while about eighty years ago.

While not angry like Pallas, the Queen's brow furrowed into a concerned frown. "It would not bode well for Lanfor if those scrolls were to fall into Parthian hands."

"My thoughts exactly, your majesty," Balthazar concurred.

Pallas took heart knowing them all to be agreement as far as the Parthians were concerned. The only way to squelch their plans for world domination would be via a united front. He started to say as such, but that irritating bard interrupted him before he could get out a single word.

"Well that's our cue," Elladan said with a glib smile. "If you can direct us to this Kaniron, I'm sure we'll beat the Parthians there by airship."

Balthazar fixed Elladan with a dubious stare. "It's due south down the coast, but I'm afraid getting there will not be quite that easy."

Elladan narrowed an eye at the Lieutenant. "What do you mean by that?"

For once Pallas had to agree with Elladan. That statement had been pretty cryptic.

Balthazar folded his arms across his chest, his face impassive as he met Elladan's stare. "If you try entering Kaniron by air, the firebirds will burn you out of the sky."

"Do you say *Firebirds*?" Pallas repeated, not sure he had heard correctly.

Queen Amerelis rose from her chair and held her palm up in the air. An image spread out from her hand of a large volcano with numerous red winged creatures circling all around the caldera. A city stretched from the base of the volcano to the water's edge some miles away.

"This is Kaniron," the Queen explained. "It was built around the great volcano of the same name. Large firebirds make their nest high above the city along the mountainside. Thus, the Kanironians have come to worship the great fire bird god, Zharpita."

Thea stepped forward and squinted at the vivid image. "That is amazing. An entire culture centered around the worship of a single bird god." She peered up at the Queen. "So, I take it they do not worship the Ralnai at all?"

Queen Amerelis shook her head. "No. Somehow their prayers must have been answered because they have learned to live in harmony with the firebirds."

While Pallas also found the symbiotic relationship amazing, they had more pressing matters at hand. "So, if an approach by air is ruled out, I suppose that leaves us to getting there by sea."

Balthazar met his statement with an affirming nod. "That appears to be the only safe way to enter the city."

"I guess we're going by ship then," Elladan stated the obvious.

Thea did not seem pleased by the thought. "Does this mean we have to pass through that Vortex?" she asked with a hint of apprehension.

Balthazar gazed at her with clear sympathy. "I'm afraid so."

Queen Amerelis dropped her hand and the image she had conjured disappeared. She then fixed her gaze on Balthazar. "Lieutenant, please procure a ship with a capable navigator for our friends."

Balthazar executed a short bow. "At once, your majesty."

He spun on his heel and started to stride away when she called after him. "Also—"

Balthazar stopped in his tracks and turned back around to face his Queen.

"—I would like you and Captain Cloud to accompany them on this mission," she stated in a matter of fact tone.

Both Balthazar and Cloud exchanged a surprised glance. The Lieutenant peered back at his Queen with obvious confusion. "Your majesty?"

Queen Amerelis did not seem the type used to having her orders questioned, but there appeared to be some sort of special bond between her and these two soldiers. She gazed down at both of them fondly, her voice softening. "I know your first service is to guard me, but we cannot allow the Parthians to get their hands on those scrolls. The very fate of Lanfor may hang in the balance."

The two knelt without any more questions and spoke as one. "As you wish, your majesty."

The Queen smiled at both of them, then turned her gaze upon the Isandorian. "What about you, young Shin Tauri?"

Seishin had been preoccupied with the scabbard she had given him. He now looked up at the Queen, his expression puzzled. "Your majesty?"

Queen Amerelis took another step down towards them. "I understand your desire to find the blade of your ancestors, but this mission is of utmost importance. Another point to consider, these folks are looking to forge weapons of near equal power to the Shin Tauri blade. Your prowess as a Shin Tauri warrior might prove quite useful in their quest."

Seishin did not immediately answer. Instead, he swept his eyes around those of their group still remaining.

Pallas had gauged the warrior's aura when he first approached them outside the throne room. He definitely had power, similar to that of a spiritblade in fact. He might even be comparable in ability to Lloyd, Pallas estimated. Considering they were down three dragons, the addition of this warrior could not hurt.

When Seishin's eyes swept over Pallas, he addressed the warrior. "If you do decide to come with us, then once we have the scrolls, I give you my word that we will accompany you by airship on the search for your ancestral blade."

Seishin held his gaze for a few moments. Though his expression remained impassive, Pallas could feel him trying to gauge his aura in return. Finally, the warrior bowed. "Then I will accompany you."

Above them all, the Queen let out a deep sigh. "There. Now that that is all settled, please feel free to utilize the facilities of Lanfor while we prepare for your journey."

They all paid their parting respects to the Queen, then followed Balthazar and Cloud out of the throne room.

5
THE GREYSTONE HALLS

"These two brought an evil artifact into our halls!"

Two royal coaches waited for them at the palace entrance. Captain Cloud escorted the first coach to the inn where Seishin was staying. Elladan, however, requested instead to go to the Greystone Halls. Curious to see them as well, Thea chose to go along. Lieutenant Balthazar ended up escorting them both.

Thea had spent the last four years living and studying at the Temple of the Ralnai. Those grounds were expansive, but the Greystone Halls put them to shame. The vast complex sat at the base of the mountain directly below the Queen's palace. A thick wall surrounded the halls, stretching across the entire foot of the mountain until it butted up against its base on either side. Numerous multi-building complexes stood inside those walls. All had an ancient feel as if centuries of learning had taken place within their halls.

Not knowing where to even begin, Thea turned to Balthazar. "Is there some sort of directory for this place?"

The lieutenant nodded down the walkway ahead to where it split and wrapped around either side of a large grassy area. A number of folks milled about there, some from different races, others merely dressed in strange attire. More than a few stood in front of a large board in the center of the circle set upon a wide stone platform.

Thea strode forth across the campus. As she drew nearer, she saw that the board depicted a numbered map of the Halls. A wide plaque stretched across the platform below with descriptions for each matching number. Thea determined that most of the buildings were part of the university. After perusing the map for a bit, however, she finally found what she was looking for.

Thea pointed a finger toward the western end of the campus. "It looks like the library is down that way sandwiched between more than a few annexes."

She started to march off in that direction, but halted as Elladan called out after her. "If you don't mind, I'd like to first make a quick stop at the vaults."

Balthazar eyed him with a look of mild surprise. "What business do you have at the vaults?"

The elven bard grimaced. "I sort of have a few things that should be dropped off there"—he paused and cast a guilty glance Thea's way—"but don't let me stop either of you if you'd rather go somewhere else instead."

Remembering their conversation from earlier that day, Thea folded her arms and smirked. "Oh no, I wouldn't dream of missing this."

Balthazar looked pointedly at the elf. "I think I'll join you as well."

Elladan winced, but gracefully recovered. "Well then, after you," he responded, magnanimously ushering Thea and the lieutenant forth.

Balthazar eyed the bard a moment longer, then led them straight across the campus. They passed through a grove of tall trees, but upon exiting Thea stopped in her tracks. A tall spire stood directly in front of them, its pinnacle reaching upward toward the sky. It stood front and center in a structure nearly as wide as the spire was tall.

Thea's breath caught in her throat. This had to be the Temple of the Gods. It was every bit as beautiful as Ves described.

Seeing her stop, the others did so as well. "You know, if you want to go inside and take a look, we can always go on without you," Elladan said smoothly.

Thea had to admit, the offer was tempting. She could feel the powerful aura of good emanating from the structure. It did make her yearn to go inside and offer her prayers. Realizing that Elladan was trying to sidetrack her, she fixed him with a sour look. "That's alright. I can always stop by here later."

Elladan shrugged, that same half-smile adorning his lips. "Can't blame an elf for trying."

Around the back of the great temple stood a circular building with a domed cap, partially built into the mountainside. That turned out to be the entrance to the Greystone Vaults.

A wide circular foyer spread out before them inside the structure. It was eloquently decorated with a black and white marble floor and tall golden columns that reached to the vaulted ceiling two stories above. A long hall stretched beyond that foyer, lined on either side by multiple arched stained glass windows.

At the end of the hall stood a tall counter. An elderly man and woman sat behind it, both garbed in grey robes. A tall arched golden gate rose behind the pair, barring access beyond that point. Thea watched with keen curiosity as Elladan approached the duo.

The woman peered down at the elf and asked in an officious tone, "May we help you?"

Balthazar stepped forward and gestured towards Elladan and Thea. "These two are guests of the Queen. They have some 'items' to be stored in the vaults."

The elderly clerks exchanged a brief glance. The man stared icily at them. "What sort of items?"

Thea took a step back and waved him off. "Don't look at me." Other than satisfying her own curiosity, she wanted no part in what the elf was carrying.

Elladan smoothly stepped up to the counter and pulled out a nondescript grey bag from his belt. "Just some things that we picked up during our travels."

Thea immediately recognized it as a portal bag. Such bags were small enough to carry, but connected to a different plane of existence. Because of that, one could store far more inside than the apparent size of the bag itself.

Thea's curiosity grew as Elladan reached into the bag. His arm disappeared down to his shoulder as he rummaged around inside. "Where is that thing?" he murmured to himself. "Ah, there you are!" he finally exclaimed, a triumphant smile upon his lips.

The elf withdrew his arm from the bag. In his palm sat a lemon sized gem, its color as black as night. Thea felt a wave of revulsion wash over her. The thing practically radiated evil.

As Elladan went to set the gem on the counter, alarms suddenly rang out all around them. Bars magically appeared in the windows up and down the hallway and a gate dropped down out of the ceiling at the other end of the corridor.

"What in Thac—" Elladan began.

Before he could finish that sentence, more grey robed clerks poured out of a side door that Thea hadn't previously noticed. The group swiftly encircled them making her decidedly nervous. Without realizing it she had fallen into a crouch, her hands instinctively straying towards the two daggers hidden beneath her robes.

Thea silently admonished herself. *You're a priestess now, not a spiritblade.* Straightening herself, she waited to see what would happen next.

Moments later, a small figure pushed its way through the circle. Unlike the others, this one had gnomish features and wore purple robes with golden trim. Obviously some sort of head clerk, the gnome adjusted his horn-rimmed spectacles, his voice rife with irritation. "What's going on here?"

The woman at the desk immediately pointed a finger at Elladan and Thea. "These two brought an evil artifact into our halls!"

The head clerk lowered his spectacles and stared over the top of them at the pair. "Is that so?"

Thea met the head clerk's gaze evenly, ready to disavow any prior knowledge of the artifact in question. Yet before she could utter a word, Elladan took a step forward and threw up his hands. She noticed they were now both empty. In all the commotion, he must have dropped the gem back into the bag. Not the worst idea, all things considered.

"Now hold on there, friend," Elladan responded, keeping his tone as pleasant as possible. "We were told the Greystone Halls were the safest place to bring such artifacts."

The gnome narrowed an eye at him. "And just who told you that?"

"Our friend, Calipherous," Elladan answered, his voice still smooth and calm.

The head clerk paused and pursed his lips at the mention of the copper dragon's name. "Calipherous, you say?"

"Aha," Elladan said with a slight nod. "We came here to Lanfor with him and the Greymantles."

The head clerk's eyes widened at the mention of the sisters' family. His brow furrowed as he turned his gaze upon Lieutenant Balthazar. "Is this all true?"

"It is," Balthazar said in a matter of fact tone. He gestured toward Elladan and Thea. "As I already told your clerks here, these folks are guests of the Queen herself."

The head clerk's cheeks reddened as he turned his gaze upon the pair behind the counter. "You could have led with that," he told them in a sour tone. The two clerks winced, appearing chagrined, yet wisely chose to remain silent.

After sufficiently staring down the clerks, the gnome returned his attention to Elladan. He gestured towards the black gem in the elf's hand. "So, what exactly do you expect us to do with that thing?"

"Consecrate them," Thea said before Elladan could answer.

Both of the gnome's bushy brows shot up his forehead. "Did you say them? Is there more than one?"

"Actually, there's five altogether," Elladan murmured in a soft voice.

"Five—" the gnome trailed off in obvious shock. He quickly recovered, however, barking orders to the clerks standing around him. "Go get five anti-magic boxes from storage."

"Ahem," Elladan cleared his throat. He held his thumb and index finger in front of him with a slight gap between them. "You might need just a few more. The last one is a full set of armor."

The head clerk's face reddened to the point where he looked about to explode. At the last moment, he managed to contain himself, and instead barked at his clerks. "Make that ten anti-magic boxes." As they departed, the gnome singled out one last clerk. "You, go to the temple and fetch one of the clerics. We'll need a magic circle for the transfer."

"I can provide that," Thea announced solemnly before the clerk could take a step.

The head clerk looked her over briefly, then gave Thea a curt nod. "Very well."

The clerks returned a short while later, all holding wooden chests of various sizes. They ranged anywhere from the width of Thea's palm to the size of a large bedroll. The top of each chest was marked with magical runes engraved in gold.

With everything ready, Thea began her spell. Lifting her finger, she traced an intricate symbol through the air in front of her. With each stroke, the mana flowed into the last line she drew. Once the pattern was complete, she released the spell with a set of words from the old language. *"Magicae Circuli Contra Malum."*

Thea felt the magic as it rushed forth away from her in all directions. A visible circle of white light formed around everyone gathered there. The effect lingered for a few moments before it finally faded from view. Still, the effects of the spell remained. Anyone inside that circle would be protected from evil influences while it endured.

The head clerk gave her an approving nod, then set his eyes upon Elladan. "Now you may take them out"—he held up a single finger as the elf reached into his portal bag—"one at a time, mind you."

Elladan hesitated, then gave the gnome a smooth smile. "Of course." He started again with the black gem, yet this time when he pulled it out, Thea felt no revulsion.

The clerk with the smallest chest stepped forward. Elladan gingerly dropped the gem inside and the clerk snapped the lid shut. The runes atop the chest flared to life in a brilliant flash. The glow swiftly disappeared, but Thea could clearly sense a distinct absence of mana where the chest stood.

The next object Elladan retrieved was a gleaming silver scroll case. Ornate symbols had been etched across the length of the case. As one of the other clerks stepped forward with a chest, the head clerk held up his hand to stop him. "Wait a moment. Let me see that."

The head clerk drew up close to the scroll case and pulled his spectacles down once more. He peered intently at those symbols until a small gasp escaped his lips. "Ah, these symbols are in royal Lanforian." He pointed at the elderly male clerk behind the counter. "Bring a parchment and a quill over here. We need to write these down for the Queen."

The gnome cast a sidelong glance at Elladan while the clerk took down the symbols. "Where exactly did you say you found that scroll?"

"That's a long story—" Elladan paused as the gnome again held up his hand—"but in a nutshell, we found it in an assassin's lair below a citadel in eastern Thac."

"Hm, I wonder…" the head clerk trailed off, not finishing his thought aloud.

Thea found the entire conversation intriguing. She wondered what the gnome wasn't telling them. After all, he did not seem the type to unduly share information. Perhaps the Queen might tell them if she asked, but for now she thought it best not to press her luck with the irritable high clerk.

As soon as the clerk finished transcribing the symbols, they put the scroll away in another chest. Elladan then reached into his bag again. This time when he pulled out his hand, he held in it a black crystal skull. The surface of the skull shimmered with a dark glow as soon as it was exposed to the light.

Suddenly, a blast of cold air rushed out over them. The magic circle Thea had cast winked out. Dark shadows rose up through the floor carrying with them a feeling of dread. Some of the clerks cried out in panic. One in particular bolted for the door, but never quite made it. The shadows fell upon him and started dragging him back down through the floor with them.

Something abruptly wrenched inside Thea. The pure vileness the skull had summoned made her blood boil with rage. That rage burst forth from her, lashing out in a wave of pure white energy. It expanded in a flash, engulfing everything in its path: the shadows, the clerks, Elladan, Balthazar.

Thea let out a sharp breath, bringing her emotions back under control. The white aura still fanned out around her, but it had dimmed to the point where she could see. The shadows were gone. The skull in Elladan's hand no longer glowed. Everyone else seemed fine. Even the clerk who had been nearly dragged away now lay on the floor, albeit sobbing uncontrollably.

The head clerk stared at Thea with newfound respect. "That was quite impressive."

"That's the power of an Auric Priestess," Elladan said with a sly wink in Thea's direction.

Balthazar, on the other hand, seemed less than enthusiastic. He gauged Thea carefully for a few moments before speaking. "While I must admit that works well against the undead, I don't think it will be quite as effective when we're facing pirates."

Thea mentally winced. *Ouch, that stung,* she thought to herself. Still, the lieutenant brought up a valid point. Other than healing that any trained cleric could provide, just what did she bring to the table on the journey that lay ahead?

After they left the vaults, Balthazar went to procure a ship for the next leg of their journey. They agreed to rendezvous with the lieutenant at the entrance to the Halls in a couple of hours.

Still smarting from the lieutenant's remarks, Thea was determined to prove her value on this mission. One place she could immediately start was to help with the research on the towers and the purple worm. Thus, she accompanied Elladan to the library here in the Halls.

The main library turned out to be huge with multiple wings and a great circular dome in its very center. That dome rose a story higher than the rest of the building. Thea and Elladan climbed the wide stairs, then passed beneath a tall archway with the golden inscription "Library of Palt." Beyond the arch, they entered a great foyer with a vaulted ceiling held aloft by thick marble columns.

Another set of archways spread out before them with a pair of marble staircases on either side that rose to the second floor. They passed through the arches and down a short corridor to a wide set of double doors. Thea gasped as they went inside. Those doors opened to a huge circular room the likes of which she had never seen.

Rows upon rows of tables and chairs formed concentric circles around a great circular ring of desks in the very center. Three stories of shelves packed with books lined the walls around the chamber. Curved staircases climbed those walls to open walkways at each level. Above it all sat a great dome with wide arched windows that lit up the whole chamber.

Sweeping past the many rows of tables, Thea and Elladan strode to the ring of desks in the center. A young woman in grey robes sat behind the ring directly in front of them, busily sorting a pile of books. She looked up as they approached. "Welcome to the Library of Palt. How may we help you today?"

Elladan addressed the librarian with one of his charming half-smiles. "We were looking for some information on the Naradon Empire."

The librarian's eyes fixed on the handsome elf, a mercurial smile crossing her lips. "Honey, we have dozens of books on just about every subject. Were you looking for anything in particular?"

"We are, in fact," Thea acknowledged more loftily than she had intended. For some reason, this woman rubbed her the wrong way. "Do you have any volumes regarding the lost towers?"

The librarian's eyes widened just a bit. "Oh, so you're the ones sent here by the Queen."

Elladan leaned over the desk, his half-smile widening. "We are, in fact. Does this mean we get special treatment?"

The librarian fixed him with a smoldering stare. "Honey, even without the Queen's blessing, it would be a pleasure servicing someone as handsome as you."

Thea found herself hard pressed to not laugh out loud. This woman was trying way too hard. "So"—she said, struggling to keep a straight face— "can we see those volumes?"

The librarian tore her eyes away from Elladan and peered at Thea with a mild hint of annoyance. "Unfortunately, you'll have to wait a bit. The Queen sent word ahead, but those volumes are currently in one of the annexes. We sent a runner to retrieve them, so they should be here shortly."

"That's fine," Thea said with a shrug. "I'll just sit here and wait." She spun on her heel and started for an empty table. "Carry on," she called back over her shoulder, her voice laced with merriment.

The librarian continued to fawn all over Elladan, constantly reaching across the counter and touching his hands and arms. A few minutes went by before the bard finally extracted himself from the lively conversation. When he finally rejoined her, Thea couldn't help commenting.

"Having a bit of trouble with the help?" she asked with thinly veiled amusement.

Elladan gave her one of those smooth smiles. "No trouble at all. Apparently she's doing a thesis on elven culture and had a few questions for me."

The corner of Thea's mouth lifted ever so slightly. "Really? Does her thesis include a 'hands on' approach?"

Elladan's face reddened ever so slightly. "Ahem, not that I'm aware. Even if it did, I told her I'm otherwise engaged at the moment."

"Engaged?" Thea arched both eyebrows, her face suddenly rather warm.

"Obviously," Elladan responded with another half-smile. "We have to find those scrolls, of course. The world is depending on us."

"Oh," Thea merely nodded, her sudden embarrassment fading. At the same time, for some reason, she also felt just a bit disappointed.

Nearly a half an hour went by before an intern showed up with the volumes they requested. The young man dumped nearly thirty books on the table in a pile in front of them. Elladan grabbed the first with a soft chuckle. "Looks like we've got our work cut out for us."

Thea let out a deep sigh. "This could take weeks," she agreed as she grabbed another of the volumes.

The two of them delved in with the idea of narrowing things down to just a few books at most. Thea's first text was entitled the

Rise and Fall of the Naradon Empire. Though rather thick, it read more like a novel than an actual historical account. After the first few chapters she decided to table it and move on to another text.

The second volume she picked up held the title *Treatises on the Naradon Empire.* That book turned out to be a dissertation by different scholars on various topics concerning the empire. One compared the empire to the previous Laurentian Empire. Another delved into the effects of the empire on the relationship between the races. Overall, it seemed to be more scholarly opinion than details on the empire itself.

Abruptly, she felt a tug on her arm. "I think I found something," Elladan whispered across the table in a conspiratorial tone.

Thea got up and went around to lean over the elf's shoulder. A map spread across two pages centered on the straits between Thac and Lanfor. The map contained seven small diagrams depicting towers, six of them in a circle around the seventh in the very center. Next to each tower stood a small key labeling each.

The tower in southern Thac stood next to the city of Mezarene. Once the summer home of the emperor and his wife, now all that stood there were ruins within the thick marshes. The key next to the tower consisted of a black diamond with the label Tower of Noctis. The tower in the Korlokesel mountains farther north had been marked with a purple diamond and the label Tower of Ameth. The northernmost tower in Thac stood next to the city of Naradon itself, now also nothing but ruins. That key displayed a clear diamond along with the words Tower of Adamantem.

Almost directly across the straits in northern Lanfor stood a tower once again in the mountains. A red diamond marked that tower accompanied by the words Tower of Sanquis. The tower in Palt they had just seen was identified by a yellow diamond and the label Tower of Amber. The southernmost tower on the Isle of Gilax had been marked in green and entitled the Tower of Viridi.

The last tower sat on a small isle in the center of the straits called Namlon. The tower there had an orange diamond next to it along with the name Tower of Tange.

The name of that isle sparked something in Thea's memory. "Namlon. Isn't that the isle that sank?"

Elladan peered up at her and nodded. "Some kind of great cataclysm struck the isle just before the fall of the Naradon Empire. It sank beneath the waves taking the seventh tower with it."

Thea stood up straight and gently tapped her chin with her finger. "Well, we've verified the location of all the towers. We even know their names if that helps."

"And colors," Elladan pointed out, "though I'm not quite sure of the significance of that just yet."

"If any," Thea added pointedly.

"True," Elladan agreed. He stood up as well and stretched his arms, barely stifling a yawn.

"Giving up already?" Thea said with mild amusement.

"Not in the least," Elladan countered with a glint in his eye. He picked up the book he'd just been reading and set it off to the side. "We should definitely take this one with us."

"Agreed," Thea said with a nod.

The two of them then sat back down and continued the long task of searching through the rest of the volumes.

6

THE DRUNKEN DRAGON

Next thing you know, people start dying, but there's no one there.

Though Donnie never spoke of it, he actually grew up on the Isle of Lanfor. An orphan, he spent his formative years with a gang of pickpockets on the streets of Kreel. He had only been to Palt once before and that had not ended well for him. Still, his time in Kreel made him wise to the ways of the street. Thus, he was keenly aware when their coach crossed into a seedier section of the city.

Donnie noted more than one questionable stare as they traveled down the busy street. Feeling more leery by the minute, he cast a wary glance at Seishin. "Where exactly is the inn you're staying?"

Seishin sat forward in his seat and peered out the window of the carriage. He took a few moments to get his bearings, then nodded in the direction they were headed. "Maybe another mile along this street, then not far down one of the side roads."

"Thanks," Donnie drawled, not quite thrilled with the answer he received. It had confirmed his suspicions though. Despite being from a distinguished clan in Isandor, Seishin must have traveled here with limited funds. That told Donnie one of two things: either the young man had a falling out with his clan or the clan itself had fallen on hard times.

As Seishin indicated, a short while later they turned down a side street. Not long afterwards, their carriage came to a halt. A large three story structure stood before them, its white exterior criss-crossed with extensive dark timbering. A sign hung off a thin pole that extended over the front door. Donnie climbed down from their coach and stepped to the side to see what it said.

The sign depicted a marginally acceptable drawing of a dragon holding a frothy mug in its claw. The lackluster scripting scrawled beneath read *The Drunken Dragon*.

"Nice place you're staying," Donnie commented as Seishin, Pallas, and Cyclone disembarked behind him.

Seishin looked at the building before them and shrugged. "One must make do with what one has," he intoned as if reciting a lesson he had learned by rote.

"Well my job is done," a voice sounded from somewhere above them. Captain Cloud hovered on that strange flying board of his just over and behind the carriage. "See you gents later," the gnome added, giving them all a quick salute. The carriage then took off again with Cloud trailing not far behind.

Donnie noted all the stares they were getting from passersby. Though none made him feel as leery as before, he assumed the sight of a royal coach was not exactly normal in this part of the city. Not wanting to draw any more attention, he gestured toward the inn. "Maybe we should go inside."

"Might as well," Cyclone said, brusquely pushing his way past the slight elf.

Donnie swiftly stepped aside as not to be bowled over by the gruff hunter. Though he didn't actually lose his balance, he felt a steadying hand on his shoulder.

Pallas stood behind him with a thin smile on his lips. "He certainly is a charmer, isn't he?"

"No argument there," Donnie responded with a wry grin.

A single step led up to the entrance. Beyond lay a noisy tavern room, the air reeking of ale and rum. Despite it being the middle of the day, a number of patrons sat at the dozen or so round tables in the center of the room. A few more occupied booths along the dark wood-framed walls. Light filtered in from a large bay window in the front of the tavern. The open hearth directly opposite lay cold and bare, not surprising given the time of year.

A long bar occupied the entire wall to one side. Behind the counter stood a weaselly looking man with short cropped hair and unshaven features. Cyclone had already seated himself at the bar and ordered an ale. Deciding it best to stick together, Donnie grabbed the seat next to him and motioned for the others to follow suit.

After shoving a frothing mug in front of the dragon hunter, the barkeep turned a wary eye on the rest of them. "What can I get you gents?"

Falling into his best street persona, Donnie pointed a casual thumb at Cyclone. "We'll have what he's having."

The man looked them over for a moment, his eyes briefly stopping on Pallas. "Coming right up," he finally said, his eye twitching ever so slightly.

Donnie could have kicked himself. The Penwick officer stood out like a sore thumb in his crimson uniform. Thankfully, this Stealle was far more observant than his younger brother. Before Donnie could say a word, Pallas stood and removed his long coat, neatly folded it and shoved it into his pack. He sat back down and met Donnie's gaze with a subtle nod.

The barkeep slammed a froth-filled mug down in front of each of them in turn, then stood back and eyed them once more with that slight twitch. "So, what brings you gents to town?"

Realizing that the man was already suspicious of them, Donnie decided to take a different tact than he normally would. "My friends and I had some business up at the palace."

The barkeep picked up a wet mug and began to dry it, trying his best to appear nonchalant. "The palace? Are you supporters of the Queen?"

"Not me," Cyclone growled, slamming down his empty mug and motioning for a refill.

"Then why go up there at all?" The barkeep asked as he grabbed Cyclone's mug and refilled it to the top.

The weaselly man's interest in their dealings with the Queen set off all sorts of alarm bells in Donnie's mind. He decided to play along to see if he could find out more. "We were trying to get her to keep her granddaughter on a short leash."

The blood suddenly drained from the man's face. He drew closer, his voice dropping to a near whisper. "The Princess? What did she do to you?"

Donnie leaned over the bar and held his hand to the side of his mouth. "Oh, just dropped a building on my friends and me."

The barkeep narrowed an eye at him, but Donnie held his stare evenly. "You're serious?" The man finally exclaimed.

"Was picking the dust from my hair for a week," Cyclone grumbled between swigs.

The hunter's grim countenance finally put the barkeep's suspicions to rest. He gave them all a begrudging smile. "Ah, so you've seen the royals for who they really are—that calls for a real drink."

The man reached under the bar and came back with a bottle labeled South Point Whiskey. "The good stuff, on the house." He laid a small glass in front of each of them and proceeded to pour them all a round.

In his time along the dark coast, Donnie had sampled more than his fair share of whiskeys and rums. South Point was indeed one of the finest. He picked up his glass and drained it, feeling it burn all the way down his throat. Setting his glass back down, Donnie let out a deep breath to cool his throat.

"Smooth," he rasped, grinning at the barkeep with a gesture toward the barely dented bottle. "Why don't you join us, friend?"

The barkeep gave him another begrudging smile followed by a nod. "Name's Ruebalt and don't mind if I do."

Ruebalt called one of the barmaids over to tend the counter, then led the four of them to an empty booth in the back corner of the room. Once they were all seated, he poured them each another glass, then drank his down in a single gulp.

"Ah," Ruebalt gasped, wiping his arm across his mouth. "That is smooth."

Donnie casually leaned forward in his chair. "So, I take it you've had a run in with the Princess?"

Ruebalt's eye began to twitch again. He poured himself a second glass and downed it, then glanced around over his shoulder before also leaning over the table. "I get some locals in here who like to talk. You know, things like what life would be like out from under the royal's thumb."

"Sure," Donnie agreed with a noncommittal nod.

Ruebalt drew in even closer. "Word must have gotten out. One night, a couple of months back, some of the Princess' goons showed up here: that boot-licking wizard fellow and the crazy chick that hangs on his arm."

Donnie frowned. "You mean Sigfus and Dari?"

"Them's the ones," Ruebalt agreed, pouring himself another shot and swiftly downing it. "Well the boys was having a meeting and talking like they usually do, when that Dari just up and disappears. Next thing you know, people start dying, but there's no one there. Folks tried to run, but that's when them bolts flew out of that wizard's fingertips. Fried them all right before my very eyes."

Ruebalt's face now twitched wildly. He poured himself a fourth shot and downed it in a single gulp. When he put it down, his hands were still shaking.

Donnie couldn't blame Ruebalt. During his own first encounter with the mage, Sigfus had tried to kill him as well. The others around the table had similar reactions. Pallas wore a dark expression. Seishin's eyes had gone wide with shock.

Cyclone was the only one who didn't appear affected. He folded his arms across his chest and snorted. "Hmph. Doesn't surprise me."

"What happened after that?" Donnie asked with real sympathy.

Ruebalt clasped his hands together to stop them from shaking. "That Dari reappears next to Sigfus and wipes off her bloody knives on my bar towel. That deranged wizard then looks me in the eye and says, 'You should be more selective of the clientele you let into this place.' After that, the two of them just saunter out of this place like nothing happened."

Pallas sat forward in his seat, his voice rife with anger. "That's outrageous. Did anyone report this to the Queen?"

Ruebalt's skin paled even further. "That'd be like slitting your own throat. No one can touch her precious granddaughter."

Pallas started to say something else, but Donnie waved him off. Ruebalt's hands had finally stopped shaking, at least enough to pour himself another glass.

Donnie waited for him to down his drink, carefully thinking his words over before he addressed the nervous man. "My friend here is right though. Actions like that cannot go unpunished."

Ruebalt glanced over his shoulder again before speaking. No one appeared to be paying any attention to them. "Oh they won't," he said with thinly veiled animosity. "Their day is coming. Soon there won't be any more royals."

Donnie held the man's stare, not batting an eye. This was exactly what he had been fishing for. Ever since they arrived in Lanfor, they'd seen signs that something wasn't right. Another rebellion was brewing right under their noses and Princess Anya's minions had lit the match.

Still playing along, Donnie reached for the bottle and poured himself another drink. He gulped it down in one swig, then slammed the glass on the table. "After all that Anya's done, I'd say good riddance."

"Same here," Cyclone echoed his sentiment. The only difference between the two of them was that the hunter actually meant it.

Oh well, Donnie thought wryly. At least he was helping sell the con.

Ruebalt eyed the lot of them for a few moments, then once again leaned across the table. "If you really mean that, I've got some friends who you should meet. What are you gents doing later?"

Donnie exchanged a quick glance with the others. Cyclone didn't seem to care, but both Pallas and Seishin appeared to be following along with his lead. He turned back to the barkeep and shrugged. "Not much. We only just arrived in town."

"Good," Ruebalt said with a wicked smile. He cast a glance at Seishin. "You're already staying here, ain't you?"

"Yes," Seishin answered simply.

"Alright." Ruebalt nodded. "I'll get the rest of you some rooms. Be down here after dinner and I'll introduce you." With that, the barkeep rose from his seat. He wobbled slightly on his legs, then straightened himself and headed back to the bar.

Once he was gone, Seishin stared uncertainly at Donnie. "I trust you're not going along with this."

"Probably just enough to see who's plotting against the crown," Pallas answered before Donnie got the chance.

Donnie touched a finger to the side of his nose. "I see who inherited the brains in the family."

The corner of Pallas' mouth upturned slightly. "Still, I wonder at the wisdom of them having another meeting here after what happened."

"Probably not the wisest course of action," Seishin agreed.

Donnie found himself liking these two more and more. "Either way, we should probably alert Balthazar and Cloud as to what's going on."

Seishin rose from his seat. "I'll slip out and go find them."

Donnie held up a hand before he got too far. "No need. I have a way of contacting Elladan directly."

Balthazar Cnidel had been a member of the Royal Lanfor Army for almost ten years now. In all that time, Bal followed orders without question, but being assigned to assist these new folks definitely caught him by surprise. Although he agreed with the importance of their mission, he was loath to leave the Queen's side—especially now with rumors of a brewing rebellion.

"Did you get us a ship?" Elladan called from the entrance to the Greystone Halls.

Bal had gone to the docks to procure them a vessel for the upcoming mission. As promised, he now stood outside the Halls waiting to pick up the gaudy-dressed elf and the holy priestess.

"The *Gossamer Lady* out of Niracom," Bal answered as he ushered the pair toward the waiting carriage. "The navigator has made the run through the Vortex multiple times."

"Sounds promising." Elladan's mouth contorted to one side in a half-smile as he climbed into the coach.

Bal had noticed him do that a couple of times during their audience with the Queen. He assumed it to be some sort of affectation—an attempt on the elf's part to be charming. Personally, he found this Elladan to be just a bit too flashy. In his experience, folks like that were all flash and no substance. It also worried Bal that this elf so recklessly carried around those evil artifacts with him. He decided he would need to keep an eye on this one.

"Let's pray this navigator has one more good trip left in him," Thea added half-jokingly as she too stepped up into the carriage.

Bal had yet to figure out the priestess. He noticed her take a fighting stance when the clerics surrounded them in the vaults. She obviously had some sort of martial training. Despite that, her power as a priestess was undeniable. The way she vaporized those shadows back in the vaults had been impressive. Though, other than the obvious healing abilities of an auric priestess, he wondered as to the extent of her battle prowess.

Bal instructed the driver to take them to the *Drunken Dragon* to rendezvous with the others. He then climbed in after the duo. They had only gone a short distance when a strange voice echoed through the cabin.

"Elladan, are you there?" The sound appeared to be coming from a broach on the elf's cloak.

Elladan lifted the broach to his lips and spoke into it. "Donnie? Is that you?"

"Who else would it be?" The voice replied, its tone dripping with sarcasm. "Seriously, is Balthazar there with you?"

"He is," Elladan said, extending the broach out to the center of the cabin. He motioned for Bal to speak into it.

Working in close proximity to the Queen, Bal had seen his share of strange magic. Thus, this peculiar method of communication did not exactly surprise him.

"This is Lieutenant Balthazar," he spoke into the broach.

The voice on the other end turned out indeed to be Donatello, or Donnie as his companions referred to him. Though not flashy like his friend, this elf dressed far too similar to the pirates from the Dark Coast. Not to mention, Bal caught a gleam in his eye directed at the Queen that seemed totally inappropriate.

Donnie went on to detail a rebel plot they had uncovered at the *Drunken Dragon*. Bal listened with growing apprehension until he finished his story. By the time he did, Bal had already decided what he must do.

He banged on the wall of the carriage behind him and called out, "Stop the coach!"

"What are you going to do?" Elladan asked as they came to a halt. Both he and Thea sat forward in their seats eyeing him expectantly.

"I need to warn the Queen's guard," Bal told the duo. "Can I count on you to go ahead and keep an eye on things?"

"Certainly," Thea answered this time, her expression grim.

"Very good." With a farewell nod, Bal practically vaulted out of the coach. He instructed the driver to continue on, then quickly scanned the skies above. Sure enough, his eyes picked out a skyrider passing by overhead.

Bal waved down the rider. The figure arched around in the sky and swept down towards him. He half expected it to be Cloud, but as they approached he recognized it to be one of Cloud's fliers.

"Can you take me to the palace? It's urgent," Bal explained as the skyrider landed.

"Sure thing. Hop on and hold onto me." She gestured toward the back of her board.

Bal leaped onto the board and grabbed the soldier around the waist. He held on tight as she took off and rose in a steep arc up towards the mountain top. Buffeted by the rushing wind and the sharp climb, Bal could do nothing else but hold on to the skyrider. Though his body remained motionless, his mind continued to race.

The audacity of these rebels astonished him though he could understand their hatred of the Princess. During his tenure with the guard, Bal had the misfortune of dealing with Anya more than once. She was spoiled, willful, and just a bit crazy. Even so, her retinue tended to be far worse.

When reports of the massacre at the *Drunken Dragon* reached the Queen's ears, she ordered Anya's murderous retainers arrested. Anya, however, had already fled with her retinue in the royal family's airship. Though chase was given, the Princess had too far of a head start and got away.

With no other recourse, the Queen anonymously paid for the funerals of all who had died. Bal thought it a mistake to do so quietly. If the rebels only knew how much she truly cared for her people, they might not see her as a monster like her granddaughter. Unfortunately, it was not his place to tell her majesty what to do.

Before Bal knew it, the skyrider was dropping him off in front of the palace. After thanking her, Bal leapt off the board and rushed into the palace. Two guards were always stationed in the entrance. Bal addressed one of them. "Where's the Lord Commander?"

The man pointed back across the grounds towards the barracks. "Where else would she be? She's working with the new recruits."

A thin smile crossed Bal's lips as swiftly crossed the grounds. Lord Commander Amaia Catolis was a strong, fit woman who found it difficult to run things from behind a desk. Sure enough, he found her decked out in full armor, sizing up the latest batch of recruits.

During his tenure in the army, Bal found it to be almost completely dominated by nobility. Amaia proved to be the one of the few exceptions to that rule. During the last war, her family had sided with the rebels. Already a captain in the army, she chose instead to fight for the crown. Despite her now tainted line, Amaia earned her position as head of Intelligence due to that devotion as well as her mental prowess.

When Amaia caught sight of Bal, she swiftly disarmed the poor recruit who had the misfortune of facing her. Whacking the man with the flat of her blade, she barked at him, "A battle is first won in the mind. Keep your wits about you!"

After handing her weapons to the training officer, Amaia briskly clanked her way over to Bal. A trace of amusement graced her lips as she brushed aside a lock of her short brown hair. "I heard you and Cloud got babysitting duty. What are you doing here back at the palace?"

Under other circumstances Bal would have enjoyed verbal

sparring with his commander, but now was definitely not the time. "Something urgent came up." He lowered his voice to barely a whisper. "We might have a lead on the rebels."

The glint of amusement in Amaia's dark brown eyes immediately faded. "Come with me." She pushed past and motioned for him to follow.

Once they reached the privacy of the commander's office, Bal relayed to her what the newcomers discovered at the *Drunken Dragon*. When he finished, Amaia stood there biting her lip. "That's not good. We've had reports of a Sentinel raid planned for that section of the city tonight."

The Sentinels were the city guard. While many of their troops were good people, their commander, Lord Viron, was another noble with no real expertise in tactics. Thus Bal understood her concern. "You're afraid they'll scare off any rebel leaders that might be attending tonight's meeting."

"They are not exactly known for their subtlety," Amaia admitted with a wry smile. She paused and tapped a finger to her chin. "It's a long shot, but maybe I can get the Sentinels to stand down."

Bal truly admired Amaia, but he doubted anyone short of the Queen herself could get Lord Viron to listen. In the meantime, he had some ideas of his own. "These new folks managed to get themselves invited to tonight's meeting. Maybe I should tag along and see if I can identify any of the rebel leaders."

Amaia gave him a genuine smile. "That's an excellent idea. You go and do that while I reach out to the Sentinel commander."

After stopping by his room to switch into street clothes, Bal hitched a ride on one of the patrol ships that swept the city. He had them drop him off on a rooftop just outside the South Side, the section of Palt where the *Drunken Dragon* stood.

Night fell as Bal made his way through the city streets. He moved as fast as he possibly could while still trying to remain inconspicuous. He drew within a few blocks of the inn when he came to a sudden halt. The next intersection just ahead had been blocked off by a large contingent of Sentinels. As he suspected, Amaia had not been able to stop the raid.

As Bal watched, more Sentinels poured in to join their colleagues. He was all too familiar with this brute force strategy. Every street in this section of the city was now being cordoned off. Once the Sentinels had finished marshalling their forces, they would begin their raid by marching through and searching every building in the area. If he were to get past them, the only alternative would be to employ a more specialized approach.

Psychic abilities ran in Bal's family. Recognizing his potential when he first joined the army, Amaia enlisted him in a very specialized group. After nearly a decade of intensive training, Bal mastered his particular area of expertise—the conjuration and control of constructs from the astral plane.

Slipping into a nearby alley, Bal quieted his mind. As he brought his will to bear, a purple aura enveloped his body. His concentration deepening, Bal used the aura as a guide to manifest a form of astral armor. Had a casual observer been passing by, that aura would have appeared to take on mirror like qualities. With the armor warping the light around him, Bal would have all but faded from view.

Now virtually invisible, Bal left the alley and cautiously padded down the street. Moving as silently as possible, he slipped around the ranks of the still gathering Sentinels and headed straight for the *Drunken Dragon*.

7

NIGHT OF THE SENTINELS

"It's not my fault they're afraid of their own town guard. Makes you sort of wonder though about this Queen Amerelis."

Thea and Elladan arrived at the *Drunken Dragon* just before dinner. Though not a small tavern, many of the tables were already taken. Pallas and the others had a booth in the back with enough seating for them all. Thea sat next to her brother facing the doorway. From there she scanned through the crowd, but could detect no trace of darkness.

As dinner progressed, small groups of folks filtered in through the front door. Some were seated in the main room, but more and more headed past the bar toward the back of the inn. Out of those, Thea detected only a few auras with traces of darkness. These were just regular folks, misguided perhaps, but not evil.

Thea shared her impressions with the others, ending with her own conclusions. "Someone must be using these people."

"Hmph," Elladan murmured. "Wouldn't be the first time. History is filled with examples of the power hungry riling up folks for their twisted purposes."

Seishin hadn't said much since they first met, but this topic apparently struck close to home for the young man. "The same thing happened in Isandor after the King died," he told them in a quiet voice.

Though Seishin's face remained stoic, Thea could see an emotional fluctuation in his aura. She'd heard rumors of trouble in Isandor before they left Penwick. "Does that have anything to do with the reported alliance between Isandor and Parthos?"

A pained expression briefly crossed Seishin's face before he could clamp it down. "The church turned half the country against the Queen. In order to prevent a civil war, she appointed the high priest to the Isandor council." A trace of anger had filtered its way into his voice. He paused a moment to rein in his emotions. "In doing so, however, she lost control of the country."

Elladan let out a low whistle. "That's some seriously underhanded dealings."

"I still don't understand how that led to an alliance with an aggressor nation like Parthos," Pallas interrupted brusquely.

This time Seishin visibly winced.

"Pallas!" Thea smacked her brother on the arm. She fixed Seishin with a sympathetic smile. "Don't mind my brother. He has no sense of compassion whatsoever."

A wan smile crept across Seishin's lips. "No, he's right. It doesn't make sense." The young warrior halted briefly to take a deep breath. "After the King died, pirate activity increased along the coast. Since Isandor lacks a strong navy, the high priest pushed for a Parthian alliance."

"Sounds like mighty convenient timing to me," Elladan drawled. He turned to Donnie. "You know the pirates better than anyone else. What do you think?"

Donnie cocked his head to one side and pursed his lips together. "I wouldn't put it past some of the clans to take part in that kind of scheme—especially if it involved looting and pillaging."

"I wonder if something similar is happening here?" Thea speculated aloud. With both her parents on the Penwick Council, she'd been exposed to more than her fair share of intrigue. Between that and her earlier impressions of the folks in this tavern, she thought she spied a web of deceit.

Pallas looked dubiously at her. "So you think some high level official is behind this rebellion? Or are you saying it's the Parthians—or both?"

Thea gazed back at him thoughtfully. "The question is who has the most to gain if the Royal House of Lanfor falls?"

"Lanfor wasn't always one country," Donnie informed them. "I wouldn't be surprised if some of the former royals still held grudges against the crown."

Elladan cast a curious glance at his fellow elf. "You seem to know a lot about Lanfor history."

Donnie winked at his friend. "Just some knowledge I picked up from my time on the coast. Just like I also know that Lanfor and the Clans are the only real competition to the Parthians in these waters."

Elladan did not appear quite convinced as to Donnie's explanation on how he knew all this. He did not get to question him further though, as Ruebalt chose that moment to join them. "The meeting's about to start. There's just one slight problem."

Thea could see the emotional turmoil in the man's aura. All sorts of warning bells went off in her head. *Have we been discovered?*

If Donnie had similar thoughts, he showed no signs of it. "Oh, and what's that, friend?" the elf asked nonchalantly.

Ruebalt leaned over the table and spoke in a confidential tone. "I was counting on a singer to keep folks out here entertained, but the guy backed out at the last minute. Said he was sick, but I ain't so sure about that."

"Well you're in luck," Donnie said with a knowing smile. He gestured a hand toward Elladan. "My friend here just happens to be an extraordinary entertainer."

"Is that so?" Ruebalt eyed Elladan skeptically.

Elladan stood and snapped his fingers. A lute appeared in his hands and he proceeded to strum a few pleasant notes.

"Not bad," Ruebalt admitted, "but can you sing?"

"I've been known to carry a tune," Elladan responded with one of those half-smiles.

Ruebalt held up a pair of fingers. "Two silver pieces an hour if you can keep the crowd occupied,"—he paused and added a third finger— "three if you get them to buy more drinks."

"Done," Elladan agreed with a nod.

Having seen Elladan perform back in Penwick, Thea was certain the innkeeper got the better end of the deal. Donnie slid down and made room for Ruebalt to sit as the bard strode across to the stage. Once there, he projected his voice over the crowd. "Evening everybody. How about we make a little noise?"

A round of cheers went up around the room.

"Drink up and enjoy the show," Elladan urged as he eased into a jaunty tune. His rendition of *Hell Hound* soon had folks up from their seats and dancing in the aisles.

Ruebalt tapped Donnie on the shoulder and yelled over the din. "Hey, your friend's pretty good."

"Don't tell him that. It'll just go to his head," Donnie cried back with a wink at Thea.

Thea chuckled softly to herself. Though his humor sometimes bordered on corny, Donnie could be quite amusing.

Rising from his seat, Ruebalt motioned for those in the booth to follow. Thea moved to one side and grabbed Pallas by the arm as he went by. "I think I'll stay out here and keep an eye on things."

Pallas' face briefly darkened as he glanced at the elf on stage. Thea had dealt with her brother's overprotective tendencies through most of teen years. She wasn't about to let him start up with that again now. As Pallas turned back to her, she fixed him with a withering stare.

Pallas met her gaze for a moment, then shrugged. "Suit yourself." He took off after Donnie and Cyclone, both who already were following Ruebalt.

Interestingly, Seishin chose to hang back as well. Her dander already peaked, Thea cast a suspicious stare at the young Isandorian. "You do know I can take care of myself, right?"

"No offense meant," Seishin said, raising both hands in a warding gesture. He leaned closer and whispered to her, "If it's any consolation, you remind me of someone and she's as tough as they come. It's merely—my choice to do the honorable thing."

Thea felt both impressed and flattered at the same time. This Seishin seemed to be quite the gentleman.

Elladan was in the middle of his performance when Thea spied Balthazar enter the tavern. Strangely, he no longer wore his uniform. When Thea and Seishin went over to meet him, he pulled them both aside.

"This place is going to be raided in a few minutes," Balthazar warned the duo.

Seishin appeared as surprised as Thea. "Isn't that somewhat counterproductive?"

"It is," Balthazar agreed, "but try explaining tactics to the Sentinels—that is the city guard."

"I see." Seishin nodded.

Thea nudged her head toward the hall at the other end of the bar. "The meeting's taking place back there. If you want to check it out, we'll make sure these innocents are not caught in the crossfire."

"It's probably too late for that," Balthazar cautioned her.

"I have to try," Thea countered. She wouldn't be able to live with herself if innocent folks got hurt in a fight between the town guards and the rebels.

Balthazar eyed her for a few moments before nodding. "Very well." With that he strode off toward the back of the tavern.

Thea touched Seishin on the arm. "Watch the door. I'll see if I can get Elladan to warn the crowd."

Seishin gave her a curt nod, then headed toward the front entrance. Thea wound her way through the crowded tables until she stood at the foot of the stage. As soon as Elladan saw her there, he stopped playing, bent down, and whispered, "What's going on?"

Thea swiftly explained the situation. Without batting an eye, Elladan rose to his feet and announced the impending raid to the crowd.

Panic immediately ensued. Everyone bolted for the door, nearly running over Seishin in the process.

Thea folded her arms across her chest and narrowed an eye at Elladan. "Well that was certainly delicate."

Elladan cocked his head to one side. "It's not my fault they're afraid of their own town guard. Makes you sort of wonder though about this Queen Amerelis."

His point gave Thea pause. Penwick had its own brand of politics, but no one was afraid of the Baron. Then again, no one loved him either. "Balthazar and Cloud seem quite dedicated to the Queen," Thea noted, "and she was rather kind to us."

"True," Elladan agreed, "but she was rather harsh on the Greymantles."

"Fair point," Thea admitted. There was definitely an iron side to this deceptively young looking Queen. Nevertheless, her aura had been basically pure with only the faintest traces of darkness. That did not seem all that uncommon for a ruler who's had to make hard decisions over the course of time—and three hundred years was an awfully long time.

Ruebalt led Donnie and the others to the back of the inn and down a cramped hallway. The very last door opened to a long, thin room with an oval meeting table at one end. More than two dozen people stood in there talking to each other in small groups.

The din died down as they entered, the folks gathered there eyeing the suspiciously. "Who's them with you?" Someone called from amongst the crowd.

Ruebalt pointed a thumb back at Donnie, Pallas, and Cyclone. "They're okay. Had a run in with the Princess just like us."

Mumbles swept through the gathering, but no one questioned him any further. Donnie noted that all the seats at the table stood empty. He pointed it out to Ruebalt.

Ruebalt's mouth twisted into a cagy smile. "The meeting don't start until our leader arrives."

"And who's that?" Donnie asked with as innocent a look as he could muster.

"You'll find out soon enough." Ruebalt responded with a hoarse laugh.

Someone across the room waved at the barkeep. Ruebalt waved back, then told the three of them, "Wait here."

While Ruebalt went off, Donnie furtively scanned the crowd. He had run with some rough crews in his time, but Thea was right— these folks didn't quite strike him as thugs.

A sudden whisper in his ear nearly made the slight elf jump. "It's Balthazar. Don't turn around."

Not turning his head, Donnie glanced out of the corner of his eye. It certainly sounded like Balthazar, but the Lanfor lieutenant was nowhere in sight.

"The city guard is just down the street and plans to raid this place," Balthazar went on. "Is the leader here?"

Donnie subtly shook his head.

"That's unfortunate," Balthazar sighed. "We were hoping to catch him, but now there's no chance."

Donnie cocked his head to one side. "Maybe, maybe not." This was not his first experience with intrigue and an idea had already popped into his head. Without another word, the slim elf weaved his way through the throng until he came upon Ruebalt. He stole up to the man's ear and repeated Balthazar's warning.

The barkeep fixed Donnie with a hard stare, his brow knit into a tight frown. "You sure?"

Donnie responded with a single nod.

Ruebalt held his gaze for a moment longer, then held up his hands and called out for everyone to quiet down. Once he had their attention he announced, "We just got word that the Sentinels is planning a raid."

Chaos erupted amongst the gathering. Everyone started talking at once. Ruebalt pushed his way through the crowd, shouting above the din as he went. "Quiet down and follow me if you want to get out of here without being thrown in the dungeon!"

The barkeep led them all across the hall and down a flight of narrow stairs to the cellar. A long stone room stretched before them, wooden racks filled with bottles lining either wall. A number of kegs lay piled up at the other end of the room, a pair of them on their sides on raised pallets in front of the wall.

Ruebalt went to one of those kegs and twisted its beer tap nozzle. His effort was rewarded with the grinding sound of stone on stone as a section of the wall swung outward. The barkeep peered at Donnie and winked. "Had these put in after the royals' last visit."

"Not bad," Donnie admitted. Perhaps these rebels were not quite as dumb as he thought.

Ruebalt raised his voice over the nervous chattering of the crowd behind them. "You all go ahead without me. I need to check on the folks upstairs." With that he pushed his way through the throng and headed back up the steps.

Donnie peered through the open section of wall. It was pitch black on the other side even to his keen elven eyes. He glanced at Pallas, but merely received a shrug in return. Cyclone was no help either, his arms folded and his expression stony.

When no one else seemed willing to move, Donnie shook his head and cautiously stepped through the opening. He hadn't gone more than two feet when an awful smell assailed his senses. He waved a hand in front of his nose and called back over his shoulder in a semi-hushed voice, "Does anyone know where this goes?"

"The sewers," an unfamiliar voice answered.

His hands on his hips, Donnie spun about and glared at the gathering of nervous rebels. "Gee thanks, I couldn't tell by the smell."

His quip was met with wan smiles and deadpan stares.

"What I meant is where does it lead?" Donnie quickly amended.

"Down to the—river," a mousy man answered with a nervous catch in his throat.

Donnie took a step to one side and magnanimously ushered the man forward. "Well then, lead the way, my friend."

Up in the tavern room, pandemonium reigned as folks practically trampled over each other to get out the front door. Something about their frantic behavior didn't sit quite right with Elladan. True the Queen had been harsh on the Greymantles, but not in a way that should generate this kind of fear. While Anya's little bloodbath didn't help matters, these folks seemed genuinely afraid of their own city guard. Elladan began to wonder if they had good reason.

As the first few patrons made it through the front door, loud shouts rang out over the noise of the frantic crowd.

"Stop right there!"

"Don't move!"

"We've got the place surrounded!"

Back by the bar with Thea and Seishin, Elladan exchanged a bewildered glance with the duo. "Well that sounds a bit over the top."

Thea appeared equally confused. "These are just ordinary folks, yet they're treating them like criminals."

Even the stoic Seishin wore an expression of mild surprise. "When I was in the Isandor army, we never treated civilians like this."

Folks stopped clamoring to reach the exit. Instead they tried to back away from the door, but were packed together too tight to retreat. Beyond the open doorway out in the street, Elladan spotted a group of armed soldiers.

"Everyone step outside now!"

"There's nowhere to run!"

"These Sentinels don't sound like they're willing to reason," Thea noted sourly.

The guards' belligerence did seem almost purposeful to Elladan. It made him wonder if someone in the Sentinels was deliberately trying to sour the populace. Either way, these aggressive tactics posed a threat to their own mission.

"Finding the leader of this little rebellion would be awfully hard from inside a dungeon cell," Elladan agreed.

"Perhaps we should move out of sight of the doorway?" Seishin observed pragmatically.

Taking Seishin's cue, the three of them retreated toward the back of the inn. In doing so, they nearly ran head first into Ruebalt.

"What's going on up here?" The barkeep's expression grew frantic as he surveyed the chaos behind them.

"The city guard has the place surrounded. There's nothing more you can do," Thea advised him with clear sympathy.

Despite her gentle attempt to dissuade him, Ruebalt did not take it well. He grabbed either side of his head and shook it back and forth. "No, no, not again! This is going to ruin my business."

Though Elladan felt truly sorry for the barkeep, now was not the best time for a meltdown. He grabbed Ruebalt by the shoulders and shook him. "Get a grip, man. Where are the others?"

Ruebalt blinked, coherence swiftly returning to his eyes. "They're safe—out the secret exit to the sewers."

"Sewers?" Thea repeated with obvious disdain. "That sounds lovely."

Elladan cast a wry look at the priestess. "Can't say I disagree, but…"

A cry from the front of the tavern cut him off before he could finish. "You back there! Don't move a muscle!"

A quick glance over his shoulder proved his worst fears to be true. The guards had pushed their way into the tavern and stood in the midst of the remaining patrons. It wouldn't be long now until they'd come after them.

"Quick, follow me," Ruebalt hissed as he pulled away.

A number of thoughts raced through Elladan's mind in that moment. If they ran the guards might still catch them. If they did manage to escape, the Sentinels would tear this place apart looking for secret doors. Neither seemed ideal, but they did have one last alternative.

"There's no time!" Elladan cried, grabbing Ruebalt by the arm. He flung the man back toward Seishin and began tracing a pattern through the air. More shouts rang out behind him, but he ignored them all, concentrating solely on that symbol. In a few seconds he had it drawn and mana flooded into the pattern.

"*Planum porta.*" As soon as the words tumbled from his lips, a blue, glowing, six foot oval appeared in the air before him. "Quick, go!" Elladan motioned to the others.

Thea immediately leapt through, her entire body disappearing into the shimmering glow of the portal. Seishin went next, dragging along a confused Ruebalt.

A strained cry sounded behind him as Elladan prepared to leap after the others. "Wait! You can't get away!"

Two of the guards had broken free and rushed along the bar for him. With a quick half smile, Elladan leaped. The moment he disappeared, the glowing blue oval whooshed shut. It vanished with a thin pop, the angry guards reaching it just a moment too late.

Darkness cloaked the sewers beneath the city of Palt, but that bothered Pallas little. A master of the spiritblade *School of Shadows*, he tended to think of the dark as his friend. However, some folks brought torches from Ruebalt's cellar, at least enough to light the passage a few yards ahead. The foul smell of raw sewage permeated these tunnels, but Pallas found it not much worse than the stench from fishing trawlers returning with their daily catch.

Though the initial tunnel forced them to forge ahead single file, it eventually emptied into a much larger passageway. Water flowed through a deep channel down the center of the new tunnel carrying the sewage along with it. Walkways flanked the channel on either side with enough space for two people to march abreast.

Donnie casually draped his arm across the shoulder of their im-promptu guide. "Which way, friend?" the slim elf asked with a toothy grin.

"We—follow the water," the man responded, thrown off guard by Donnie's forwardness.

Pallas fell in behind the duo, noting how easily Donnie played the part of a dubious character. Between that and his knowledge of the pirate coast, Pallas wondered at the elf's shady past. Cyclone, on the contrary, remained aloof as always. Nothing seemed to faze the hunter, not even the Queen of Lanfor nor the huge gold dragon that slept behind her throne. He only hoped these two would stick to their word to help track down the rebel leaders.

They came to an abrupt halt as the passage ahead split in two. Seemingly confused, their guide called out to one of the others. "Which way is south?"

Whispers rose up among their companions until one of them finally pointed to the left branch. "That way, I reckon."

The more Pallas observed of these so called rebels, the more he realized his sister was right. These were just ordinary folks embroiled in something far beyond their understanding. He doubted any of them had a clue as to the ruin they might bring down upon them-selves and their loved ones.

Pallas had already seen far too much of that in his life. Even now, the dreams still haunted him.

Thick smoke hung like a grey veil in the air. Scarlet flames leapt from windows and danced across rooftops. Corpses lay strewn all about. Cries and shouts echoed around every corner. Steel rang on steel. Dark shadows fled down side streets accompanied by the cries of death.

Pallas had only been six at the time, but visions of the pirate invasion were forever etched within his brain. No one should ever have to live through that kind of death and destruction. He was certain these rebel leaders, whoever they were, cared little for the wellbeing of these people.

Maybe an hour had passed when they finally reached the end of the sewers. Dim light flooded in from the night revealing where the tunnel ended. It also outlined a pair of figures that stood just outside the entrance.

The mousy man acting as their guide drew to a halt and hissed to the folks behind them, "Put out them torches."

"I take it they're not one of yours?" Donnie whispered as darkness enveloped them.

"We don't stand guard over anything," the man hissed back emphatically. "Them's got to be Sentinels." His utterance of the name immediately silenced the anxious murmurs from the crowd behind them.

These folks sure seem afraid of their own city guard, Pallas thought dourly. Had he been in charge, he'd have thrashed the guards soundly for generating that kind of fear in these townsfolk. These Sentinels were abusing their positions and deserved to be taught a lesson.

Stealing up next to Donnie, Pallas quietly assured their nervous guide, "Don't worry, we'll take care of them."

"They ain't exactly pushovers," the man replied, his voice rife with skepticism.

"Neither are we," Donnie responded glibly.

Donnie and Pallas stole down the tunnel on silent feet. When they reached the very edge of the darkness, Pallas placed a staying hand on the elf's shoulder. "I'll take the one on the left," he whispered into Donnie's ear.

Before Donnie could respond, Pallas took a deep breath and

stilled his mind. He felt himself melting inward, deep into the very core of his being. There in the midst of the darkness shone a light like a brilliant star—the spark of life that fueled the gifts of the spiritblade. As Pallas tapped into its power, he envisioned himself fading into the shadows. Warmth flooded his entire body and in moments any trace of him faded from view.

"Neat trick," Donnie whispered. "One of these days I have to learn this spiritblade stuff."

The duo moved forward again, closing on the two Sentinels. Had Pallas been worried in the slightest, their quiet chatter stayed his concerns.

"What are we even doing out here?" The first guard grumbled.

"Hey, I ain't complaining," the second guard answered. "It's nice to be far from the action for a change."

"I don't exactly call rounding up these low life's action," the first guard countered.

"Well—"

Whatever the second guard was going to say died on his lips as Donnie struck. Pallas made certain he struck at the same time, and in a matter of moments, both men had been laid out cold. Dragging them back into the tunnel, they hog-tied and gagged them.

By the time they had finished, the rest of the crowd caught up with them. "You two aren't exactly pushovers either," the mousy man admitted ruefully.

Donnie gave him a sly wink. "We do alright, but I'd be careful not to rile our grumpy friend back there."

The mousy man cast a glance toward the back of the crowd. Cyclone stood there with his arms folded, a menacing scowl upon his lips. The man attempted a weak smile, but the hunter merely glared at him.

"I see what you mean," the man shuddered as he confided in Donnie.

8

SINS OF THE FATHER

Bal finally had the chance to make up for his family's transgressions.

As soon as Elladan stepped through the portal he found himself in a dark alley. A well-lit city street could be seen on the one end, but the other turned an abrupt corner a few yards down. Thea, Seishin, and Ruebalt stood there in the shadows, the latter looking rather tense. Shouts could be heard off in the distance along with the sound of heavy boots and the clanking of armor. As they listened the shouts grew closer.

Ruebalt turned a wary eye toward Elladan. "Thanks for getting us out of there, but we're not out of the woods just yet."

"Do you know where we are?" Thea asked in a hushed voice.

The barkeep stopped and grabbed his chin. "Mm, I'd say about three blocks over from the Drunken Dragon."

"Still close enough to be caught in a sweep," Seishin observed in a matter of fact tone.

He was right, Elladan realized. They needed to move and quickly. The question was to where? "I can portal us again," he announced to the others, "but I think it best if we find a place to hide until things settle down."

"I have a place in the Olde Town section of the city," Ruebalt offered.

Thea fixed the man with a deadpan stare. "Isn't that the first place they'd look for you?"

"Not likely," Ruebalt snorted. "The Sentinels are notoriously lazy. They'd rather sit outside my inn and bully my customers than go to the trouble of tracking down a single soul like myself."

"It's a typical suppression tactic," Seishin affirmed. "Throw out a wide net and reel in as many folks as you can in one haul."

"How effective is that?" Thea asked.

"Not very if you're looking for specific people," Seishin admitted.

Ruebalt moved in closer to them, his hand going to the side of his mouth. His voice dropped to a conspiratorial whisper. "Even if they did come looking for me, I have a secret room they'd be hard pressed to find."

That did make the innkeeper's place sound a bit more appealing. Despite that, Elladan wasn't so sure that the city guard wouldn't show up there looking for him. If what Ruebalt had told them was true, however, then that would prove the city guard was more interested in stirring up folks than actually catching rebels.

More shouts echoed from the street outside the alley. This time they were much closer.

Elladan traded glances with Thea. "Well one thing's for sure—we can't stay here."

Thea shrugged though her expression remained skeptical. "Probably not the best idea."

Elladan cocked an eye at Ruebalt. "Which way?"

The barkeep hesitated a moment to get his bearings, then pointed toward the dark end of the alley. "West."

Elladan drew in a deep breath and began once again to cast *portal*.

Beyond the end of the sewer tunnel the channel emptied into a wide river—the River of Liath according to the locals. Calm waters carried away its foul contents to the Bay of Glas a few miles downstream. A well-lit bridge spanned the waters to the far side easily over a mile away. Bright city lights twinkled along the length of the opposite bank.

The brilliant glow from the city skyline drowned out the stars in the inky black sky. The only lights visible above were from passing airships or those glowing boards of the skyriders. Shouts emanated from the city behind them. It sounded as if the Sentinels were still cracking down on the quarter they had just left. Wanting to avoid any confrontations, the rebels chose to stick to the darkness along this side of the river.

Hugging the bank, they traveled downstream perhaps a mile before stopping before a dark warehouse. Stealing up to the loading doors, their mousy guide rapped on it in a distinctive pattern. A few seconds later the double doors cracked open and light spilled out into the darkness.

Three robed figures stood just inside, their features shaded by the light behind them. "Get inside, quick!" barked the center figure, the voice husky, but definitely female. As soon as everyone filed inside, one of the other three pulled the doors closed behind them.

Pallas' eyes swiftly adjusted to the light. All clothed in dark green robes, the two on either side of the woman turned out to be men. One was bald and pudgy while the other appeared muscular with close-cropped dark hair and a matching beard and mustache. Of the woman, only her face could be seen beneath her hood along with a shock of raven black hair.

Subtly gauging their auras, Pallas could sense they all had some amount of power. He also detected more than a tinge of darkness in each. These three were definitely not the good guys.

The rebels distanced themselves from Pallas, Donnie, and Cyclone, while their mousy friend reported to the woman. At the same time, the two men in robes stood directly in front of the trio. Though the hairs bristled on the back of his neck, Pallas chose to quietly wait and see what would happen next.

Cyclone, on the other hand, showed no such compunction, instead reacting with a derisive snort. The muscular man and the hunter scowled at each other until the woman came and pushed both her fellow rebels aside.

"None of that now," she scolded her allies. "These three helped our folks escape."

Apparently never one to miss an opportunity to flirt, Donnie flashed her a toothy smile. "It was the least we could do, milady."

Arching an eyebrow, the woman ran her gaze up and down the slim elf. "Milady, is it? So, a bit of a rogue and a charmer I see." She pulled down her hood and brushed back the locks of her long raven-colored hair so that it draped down her shoulders. She was quite beautiful in fact, though Pallas noted a coldness in her pale blue eyes that gave him pause.

While Donnie and the robed woman flirted with each other, Pallas heard a soft whisper in his ear. The voice belonged to Balthazar. "I've got this from here. If I know Cloud, he's flying around the area. Flag him down and tell him what we've found."

Pallas responded with a barely perceptible nod, then reached over and tapped Donnie on the shoulder. "While we're glad to have offered our assistance, I think it best than none of us overstay our welcome."

The woman turned her gaze upon him and also looked him up and down. There was a hunger in her eyes that made Pallas quite uncomfortable. "Good looks and brains to boot. What a refreshing combination."

"Your friend is right," she told Donnie. "We cannot tarry here, but your resourcefulness is appreciated." She reached out and touched him lightly on the shoulder. "Perhaps we'll be able to use your services in the future."

Donnie took her hand and kissed it, then backed away with a smooth bow. "As you wish, milady."

With one last enticing smile, the woman spun about and rejoined the rest of the rebels. The muscular man eyed them warily while the pudgy one cracked open the loading door to let them out.

Once the door slammed behind them, Donnie grabbed Pallas

by the arm. "What was that all about? I was getting somewhere with their leader."

Before Pallas could frame a retort, Cyclone beat him to it with a derisive click of his tongue. "Tsk. I don't think that 'somewhere' was going to help us."

Gruff as Cyclone could be, Pallas was coming to appreciate his brusque sense of humor. Stifling a laugh, he related Balthazar's words to the two of them. He then added what he had seen of the rebel leaders' auras.

When he finished, Cyclone nudged his head away from the warehouse. "You two go ahead. I'll make sure they don't get away."

Pallas watched with keen interest as the hunter picked up an iron pole from a pile next to the warehouse. Lacing it through the handles of the double doors, he braced himself and pulled on either end. Beyond plain sight, Pallas observed a marked flare in the hunter's aura. With a metallic creak, the pole gave way and bent around the handles, effectively sealing the doors shut.

Pallas traded an astonished look with Donnie. "That was rather impressive."

Donnie responded with an offhanded smile. "You should see him when he's really angry."

Pallas shrugged. "As long as it's not directed at me."

Leaving Cyclone to guard the door, the two of them headed back up the riverbank while searching the skies around them. They had only gone a short distance when Donnie suddenly pulled up short.

"What's wrong?" Pallas hissed, glancing around for signs of danger.

Donnie pointed back the way they came. "I thought I saw something take off from the top of the warehouse."

Pallas followed his gaze, but saw nothing. "What was it?"

Donnie shook his head. "I'm not certain, but whatever it was, it headed upriver."

Pallas didn't like the sound of that at all. If the rebel leaders escaped from the warehouse, the gods only knew where they'd night go next. "Maybe we should warn the others?"

"Good idea," Donnie agreed. The slim elf touched the broach on his cloak and proceeded to contact Elladan.

Bal thought all was lost until Donnie's quick thinking enabled the rebels to circumvent the Sentinels' net. While he still didn't completely trust the elf, perhaps Donnie's intentions were not as dubious as he originally thought. As luck would have it, the rebels led them directly to this group in green robes. Though obviously higher ranking than the others, the way the two men deferred to the woman marked her as their leader. With any luck she was high enough up the chain to lead him to the brains behind the rebellion.

Once Donnie and the others left, the woman in charge spoke briefly to the gathering of rebels. Her speech contained nothing of merit other than assuring them that the "fall of the royals" was "inevitable." After urging them to wait here until the fervor died down outside, she and her two robed comrades retreated to the back of the warehouse and up a flight of stone stairs.

Still cloaked in his light-bending astral armor, Bal cautiously followed the trio up a second flight to a door that opened to the roof. With no way to make it through without alerting them to his presence, Bal let the trio pass through, then counted to ten before following.

With the moon not risen yet, darkness bathed the warehouse rooftop. Thankfully it was mostly flat. Bal easily spotted his quarry about a dozen yards ahead. As he hastened to catch up, Bal noted many lights and noises still emanating from the South Side up river. The trio in front of him noticed it as well.

"They're really stepping up their game. You should've thought twice before coming out here yourself, Lillon," the pudgy man chided. His voice had a distinctive nasal quality to it.

Lillon responded in a tone that was both reproachful and condescending. "You worry too much Celdon. They are doing our work for us—stirring up more hatred for the royals."

"I thought that's what we were paying Lord Viron for," the muscular man pointed out, his voice a low baritone.

"It doesn't make it any less delicious, Burkon," Lillon practically purred with delight.

Bal's jaw tightened at the mention of Lord Viron. *So the head of the Sentinels is in league with the rebels.* That information alone made this mission worthwhile. Still, he wanted more.

Bal had a personal interest in ending this rebellion. Like Amaia, his parents had chosen the wrong side during the last insurrection. With Bal hidden away when they died, everything they owned had been forfeit to the crown. Left with nothing, he resorted to living off the streets until Amaia found him.

Bal came to a sudden halt as his quarry reached the edge of the roof. All three abruptly sat down and Lillon spoke a single word. *"Fugere."*

Without warning the trio suddenly lifted into the air. In the darkness it appeared as if a thin piece of the roof had risen up with them. It suddenly struck Bal that they must be sitting on some sort of flying carpet. He watched dumbfounded as the trio started to pull away.

Reacting out of pure instinct, Bal caught the edge of the carpet and rolled up onto it in a prone position along the back. Thankfully the magic that kept the carpet aloft also masked his sudden movements.

"Stick to the river," Celdon moaned as the glow from the orb of a skyrider's board cut across the sky in front of them.

"This is not my first rodeo," Lillon hissed back as she angled the carpet down toward the River of Liath.

Steadily descending until just a few feet above the water, they then angled east along the center of the river. Lillon stuck as close to that track as possible, only swerving occasionally to avoid any boats in their path. The trio remained silent as they navigated upstream leaving Bal to his own thoughts.

Because of his lost heritage, Bal had struggled with fitting into an army dominated by nobility. In truth his only friends were Amaia and Cloud. Due to his race, the gnome had also been treated like an outcast. Yet now Bal finally had the chance to make up for his family's transgressions. In taking down the leaders of this rebellion, he could wipe the slate clean once and for all.

Upon reaching the outskirts of the city, Bal thought the rebels might veer away from the river. To his surprise, they continued eastward past empty farmland and the occasional village. With little chance of being overheard, the rebels once again became talkative.

"That was too close," Celdon grumbled.

"Grow a spine, Celdon," Lillon warned, her voice taking on a dangerous edge.

"That's easy for you to say. You weren't there twelve years ago," Celdon complained, either not noticing or purposely ignoring Lillon's growing anger with him.

"Celdon raises a fair point," Burkon interjected before Lillon could retort. "Heads rolled from the top down. We were lucky to get away with our necks intact."

"Tsk," Lillon clicked her tongue. "You two were small fish back then—too small to fry. I trust you like being big fish now—but that doesn't come without risk."

Bal found it surprising that these two had been part of the last rebellion. By all reports, every last rebel had been captured or killed. Of course, that's probably what the royal forces wanted everyone to think. The Queen probably knew the truth as did Amaia.

What concerned Bal more at the moment is where did this Lillon come from? And more importantly, why was she the implicit leader here if these two had seniority?

"There is risk and then there's foolishness," Celdon's tone grew belligerent. "The old leaders found that out the hard way," he added, running a finger across his portly neck.

Lillon responded with a sharp laugh—probably not what Celdon expected. "They were like bulls in a porcelain shop. This type of operation requires finesse," she said smugly.

"You mean a woman's touch," Burkon amended.

"Why Burkon, how utterly sexist of you," Lillon replied, her tone rife with mock offense. "Call it what you will," she continued before either man could comment, "but the people are slowly turning against the royals. Anya was a nice touch if I must say so myself," she practically crowed. "A bit of dirt about the Drunken Dragon in the right ear, mixed with her predilection toward violence, and voila, the royals suddenly look like butchers."

"We lost a few of our own in that massacre," Celdon scolded.

Lillon, however, did not seem to care in the slightest. "You can't make an omelet without breaking a few eggs," she responded rather glibly.

Bal felt his own anger building. Lillon had set up the Princess, and Anya, or more likely Sigfus, had been fool enough to fall for it. Bal amended his original impression of this Lillon. She was far more dangerous than he had previously imagined.

"Using the Sentinels to rile the people was an excellent stroke as well," Burkon admitted somewhat begrudgingly.

"Exactly," Lillon replied, sounding overly pleased with herself. "It all paints a picture of the Queen as a monster. It won't take much now to push the people over the edge."

"I just hope we all live to see it," Celdon grumbled.

The more Bal listened to these three, the more he realized just how much they despised each other. With any luck, he could use that to his advantage when the time came.

Ruebalt's home turned out to be a modest three story dwelling situated along the riverside in the Olde Town section of the city. Just over the border from the South Side, it took Elladan nearly a half dozen portals to get them there safely.

All of the houses here appeared quite old. Butted up against each other and the street, there were no alleys of any kind nor any front lawns. Even so, each house seemed rather charming with their neatly decorated balconies, flowered window planters, and colorful awnings.

Despite his earlier statements on the city guards' laziness, Ruebalt rushed to his front door. "Quick, follow me," he gestured as he went inside.

Elladan grabbed the door and ushered Thea to go first. Thea peered at the handsome elf with thinly veiled amusement. "Are you this gallant with all the ladies?"

"I do my best," Elladan replied with that patented half smile of his.

Dark pervaded the barkeep's house, the only light a soft glow from some embers in an open hearth. Thea quickly brightened things up with a soft prayer. In response a white aura flared to life around her body.

"Well that's pretty handy," Ruebalt said with an appreciative nod.

"You're welcome," Thea responded as she quickly took in their surroundings. The small foyer where they entered opened into a modestly furnished living/dining area with an open hearth. A thin set of stairs with a small landing turned and climbed to a dark second floor above. A small dining table stood on the other side of the living area with an open doorway just beyond.

Grabbing a lantern from above the hearth, Ruebalt used the embers and a stick to light it. He then marched toward the open doorway gesturing once more for them to follow. "This way."

Thea fell in behind the anxious man as he led them through the kitchen and into a short hallway beyond. Three doors stood in that hall: one to the left, one to the right, and a third door at the very end. That one had a glass pane and obviously led out back.

Ruebalt opened the door to the left revealing a steep flight of stairs beyond. "Down here," he said with a quick glance at Thea, then hurtled down the stairs at a breakneck pace.

Thea hiked up her robes, prepared to rush after him, but paused as she felt a hand on her shoulder.

"Maybe Seishin should go first?" Elladan asked softly.

Thea frowned at the elf, a sarcastic retort on the tip of her tongue. She quickly bit it back, however. It had been forever since anyone had treated her like a lady. Though definitely not used to it, she found it somewhat appealing.

"No, I'm fine," she said with a bemused smile.

A surprisingly dry basement awaited them at the bottom of the stairs. Ruebalt stood at the other end of the room behind a few rows of shelfs. He appeared to be fiddling with the stones in the wall. A moment later, a section of wall swung back revealing a secret door.

Ruebalt held the lamp aloft illuminating another room beyond. "We shouldn't be bothered in here," he said with a toothy grin.

The rebel barkeep's hidden room was far cozier than Thea imagined. Furnished with a desk, some chairs, a bookshelf, and a small couch, it was easily as large as her bedroom back home.

Ruebalt used the one lamp to light a second one waiting for them, then set the two down on opposite sides of the room. Afterwards he pulled the door closed, then turned to his guests and spread his arms wide. "Make yourselves comfortable lady and gents. We might be waiting for a while."

While Elladan and Seishin took him up on his offer, Thea perused the contents of the bookshelf. The barkeep's collection appeared quite eclectic, composed of everything from Laurentian poetry to Dreamweaver's multi-volume account of the Thrall Wars.

Thea arched a single eyebrow. This man had far more depth than she ever imagined. It was then that she noticed the open book sitting on his desk next to some pieces of fine silverware—far too fine for the owner of a simple inn. Standing on her toes and craning her head for a better look, she saw that the pages of the book appeared to be handwritten.

Intrigued, Thea definitely thought it warranted a closer look. The question was how to do so without alerting their host. A sudden idea crossed her mind. Pulling Dreamweaver's first volume from the shelf, she walked it over to Elladan. "Look at what our good friend has here."

When Elladan saw the volume in her hand he practically crowed. "Well now, my friend, you have exceptional taste."

The barkeep practically beamed with pride. "It is one of my favorite works, but I hear the passages are better sung."

"Say no more," Elladan exclaimed. With a snap of his hand, he summoned his lute. Strumming a few chords, the bard eyed his audience expectantly. "Any passage in particular?"

Ruebalt wore a torn expression. "There are so many. Which one to pick…which one to pick…" he mumbled, twiddling his fingers together nervously.

Silent until now, Seishin made a quiet suggestion. "How about the final battle between Tibarn and the Lord of All Demons?"

"Yes!" Ruebalt practically squealed with excitement. "The battle to end all battles."

Considering his ancestry, it came as no surprise that Seishin chose that particular passage. Both he and Ruebalt appeared rapt as Elladan began the long-versed passage. Waiting for a few moments, Thea then slowly backed away.

Reaching the desk she skirted behind it and picked up one of the forks lying there. From the weight and sheen she was positive this was pure silver. More than that, the handle had a crest inscribed into it—the image of a blue and gold shield.

Placing the fork down where she found it, Thea then bent over the open book. The page listed a number of items that Ruebalt had been given from someone named Celdon. The silverware was on that list along with a price for each piece.

With their host still captivated by Elladan's performance, Thea sifted through more pages. In them she found the details of the deal the two had struck. Ruebalt would sell these items for Celdon and the two would split the profits. It had to be done clandestinely, however, or someone named Lillon would have their heads.

Farther on, Ruebalt speculated as to the source of these expensive items. He believed they came from the estate of a former noble house. He further speculated that estate was being used as a hideout by the rebel leaders.

Thea's curiosity was piqued. If they could identify the crest on that silverware, then they might be able to pinpoint the rebel leaders' whereabouts. The question was what to do with that information?

The rebels they had seen thus far were not bad people, but then again neither was the Queen. If they chose to pass this information on to Balthazar or Cloud, would they be betraying a group of relative innocents?

Across the room, Elladan had nearly finished his account of the final battle. Not sure just quite what to do, Thea quietly put the book back. She then furtively crossed the room and seated herself beside Seishin.

A quick glance at Ruebalt proved him to still be solely focused on Elladan's rendition. Thea let out a brief sigh. Her relief turned out to be short-lived, however. She had not been seated for more than a minute when a familiar voice interrupted the bard's performance.

The voice emanated from the broach on his cloak. "Elladan? Elladan are you there? It's me, Donnie."

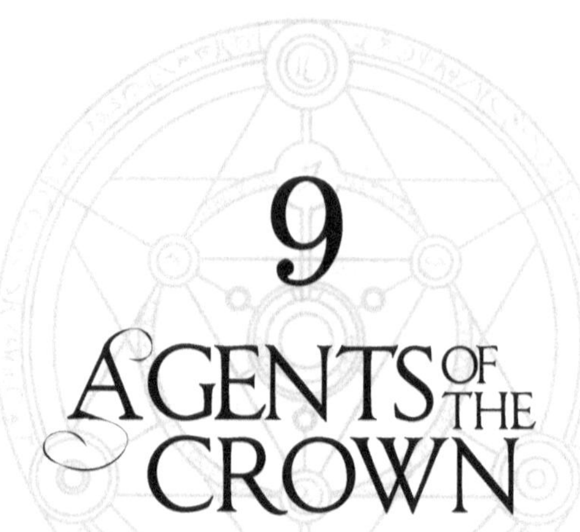

9
AGENTS OF THE CROWN

Muffled voices wafted down the stairwell from somewhere above.

Cloud Stryder sailed through the night skies over the South Side, shaking his head as he watched the chaos unfold below. Not that he had any sympathy for rebels. His parents lost their lives during a rebel uprising, their shop burnt to the ground by insurgents. However, the way the Sentinels had executed this raid was just plain stupid.

In truth, Cloud found most humans to be idiotic. In his experience, most did not use the brains the gods had given them. Yet this Lord Viron seemed stupider than most. Raiding an entire section of the city and treating each inhabitant like a criminal was not the ideal way to engender trust. The people were already mistrustful of the monarchy and this treatment didn't help matters.

We could put an end to him, Ragnarök offered.

Cloud entertained the thought for the briefest of moments, but then shook his head. *No,* he thought to the sentient sword, *that would probably cause more trouble than it's worth.*

More's the pity, Ragnarök replied, its disappointment clear. The sword always managed to see the simplest solution to any problem. More than not, however, that solution ended with someone dying by its blade.

Despite his misgivings, Cloud had a job to do. Commander Amaia had informed him of Balthazar's mission here in the South Side. Amaia was one of the more intelligent humans he had met since joining the Lanfor Royal Air Force. She was also the only human besides Balthazar and the Queen that treated him like an actual person. Thus, at Amaia's request, he sent out his skyriders to monitor the situation from above.

Cloud instructed his people to report any sightings of Balthazar or these new folks they had been ordered to babysit. He held no illusions as to their assignment with these folks. Their mission was critical and the Queen didn't trust them to carry it out on their own.

The light from the wind crystal of another skyboard caught the corner of Cloud's eye. A minute later one of his riders flew up to parallel his trajectory. "Captain Cloud," she gave him a quick salute, "we found three of those newcomers down by the river. They claim they have the rebels locked up there in a warehouse."

Interesting, Cloud thought to himself. *Maybe these folks aren't so useless after all.*

"Go flag down the *War Hammer* and tell them what we've found," he instructed her. The *War Hammer* was the flagship of the Queen's Royal Air Guard and captained by Commander Amaia. Based on what Amaia had told him, it should be airborne by now and enroute to help monitor the fiasco beneath them.

"Yes, sir!" The rider gave him a crisp salute. She then banked her board away and took off eastward in the direction of the palace.

Cloud had just gone back to observing the madness below when another rider came flying in from the west. "Captain Cloud, we picked up three of the new folks over on the border of Olde Town. They claimed to have found critical information about the rebellion."

Cloud's brows knit into a frown. They had better not be wasting his time. "Very well, lead the way" he gestured to the man.

The rider banked his board around and took off the way he came. Cloud kicked up the wind crystal on his board and sped after him.

About an hour outside of the city the rebels finally veered from the river. The forest here was thick with vegetation, but Lillon steered them over the treetops on a heading due north. The moon had risen, its silverly light quietly bathing the surrounding countryside. Thus when the forest finally gave way, Bal easily spotted their destination.

A castle rose before them in the night, its windows as dark as the night around them. A wide moat encircled the structure with a solitary stone bridge extending partway across the waters. That bridge, however, dead-ended a few dozen yards from the castle walls. The drawbridge that spanned the rest of the moat currently stood in the upright position between two fortified towers. That effectively cut off ground level access to the keep.

"Ah, home, sweet home," Celdon noted in a sour tone.

"If this castle isn't to your liking, I hear they have room in the palace dungeon," Lillon responded with mock concern.

Celdon chose to ignore her retort, instead gesturing toward the keep with a snide remark. "Well at least your pets seem to like their new home."

Bal followed the man's gaze and abruptly froze. Perched atop the spires of the keep sat a number of long necked creatures, their bat-like wings neatly folded against their backs. Despite their large size, however, they were still too small to be dragons.

Wyvern. The word sent a chill up Bal's spine.

Unlike their larger cousins, wyverns had no forelegs nor breath weapons. At the same time, they shared one trait with them: ultra-keen senses. Despite being near invisible, if they drew too close the wyverns were certain to detect his presence.

Bal needed to do something fast. Swiftly scanning the landscape below, he noted a small outcropping of land surrounded the base of the castle. Thick brush grew wildly along the bank.

Forcing down his sudden nerves, Bal waited until the last possible moment. They had crossed the moat and almost reached the walls when he pushed himself off the back of the carpet. Plummeting toward the bank below, Bal curled his body into a ball. The thick brush tore at his clothes and scratched his skin, but also thankfully broke his fall.

Though his landing hadn't made much of a racket, Bal nonetheless went still. Carefully peeking out of the bushes he saw that the rebels had passed out of sight. Even so, Bal remained motionless for a few minutes. While he waited, he took in his surroundings.

Well the front entrance is out of the question, he thought to himself wryly.

Bal carefully gauged the castle walls. He estimated them to be at least thirty feet tall. *I could reform my astral armor to climb that,* he considered briefly, *but then I'd no longer be invisible. With those wyverns around, it would be far too risky.* After a bit more deliberation, he finally decided the best bet was to look for another way inside.

The dutiful lieutenant cautiously picked his way through the brush as he circumnavigated the exterior of the castle. Not finding anything but thin cracks along the front wall, he warily circled the tall corner tower and continued down the west side. Here the cracks were a bit wider, some even accompanied by dark patches that resembled scorch marks. Though, none were wide enough for a person to fit through.

About three quarters of the way down, Bal spotted a pair of short towers similar to those that bordered the drawbridge. As he drew closer, he spied a section of brush beneath them illuminated by silvery light. His hopes rising, he hurried forward to find an archway between the towers. His elation died, however, when he found it blocked by a solid iron portcullis.

Then again, maybe not so solid, Bal thought on closer inspection. Clinging vines had overgrown the base of the portcullis. Pulling them aside, he found signs of rust here and there.

Peering through the iron wrought gate Bal swiftly scanned the grounds beyond. The courtyard here was also overgrown with weeds and brush, yet the keep itself stood only about a dozen yards away.

If I can just get through this gate, Bal thought to himself, *I might be able to slip inside before those wyverns spot me.*

Stepping back, Bal focused his mind and dispelled one of his light-bending gauntlets. Bringing his will to bear, that same purple aura enveloped his now visible arm. Using its energy, he manifested another form of astral armor. Though it didn't exactly look like armor, if one looked close enough, they might have seen the vague outline of a translucent purple gauntlet.

Bending down, Bal touched the base of one of the bars. The iron immediately started to sizzle where his hand connected with it. Within moments, it began to melt. Five minutes later, he had melted away enough of the bars for him to fit beneath the portcullis.

Resummoning his light-bending gauntlet, Bal crawled on his belly beneath the bars. Carefully rising to his feet he cast a quick glance upwards. The wyvern perched on the nearest spire sat almost directly above where he stood. Bal gulped, but the creature's attention seemed fixed on the countryside beyond the castle.

Not wanting to press his luck, Bal headed straight for the keep. As soon as he reached it, he flattened himself against the wall and let out a soft sigh.

That could have gone worse, Bal admitted to himself.

Assuming the front doors would be watched, the cautious lieutenant stole his way around the side of the huge building. At the very back of the keep he found a one story structure with an extra wide door butted up against it.

Silently slipping inside, Bal discovered a long aisle lined on the one side with a dozen or so dark stalls. The earthy scent of horses mixed with dung and dried hay filled the air. Strangely, the wall and ceiling at the other end of the building was gone.

Bal cautiously padded over to investigate. Debris lay strewn all around at this end of the stables. Half the last stall was gone along with part of the wall of the keep. Peeking outside, Bal saw that a portion of the back outer wall had been blown inward.

Well that would have been nice to know a few minutes ago, Bal thought wryly.

Stealing over to the hole in the keep, Bal warily peered inside. Moonlight revealed the remains of what once might have been a kitchen. Everything appeared shattered: the counters, the hearth, and most of the cabinets.

A stark realization dawned upon Bal. *This must have been a rebel stronghold during the last rebellion.* Even so, that didn't explain why it had remained in ruins after all these years. His own family's estate had been bequeathed to and restored by another noble line. He wondered why the same had not been done with this place.

It's not like it makes any difference at the moment, Bal chastised himself.

Focusing once again on his mission, Bal gingerly stepped over the debris and entered the keep. It was eerily silent. Pale moonlight filtered in behind him and through a couple of shattered windows. That still left far too many dark corners for Bal's liking.

Three open archways led from the kitchen, the doors having been ripped from their hinges long ago. Moving slowly, Bal checked each in turn. Beyond the first arch stood the remains of a mess hall, its tables and chairs now all smashed and rotted. The second doorway led to a large pantry. The final door opened to a hall which crossed with a wider hall a few yards beyond.

Bal warily padded into the hallway. It was even darker here than in the kitchen. Slowly making his way to the intersection, Bal spied a set of stairs leading upward from the back of the keep. The hall continued beyond those stairs disappearing into the darkness.

A cold breeze suddenly passed over Bal's shoulder. He glanced behind him, but saw nothing.

Must be the wind blowing in through the kitchen, Bal told himself. Still, considering all that had happened here, it wouldn't have surprised him to find this place haunted.

Steeling his resolve, Bal crept out into the main hallway and slowly began to ascend the back stairs. A sudden creak beneath his feet made him freeze in place. Some of the stair boards must have rotted over time.

I should have anticipated that, Bal berated himself. The young lieutenant remained motionless for what felt like an eternity. Thankfully, no one appeared to investigate the errant noise.

Not realizing he had been holding his breath, Bal let out a short sigh, then carefully continued his climb upward. The stairwell opened to another hall that paralleled the main one below. Enough light filtered in here from side doorways for him to see most of it.

Thick rubble blocked the next flight of stairs upward. In fact, many of the rooms along this hall had collapsed inward. The few that had not were filled with empty cots. Bal counted nearly a dozen in total. All looked relatively new with many recently used.

Bal felt elated. *That cinches it. This is definitely a rebel hideout.*

Continuing toward the front of the keep, Bal came across another set of stairs. Muffled voices wafted down the stairwell from somewhere above.

With extra caution, Bal ascended those stairs up to the next floor. At the top he found another hall. Bright light streamed in through the last doorway at the front of the keep. The voices he had heard from below drifted down the hall from that room.

Silently padding over to the door, Bal flattened himself against the wall, then peered around the corner. A long table took up most of the room. Three bright candelabras stood across its length providing the light he had seen from the hall. Moonlight streamed in as well from a wide window at the other end.

Seven figures sat around that table, all dressed in those same green robes. Their hoods draped around their shoulders, Bal recognized Lillon at the head of the table. Burkon sat immediately to her right with Celdon directly across from her at the end closest to Bal. Two men and two women were seated between the trio.

Bal briefly studied their features. One of the men and one of the women had pointed ears.

They're elves, he realized with mild surprise.

While elves were not uncommon in Lanfor, he had always assumed that Parthos was behind these rebellions. After all, they had the most to gain if Lanfor were to fall. Yet the Parthians and the elves held an unabiding hatred for each other ever since the Wars of the Great Forest.

Bal's musings were cut short as Celdon whined across the table, "I tell you, Lillon, we need to move the plans back. Those idiots in the city are going to give us away."

Lillon glared across the table at the pudgy man, her fingers rapping impatiently against the table. "As I told you before, I have things well in hand. We will proceed on schedule."

The man Bal hadn't seen before sat forward. Splaying his hands across the table, he glanced around at his comrades. "What about this new airship?" he asked in a gruff voice. "We still have no idea who's on board."

Lillon opened her mouth to answer, but Burkon beat her to it. "It's flying a Penwick flag, an inconsequential city on the other side of the channel. It should be of little concern." He ended with a nonchalant wave of his hand.

The elven woman seated next to him chose that moment to speak. Her voice had an almost sing song quality to it. "I've heard rumors that a trio of bronze dragons were seen flying from that ship to the palace."

The folks around the table practically exploded in fear. Many of them jumped out of their seats.

"Bronze dragons?" the new man hissed.

"Three of them?" the woman next to him gasped.

"The ones that crushed the last rebellion?" Celdon cried from the near end of the table.

Bal had heard about that from Amaia. It was actually the Greymantles' parents who helped stop the rebels twelve years ago.

Lillon rose to her feet and yelled over the commotion that followed. "Silence!"

Everyone quieted down and stared at her, their mouths agape.

"It's not the same ones," she continued now that she had their attention. "Our people in the palace saw them and they are barely adults, if that."

Our people in the palace? Bal felt a chill race up his spine. He did not like the sound of that at all. If the castle had been infiltrated by rebels, the Queen might be in imminent danger.

"Now sit down and grow a spine, before I have Burkon here lash a two-by-four to your backs," Lillon warned, her eyes seething with anger as they flickered around the room.

Grumbles arose from the rest of the rebels, but they retook their seats without challenging her further.

The trip to Olde Town and back again took Cloud about half

an hour in total. As it turned out, these newcomers did have useful information—information that Commander Amaia needed to hear as soon as possible.

The *War Hammer* sat next to the warehouse as Cloud drew up with three of his riders, each bearing one of the newcomers. The warehouse doors had been cracked open with a line of rebels filing outward. Royal guardsman herded the traitors over to the waiting airship.

Cloud spotted Commander Amaia overseeing the entire operation from the ground. Beside her stood the rest of the newcomers: the slim elf, the officer in red, and the dragon hunter. He'd yet to form an opinion of the officer or the elf, but the hunter had proven to be downright belligerent. Regardless, if he could fight half as well as he threw around threats, Cloud wouldn't hold that against him.

Signaling his riders to drop off their passengers, Cloud drew up and hovered in front of Amaia. "Commander, I think you're going to want to hear this." He and Amaia were long past formalities. It was one of those things he liked about her.

Amaia narrowed an eye at him. "Does this have anything to do with Lieutenant Balthazar? He was not in the warehouse nor were the rebel leaders."

Cloud could sense the concern in her voice. She knew as well as he that Bal could handle himself. Still, who knew what he might be up against if he had followed these missing rebels.

"I did see something take off from the roof after we trapped the rebels inside," the slim elf offered.

Well at least he's somewhat observant, Cloud noted silently. "Where was it headed?" he asked aloud.

The elf pointed toward the east. "Over the river in that direction."

Amaia peered sharply at Cloud. "Could what you've found give us a clue to where they're headed?"

"It might." Cloud nodded.

Out of all these newcomers so far, the priestess seemed to be the most intelligent. Cloud engaged his wind crystal and floated over to her. "Tell the Commander what you told me."

The priestess repeated everything she had found in the rebel's books. She finished by showing the silverware to Amaia.

Amaia eyed the crest closely. After a moment or two, she visibly paled. "It couldn't be."

Cloud wondered if that might be her reaction. He thought he had seen that crest before—the crest of Lord Catolis, Amaia's father. Amaia had personally overseen the capture and demise of her traitorous clan. Cloud imagined that could not have been easy, but it definitely proved her loyalty to the crown. It was another thing he liked about her.

Getting over her initial shock, Amaia's expression turned stony. She spun about and called out to the guardsmen. "Hurry loading the prisoners on board. We're taking off again immediately."

The flashy looking elf in white peered curiously at Amaia. "Do you know where they are?"

"I believe I do," Amaia responded, her eyes now burning with anger.

10
REDEMPTION

The wyvern swiftly closed the gap, its maw open wide.

althazar had heard enough. This group comprised the rebel leaders with Lillon in charge of them all. The question remained as to who was backing them, but that information would have to wait. With the Queen at risk, it was far more important to find these infiltrators in the palace. In order to do so, he'd need to take these traitors alive—or Lillon at the very least.

Over by the window at the other end of the room, Bal spied the rebel's flying carpet. The sight sparked the beginnings of a rudimentary plan in his mind. Though far more fragile than Bal would have liked, with the looming danger to the Queen he felt he had little choice.

Resigning himself to the circumstances at hand, the young astral knight carefully backed away down the hall. Once again focusing his will, this time he did not dispel his armor. Instead he pushed the energy out of his hand and shaped it with his mind. When he was done, he held a translucent purple crossbow. Not quite finished just yet, Bal focused on the other hand, this time sculpting three ethereal bolts.

Down the hall, the rebel leaders had resumed their discussions. From the sound of it, things had taken a less volatile turn. Bal padded back to the edge of the doorway and peered inside.

"…and the Olde Town crew I'm overseeing are prepared for the coming revolt." The droning voice belonged to Celdon who had risen from his seat to address the table. "Yet, unlike some folks, they've managed to keep a low profile," he added loftily with a pointed look at Lillon.

Lillon chose to ignore the dig, but Celdon's presentation helped Bal in two ways. First, it confirmed that there was more than one rebel cell in the city. Second, in his current position, the portly man made an excellent target.

As Celdon went on with his report, Bal swung around his crossbow. Taking aim at the man's corpulent back, he pulled the trigger and let the bolt fly. Noiselessly hurtling across the room, the projectile hit its mark with nary a sound and disappeared into Celdon's body. The only indication that anything had happened was a slight pause in the pudgy man's speech.

As Celdon continued to drone on, Bal took aim at his other marks: the two elves next to Burkon. Like Celdon, the man hardly reacted, but the elven woman seemed to notice something. She spun about, her eyes focused on the hallway. Bal ducked back around the corner, his heart pounding in his chest.

"Is something wrong Selone?" He heard Lillon ask.

"It's—nothing," Selone answered hesitantly. "I just thought I heard something in the hall."

Bal fought down a rising panic. This Selone was obviously some sort of sensitive. He would have to be extra cautious around her.

Burkon got up and stuck his head through the open doorway. Bal held his breath as the big man peered up and down the hall. Thankfully, he looked right past him. Burkon turned about and let out a hearty laugh. "I think the ghost stories about this place are starting to get to you, Selone."

Bal chanced another peek around the corner of the door. He was just in time to see Burkon walk up behind Selone and drape his arm around her shoulders. "Maybe you'd like some company this evening?"

Selone slowly turned her head and peered at the hand on her arm. A look of disgust crossed her face as she picked it up with two fingers. Holding it as if it carried some sort of disease, she lifted it away and abruptly dropped it. She then twisted about in her chair to fix Burkon with an icy stare.

"Not in your wildest dreams," she intoned haughtily.

The dissension between Burkon and Selone had caught the attention of everyone at the table. Seeing his chance, Bal took the opportunity to slip into the room past the big man and steal over to the window where the carpet laid.

Burkon sat down with a boisterous laugh. "One of these days you're going to wish you had taken me up on my offer."

Selone upturned her nose at the man. "In half a century you'll be nothing but a memory."

"Alright, you two, that's enough," Lillon snapped. "Burkon, keep it in your pants," she chided. "Selone…" she began, but never got to finish her sentence.

Crouching down by the carpet, Bal put his plan into motion. Focusing his will, he pushed with his mind at each individual bolt and turned them solid one by one.

"Ahhh!" Celdon was the first to cry out, the pudgy man clutching his abdomen as he doubled over.

"What's wrong now?" Lillon chastised him. "Eat too much again?"

A moment later, the elf beside him also cried out and doubled over.

Selone shot up out of her seat. "Something's wrong…" she began when it hit her as well. She cried out and fell to her knees, folded over in pain.

Everyone else leapt from their seats. Those closest to their ailing comrades tried to determine what was wrong. Burkon in particular bent over Selone.

In the midst of all the pandemonium, Bal struck. Rising from his crouched position, he rushed up behind Lillon and conked her on the head. Catching her unconscious body, he grit his teeth and pushed again, this time extending his aura out until it encompassed her inert form.

With Lillon now virtually invisible, Bal dragged her back onto the carpet. Setting her down next to him, he knelt and placed his palm on the rug. Steeling himself, he gave one last final push. His body ached, rebelling against the strain, but in the end his aura responded stretching to cover the entire carpet.

"Phew," Bal gasped when he was done, his breath coming in short ragged bursts. Behind him he heard someone yell.

"Wait! What happened to Lillon?"

"Fugere," Bal said the word without looking back. The carpet immediately responded to his wishes, rising up into the air and shooting out of the window in front of them.

Balthazar laid flat on the flying carpet as they sped past the walls of the keep and the moat beyond. Holding onto Lillon's inert form, he verbally steered them off at an angle keeping as close to the tree tops as possible.

Knowing that pursuit wouldn't be far behind, he cast a quick glance over his shoulder. As he expected, a number of dragon-like forms separated themselves from the spires of the keep. Their large wings spread wide, they shot past the moat in mere seconds. From there the wyverns fanned out further. Unfortunately, one was headed in their direction.

Bal knew there was no way they could outrun a wyvern. Worse, the strain of keeping the carpet, his captive, and himself invisible had become almost unbearable. Frantically scanning the forest below, he prayed to the gods for a miracle. Not far ahead, the trees began to part. Beyond that lay the River of Liath, its waters sparkling in the silver moonlight.

Behind them the wyvern was coming up fast. It would be close, but they might just make it. Clearing the treetops, Bal angled the carpet downward. They'd drawn within fifty yards of the riverbank when a sharp cry cut through the night.

Bal's heart leapt into his throat. *It must have caught our scent!* They'd run out of time. The creature would be on them in less than a minute. They only had one chance.

Tightening his grip on Lillon, Bal waited until they were far enough out over the water. Wrapping his arms around Lillon's inert form, he commanded the carpet to keep going, then rolled off the side.

The duo plunged into the river with more of a splash than Bal would have liked. On top of that, the cold waters had shocked the rebel leader awake.

Lillon shrieked in terror as they resurfaced, her arms around him in a death-like grip. "Don't let go! I can't swim!"

Bal might have found that amusing if not for their current situation. They had landed near the center of the river, too far from either shore for his liking. To make matters worse, he had lost control of his aura and the commotion had drawn the wyvern's attention. Peeling off from its pursuit of the carpet, the creature banked around and dove down directly towards them.

Though the situation seemed hopeless, Bal was not the type to give up so quickly. After all, he had spent much of his energy escaping from the castle in the first place. Moreover, with Lillon holding onto him, his options were rather limited.

The wyvern swiftly closed the gap, its maw open wide. Lillon shrieked again as she saw their impending peril. "What are you doing you stupid reptile? You work for me!" she screamed at it.

"Somehow, I don't think it cares," Bal muttered to the indignant rebel. "Oh, and you might want to take a deep breath."

"What do you—" Lillon's response was literally drowned out as Bal dragged them both under.

A moment later, a large shadow whizzed over the top of the water where they had just been. As soon as it was gone, Bal propelled them both back to the surface.

"Wh—what was—that for?" Lillon sputtered, coughing out river water in between her words.

"I thought it better than ending up in some monster's belly," Bal responded wryly. Unfortunately, the tactic would only work for so long.

A hundred or so yards away, the creature cried out as it banked around and began another run. Other cries echoed in response. The rest of the wyverns were headed this way. They were done for unless they could find some way to call them off.

"So how do you control these creatures?" Bal asked the still sputtering Lillon.

"I have a crystal of course"—she responded somewhat indignantly— "but I do need to make eye contact to use it," she admitted in a soft voice.

That figures, Bal thought with more than a little irony. Unfortunately to get that close would definitely be the end of them.

The wyvern was coming up on them fast, its maw open once more in anticipation. Bal prepared to dive yet again when something suddenly shot past them. A winged figure the size of a man raced across the top of the waters directly for the incoming wyvern.

Bal blinked. *Am I crazy? Or are they?*

The last moment before they collided, the wyvern snapped at the oncoming figure. The smaller flyer proved faster though, slipping beneath the creature's maw.

Bal caught the glint of moonlight on steel just before the wyvern cried out in pain. The creature abruptly veered off course. It hit the water with a tremendous splash a few dozen yards from Bal and his captive.

Bal couldn't believe his eyes. Whoever, or whatever, that was, it took out the wyvern in one shot. He had no more time to think about it, however, as the wake from the wyvern's fall came rushing at them.

"Hang on!" He cried to Lillon, diving beneath the surface once more.

When they resurfaced, the night sky had lit up around them. A squad of skyriders, easily two dozen strong, now hovered over the river and nearby forest. The remainder of the wyverns had peeled off and were headed back in the direction of the keep.

A wave of relief flooded over Bal. By the grace of the gods, they had somehow survived.

A light suddenly shone on the waters around them. A familiar voice called out from above. "Nice night for a swim."

Bal peered upward to see Cloud hovering just above them. The normally stoic gnome wore a slight smirk. Bal grimaced back at his friend. "I hadn't exactly planned it that way."

"Apparently," Cloud replied, this time totally deadpan. "Guess you'll be wanting a lift?"

"That would be nice." Bal half laughed.

Cyclone was a dragon hunter from a long line dating back to well before the Thrall Wars. Trained from the moment he could hold a spear, he relentlessly plied the family trade after his father died hunting a red. All that changed, however, after meeting Ruka, Ves, and Maya.

The bronze sisters showed honor and bravery, qualities Cyclone had never seen in a dragon before. They even risked their own lives to save his—more than once. Staying his hand, an unlikely partnership had formed between the hunter and the three dragons. That, along with the opportunity to fight pirates, was why he had journeyed with them across the sea.

Leaning against the rail at the prow of the *War Hammer*, Cyclone had been the first to spot the winged creature buzzing the river ahead. Immediately recognizing it as a wyvern, the hunter stood erect and slowly stretched his muscles.

Probably not worth my time, he thought to himself. *Just the same, I could use the workout—and it might be fun robbing it of its prey.*

Before anyone else on the ship even noticed, the hunter had sprouted wings and sped across the water toward the airborne reptile. Up ahead, the wyvern had banked around for another pass at its target.

Cyclone spied something bobbing in the middle of the river up ahead. *Make that two somethings,* he swiftly amended.

Determined that the creature would never reach its intended prey, Cyclone surged forward. His halberd readied, he aimed himself directly at the wyvern's open maw.

Fixated on its intended prey, the creature didn't notice him until the very last minute. Too late it snapped at him, allowing the hunter ample time to corkscrew around its maw. Ending up beneath the flying reptile, Cyclone sliced open its soft underbelly as he sped by. The creature let out one last sharp cry, then plummeted into the dark river waters below.

Cyclone momentarily thought about stopping, but he had heard the cries from more wyverns ahead. Behind him downriver, the lights from several skyboard riders had peeled off from the ship.

They can take care of whoever's in the water, Cyclone told himself. Without another thought, the hunter took off to meet the approaching wyverns.

Half an hour later, Bal sat on the deck of the *War Hammer* wrapped in a towel and sipping hot tea. He had been surprised to find all the newcomers there, sans Cyclone. The dragon hunter had been the one to save them, and as of this moment was out hunting the other wyverns.

The rest of his new charges had gathered around to explain the circumstances of their timely arrival. Donatello was talking at the moment. "After we couldn't find you in the warehouse, we figured you must have flown off with those robed folks."

"But how did you trace us to the keep?" Bal asked in between sips of hot tea.

"That was mostly Thea's doing," Elladan gestured towards the priestess. Thea briefly explained about the deal between Ruebalt and Celdon and the silverware bearing the crest of Lord Catolis.

That explained much. The keep where the rebels had holed up must have belonged to Amaia's family. After she had dealt with her traitorous relatives, she no longer wanted anything to do with it. That accounted for the castle's state of disrepair. Still, it made Bal wonder why she hung onto it at all.

Bal put down his tea and let out a short sigh. "Thank you. Your timing couldn't have been better."

Donatello flashed him a toothy smile. "According to Cloud, you were nearly fish food."

"More like wyvern food," Bal responded with a begrudging smile. The slight elf had a cheesy sense of humor, but he was starting to grow on Bal.

"Which turned out to our advantage," a voice called across the deck. Commander Amaia had reappeared from below and now strode over to join them.

Bal peered at her uncertainly. "How so?"

Amaia laughed, something she did not do very often. "It appears she didn't appreciate being nearly fed to her own wyverns. So she turned on the entire cause—even named the rebel spies in the palace."

Bal breathed another sigh. "So the Queen is safe."

Amaia placed a hand on his shoulder. "Thanks in great part to your efforts. You've done an excellent job, Lieutenant."

Though Bal appreciated the compliment, he couldn't shake the feeling that he nearly failed. Too much depended upon his success—especially with this upcoming mission.

"As for the rest of you," Amaia turned to survey the others, "the Queen would like to express her gratitude. You've done a great service for Lanfor this day."

"It was our pleasure," Elladan responded for the group.

"Perhaps this might convince her majesty of the benefits of an alliance with Penwick?" Pallas added adroitly. The Penwick officer had not struck Bal as the diplomatic type, but he seemed to be learning fast.

Amaia pressed her lips together into a thin smile, then nodded. Perhaps, indeed. I will take it upon myself to mention it to her."

"That would be most appreciated," Pallas said with a slight bow.

These newcomers were indeed a strange lot, but they had proven themselves to be rather resourceful. Cyclone at the very least harbored a lot of power.

Bal peered out over the dark forest, but saw no sign of the dragon hunter. He silently wondered how he was fairing with the rest of the wyverns.

Cyclone caught sight of the approaching wyverns over the forest north of the river. He counted three altogether. Two flew in from the northeast while the last one came in from the east, paralleling the river. It wasn't long before they spotted him. Not realizing what they were up against, the creatures headed straight for him.

This should be fun, the dragon hunter thought to himself. Three wyverns altogether might at least provide him with some sort of challenge.

Weighing his options, Cyclone decided to first handle the wyverns closest to each other. Veering northeast, the hunter swooped down until he just barely skimmed the treetops.

Both wyverns took the bait, dropping down until they were level with him. As they closed in, they let out a sharp cry, a tactic which was supposed to freeze their prey.

Cyclone let out a derisive snort. *How predictable.*

Much like their larger cousins, these creatures relied too much on fear. In his experience, most did not know what to do with a creature that fought back.

The dragon hunter continued on a collision course with the two wyverns. One hundred yards…sixty yards…thirty yards…at the last possible moment, he dove down below the treeline. Unable to stop themselves, the two wyverns passed overhead.

That's when Cyclone struck.

Arching sharply upward, the hunter burst out from the trees directly below one of the creatures. With a huge swing of his halberd, he sliced the wyvern clear through the abdomen. A pitiful cry escaped the creature's maw as it lost altitude and slammed into the trees ahead.

Cyclone didn't wait to watch, however. Instead he plunged after the second wyvern. Too stupid to realize its fate, the flying reptile banked around to meet him.

A smug smile spread across the hunter's lips. *You're making this far too easy.* Closing fast, Cyclone prepared to spiral beneath the foolish creature. Just as he was about to dive, the wyvern pulled up and lashed out at him with its tail.

The whip-like tail slammed into him sending the hunter spinning backwards end over end. He plummeted into the trees below taking out more than a few branches before finally crashing into the forest floor. A resounding *thud* rang out around him with brush flying everywhere.

Laying there stunned for a few seconds, Cyclone finally bolted to his feet. Angrily brushing the vegetation from his body, he chastised himself aloud. "Damn! I should have seen that coming." He was so used to fighting actual dragons that he had neglected to account for the maneuverability of their smaller cousins.

Grabbing his halberd from where it lay on the forest floor, the hunter set his jaw. "Let's try that again." With an angry flap of his wings, he took off and quickly rose above the trees.

The last wyvern had reached them by now and both were circling about a hundred yards out on either side from where he went down. As soon as they saw him, they let out triumphant cries and banked in his direction. Hemmed in on both sides, the hunter prepared for the double assault.

Cyclone had seen these tactics before. One of the creatures would have to veer off or they'd run the risk of colliding with each other. The question is which one would peel off and which one would attack? If he guessed right, he would have a fighting chase. If he guessed wrong—well then he wouldn't have long to worry about it.

About fifty yards out, both creatures pivoted in opposite directions. They obviously had hunted together and knew what the other would do.

This is going to be close, Cyclone thought to himself grimly. He was only going to get one chance at this and he'd have to make it count.

Closing his eyes and stilling his mind the hunter tapped into the rage at the core of his being. Anger constantly seethed in there just below the surface. The air around him began to stir. Tiny arcs of electricity swept across his body and his hair rose of its own accord. When his eyes snapped open, they had turned a crimson red.

Both wyverns were nearly upon him, one having just barely veered off. The other was only a few yards away now, its maw gaped to engulf him whole. Moving almost faster than the eye could see, Cyclone evaded that maw, placing himself between the two passing creatures.

Swinging his halberd as hard as he could, he carved a great circle through the air. The sharp-edged blade passed through one wyvern's neck on the downswing and sliced through the other's neck on the subsequent upswing. Their necks nearly cloven straight off, both creatures arced downward into the trees and disappeared into the dark forest below.

While Cyclone tracked down the rest of the wyverns, the Queen's forces descended upon the keep. Most of the rebel leaders were captured with the exception of Burkon who fought to the very end. Also, Selone had somehow disappeared. A sweep of the entire keep turned up no sign of the elven mage.

Not even Celdon seemed to know her whereabouts. The pudgy man proved quite cooperative in all other respects, however, confirming and adding to what Lillon had already told them. Overall, a group of nobles had been funding the rebellion. Furthermore, each came from a royal line subjugated during the unification of Lanfor.

Once Cyclone and the skyriders returned, the *War Hammer* set out on the voyage back home. Bal had warmed up and changed by the time the city lights of Palt appeared on the horizon. He found the newcomers at the prow taking in the spectacular view.

Cloud hovered there as well apparently conversing with their new charges. Bal found that rather surprising. Cloud usually talked to no one other than himself and Amaia.

As Bal joined them at the rail, Pallas fixed him with a probing stare. "Do you know how the Queen intends to handle these traitorous nobles?"

Taken aback by the unexpected question, Bal exchanged a furtive glance with Cloud. The gnome shook his head in response. "I'm not answering that one."

Bal let out a short sigh and returned his gaze to Pallas. "While I'm no politician, even I know going after those lords would be difficult. It could put a strain on the relationship between the fiefdoms that make up Lanfor."

Though Lanfor was a unified kingdom, relations between the

crown and the fiefdoms could be tenuous at times. The Queen would need to tread lightly if she wanted to avoid another civil war.

"So what do you think her majesty will do?" Elladan pressed the hesitant lieutenant.

"My guess is she'll use her spy network to investigate these lords first," Donatello interjected before Bal could answer.

"That's probably true," Bal agreed with an approving nod. The slight elf was definitely more astute than he had given him credit for. "If it could be proved that some outside force is behind this insurrection," Bal continued, "it would unite rather than divide the kingdom."

"And by outside force you mean Parthos," Donatello corrected him with a toothy grin.

Bal pressed his lips together and nodded. "That's a possibility."

While no self-respecting Lanforian would ally themselves directly with Parthos, Bal couldn't think of no one who would have more to gain if the Royal House were to fall. "Still, while I definitely appreciate all your help in this matter, the rest of it will have to fall to the Queen and Commander Amaia. I believe our hands will be more than full with the upcoming mission."

While Bal hadn't intended to end all conversation, his weighty words had that effect. A somber mood fell over the group as they contemplated what awaited them down the dark coast.

11
DODGER

Once the rebel leaders had been captured and interrogated, Pallas felt both vindicated and relieved. As he suspected, they cared nothing for the people of Lanfor. Their only concern was toppling the Royal House, even at the cost of their own supporters. Causes like that were destined to fail sooner or later. Pallas was only glad to have had a hand in stopping it before more innocents got hurt.

The fallout from their mission came swiftly thereafter. By the time they landed in Palt, all the rebels within the palace had been rounded up. Besides that, the Queen deployed the rest of her forces to take down the rebel cells in the city. As for the Sentinels, they had been ordered to stand down and release the citizens they unjustly arrested.

Overall things had gone well with two minor exceptions. First, the head of the Sentinels, Lord Viron, disappeared before he could be apprehended. Second, the *Drunken Dragon* had been closed indefinitely, leaving Pallas and the others without a place to stay. Hearing of their plight, a grateful Queen had them put up in the palace overnight.

The next morning they all received invitations to join the Queen for breakfast. When they arrived at the dining hall, however, they found Balthazar and Cloud waiting for them in the doorway.

"The Queen and Commander Amaia send their warmest regards," Balthazar informed them, "but they will not be able to join us this morning."

"Apparently dismantling a rebel network takes more than just a single night," Cloud added with an ironic snort.

Balthazar ushered them into the dining hall. "Either way, the Queen insists we eat without her."

Pallas had thought the guest rooms opulent, but the dining hall put even those to shame. An immense table stood in the center of the chamber with easily enough seating for twenty. About a dozen candles and half a dozen floral centerpieces stretched along the table's length. A huge chandelier hung overhead with easily three dozen candles around its circumference. None were currently lit, however, as the morning sun streamed through three tall arched windows on one side of the room.

Two huge mirrors bordered either side of a wide hearth directly opposite those windows. Numerous side tables stood against the walls, each teaming with an outrageous variety of buffet style breakfast foods. The place settings were finer than the most expensive dishware Pallas' family owned. It made them look like paupers in comparison.

From their expressions, Thea and Seishin shared Pallas' awe, but none of the exquisite finery seemed to faze Elladan, Donnie, or Cyclone. The three of them hefted food upon their plates and dug into their meals with gusto. Sharing a glance and a shrug, the two Stealle siblings and the man from Isandor followed suit—albeit with a bit more finesse.

Once they had all been seated, Balthazar brought them up to date on the ship he had found to take them down the coast. When he was done, he asked if anyone had questions.

Elladan, who had been listening quietly for a change, put down his fork and eyed the lieutenant. "You said this *Gossamer Lady* is from Niracom? Where is that exactly?"

"It's a city in the Ice Plains at the northern tip of Laurentia," Balthazar responded.

"Isn't that a bit far north from the Vortex?" he asked, his tone laced with skepticism.

"That's a fair question," Balthazar admitted. He rose from his seat and paced around as he answered. "The truth is their country thrives on trade all up and down the coast. They are some of the most experienced sailors you will find on the entire continent."

"And their navigator has made the run through the Vortex multiple times?" Donnie pressed the point.

Balthazar stopped and met the elf's gaze evenly. "According to the ship's captain."

Some of the best sailors Pallas knew were merchants. A good navigator and crew were essential if one intended to be successful at maritime trade. Still, one thing puzzled him. "Pardon me if this is a naïve question, but don't any Lanfor navigators have experience with this Vortex?"

Balthazar sat down again and met his gaze with a shrewd nod. "Of course there are. I assumed that we would need to keep a low profile on this mission. To that end, I thought a non-Lanfor vessel would be best."

"I like the way you think," Donnie said with a wry expression. "To that same end, some of us should definitely think about changing our wardrobe." He looked pointedly at Balthazar, Cloud, and Pallas.

"Don't worry," Balthazar assured him. "Cloud and I have traveling clothes for the occasion."

"As do I," Pallas added with a wry smile of his own.

After breakfast, the Penwick officer went back to his guest room and packed away his uniform. He then donned a traveling coat— a midnight blue longcoat that was the exact opposite of Penwick colors.

Pallas almost didn't recognize himself as he looked at the image in the mirror. He had worn some sort of Penwick uniform ever since joining the navy as a cabin boy at the age of twelve. He almost never took it off, sometimes even sleeping in it.

Yet, not wearing the uniform now seemed strangely liberating. Perhaps those colors had been a subconscious reminder of the constant need to protect his city. Then again, maybe that wasn't it at all. All the same, Pallas felt as if a great weight had been lifted from him.

Between his parents, Lloyd, and his brother's new friends, he had left Penwick in good hands. As for their mission, they had lost the dragon girls, but had gained competent allies from both Lanfor and Isandor. For once, Pallas did not feel as if everything rested squarely on his shoulders.

If the Palt docks looked huge from the air, from down here they looked enormous. Everywhere you looked there were dozens of vessels—galleons, frigates, and brigantines with a few smaller ships mixed in. Across the harbor stood a line of warships, each a man of war comparable in size to the best in the Penwick Navy. Nevertheless, one was bigger than all the rest.

Pallas pointed it out to Balthazar. "What ship is that?"

"That's the King Flandril's Revenge," Balthazar answered flatly, "the first ever ship of the line."

Donnie tilted his head sideways as he scrutinized the huge vessel. "I can't imagine it's very maneuverable."

"It's not meant to be," Balthazar informed him. "It's got twice as many guns as a man of war."

Pallas let out a low whistle. "So one broadside from that thing would sink most ships."

"That's the general idea," Balthazar said with a grim nod.

They followed the Lanfor lieutenant through a maze of docks to a long, three masted schooner at one of the smaller piers. The words *Gossamer Lady* stretched across its front the hull in finely scripted letters.

Pallas immediately noted how low it sat in the water, maybe ten feet over the water line. These types of ships normally had a long keel making them very stable. If she were rigged right, she would make the perfect vessel for traversing the rough waters of a storm like the Vortex.

Balthazar led them aboard ship where the crew was already preparing to set sail. The men and women from Niracom appeared to be mostly blonde and fair-skinned, though Pallas did spy a redhead here and there. He felt a momentary pang in his heart as his thoughts strayed to Alys. He hadn't realized he would miss her so much.

His thoughts were shattered as a tall woman with fair skin and ice white hair came up to greet them. Despite the color of her hair, Pallas estimated her to be not much older than himself.

"Welcome aboard," she addressed their group. "I'm Captain Silyna." Her eyes wandered over the lot of them until they fell on Thea. "Welcome good priestess. Our priest grew ill and cannot travel with us, but we would love to have a service before entering the Vortex. Would you be so kind?"

Thea stepped forward and peered up at the captain. Though his sister was not exactly short, Silyna stood a full head taller than her. "It would be my honor, of course. Might I assume you worship Niracom?"

Niracom was the Ralnain God of Ice and the obvious namesake of their city. "We do," Silyna answered. "I see from your robes you are a Priestess of Arenor, but that would do just fine under these circumstances."

Thea gave the woman a warm smile. "No, that's alright. I am versed in the ceremonies of all the Ralnain Gods. I can perform a service for Niracom."

Silyna practically grinned from ear to ear. She reached out and placed an arm around Thea's shoulders. "That would be most excellent! You must feast with us after the service." She extended her free hand to all of them. "You all must, in fact. We will dine like there is no tomorrow, for one doesn't enter the Vortex lightly."

Elladan narrowed an eye at the tall captain. "I thought you had plenty of experience with the Vortex?"

A shrill laugh sounded from behind them all. Pallas spun about to see a dark-haired elf crossing the deck planks towards them. He wore a patch over one eye. "The Vortex ain't like nothing you've ever seen. Swells that come out of nowhere. Winds that change on a moment's notice. There's no such thing as a straight course once you enter."

Elladan made a face at the new elf. "Are you trying to make it sound impossible?"

Silyna clasped Elladan on the back with her free hand. "Pay no attention to Lonnin. He likes to embellish everything." She then presented the one-eyed elf to the group. "Folks, this is our navigator, Lonnin. Don't let the eye patch fool you. He's got a better sense of direction than most folks with two eyes." She finished with a hearty laugh.

Lonnin greeted them all in turn, but when he got to Donnie he did a double take. "Why if it isn't Dodger. I haven't seen you in a human's age."

"Lonnin." Donnie responded with a curt nod, looking rather uncomfortable.

Elladan, on the other hand, appeared quite intrigued. He strode over to his elven friend and placed an arm around his shoulder. "You know Donnie here?" He asked the one-eyed elf.

Lonnin let out another shrill laugh. "Donnie? Going by another name now, are we?" He squinted with his one good eye at the slim elf. "After what happened with *Black Pearl*, that doesn't exactly surprise me."

Pallas had definitely heard that name before, but couldn't quite place it. He frowned at Lonnin. "Black Pearl—is that a person, place, or thing?"

Lonnin chortled. "Oh she's definitely a person…"

"…which is a story we can save for another time," Donnie cut him off. "Right now we should weigh anchor while the day is still young."

"Dodger, or Donnie, here is right." Silyna interrupted before anyone else could speak. "That's enough jabbering for now. The priestess here can have the first mate's quarters next to mine. We've also got a stateroom with four beds. As for the rest of you, it seems like some of you have sailed before. You can hang a hammock below and sleep with the crew."

After a brief discussion, they decided to leave the stateroom to Cyclone, Elladan, Balthazar, and Cloud. Pallas, Donnie, and Seishin headed below as the *Gossamer Lady* weighed anchor.

Leaving the Bay of Glas behind, the *Gossamer Lady* swiftly turned south down the coast. Before long, the isle of Lanfor disappeared from the northern horizon. Ahead of them stretched across the sky rose the massive dark clouds that made up the twin storms of the Vortex.

While the others settled in, Elladan made a quick trip of dropping off his stuff in their cabin. Intrigued by this Lonnin, Elladan then went in search of him. He found him at the ship's wheel just in front of the sterncastle along with Pallas.

"So what should we actually expect once we start to "thread the needle'?" Pallas was asking the one-eyed elf.

Lonnin cackled with that shrill laugh again. "I told you before, it's like no storm you've ever seen." He pointed out of the box ahead of them. "Beneath them twin storms is two gigantic whirlpools that'll suck you to a watery grave if you get too close."

Elladan's heart nearly skipped a beat. "Woah, woah, woah. Giant whirlpools? No one said anything about giant whirlpools."

Lonnin snickered, obviously enjoying the rise he'd gotten out of him. "And between them ain't much better. Howling winds, driving rains, forty foot swells that come out of nowhere. Even when you aim for the calm spots, they may not be calm when you get there."

Elladan felt a shiver go up his spine. "How in Thac do you steer through something like that?"

A seasoned sailor, Pallas didn't seem nearly as thrown as Elladan. Instead, he eyed the navigator intently. "There's a trick to it, isn't there?"

Lonnin touched the side of his nose with a single finger, then pointed it at Pallas. "Aye, there is indeed. For starters we'll use trysails and a storm jib."

Having grown up on sailing ships, Pallas knew those terms only too well. A trysail was a small fore-and-aft sail hoisted in place of the larger main sails. In a storm, it would help to keep the ship's bow to the wind. The small heavy sail called a storm jib would be placed in front of all the other sails to help maneuver the ship in high winds.

"If things get really bad, we'll deploy a sea anchor," Lonnin added with a wicked grin.

Elladan blinked. "Won't that stop the ship entirely?"

Pallas fixed him with a withering stare. "Not a real anchor. A small parachute at the end of a line off the bow. It helps to keep the bow above water."

"Oh," Elladan responded, feeling suddenly very foolish.

Lonnin put an arm around Elladan's shoulder. He pointed at the storms ahead of them, weaving his free hand back and forth as he talked. "The real trick is to stay as close to the center as possible. The channel varies from a half mile to a mile wide in spots. So, you can't turn directly into the swells or you risk getting pulled into one of them whirlpools."

Elladan peered at Pallas and saw the grim look on his face. "Are you sure about this?"

Pallas merely shrugged. "You can never be sure when it comes to the sea."

"Well that's not very reassuring," Elladan chastised him. He glanced back at Lonnin. "How many times did you say you made it through there?"

Lonnin mumbled to himself as he counted on the fingers of his hands. "If we make it through this time, it'll be ten altogether."

"That's fairly good odds," Elladan admitted. While still not thrilled, it did make him feel somewhat better.

Deciding it best not to dwell on it, Elladan swept his eyes across the nearby deck. Seeing no sign of Donnie, he fixed the one-eyed elf with a half-smile. "Well, now that we won't be interrupted, who is this Black Pearl and what does she have to do with Donnie—I mean Dodger?"

Lonnin chortled again. "Oh ho, now that's a story." Elladan and Pallas both drew closer as the one-eyed elf delved into Donnie's sordid past.

Donnie's mind drifted terribly as he searched below decks for an empty spot to hang his hammock. It had been ages since he had heard the name *Black Pearl*, a name that brought back a flood of memories. Mor'Findl had been many things to him, but foremost she was his owner. He had been her indentured servant, sold into slavery by his arch nemesis, that scoundrel Wraithbone. In spite of that, his time as part of her crew had not been all bad.

Mor'Findl had taken him under her wing in more ways than one. Some had been quite pleasant in fact, while others turned out to be very challenging. Donnie had learned the blade from a master, but Mor'Findl took his training one step farther. She had developed a unique fighting style during her years as a buccaneer on the high seas. Her striking appearance along with the deadly combination of swordplay, acrobatics, cunning, and wit had earned her the nickname of *Black Pearl*, a thing both deadly and beautiful.

The slim elf paused as he spotted an empty space between two support beams. He doffed his pack, pulled out a rolled hammock he had purchased prior to their departure, and began tying it to the first beam. As he did so, his mind wandered back to his days with the pirate clans.

Donnie had always been a quick learner; it was one of the main reasons he had survived this long. He quickly adapted to Mor'Findl's style, in the end rivaling even she herself. His reputation grew amongst the Pirates of the Coast until eventually most of them had heard the name 'Dodger.' Twenty years went by more swiftly than he realized until that fateful day when he saved Mor'Findl's life. That day he earned his freedom and said goodbye to pirate life forever.

Right, Donnie snorted to himself.

Despite his best efforts, he once again found himself headed down the coast toward the shores of the Saricordi, the Clans of the Coast. Though twenty years had passed, Mor'Findl was an elf like himself. Unless something untoward had happened to her, she would still be very much alive and kicking. Donnie found himself wondering if he would run into her again; he wondered if he wanted to.

Old feelings began to stir inside the elf, but he immediately squelched them. Every woman he had grown close with ended up the worse for it. Xira had paid with her life, Miranda had been taken, and Alana had been turned into a vampire forcing him to end her existence.

Donnie shuddered at the thought, tears coming unbidden to his eyes. Despite the fact that he had saved her, Mor'Findl nearly died because of his own stupidity. No, he was far better off the way he had lived these last few decades—as an itinerant artist, dallying with the fairer sex, but never allowing himself to get involved.

The slight elf finished tying down his hammock and swung himself up into it, sinking down into the stretched cloth cocoon. He swore he would keep to himself as much as possible on this voyage. It would be safer that way for everyone.

Donnie quietly hung there in his hammock, the sway of the ship his only comfort as he wrestled with his dark thoughts.

12
THE VORTEX

*Beyond the currents lay a huge gaping hole, darker than anything
Pallas had ever seen.*

Aday and a half later they reached the outer edges of the storm. The dark clouds of the Vortex towered over the seas ahead, entirely blotting out the sky. The seas grew choppy, constant flashes of lightning cut across the clouds, and the sounds of thunder created a cacophony off in the distance.

A couple of hours out, Thea held a service for the entire crew. Pallas decided to attend since it would be her first since being ordained. His sister appeared quite majestic in front of the crowd. She glowed with a holy radiance that caught him by surprise.

It was a far cry from the teen she'd been only five years ago. That girl had been rambunctious—traipsing all over Penwick with her friends, obsessing over pirate treasure. She had also been a rather proficient spiritblade, even surpassing him in her ability to channel spiritual energy. Thus, it should have been no surprise that she'd be adept at channeling the energy of the gods.

About an hour out, Pallas stood next to Lonnin at the ship's wheel. The one-eyed elf pointed out a spot in the clouds ahead. The howl of the wind had grown rather loud, forcing them both to yell over it. "You see there, lad? There's a break in the clouds where the two storms meet."

Pallas followed the elf's gaze and did in fact see a subtle lessening of gray mist in the thick wall of clouds. "So now what?" Pallas cried back.

"Now we batten down the hatches," Lonnin responded with a wink of his one good eye.

Pallas watched with silent admiration as the crew of the *Gossamer Lady* prepared for the storm. Though not quite as regimented as the Penwick Navy, they had a certain efficiency to them. Shortly there-after, the main sails had been strapped down, replaced with trysails and a storm jib. The storm anchor had been readied at the bow and anything not battened down was moved below decks.

The sea around them had grown quite rough when Captain Si-lyna's voice bellowed over the howl of the wind, "All passengers to their quarters!"

While the rest of their group made their way off the deck, Pallas and Donnie confronted the captain. "If you don't mind, we'd like to stay and help," the slim elf told her, pointing with his thumb to himself and Pallas.

Silyna eyed the both of them for a moment, then gave them a curt nod. "Much appreciated."

Donnie headed toward the bow while Pallas went back to Lon-nin's side. He watched with growing admiration as the elf expertly maneuvered them over the growing swells. Ahead the break in the clouds widened as they approached the outside edge of the storm.

Rain began to fall across the deck as the gap in the storms loomed overhead. Both elf and human held their breath as the stiff winds drew the *Gossamer Lady* into the Vortex.

Despite Lonnin's warnings, the ferocity of the storm caught Pallas by surprise. Powerful winds drowned out all sounds except for the continual crashes of thunder. Driving rains drenched the deck. The constant drops and lifts of the swells played havoc with his equilibrium. Had he not lived his entire life at sea, he might have completely lost the contents of his stomach.

Either as a testament to Lonnin's skill or perhaps due to pure luck, no waves had come crashing across the deck thus far. They had just cleared a large swell off the port bow, when an even larger swell came at them from their starboard. With no time to steer the ship into that swell, all they could do was hold on tight and pray that the *Gossamer Lady's* keel would keep them from rolling over.

The swell hit the ship broadside, lifting it way up and threatening to turn it over. The *Gossamer Lady* tilted at a crazy angle forcing Pallas to grab for the nearest rail. The ship teetered to the point where he thought they would surely capsize, when the wave finally broke across the deck. Somehow the ship righted itself, but the torrent that washed over them was so strong that it nearly dragged Pallas with it.

Unfortunately, not all the crew had been so lucky. After the last of that wave passed over them, Pallas saw that Lonnin no longer stood at the ship's wheel. The wheel spun back and forth aimlessly with no one there to man it.

Pallas swept his eyes all across the deck, but the one-eyed elf was nowhere in sight. A sudden chill traveled up his spine as the realization struck him. *Lonnin must have been swept overboard!*

Pallas felt torn in two. Someone needed to take the wheel, but their chances of "threading the needle" without the elf were slim at best. If being a captain had taught him anything though, it was how to make split second decisions. Wincing at the loss of the one-eyed elf, Pallas started for the wheel.

He hadn't gone more than two steps when a figure suddenly swung across the deck. Landing in front of the errant wheel, they grabbed it with both hands, then wrenched it with their entire body. The wheel fought them for a moment or two, then by the grace of the gods, finally stopped spinning. With the wheel now under control, the figure spun its head about and flashed Pallas a toothy grin.

It's Donnie!

Pallas should have known that only the wiry elf could have tried such crazy acrobatics in the midst of a raging storm. Donnie gave him a quick wink, then nudged his head toward the railing behind him.

Pallas responded with a curt nod, then spun about and half ran, half skidded to the ship's rail. Between the driving rain and rolling swells it was hard to see anything in the darkness beyond. Yet, Pallas thought he saw something during the intermittent flashes of lightning.

Taking a deep breath, he stilled his mind, all else around him fading away. Swiftly connecting to his spark of spirit, he tapped into its transcendent power. Responding to his unspoken thoughts, the energy rushed forth from the core of his being. It coalesced around his eyes, leaving him with a sharp tingling feeling.

Peering through the darkness with his augmented sight, Pallas spotted two heads bobbing between the tall swells. One of them had dark hair. Pallas felt a rush of excitement. *That's got to be Lonnin!*

His elation was short lived, however. Even if he could save the elf, there was no way he could get to both drowning sailors in time. With no other choice, Pallas launched himself over the rail and knifed into the rough waters below.

Once again reaching inward, Pallas touched that brilliant light of spirit within his mind. This time the energy rushed forth and fanned out to all his limbs. His arms and legs felt as if they were on fire as he resurfaced. With a great heave he took off, plowing forward through the rising swells. In under a minute he reached the spot where he last saw the drowning elf—just in time to see a dark-haired head disappear under the raging waters.

Pallas dove in after him and swiftly caught up to the sinking form. Wrapping his arms around Lonnin's torso, he stopped the elf from sinking further.

Pallas' heart suddenly leapt into his throat. Lonnin felt limp in his arms as if the life had already been drained from him. He needed to do something quick or the elf was as good as dead.

Despite the dire circumstances, it was strangely peaceful here below the waves. That helped Pallas to once again still his mind. Melting inward one last time, he touched the brilliant light that was his spirit. This time though, instead of allowing the energy to rush forth, Pallas let it build up inside him. He held onto it there, waiting until the critical moment he would need it.

It felt like an eternity until they bobbed back up to the surface. Pallas thought he was going to burst from holding the energy back that long.

Winds and rain whipped over them. Lightning flashed in the clouds above. Swiftly scanning the stormy seas, his eyes finally fell upon the *Gossamer Lady*. It was farther away than Pallas anticipated, but at this point he really had no choice.

Releasing the energy all at once, he guided it around him and the elf in his arms. The energy swirled about them, creating a portal to the astral plane. A split second later, the two of them reappeared about ten feet above the rolling deck of the *Gossamer Lady*.

Pallas shielded the elf with his own body as they fell to the deck with a resounding *thud*. Ignoring the pain, he rolled Lonnin over and checked to see if the elf was still breathing. He was not.

Thea. She's his only chance now, the stark realization hit Pallas. Swiftly rising, he lifted the elf off the deck with him. A second pair of arms were suddenly there wrapping themselves around Lonnin's other side.

"Taking him to your sister?" Donnie yelled over the howl of the storm.

"Yes!" Pallas cried back with a grateful nod.

As man and elf struggled toward the sterncastle, something came flying over the deck and landed directly in front of them. Halting in their tracks, Pallas stared with disbelief.

That's Cyclone!

The hunter's bronze wings draped around him shielding whatever he was holding in his arms. They swiftly retracted as he stood, revealing his burden to be the second sailor that had been washed overboard.

Pallas was stunned. *Just how strong is this guy—flying through these ungodly winds to pull that woman out of the waters?*

Quickly recovering his wits, Pallas waved for the hunter to follow them. Cyclone nodded and fell in beside them as they dragged the two drowned sailors toward the cabins where his sister rode out the storm.

Thea was no stranger to the seas. With her father being Admiral of the Penwick Navy, she had grown up on and around sailing ships. She had also spent much of her youth at the merchant docks, searching for clues to the whereabouts of Eboneye's treasure.

Even so, she had never ridden through a storm like this. Thea sat on her bed trying to pray as the entire cabin swayed back and forth. Between the heavy rocking, driving rains, howling wind, and the crash of thunder, concentration seemed to elude her.

That last swell in particular sent her tumbling off of her bed across the room to the cabin wall. Thea wondered what the navigator was thinking. If they capsized in this storm, they were all as good as dead. She had just settled back down to try and pray when she heard yelling in the corridor outside her cabin.

"Thea!" Someone called her name.

That sounds like Pallas!

Leaping from her bed, Thea rushed to the door and swung it open. Pallas and Donnie stood in the doorway holding the navigator between them. Cyclone stood behind the trio carrying another sailor in his arms. They were all completely drenched.

She immediately ushered them all inside. "Quick, place them here on the bed."

"What happened?" she asked, still incredulous as they all piled into the room.

"That last wave washed them overboard," Pallas exclaimed as they set the elven navigator down. "Lonnin here is not breathing."

"Neither is this one," Cyclone said as he laid the other sailor down beside the drowned elf.

"Step back," Thea ordered, pushing them all out of the way. She had already begun her prayers to Arenor as she scanned the bodies of the two sailors. Their diagnosis had been correct—neither were breathing.

Thea was intimately familiar with death. She still remembered what it had felt like when she had died. Her spirit had left her body and floated through the ether. Alys and her other friends had been there as well. Angels surrounded them all, singing a glorious tune. Alys had joined in with them, but Thea had another experience altogether.

As Thea floated in the near empty grayness, a tall man approached her from out of the void. Gold and white robes partially covered his muscular frame and a brilliant nimbus shone around him as if he were the embodiment of the sun. His appearance of indeterminate age, a mane of lush blonde hair flowed down to his broad shoulders.

This man's presence felt extremely powerful, yet peaceful at the same time. Dumbfounded, Thea stood there in awe as the man strode up to her and smiled. When he spoke, there was a deep echo to his voice, as if his very words carried power.

"Child, your time is not yet done. You still have much to do should you choose so in the material plane."

When Thea finally found her voice, it sounded quite small next to his. "Me? What's so important that I must do?"

His golden eyes danced with amusement, filling her with a feeling of warmth. "That is not something I can tell you my child, but I promise you it will come to pass." He reached down and took her hand causing Thea to tremble inside. "All that I ask is that you give thought to my words. If you find them worthy, then consider swearing yourself to my cause."

Thea gulped. Part of her yearned to do just that, but her mind rebelled at making a blind commitment—even to such an incredible being. "And what cause is that?" she forced herself to ask.

The splendorous man raised both his arms, the ether around them glowing brighter in response. "Why the cause of the light." He executed a graceful bow. "I am Arenor—he who holds the light in wait for the return of its true owner."

Thea's eyes went wide with astonishment. "Arenor, the Hand of Light? The Ralnain god?"

"The very same," Arenor answered, the corners of his mouth crinkling ever so slightly.

Thea felt stunned. The Ralnain god of light had just asked her to join his cause. Just what did that mean? More than that, was she even worthy? Her friends had just died because of her dark obsession. How could she be forgiven for something like that? How could she possibly serve the light?

The sound of beautiful music washed over her, partially soothing her inner turmoil. Thea peered over to see Alys happily singing with the angels. The sight nearly brought her to tears.

"What of my friends?" she asked, not turning to look at the god.

Arenor strode forth to stand beside her. "It is always their choice, but I believe your friends will return as well." He paused and nodded at Alys. "Like yourself, that one also has much to do if she so chooses."

Thea found herself suddenly overcome with emotion. Tears freely flowed from her eyes as she realized the mistakes she made didn't have to be the end for her friends. Still, she had never thought about serving the divine. She had always thought she would follow in her father's footsteps.

Casting a sidelong glance at Arenor, she found herself strangely drawn to him. Perhaps this was her way of making amends—a way to make up for leading her friends down such a treacherous path.

Taking a deep breath, Thea made up her mind. She bent down on one knee and gazed up at the god before her. "Very well. I will return and in doing so choose to serve the cause of the light."

Arenor smiled as he reached out a hand to her. "Very well, my child. So it shall be."

As Thea took the god's hand, she felt enormous power flow from it into and throughout her body. She had never felt so serene in her entire life.

Thea now drew on that same power as she touched the two life-less forms before her. White light flowed through each of her hands down into the two drowned sailors. In her mind she heard Arenor's voice as she willed the light to heal them.

Let the light lift you.

A few moments passed before both began to cough. First one, then the other turned their head to the side. Water poured from their throats as their lungs cleared and their hearts began to beat once more.

Thea let out a grateful sigh. She had wielded the light today and saved two lives in the process. It was a far cry from the life she had lived before meeting Arenor, but times like this justified her decision. She had chosen right in serving the light.

Even though they had saved both sailors, neither were in any condition to brave the storm. Pallas and Donnie left them in Thea's capable hands, then went back outside to see if they could lend a hand.

Silyna had the wheel, but was not a seasoned expert like Lonnin. As another swell approached them from their starboard, she angled the ship directly for it.

Pallas froze in place. *That's exactly what Lonnin had warned us against!*

Visions from the pirate invasion of Penwick once again clouded his mind. Pallas had been too young then to be of much help, but he wasn't a helpless child anymore. He had spent his life since then training for moments just like this.

Pallas lunged across the deck and grabbed the wheel away from Silyna. He pulled it hard in the opposite direction angling the ship as it rose up the giant swell.

"What are you doing?" Silyna cried, trying to grab the wheel back from him.

"Saving our skins!" Pallas yelled over the wind, blocking her from the wheel with his body.

The ship rode up the side of the wave, tilting again at a dangerous angle. Just as it felt like they were going to tip over and end up in the murky depths, the *Gossamer Lady* reached the top. She righted herself, then sailed gracefully down the back of the giant swell.

Unfortunately, their course had taken them too far east. All aboard could see the fast currents now—the outer edge of a giant whirlpool. The rush of water drowned out even the howl of the wind and the crashes of thunder.

Beyond the currents lay a huge gaping hole, darker than anything Pallas had ever seen. It looked like something straight out of the Abyss—a rip in the fabric of the world that would drag them down into the darkness.

Pallas took a deep breath, willing himself not to panic. Following his innermost instincts, he cut the wheel at a curt angle in the opposite direction. The ride was not smooth to say the least. Swells came at them from all directions, but Pallas ignored them and stuck to their course.

By the grace of the gods, they stayed afloat and slowly left behind the enormous gaping maw. With the *Gossamer Lady* once again 'threading the needle', Donnie tapped Pallas on the shoulder.

"I think you can let go of your death grip on the wheel," he yelled into his ear.

Pallas peered down and saw his knuckles had turned white. He slowly loosened his grip on the wheel and flexed each hand in turn, letting the blood rush back to his fingers.

Feeling a hand on his other shoulder, Pallas turned to meet the intense gaze of Captain Silyna. As a ship's captain himself, Pallas felt a bit like he had committed mutiny, even though it had saved their lives. Taking a step back, he proffered the wheel to her.

Silyna waved him off, however. "No, you keep it," she cried above the howl of the wind. "I panicked and nearly got us all killed."

Pallas gave her a grim smile. "Only if you and Donnie be my extra eyes."

"Done," Silyna exclaimed with a grave nod.

For the next few hours, Pallas, Donnie, and Silyna manned the wheel together. Never veering more than forty-five degrees from their course, Pallas handled approaching swells as Lonnin had taught them. It was a rough ride, but in the end they reached the southern end of the storm.

Once back into the open seas, shouts of triumph sprang up all across the deck of the *Gossamer Lady*. Exhilarated from beating the Vortex, Silyna, Donnie, and Pallas joined the shouting and exchanged hugs.

A wave of exhaustion suddenly overcame Pallas. He felt so tired that he wanted to go to sleep right there on the deck.

"Take him to my cabin," Silyna instructed Donnie. "He's earned a good rest."

Pallas barely remembered the walk to Silyna's cabin. Once Donnie helped him to the bed, he fell over and in moments was fast asleep.

13
GHOSTS OF THE PAST

Of all the women in the world, he had the misfortune of falling in love with a pirate queen.

epairs to the *Gossamer Lady* took up most of the next morning. One of the yardarms on the foremast had cracked in the fierce winds. The torrents that raged across the deck had washed away a part of the port rail. Also, the tip of the bowsprit had snapped off while riding those giant swells. Thankfully Silyna had the foresight to have a couple of crew members with carpenter skills and carry extra wood onboard.

Once underway again, they headed southeast and swiftly drew within sight of the shoreline. Seishin leaned over the newly fixed rail, his eyes fixed on the lush greenery that laid just beyond the sand filled beaches. Beyond those, craggy peaks rose to meet the blue of the afternoon sky.

The young warrior never expected to be headed back down the coast so soon. He had only left a few weeks ago not knowing if, or when, he would return. Sending someone as ill prepared as himself to find the legendary Shin Tauri blade seemed like a fool's errand despite the wizard Aldurin's assurances. His Uncle Draigo would have been far more suited to the task.

The veteran General had led the Isandor Royal Army for well over two decades. He had been best friend and advisor to the King himself before his majesty had been assassinated. Even more importantly, Draigo was a Shin Tauri master. With demon hordes about to descend upon their world, his uncle would have been a far better choice to seek out the all-important blade.

"Breathtaking sight, isn't it?"

Roused from his musings, Seishin glanced over to see the slim elf, Donatello, leaning on the rail beside him. Seishin gave him a slight nod. "Man is as nothing to the beauty of nature, thus it holds us in awe."

A knowing grin spread across the elf's lips. "Spoken like a true Shin Tauri."

Seishin's brow furrowed. "You've met others I take it?"

The corner of Donnie's mouth lifted ever so slightly. "Let's just say I've spent some time here along the coast."

The elf went silent, his expression growing distant. As the quiet persevered, Seishin's mind drifted back to his own troubled thoughts.

Despite his personal misgivings, his uncle would not have gone on this quest in his stead.

With the implicit church takeover of Isandor, the Queen herself had sent Seishin in search of his uncle. The time honored General was perhaps the only one who could rally the people of Isandor back to the Queen's side. Seishin had spent months following the cold path of his missing uncle. He had nearly died more than once along the way, until lady luck brought him to Draigo hidden amongst the pirate clans.

"It's a woman, isn't it?" Donnie once again interrupted his thoughts.

Seishin kept his expression neutral as he met the elf's gaze. He had not been thinking about Korti at that moment, but losing her was indeed his greatest source of pain. "What makes you say that?"

"It's always a woman." Donnie winked.

Seishin arched an eyebrow at the elf. Despite his brash assumptions, he was not wrong. Had Seishin not gone on this journey, he would never have met the love of his life—Kortiama Ozden, Lord Captain of the Dasati Nation of the pirate Clans of the Coast. Of all the women in the world, he had the misfortune of falling in love with a pirate queen. Strangely enough, she loved him back for all the good it did them.

Seishin still remembered the pain in her eyes as she pulled away from their last embrace. Her words cut through him like a knife. *Do what you need to do. I have my own people to worry about.*

Wounded to his very core, Seishin hadn't known how to respond. He didn't choose this path, but he was honor bound to it—for all their sakes.

Her parting words had left him equally perplexed. *If you manage to live, you know where to find me.*

Had that been an invitation or an epitaph? Seishin still wondered.

"Ow. That bad?" Donnie asked in a soft voice.

"Two different worlds"—Seishin shrugged in an attempt to mask the still fresh pain—"and she wasn't exactly happy with me for going on this quest."

"Double ow." Donnie winced. He reached out and placed a hand on Seishin's shoulder, his eyes filled with sympathy and something more—his own pain perhaps.

Seishin felt a sudden kinship with this strangely empathetic elf. From his reaction, he could only assume that Donnie was intimately familiar with heartbreak. Though not typically one to share thoughts or feelings, Seishin believed it only polite to reciprocate in turn.

"What about you?" he asked the slim elf.

A pained expression flashed across Donnie's face, only to be quickly replaced with an ironic smile. "Well now, that's a long story."

Thea stood in her stateroom admiring herself in the mirror. She had doffed her white cleric robes in favor of something a little less conspicuous for this next leg of their journey. Now garbed in a white shirt laced up the center, she had matched it with a long skirt the color of the sea. Being no novice to needle and thread, she cut out a high slit for each leg so it wouldn't impede her in battle. She finished the outfit with knee high black leather boots and a sea blue jacket cut off just above the waist.

A thin sword and scabbard hung off her belt. She pulled the slender blade from its sheath and held it lightly in her hand. She hasn't used one of these in earnest since before dedicating herself to the god of light.

As if by second nature, the energy of her spirit flowed forth and encircled the blade in blue flames. A hint of a smile came unbidden to Thea's lips. She hadn't completely lost her touch.

Picking up one of the knives she typically carried under her robes, Thea sheathed that blade as well in a small scabbard behind her back. She then rounded out the outfit with a dark grey cloak draped over her shoulders.

Pausing to take one last glance in the mirror, Thea recognized a side of herself she hadn't seen in over four years—a part she had given up when making her pledge to the god of light. A sudden longing pulled at her insides. *Do I really miss it that much?*

She had to admit, it had been an exciting life. *Sure, right up until it got you and your friends killed,* the voice of reason suddenly spoke up inside her.

The sobering thought quelled any further longings Thea might have been feeling. Arenor had come directly to her. She had learned the ways of the cloth, excelling at wielding the light as a weapon and for healing. Her talent was undeniable—plus who was she to question the gods?

Thea cast a wry smile at the reflection in the mirror. She had been a silly girl hunting silly pirate treasure back then. She knew far better now. Dismissing the subject, she pulled the hood of her cloak over her head and exited the stateroom without looking back.

Pallas had been so exhausted from navigating the Vortex, that he slept until the noon of the next day. When he awoke, he still felt groggy. Pushing himself up onto his elbows, he peered around the ship's cabin.

Where am I? He thought to himself. *This looks like the captain's quarters, but it's certainly not mine.*

All at once it came rushing back to him. The storm, the rough seas, Lonnin getting washed overboard—he was aboard the *Gossamer Lady!*

As if to confirm his suspicions, the door to the cabin opened and a tall woman with ice white hair entered the room. "Ah, I see you're finally awake," Silyna said, closing the door behind her. "I thought you were going to sleep the entire day away."

Pallas' hand went to the back of his neck. "Yeah, well despite all that, I still feel like I slammed head first into a bulkhead."

Silyna snorted. "That's from holding the wheel so tight for so long." She strode over to the side of the bed and motioned for him to move. "Scoot over. I think I can help with that."

"That's not really…" Pallas began.

Before he could object any further, Silyna slipped onto the bed behind him and started to need the knots in his shoulders.

"…necessary…"

She then moved up to his neck.

Pallas felt a bit awkward at first, but her hands were very strong and he melted under their touch. "I didn't realize…I had tensed up… so much…."

Silyna leaned forward and murmured in his ear, "I could relax you more if you'd like."

Pallas had been half dozing beneath her touch, but her words jolted him wide awake.

"After all, I owe you for saving my ship," she added, her voice low and throaty.

Perhaps he had, but it didn't make up for all of his past failures. Vivid images of the pirate raids in Penwick once again flashed through his mind. Yet this time it was overlaid with the dead bodies of his sister, Alys, and the rest of their friends.

His heart hammering in his chest, Pallas gently rebuffed her offer. "I—really didn't do all that much."

"I think Lonnin would disagree," Silyna murmured, pressing against him and nibbling on his ear. Her amorous advances washed the visions out of his mind.

Pallas felt himself begin to cave. Silyna was an exotic beauty and the warmth of her body felt good against his. His head started to turn of its own accord when another image flashed before his eyes. This time it was a vision of dancing green eyes and coppery tresses.

Pallas abruptly stopped himself. Somehow he didn't think Alys would be too happy if he dallied with someone else while he was away. He gently extracted himself from Silyna's embrace, then rose from the captain's bed and turned about to meet her gaze. "I'm extremely flattered, but I'm afraid I can't."

Silyna sat back in her bed and stretched her lithe, muscular frame. "Whoever she is, she's a lucky woman."

Pallas' brow knit into a questioning frown. "How did you know?"

A shrewd smile spread across Silyna's lips. "I don't get turned down very often, but when I do it's because there's someone else."

"I bet you don't," Pallas said with an appreciative nod.

Silyna slowly rose from her bed. "Anyway, there has to be something I can do to repay you."

Pallas' stomach chose that moment to emanate a rather loud grumble.

A hearty laugh escaped Silyna's lips. "There's my answer! You must be famished. I'll have the cook whip you up a grand meal."

Pallas placed a hand over his stomach and gave her an embarrassed smile. "That would be most appreciated."

"Wait here. I'll bring it to you." She clasped him on the shoulder as she went by, then exited out the cabin door.

I must be crazy, Pallas thought as he watched her go. Nonetheless, it confirmed that his feelings for Alys were very real. He swore that when this was all over, he would sweep that young lady off her feet and show her just how much he cared.

When Thea walked out onto the deck, she noticed Donnie and Seishin standing at the rail together. Thea eyed the newcomer with keen curiosity. He came across as a quiet, unassuming young man, but the spiritual energy that swirled around him was rather impressive. It felt familiar somehow, as if he were some sort of spiritblade, yet she could detect subtle differences.

Father had told them stories about spiritblade origins, how their great-grandfather brought the craft back with him from the mainland. Perhaps that was what she felt—the distant link between spiritblades and the Shin Tauri?

One other thing Thea noticed. Beyond plain sight she could see the weight that Seishin carried upon his shoulders. Being a descendant of the legendary Tibarn could not have been all that easy. In Penwick circles, Thea's parents were just short of living legends. Thus, she knew a thing or two about living in the shadow of your family's name.

A low whistle interrupted her musings. Thea turned to see Elladan approaching her with an appreciative smile. "Wow! If I didn't know any better, I'd think you were a pirate princess."

The side of Thea's mouth curved upward into a slight smirk. "Well in that case you better keep an eye on your purse."

Not missing a beat, Elladan placed a hand over his heart. "I fear you may have already stolen far more than that from me, good lady."

Thea felt the heat rise to her cheeks. The elven bard was incredibly handsome and she definitely enjoyed their time together. Still, tempting as she found him to be, she hadn't decided if she wanted anything more just yet.

"Right…" Thea drawled, using sarcasm to deflect her discomfort.

"So why the change in look?" Elladan asked. "Not that I'm complaining, mind you," he added smoothly.

Thea gazed down at her outfit, her lips pursing into a puckered smile. The tight fitting skirt and boots did accentuate her long legs, one of her best features in her opinion.

"It was Donnie's idea," she confided in him.

Elladan's nose and brow crinkled. "Really? Since when did he start giving out fashion advice?"

Thea fixed him with a sour look. "Not like that. Apparently Kaniron culture frowns on the Ralnai."

Donnie's keen elven ears must have heard them talking about him. "Come over and join us." The thin elf waved from the ship's rail.

Elladan offered Thea his arm and spoke in a mock snobbish tone. "May I escort you, my lady?"

Thea snorted with amusement. "Why of course my good man," she responded in a matching voice. She laced her arm through his and together they sauntered across the deck.

The rest of the day passed by uneventfully. Lonnin and the other sailor had fully recovered from nearly drowning, and Pallas finally showed up on deck sometime in the early afternoon. The *Gossamer Lady* made good time down the coast. According to Silyna they would reach Kaniron sometime late the next morning. The farther south they sailed, however, the more nervous Donnie became.

Kaniron would be crawling with pirates. The Church of Zharpita was filthy rich and didn't seem to care much about with whom they traded. Thus, they were the perfect clientele for the clans. Visions of running into someone from Mor'Findl's old crew left Donnie feeling anxious all day. So much so in fact, that he retired down below not long after sunset.

Even so, Donnie was not a light sleeper. Years of the pirate life along with outraged husbands and fathers had taught him to always sleep with one eye open. Thus, he reacted out of pure instinct when he felt a presence in the dark hovering over him.

In one swift motion Donnie leapt from his hammock and drew his rapier. The point of his sword drew within inches of a chiseled chin.

Dim light spread in small circles from strategically placed lanterns around the hold. The figure took a step into that light and stopped at the very tip of his blade.

It's Cyclone! Relief flooded through Donnie as he recognized the hunter. Dropping his blade and hissed at the hunter, "What are you doing down here? You nearly scared me half to death!"

Cyclone's face remained impassive. "We have a problem."

Donnie's heart leapt back into his throat. "What kind of problem? Pirates? Parthians?"

Cyclone shook his head. "Neither. It's Ruka."

Donnie wasn't quite sure he'd heard him right. "Did you say—Ruka?"

Cyclone responded with a curt nod. "I summoned her."

Donnie's eyes nearly bulged out of his head. "You what?"

"Shhh," Cyclone admonished him, putting a finger to his lips.

A few figures stirred in their hammocks around them. The duo remained frozen in place until that movement subsided.

"You what?" Donnie repeated softer this time.

Cyclone merely shrugged. "What the Queen did to the sisters was out of line—would have summoned them all if I could."

Donnie's head spun with the implications of what Cyclone had done. The Queen of Lanfor would be furious when she realized Ruka was gone. On top of that, how would Balthazar and Cloud react when they found out.

After all, it's not like they could send her back at this point Donnie realized. For better or worse, they'd have to deal with the repercussions of what Cyclone had done.

Taking a deep breath, Donnie eyed the hunter warily. "So, other than the mess you created, what's the problem?'

"She won't wake up," Cyclone said simply.

Donnie narrowed an eye at him. "What do you mean?"

"Just what I said," Cyclone snorted. "I summoned her and she won't wake up." He pointed a thumb at the ceiling of the hold. "Right now there's a large bronze dragon sleeping on the poop deck."

Donnie's jaw nearly dropped to the floor. "Well that's just wonderful." After a moment's pause, however, he realized what must have happened. "The Queen's spell is still on her."

"That's what I thought," Cyclone agreed.

It finally made sense to Donnie why Cyclone had come to him. "Okay, I'll take care of it. You just make sure no one else comes out on deck."

Cyclone curtly nodded his agreement.

As the hunter left, Donnie went to his pack to find the special gloves that dispelled magic. He found them in a treasure chest in the Golem Master's monolith and had made rather good use of them ever since.

"Summoned Ruka," Donnie muttered to himself as he rummaged through his belongings. "Why can't trouble just leave me alone for once?"

Donnie quietly stole out onto the deck. It was past midnight, the night black with no moon to brighten the darkness. The only light came from twinkling stars far above in the inky firmament and a couple of lanterns placed at strategic locations around the ship.

For the moment Donnie ignored the sterncastle where Ruka's hulking form lay. Instead he focused on the sailors at the wheel and in the crow's nest above. Neither had yet seemed to notice the large form laid out on the elevated sterncastle behind them.

Donnie breathed a heavy sigh. At least he had that going for him.

Noiselessly padding across the deck, Donnie slipped past the sailor at the wheel and climbed the stairs leading up to the sterncastle. There he spied Ruka's large shadow spread out in the middle of the deck. Scanning the sterncastle as he stole across it, Donnie made certain no one else was about. Thankfully, they were all alone up here.

Upon reaching the slumbering dragon, Donnie noted her head tucked down into her chest. A feeling of tenderness overcame the slim elf. *She seems so peaceful like this. I just hope she wakes up in a good mood.*

Pulling on his red and black striped leather gloves, Donnie steeled himself as he reached out and touched the sleeping dragon. There was a momentary flash, and then Ruka began to stir.

All of a sudden, her head lifted and spun about to face him. "What? Where?" She sputtered, still seeming a bit groggy.

"Shh," Donnie held a finger to his lips. "You're on a ship sailing down the mainland."

Ruka took that in for a few moments, then spun her head back and forth. "Ves! Where is that traitor?"

Donnie threw up his hands in front of him in a calming gesture. "The Queen put her to sleep as well. She's back in Palt, just like you were."

Ruka let out a derisive snort. "Serves her right." She paused another few moments, then peered intently at him with her large green dragon eyes. "What about Maya?"

Donnie met her gaze with a wan smile. "Same as Ves, I'm afraid."

A long silence ensued as Ruka held his stare. All of a sudden, she began to glow. The brilliance grew brighter and brighter as her dragon form shrunk in size. In less than half a minute, the glow was gone.

Ruka now stood there in the human form to which he had grown accustomed—the form that so painfully reminded him of Miranda. She sauntered up uncomfortably close and peered up into his eyes. "So did you miss me or something?"

Donnie shuffled uncomfortably on his feet. This is exactly the kind of situation he had hoped to avoid. "It was Cyclone's doing. Remember, I no longer have your dagger."

A flash of amber flickered across her eyes. As if in answer, the sound of thunder rolled across the sky somewhere off in the distance.

Donnie inwardly flinched. He could feel the anger radiating from her. It only lasted for a few moments, however, and then it was gone.

Ruka stepped back and stretched, her tone now completely nonchalant. "Well at least someone has the good sense to appreciate me."

Donnie felt the momentary sting of her words. He opened his mouth to protest, but then caught himself. "I'm just glad you two are getting along so well," he lied.

"Are you?" she asked. He could feel the weight of her stare boring into his very skin. She looked so much like Miranda, that the draw he felt to her was physically palpable. Still, if he gave into that desire, it would only bring her more pain and suffering.

"Yes," he lied again.

"Good," she responded, her tone harsh. She spun about and stormed off, but stopped after taking only a few steps. She turned back again, her tone suddenly quite sheepish. "So, um, where's Thea staying?"

Donnie pointed a thumb at the deck below them. "In the first mate's quarters, just below the captain's."

"Thanks," Ruka said wanly, then spun around yet again and glided off across the deck. Moments later she disappeared down the stairs.

Donnie's shoulders slumped as he let out a heavy sigh. He trudged slowly across the deck, his heart aching for having hurt her yet again.

14

THE FIREBIRDS OF KANIRON

Flames danced around the entire creature leaving
a scarlet trail behind it.

Elladan eagerly awaited for Thea to join them at breakfast the next morning. The more time they spent together, the more he came to appreciate her wit and
charm. Even so, that new outfit she appeared in yesterday sent him for a loop. When he clutched at his
heart in jest, he was only half-kidding. She looked positively stunning.

Everyone had already gathered around the captain's table by the
time Thea arrived. Things took an unexpected turn, however, when
Ruka came strolling alongside her into the ship's galley.

Elladan's jaw nearly dropped to the floor. "Ruka? What are you
doing here?"

The corner of the girl's lips curved ever so slightly upward. "I
guess someone just couldn't do without me." She ended with a pointed glance at Donnie.

Everyone turned to look at the elf. Donnie threw up his hands in a warding gesture. "Don't look at me!" Despite his denial, Donnie's face appeared riddled with guilt.

"Tsk," Cyclone clicked his tongue. "I did it."

All eyes now turned towards the hunter. Cyclone fixed his gaze on Cloud and Balthazar. "No offense, but your Queen had no right to do that to the sisters."

Though Cyclone was brusque as usual, Elladan actually agreed with him. Unfortunately, they had little choice back then. Finding the scrolls had to take priority and they needed the Queen's help to do so. Ruka was here now though and this time Elladan would stand beside her. He only hoped her presence wouldn't cause a rift in their newly formed group.

The entire room around them had fallen silent. Cloud and Balthazar exchanged a brief glance, then the gnome shrugged. "It's not my problem."

Balthazar, on the other hand, said nothing, instead looking past Cloud toward Ruka. Though his expression remained impassive, Elladan caught a glimpse of mixed emotions in the lieutenant's eyes.

Ruka placed a hand on her hip and met Balthazar's gaze evenly. "Well, are we going to have a problem here?"

Elladan inwardly winced. At times Ruka could be as tactless as Cyclone. Just when he thought he'd have to step in, however, Balthazar spoke up.

"No, what's done is done," Balthazar said in a measured tone. A thin smirk had begun to spread across Ruka's face, when he added, "All that I ask is that when this is over, you return with us to Lanfor to face the Queen yourself."

The smirk immediately disappeared from Ruka's face. "Fat chance of that happening," she replied with a derisive snort.

"I'll go with you," Cyclone muttered in a low voice before anyone else could speak.

"As will I," Donnie immediately chimed in.

"And I," Thea said, draping a protective arm over Ruka's shoulder.

"Count me in as well," Elladan said, raising a hand. He already decided he would stand with the sisters and wasn't about to back down now. Plus, if he were being honest, he didn't really want to part with Thea either.

A touch of moisture appeared in the corner of Ruka's eye. She quickly brushed it away, covering her momentary emotional lapse with an emphatic, "Fine!"

Elladan let out a heavy sigh. *Well that could have gone worse*, he thought wryly.

All this while, Silyna had sat back and watched without comment. Now the captain sat forward in her seat and called across the table to Balthazar. "Looks like I'll need to charge you for one more passenger."

Before Balthazar could reply, however, Ruka cut him off. "I can pay my own way, thank you."

Though Silyna appeared dead serious, Elladan had a lot of experience reading people. He couldn't quite place it exactly, but something in her demeanor made him think that she was joking. Before he could say anything, however, Pallas almost too casually elbowed the captain in the arm.

"I think Silyna here is pulling your leg."

Silyna eyed Pallas for a moment or two, then smacked him across the arm and broke out into a boisterous laugh. "Guilty as charged."

Amazingly, Pallas grinned back. The two of them appeared awfully chummy.

Elladan didn't think Pallas could smile, let alone grin. The puzzled bard exchanged a dubious glance with Thea. She responded with a raised eyebrow, her eyes mirroring his own astonishment.

Thankfully things settled down after that. Thea grabbed the seat that Elladan had saved for her right next to him. Ruka then shushed Donnie over and parked herself on the other side of Thea.

Donnie remained uncharacteristically quiet after that for the rest of breakfast.

Later that morning a tall peak appeared south of them along the coast. Black plumes rose into the air from the mountain's flattened summit. As they drew closer, small red shapes could be seen flitting about its smoking caldera.

A few hours later, they rounded a cape and sailed into a bustling harbor. Numerous ships cruised in and out of that port with a few dozen more docked at the piers. A sprawling city spread out beyond the harbor, its tall buildings styled in classical architecture with a touch of Laurentian influence. The city ended at the base of the volcano only a few miles inland.

Earlier that day, Silyna had briefed them a bit more about Kaniron. In order to even enter the city, you'd need a Priestess of Zharpita to travel with you. Otherwise you risked an attack by the firebirds. Those birds could now be seen everywhere over the city, even as far out as the harbor.

The hairs on the back of Elladan's neck bristled as one of them approached the ship. It was far larger than he expected, its body covered in multicolored feathers ranging from yellow-orange to a fiery-red. Flames danced around the entire creature leaving a scarlet trail behind it. The huge bird strafed the waters a hundred or so yards off their bow, then climbed back into the sky and circled in the air high above them.

"That thing's nearly as large as a dragon!" Donnie declared in obvious awe.

"Not quite," Ruka corrected him, her tone betraying that she was far from impressed.

Silyna had the *Gossamer Lady* draw to a stop and weigh anchor. A couple of crew members carried a large cauldron onto the deck and filled it with oil. They then lit it and stood back letting the smoke rise into the air. They didn't have long to wait.

A small keelboat sailed out from the harbor and soon pulled up alongside them. Elladan and the others followed Silyna to the ship's rail. A lone figure in red robes stood in the center of the keelboat's deck. The priestess called out from under her hood in a snappish tone, "What business do you have in Kaniron?"

Silyna kept her own voice as neutral as possible as she yelled her reply. "We are traders from up north and have goods to sell in the city."

The priestess pulled a clipboard from under her robes filled with a thick stack of parchments. She briefly rifled through the pages, then stopped and pointed to a specific line. "Ah, here you are—the *Gossamer Lady*. I see that you've been here before."

"Many times," Silyna agreed with a forced smile. "And the price of entry never gets cheaper," she murmured to the others under her breath.

Elladan had to stifle a laugh. In his experience taxes and fees only went up, never the other way.

The priestess swept her gaze across all those at the rail until finally settling again on Silyna. "Is this your crew?" she asked with obvious suspicion.

Elladan cleared his throat and motioned to the others gathered at the rail. "We are a traveling group of artists and entertainers hoping to perform in your city," he replied, sticking to the guise they had previously decided upon.

The priestess grew quiet for a few moments, then responded with a harsh, "One thousand gold crowns for the lot of you."

Silyna's jaw nearly dropped to the deck in astonishment. "One thousand gold crowns? We've never paid more than two hundred and fifty!"

Elladan placed a hand on Silyna's arm and murmured to her in a soft voice, "Don't worry, we'll handle this."

"Would you accept half that?" he called to the priestess in as friendly a tone as he could possibly manage.

"Our tribute to Zharpita is non-negotiable," the priestess declared flatly. To illustrate her point, she raised her staff. That same firebird circling overhead suddenly swooped down toward them once again.

Cyclone emitted a deep growl and started to reach for his halberd. At the same time, Ruka's eyes flashed yellow, accompanied by the distant roll of thunder.

Thea placed a restraining hand on Ruka while Pallas whispered to Cyclone, "There will be time enough for that later."

Thankfully the two of them listened. The giant bird strafed over them just missing the *Gossamer Lady's* main sail, then climbed back up into the sky to resume its circling.

Elladan had quite a bit of experience in brokering deals, but this priestess seemed to be a difficult case. He had just decided to change his tact when Donnie chose to stick in his two bits.

"Excuse me Mistress…" he called down to the priestess, flashing her one of his best sparkling smiles. The priestess' hood turned in Donnie's direction. Elladan hadn't expected her to react well to the elf's charm, but in this case he turned out to be wrong.

After a moment's pause, the priestess lowered her hood. Despite her waspish nature, she turned out to be a dark-haired beauty with smooth skin the color of golden-honey. She fixed her dark brown eyes on Donnie and responded, "Vitalis. Priestess Vitalis."

Though she stressed the word 'priestess' as if somewhat annoyed, that didn't dissuade Donnie in the slightest. "Vitalis? What a perfect name to grace such a ravishing beauty as yourself."

Elladan had to stop himself from smacking his forehead. Donnie was really pouring it on thick. Down the ship's rail Ruka stepped back, turned around, and pretended to throw up.

Donnie ignored her and continued to try and woo the priestess. "Tell me, Vitalis, it is only gold crowns that you accept as payment?"

If anyone else had made that pitch, their ship would be going up in flames by now. Yet, Donnie had a way about him. His boyish good looks and roguish charm seemed to appeal to many a woman.

Vitalis, apparently, was no exception. The hint of a smile crossed her lips. "What exactly did you have in mind?"

Donnie used his fingers to form a square in front of his face, and peered at her through them. "With those soulful eyes and that gorgeous complexion, you'd make a stunning subject on canvas." He dropped his hands and fixed her with a smoldering stare. "Perhaps you would allow me to paint your portrait?"

Elladan nearly bit his lip. That was Donnie's 'go to' move. He'd won over more than his fair share of wives and daughters by offering to 'paint their portraits.'

Vitalis' face flushed ever so slightly, but she didn't seem quite convinced as of yet. "Are you any good?"

Donnie pressed his lips together and tilted his head to one side. "Mm, I do have a bit of a reputation. Perhaps you've heard of me? Donatello?"

Vitalis' eyes went wide with surprise. "The Donatello?"

Donnie spread his hands apart and gave her a modest shrug. "In the flesh."

The original Donatello had not been an elf and as such was many centuries dead. Apparently, Vitalis did not know that. Elladan only hoped she didn't find out before Donnie's little charade played out.

The priestess' face had now turned completely red. She fanned herself with her hand before responding, "Well then, you may come aboard." She paused a moment as her brow knit into a frown. "I warn you though, if you do not live up to your reputation, there will be consequences."

Donnie responded without missing a beat. "Fear not, milady. Of my many patrons, I have as of yet to leave one unsatisfied."

Before anyone else could say a word, the slim elf went jaunting off towards the rowboats. As soon as he disappeared over the side, Ruka went storming off towards the cabins. Elladan's keen hearing caught her muttering under her breath, "I hope he catches a disease."

A little over an hour passed before Donnie returned. As he climbed out of the rowboat, he announced triumphantly, "Five hundred gold crowns in total."

Silyna gave him an appreciative stare. "That's rather impressive."

Donnie flashed her that roguish smile, but Elladan threw an arm around his shoulders, and cut him off before he got any more ideas. "It might be, but if I was him, I wouldn't go anywhere near Ruka right now."

Donnie eyed him warily. "That bad?"

"Worse," Elladan answered with his patented half-smile.

Donnie took a deep breath, then shrugged. "Oh well, it wouldn't be the first time she's chewed my head off."

Thea had gone to the cabins to console Ruka. She just returned in time to hear those last few words. "To be honest, Donatello, you'd be lucky if that's all she chews off."

Donnie peered at Thea and winced.

Not long afterward, Vitalis came aboard the *Gossamer Lady*. With a wave of her staff, she sent the firebird overhead flying away. The ship sailed uncontested into the harbor and headed for the docks along the shore.

After Thea's warning, Donnie chose wisely to distance himself from the Kaniron priestess. He disappeared with Seishin off toward the bow of the ship.

Elladan went to the port rail to watch the approaching city with Thea. They hadn't been there very long when a seemingly bored Vitalis strode over and casually leaned against the rail.

Thea chose to ignore the priestess, but Elladan did his best to make small talk. After a few minutes, he noticed her eyeing him with more than just a passing interest.

"You know, you're just as handsome as your friend," she finally told him.

Normally Elladan would have been flattered, but strangely he found himself with no interest whatsoever. He cast a quick glance at Thea and found her watching him with an arched eyebrow.

Not missing a beat, Elladan grabbed her hand and held it in his as he responded to Vitalis. "So I'm told."

Vitalis peered from Elladan to Thea, then let out a soft sigh. "Ah well, you can't blame a girl for trying."

Seishin stood at the prow of the ship staring at the approaching shoreline. Donatello leaned against the rail next to him, his new friend seemingly lost in thought. Seishin couldn't even begin to imagine flirting the way Donnie did. Where the elf was extremely outgoing, Seishin was the polar opposite. In that respect, Donnie reminded him of Kortiama.

Korti had a dynamic personality similar to the gregarious elf. She flirted with Seishin outrageously when they first met. She had even kissed him first. Little did he know at the time that her reckless abandon stemmed from a desire to run away.

Perhaps that was Donnie's problem. Korti had fled from the pressures of being Lord Captain of the Dasati. Maybe the elf was running from something similarly traumatic in his past.

As the docks drew closer, Seishin spied the flags of the nearest ships. The colors over one in particular caught his attention. He nudged Donnie in the arm. "Well, the pirates are definitely here in Kaniron."

Roused from his brooding, Donnie followed Seishin's gaze. "An ebon stingray on a field of white? That's a Dasati ship."

"I'm all too well aware," Seishin said with an audible sigh.

Donnie leaned his elbow against the rail and eyed him with a probing stare. "This wouldn't have anything to do with that girl we talked about earlier?"

"Maybe," Seishin replied with a noncommittal shrug. Before the elf could ask anything else, Seishin pointed out another ship a couple of piers away from the first. "What about that one? I've seen that flag before while defending the coast."

Donnie leaned over the rail and peered intently at the vessel. "Hm, an azure shark on a field of gray—that would be a Galocerd ship."

That made two pirate clans in port. "I wonder if there are any others?" Seishin said straining his eyes to see further down the docks.

The two of them continued to scour the piers and in the end spotted one more pirate ship. That one flew a flag with a bright emerald eel on a field of deep blue which Donnie identified as belonging to the Javanicor.

"So three clans here all at once," Seishin mused aloud. "I wonder which one sold the scrolls to the church?"

Donnie's eyes lit up with an idea. "You know, if we do a bit of digging in the right places, we might just be able to find that out."

A short while later they pulled into port. Seishin and Donnie headed back to the main deck just in time to watch Vitalis disembark. Upon seeing Donnie, she blew him a kiss. "Thanks for the 'portrait' lover boy."

Across the deck from where they stood, Ruka's face twisted into an angry snarl. She took a step toward the priestess, but Thea caught her by the arm.

"She's not worth it," Thea hissed.

Ruka cast an angry glance at her friend, but then stopped, folded her arms, and merely glared at Vitalis.

Vitalis returned her glare with an amused smile, then turned her attention toward Elladan. "Well handsome, if you ever get tired of your 'milk toast' girlfriend, you can find me up at the temple."

Thea arched an eyebrow at the priestess, then pointedly removed her hand from Ruka's arm. "Then again, maybe I spoke too soon."

A vicious grin spread across the teen's face. Vitalis visibly paled at the sight. The priestess swiftly turned about and hastened down the gangplank. Ruka and Thea exchanged a glance, then both women burst out laughing.

Seishin found the situation disturbing, yet amusing, at the same time. Vitalis acted rather unbecoming for a holy person. He would have expected her to behave with far more decorum, much like Thea. He didn't blame Ruka at all for her outburst. In fact, where Donnie's flirtatious side reminded him of Korti, Ruka displayed a remarkably similar temperament to the woman he loved.

When Seishin discovered Korti's real identity, he had followed her to the Dasati village. Unfortunately, he had gotten himself captured. When Korti came to see him in the dungeon, she tore into him with a fierceness that made his head spin.

With Vitalis gone, Silyna approached their group. "We'll be here in Kaniron for two days at most—one to offload our current cargo and another to find cargo to bring back north."

Donnie flashed the captain a bright smile. "That should be more than enough time to…"

Silyna cut him off with a wave of her hand. "Whatever you're planning on doing—and I don't want to know what—just get it done by then." With that, Silyna strode away to attend to her ship.

With the captain gone, Elladan swept his eyes around their group. "Maybe we should pull up some seats and talk about what exactly we're planning on doing?"

Everyone found either a barrel or crate to sit on except for Cyclone. The hunter chose instead to lean against a nearby stack of crates.

Meanwhile, Elladan continued on. "So our objective is to liberate the scrolls from the church. Considering they are the seat of power here, I wouldn't expect it to be all that easy. Does anyone have any suggestions on how we want to proceed?"

"It would probably be best to get the lay of the land before rushing into anything," Balthazar offered.

"I couldn't agree more," Donnie chimed in with a nod to the lieutenant. He then shared their sighting of the pirate ships here in port.

"After a big sale, they'll definitely be celebrating. Something useful might slip out of those loose lips."

Ruka fixed him with a scathing stare. "You planning on sneaking aboard their ships to spy on them?"

Donnie flinched and gave her a hurt look. "That's not exactly what I had in mind."

Seishin thought back to his time in the army. They had more than their fair share of run-ins with pirates along the coast. If the pirates liked anything more than raiding, it was getting drunk. Seishin spied a couple of taverns on the waterfront here and pointed them out. "I was thinking wherever there's alcohol, you'll find pirates."

Donnie clasped Seishin on the shoulders. "He isn't wrong," the elf exclaimed with a broad grin.

Pallas rose from his barrel seat. "Seeing what you can find out at the taverns is not the worst idea," he admitted, "but if the church has the scrolls, we should definitely scope out the grounds there at the same time."

Still seated on the crate next to him, Thea chimed in. "If this is anything like Penwick, there will most likely be vaults somewhere on the grounds where they keep their valuables."

Pallas nudged his sister in the arm. "Oh, so now I get it."

"Get what?" Thea responded with a dubious stare.

"Why you joined the church," Pallas said, his expression neutral.

"Why's that?" Thea prodded him.

"So you could get into those vaults and search for treasure," Pallas replied, his lips curving into a smug smile.

Thea hauled back and punched her brother hard in the arm. "Jerk!" she exclaimed as she did so.

Pallas grabbed his arm and rubbed it while laughing. It was the first time Seishin had seen Pallas laugh since he met him. It was also the first time he'd seen Thea act in such an aggressive manner.

Donnie leaned over next to him and whispered in his ear the word, "Siblings."

Seishin nodded as if he understood, but in truth he didn't. Family life in Isandor seemed far more reserved than that of western culture.

"Either way, you raise an excellent point," Balthazar said with a nod to Thea. "We will have to keep an eye out for something like that."

Thea gave her brother a dirty look, then subsequently smiled at the Lanfor lieutenant. "Thank you. There will definitely be areas open to the public, but you can count on the restricted ones to be guarded."

"That shouldn't be a problem for Bal," Cloud chimed in for the first time since they began this conversation.

Considering what they'd heard of his escapades in the rebel fortress back in Lanfor, Seishin didn't doubt Balthazar's abilities in the slightest. Balthazar, on the other hand, seemed far less certain of himself than his comrade.

"Maybe, but we'll have to see." He paused a moment, then shifted his gaze toward Cyclone. "You've been quiet this entire time. What do you think?"

Seishin hadn't quite decided what to make of Cyclone. The hunter was rather rude, especially in his dealings with the Queen of Lanfor. Despite that, he seemed very capable as evidenced by his handling of those wyverns. Seishin sensed a lot of power hidden deep within the hunter. He suspected they hadn't seen half of what he could do just yet.

Cyclone pushed away from the crates and smacked his fist into his palm. "All this sneaking around is well and fine, but sooner or later it always comes down to busting heads."

"Yeah, well that's what we're here for," Ruka agreed with a wicked smirk.

"Hmph," the hunter snorted, folding his arms across his chest once again.

Elladan rubbed his hands together effectively drawing everyone's attention. "Well then, now that we've all had our say, how about we decide who's going where?"

15
PIRATES OF THE COAST

"So what does this have to do with the end of the world?"

The area around the docks bustled with people moving about at this time of the afternoon. Passengers disembarked ships. Dockworkers moved goods between vessels and dockside warehouses. Patrons frequented the bars and shops along the quay.

Donnie also noticed a fairly significant presence of those priestesses dressed in red robes. Accompanying them were armored guards wearing the insignia of a flaming red bird. Silyna had been right; the Church of Zharpita definitely held a tight grip over comings and goings from Kaniron.

The slim elf weaved his way through the crowded docks, leading both Cyclone and Ruka toward the pier where he'd spied the Galocerd ship. Donnie decided to try the tavern nearest to that clan and asked Cyclone to go with him for backup. Surprisingly, Ruka decided to go as well, though the way she phrased it stung a bit. *"I want to be there when he makes a fool out of himself again."*

The first tavern off the Galocerd dock bore the curious name of *The Red Cauldron*. Donnie supposed most of the businesses around here used words like 'Red' and 'Fire' in their names. The inside was laid out much like the *Drunken Dragon* with a long bar against one wall and a dozen or so tables in the center. The main difference appeared to be a separate area in the back filled with private booths.

The clientele here also appeared a bit seedier than those in Lanfor. Besides reeking of rum and ale, the scent of unwashed bodies wafted throughout the tavern.

Ruka wrinkled her nose in an unpleasant manner. "Smells real nice in here."

Donnie spied a group that could be the Galocerd off by themselves at the booths in the back. Before he could point them out, however, Cyclone headed to the bar. Donnie followed close behind trying to remain inconspicuous. He slid into the seat next to the hunter while Ruka parked herself on the other side.

A burly looking man covered in tattoos stood behind the bar wiping down an empty glass. He strode up to them his eyes settling on Ruka. "Ain't you a bit young to be sitting in here girly?"

Donnie winced, expecting Ruka to explode. He stood to jump in, but Ruka surprised them all with her response.

She put her elbow up on the bar, her voice deadly calm. "Tell you what. You beat me in arm wrestling and I'll leave."

The barkeep eyed her for a moment, then burst out laughing. "That's a good one. You've got guts, kid. I should let you stay here just for that."

For a moment, Donnie thought things had been settled, but Ruka wouldn't let it go. Her eyes flashed as she growled at the barkeep. "What's the matter? Chicken?"

The barkeep's brow knit into a frown, his gaze narrowing. "You can't be serious, lass."

"Deadly," Ruka replied, holding his gaze without blinking.

Taken aback, the burly man put down his glass and raised both hands in front of him. "Look lass, I don't want to break your arm." He glanced at Cyclone, then gestured towards him. "What if you let your friend here stand in for you. He looks kind of sturdy. At least he'd have a fighting chance."

"Tsk," Cyclone clicked his tongue at the man. "You must have a death wish."

By now, some of the other patrons had begun to gather around them. This was exactly what Donnie wanted to avoid. He leaned across the bar and caught Ruka's eye. Flashing her one of his best smiles, he tried to reason with her.

"Do we really need to do this here and now?" He nudged his head toward the gathering crowd.

Ruka stared him straight in the eye, her pupils momentarily flashing yellow. Thunder rolled somewhere off in the distance.

Donnie knew better than to argue with her when she was angry. He threw up his hands in defeat. "Okay, okay."

With the crowd egging him on, the barkeep finally gave in. He leaned an elbow on the bar, his thick arm dwarfing Ruka's in comparison. Since her arm was so much shorter than his, someone gave her a wooden box to rest her elbow on.

By now half the tavern had gathered around the bar. Donnie gave up all hope at that point of eavesdropping on the Galocerd. Cyclone officiated the arm-wrestling match, holding both opponents' fists in place until he barked the word, "Go."

At first the barkeep barely tried, but Ruka started to bend his arm backward. His thick brow raised, he began to fight back. He managed to bring her arm back to center, but didn't get much farther than that.

Donnie's sharp eyes detected the faint golden glow that suddenly appeared around Ruka. A moment later, she gave a sharp push and slammed the burly barkeep's hand into the bar top with a tremendous *thud*.

The crowd around them went deathly silent as the barkeep yelped in pain. "Ow!" He pulled his arm away, staring at Ruka incredulously as he cradled it. "I think you broke my arm."

A moment later, the crowd went wild. Folks cheered, gathering around and slapping Ruka, Cyclone, and Donnie on the back. The next thing they knew, everyone was offering to buy them a round. The barkeep waved them all off, however. "Drinks are on the house for these three!" he yelled over the din.

"What'll you have?" the barkeep asked Ruka as everyone started to drift away.

Ruka pursed her lips together for a moment until a sly smirk crossed her lips. "I'll have a glass of Ole' Dragon Fire."

"Make that two," Cyclone agreed, holding up two fingers.

Donnie blinked. Ole' Dragon Fire was like drinking pure alcohol. Of course Ruka wouldn't be affected by it and neither would Cyclone most likely. Still, he wasn't about to let them outdo him.

"Make that three," he said, holding up three fingers.

Having created a makeshift sling with his bar towel, the barkeep pulled out three glasses with his good arm. He then grabbed a bottle from the back of the bar and filled their glasses, setting the bottle down in front of them.

Donnie cautiously sipped his glass, the few drops of liquid practically searing the inside of his throat. "Smoo—th," Donnie croaked, wiping off the sweat that broke out across his brow.

Ruka gave him a wicked grin, then lifted her glass and downed it in one gulp. Slamming the glass down on the bar, she let out an extremely loud burp. "Ah, that's the stuff," she exclaimed, wiping her arm across her lips.

Her performance elicited a huge grin from the barkeep. "Lass, you are something else."

"She certainly is," said a voice from down the bar. Donnie turned in his chair to see a blue-haired woman approaching them. Two large sailors trailed behind her.

Donnie recognized them as folks from the group in the back of the tavern—the group he had assumed were Galocerd.

The woman parked herself in the seat next to Donnie, her eyes squarely fixed on Ruka. "You wouldn't be looking for work now, would you, hon?"

Ruka regarded the woman dubiously, but did not immediately answer. That gave Donnie the opportunity he needed to interject.

"Sorry, she's with us," he said, pointing a thumb toward the reluctant teen.

The woman shifted her gaze to Donnie and stared him in the eye. "And who is us?"

Donnie dropped his voice down to a whisper. "A fellow clansman."

The woman's eyes narrowed, her face clouding over with suspicion. "What clan?"

"The silver barracuda of course," Donnie responded glibly.

The woman sat back in her seat and laughed. "So you can memorize a flag. Big deal." She sat forward in her seat once more, her eyes locked on his. "Do you know the name of that clan, I wonder?"

Donnie glanced over both shoulders. Everyone else had stepped away except for Cyclone, Ruka, and the woman's two escorts. Even the barkeep had adjourned to the other end of the bar, knowing better than to listen in on clan business.

Donnie leaned in until his face was less than a foot from the woman's. "Sphyrena," he said in a soft voice.

Her eyes narrowed even further. "What ship?"

"Spirit of the Sea," Donnie replied without missing a beat.

The blue-haired pirate sat up on her stool and let out a loud laugh. "Hah. Mor'Tindl's ship." Her eyes fixed on Donnie once more, but her expression had changed to one of curiosity. "And just who might you be?"

"Dodger," Donnie said simply.

"Tsk," the pirate woman clicked her tongue. "There are many of those. Let's see just how good you are."

She stood up and Donnie followed suit. The woman made a quick move to disarm him, but Donnie had been ready for it. He caught her wrist, then spun her about, at the same time pulling her weapon from its sheath. She tried to push away, but he used her own strength against her. He spun her back around, then dipped her and tilted her forward until their faces nearly touched.

The two large sailors behind her moved in, but the woman waved them off. "Very impressive," she said to Donnie, her breath warm upon his face.

Donnie stared into her deep blue eyes for a moment or two before responding. She was quite pretty in fact, her skin smooth and her face heart shaped. Yet this was neither the time nor the place for that.

Donnie lifted her up and let her go, proffering her weapon hilt first. "That's because I'm the original."

The woman's face was just a bit flush and her eyes dilated ever so slightly. Donnie could tell he had sparked her interest just before Ruka ruined the moment.

"Sure. The original idiot," Ruka scoffed from behind him.

The woman snorted with amusement, the moment passed. "I've heard tell Mor'Findl had a special name for the Dodger." She tapped her chin with her finger. "What was it again?"

Donnie winced. Mor'Findl had a wicked sense of humor. Though they were quite close, she berated him in front of the crew on a daily basis.

"Little fool," he said in a soft voice.

"What was that again?" the woman said, putting a hand up to her ear.

Donnie huffed. She had heard him the first time. Still, if he could get them on their side, he might be able to find out what he needed to know about the scrolls.

"Little fool," he repeated louder.

Behind him he heard a loud *thump* followed by raucous laughter. Ruka had fallen off of her chair and now rolled around on the floor laughing hysterically.

Donnie grimaced and tried his best to ignore her. "And to whom do I have the pleasure of speaking?" he asked the blue-haired pirate.

A thin smile spread across the woman's lips. "Captain Burke, but you can call me Illyria." She stood aside and gestured toward the back of the tavern. "Why don't we go somewhere where we can talk more privately?"

It was not how Donnie had originally seen things going, but he could roll with it. He gave her a gracious nod and ushered her forward. "After you, Illyria."

A few more Galocerd pirates sat in the back booths. Illyria sat in the empty booth next to them, and waved for Donnie and his friends to sit across from her. Donnie did so, but Ruka and Cyclone chose to remain standing.

Illyria gave them both a brief nod, then turned back to the slim elf. "So what can I do for you, original Dodger?"

Donnie had been thinking about how he would spin this on the way from the bar. Knowing the clans as well as he did, he decided to use the mercenary approach. "We were sent by some buyers to find a certain item. They're not concerned about how we find it."

Illyria's eyes sparkled with interest. "Sounds like my kind of buyers. Go on."

Donnie leaned in closer across the table, dropping his voice to a near whisper. "The item in question is a set of scrolls—the works of a certain well-known blademaster."

Illyria leaned in toward him as well, her voice also low. "And just how much is this buyer of yours willing to pay?"

Donnie glanced around. The rest of the Galocerd appeared to be minding their own business. "One hundred thousand gold crowns. More if necessary."

Illyria's eye twitched ever so slightly. "That's the right ballpark. Unfortunately the scrolls were already sold."

Now they were getting to what he needed to know. Donnie looked through narrowed eyes. "To whom? The Parthians?"

Illyria snorted. "No, at least not quite yet—though rumor has it they'll be here any day now."

Donnie breathed a sigh of relief. At least the scrolls were still here in Kaniron. "So the Church of Zharpita then."

Illyria glanced around, then nodded. "Bought and sold by those accursed Dasati."

"For a pretty penny I'd wager," Donnie pressed.

"Twice what you just quoted me from what I hear. And the Parthians are willing to pay two and a half times more than that," Illyria expounded, her expression wistful at the thought of all that money.

Donnie let out a soft whistle. "That's a small fortune."

Illyria snorted again. "Tell me about it."

Donnie sat back in his seat and mulled over what he had just heard. The crew of the *Gossamer Lady* had done an excellent job getting them here, but they might need something more for what would come next. He gently rapped his fingers on the table of the booth. "How fast is your ship?"

Illyria pressed her lips together and shrugged. "We can outrun anything in this harbor short of the *Black Cat*," she said confidently.

Donnie had heard of the *Black Cat*. It was a Dasati ship. It had to be the one they had spotted in the harbor.

"Good," Donnie said with a subtle nod. He leaned forward once more, his voice low and tentative. "Say we were to liberate these scrolls. Would you be interested in splitting the profits? I'm sure I could get my buyers to match the Parthian's bid."

Illyria tilted her head to one side and eyed him dubiously. "Why not just sell it to the Parthians?"

"I don't deal with Parthians," Donnie said vehemently. He really meant it too. The Parthians were conquerors and destroyers. He had already lost so much in his life, he wasn't about to give more power to people like that.

"Suit yourself," Illyria shrugged. "Fifty, fifty," she said, her eyes twitching again ever so slightly. If there was anything the clans loved almost as much as making money, it was bargaining about it.

Donnie rapped his fingers on the table once more. "I was thinking more sixty, forty."

Illyria fixed him with a smug stare. "I have the ship, unless the Spirit of the Sea suddenly pulled into port."

Donnie winced. "Not likely. Mor'Findl and I parted ways awhile back."

A satisfied smile crossed Illyria's lips. "Well then, assuming you can even get the item, you've got no chance of getting away without my help."

Donnie waved a nonchalant hand at her. "Oh, don't worry, we'll get the item. I've got a guy who's practically a ghost when it comes to this sort of stuff."

Illyria sat back, put her feet up on the bench, and folded her arms across her chest. "Well then, my offer still stands. Fifty, fifty."

Donnie hesitated a moment, then finally shrugged. "You drive a hard bargain." He held his hand in front of his mouth and spit in his palm. He then stretched his arm out across the table toward Illyria.

Illyria hesitated a moment, then swung her feet back down again. She spit in her hand as well, reached out and gripped his hand with hers.

"Done," she declared, giving his hand a stronger shake than he had anticipated.

While Donnie and the others went to seek out the Galocerd, Seishin elected to hunt down the Dasati. Considering his past history with the clan, he should have avoided them at all costs. Sadly, he just couldn't help himself—any chance of hearing about Kortiama was worth the risk.

Though Seishin could handle himself in a fight, words were definitely not his forte. Thus, he asked Elladan to join him and the bard invited Thea in turn.

The inn nearest the Dasati ship bore the name *The Burning Phoenix*. Seishin had seen numerous taverns just like it along the coast, though this one appeared bigger than most. Even so, the dimly lit, smoke-filled common room reeked of ale and rum. Despite the poor lighting, heads turned as they walked in the door.

"Don't look now, but I think we're drawing a bit of attention," Elladan murmured beneath his breath.

Not used to being noticed himself, Seishin hadn't given much thought to the appearance of his comrades. In hindsight, walking in with the well-groomed elf in white might not have been the most clandestine approach. Thea in her new 'pirate' outfit seemed to be drawing her share of interest as well.

Murmurs rippled through the place all the way to the back of the room. After a few moments, a voice rang out over the din. "Well look here at what the cat dragged in!"

The room grew silent as a slim woman rose from a booth at the back of the inn. Her tan complexion drew a stark contrast to the puffy white shirt that fell across her bare shoulders. Long, light-brown hair spilled out of one side of her bright red bandana, and a pair of curved swords hung from the dual belts strapped to her waist.

Seishin froze in place. He knew this woman far too well. "That's Korti's sister, Solais," he whispered out of the side of his mouth.

"That's a funny coincidence," Elladan murmured back. "That's the same woman that challenged Thea's dad to a duel back in Penwick."

Solais downed the contents of her mug and slammed it down on the table next to her. Her eyes lifted and locked with Seishin's. She held his stare for a few moments before her mouth twisted to one side. "Well don't just stand there gawking."

The Dasati's invitation quelled the interest of the other patrons. Only someone with a death wish got involved with the clans.

Seishin exchanged a brief glance with Elladan and Thea, then led the way across the room. Solais had seated herself once again by the time they arrived, lounging casually with her boots up on the table. She sat alone, but the folks in the booths behind her watched them warily as they approached.

Solais snorted as Seishin stopped in front of her. "Last time I saw you, you were up to your neck in sand."

After being caught by the Dasati, Seishin had been sentenced to death. Surrounded by pirates and her hands tied by clan law, Korti had watched on helplessly as the tide came in.

"I've had better days," Seishin admitted. It was not in his nature to engage in verbal sparring.

Thea, on the other hand, had no such compunction. She regarded Solais with a lifted chin. "Last time we saw you, my father sent you packing."

Her words must have struck a nerve. Solais swung her feet down off the table, the smug smile on her face fading. "I still beat your brother," she fired back sounding defensive.

A knowing smile spread across Thea's lips. "Trust me, sweetie, I could see what both of you were doing and you got lucky."

Seishin found that quite surprising. He had crossed blades with Solais before and she nearly bested him. He had to wonder just how good these Stealle's were with the sword.

No longer smiling, Solais waved Thea off with a lackluster, "Whatever." She then fixed her gaze on Seishin. "So what brings you here, Shin Tauri?" She spoke those last two words in as derogatory a tone as possible.

Seishin ignored the intended slight, their mission far more important than petty slurs. He swept his eyes around the room before speaking. No one was paying attention to them except for Solais and the other Dasati. "I'm sure your sister told you why I left. Well this is related to that."

Mixed emotions played across the pirate's face. Yet before she could respond, a barmaid interrupted them. She weaved her way around them and replaced Solais' mug with a filled one. Before leaving she asked Solais, "Should I get a round for your friends?"

"They're no friends of mine," Solais grumbled.

Seishin shook his head. He should have known Solais would be too petty to think about the bigger picture.

Elladan, however, was not so quick to give up. "Now, now, we haven't established that just yet. You might find we want the same things."

Solais lifted her mug into the air and waved it at Seishin. "So you also want this one to stay away from my sister?"

Thea's face took on the expression a parent might get with a petulant child. She put her hands on the table and leaned over the recalcitrant pirate. "Not exactly, but if you care for her that much, I'm sure you won't want this world to end with her in it."

The two women locked eyes for what seemed like forever. Both had power and Seishin could see it flare between them.

The folks in the other booths had started to rise from their seats. Seishin's hands strayed to his sword hilts in preparation for a fight.

Yet before things got out of hand, Solais finally capitulated. "You raise a good point." She waved for the three of them to sit down and turned to the still waiting barmaid. "Get us a round of drinks."

"Right away," the barmaid responded, her voice just a bit too high pitched. She immediately took off across the room, obviously glad to get as far away from there as possible.

Once they were seated, Solais narrowed an eye at Seishin. "To answer your question, my sister did tell me about the fool's errand you were on. So what does this have to do with the end of the world?"

Elladan gave her a brief rundown of the demon tower and the impending invasion. He also detailed how the Princess Anya with her airship, dragons, and a platoon of troops nearly died assaulting the tower. He ended with the need for demon killing weapons and their quest to find the scrolls.

Solais listened quietly the whole time, her expression impassive. When Elladan finished his story, she sat there silently mulling over his words.

Not wanting her enmity of him to cloud the situation, Seishin felt compelled to speak. He sat forward in his seat and caught Solais' eye. "Look, whether my 'fool's errand,' as you put it, is successful or not, those scrolls could help us stop the demons."

Thankfully his words seemed to have the desired effect. Solais gave him a begrudging smile, then nodded. "To be honest, I'd rather not have them fall into Parthian hands."

Thea leaned forward as well, her expression hopeful. "So you'll help us?"

Solais shrugged. "Not sure what anyone can do at this point. The Galocerd already sold the scrolls to the Church of Zharpita. That place is locked up tighter than an Isandorian prison."

"What about the Parthians?" Seishin asked. That was the part they didn't already know.

Solais paused and took a swig from her mug, then wiped her mouth with her sleeve. "Due here tomorrow."

Elladan exchanged a relieved look with Seishin and Thea, then rubbed his hands together. "All the time we need."

Solais' brow creased into a deep frown. "Now I know your daft. Didn't you hear a word I said?"

"Actually, he's not wrong," Seishin responded in lieu of Elladan. "We know someone who can get in and out of just about anywhere."

Solais sat forward and locked eyes with him, trying her best to stare him down. When Seishin didn't flinch, however, her resolve began to waver.

Solais sat back in her seat, and casually rubbed her fingers to-gether. "Say I was to believe you. What do you want from me?"

"We assume you're here with the *Black Cat*?" Seishin asked warily. He found it hard to believe that Solais was actually coming around.

Solais kicked her feet back up onto the table across from them. "Captain, actually," she responded with obvious pride.

Seishin was duly impressed. "Congratulations on the promotion."

"So just how fast is she?" Thea interjected, her voice filled with a renewed sense of urgency.

Solais laughed. "Only the fastest ship in these waters."

"Good," Thea responded, ignoring Solais' boast, "because once we're done we'll need a fast getaway."

Solais dropped her legs again and eyed them all with clear skepticism. "If you survive and have the scrolls, I'll get you out of here and no one will catch us."

Thea abruptly spit on her hand and put it forward toward Solais. "Deal?"

Solais appeared impressed by the gesture. Seishin was as well. He wondered how Thea knew this particular habit of the pirate clans.

Solais responded by spitting on her own hand and then took Thea's in hers. "Deal."

16
ROMANCING THE PRIESTESS

"Isn't that outfit just a bit tiny for a priestess of the cloth?"

After their separate encounters with the pirate clans, the companions met back aboard the *Gossamer Lady*. Still busy with offloading cargo, Silyna let them use her cabin. They all gathered around the captain's table except for Cyclone who remained standing and Ruka who chose to throw herself on Silyna's bed.

Elladan and Donnie took turns detailing their individual meetings with the clan captains. During Donnie's account, Ruka interjected some very amusing details that the elf left out. Thea found it difficult suppressing a laugh at the mention of Mor'Findl's affectation for Donnie.

On a more serious note, the discrepancies between the two pirate captain's stories stood out like a sore thumb. "Interesting how this Illyria claimed the Dasati's sold the scrolls while Solais said the exact opposite."

"Pirates are exactly known for their honesty," Donnie quipped with a wry smile, "especially where money is concerned."

"Still, I don't see what they would gain by blaming each other," Thea pressed.

"From what I heard when I was with Kortiama, not all the clans get along," Seishin offered. His expression was grave, but Thea detected a flash of pain in his eyes as he mentioned that name.

She fixed him with a compassionate stare. "You mentioned this Kortiama before. I believe you said she's Solais' sister?"

"She is." Seishin responded with a grim nod.

Thea could sense his pain growing and would have left things there, but Elladan's curiosity had been sparked by the conversation. "Is she another Dasati captain?"

Seishin rose from his seat before answering and stood before the large windows in the back of the cabin. Thea could feel him exerting control over his emotions as he stared out into the bay. He clamped down on them until the pain all but disappeared—buried deep for the moment at least.

"She's the Lord Captain of the Dasati clan," Seishin answered in a soft voice.

"The Lord Captain?" Donnie exclaimed. He rose up from his seat and clasped Seishin on the shoulders. "Woah, my friend! You certainly don't do things halfway."

Donnie may have understood the title, but Thea had never come across it before. The clans tended to be quite secretive. Thus, not much was known about their society outside their ranks.

Elladan must have been thinking the same thing. He cast a curious glance at Donnie. "Lord Captain sounds like a pretty high ranking title."

"You don't get any higher in the clan," Donnie replied, slapping Seishin on the back once more. Donnie might have been thrilled by the discovery, but Seishin did not seem enthused in the slightest.

In an intuitive flash, Thea abruptly realized what must have happened. Seishin obviously loved this Korti and from what she could glean the feeling was mutual. Korti, however, was the head of the clan and the clans didn't like outsiders. Solais had said the words

Shin Tauri like it was a curse, so they probably liked them even less. On top of that, her greeting to Seishin intimated that they'd tried to drown him.

Based on all of that, Thea could only assume that Seishin and Korti were star-crossed lovers. The pain she had sensed in his aura finally made sense. She stared at him with new understanding, her heart going out to this brave young man who'd fallen in love with the impossible.

While Thea came to this realization, Pallas rose from his seat and stood next to Seishin and Donnie. "Not that clan politics is uninteresting and all, but I think we're straying from the main topic."

Seishin turned toward Pallas and nodded. "I agree," he said simply, but he looked quite relieved to be changing the subject.

They all sat back down as Pallas reported on their visit to the Church of Zharpita. "The grounds are huge, easily the size of the Temple of Arenor back home," he alluded to Thea. "Much of it appears to be garden-like with the temple itself in the back near the base of the volcano."

Thea had to wonder at that choice of location. Either the priesthood had ultimate faith in their fire god or there was something else at play here.

"Around the temple itself," Pallas went on, "there's an outside terrace with stone statues of the firebirds. A wide set of stairs lead up from there to the main entrance. Beyond that entrance, there's an outer courtyard and an inner courtyard. Past that are the doors to the inner shrine. Those were blocked by guards and no one was allowed beyond."

Thea found that highly suspicious. Back in Penwick, all shrines and altars in the temple were open to the public. "So no one was allowed into the inner shrine?"

"Not that I saw." Balthazar answered this time.

"We split up at that point," Pallas continued. "I took the stairs on the one side that led up to a gallery dedicated to Zharpita. The place was filled with murals and statues to their bird god."

"It was the same thing on the other side," Cloud added, "except that it was firebirds instead."

"Did you see anything else up there?" Thea asked.

"There was a corridor at the back of the galley," Pallas answered, "but it was cordoned off and guarded."

"Same thing on the other side," Cloud agreed.

Thea tried to picture the layout in her mind. "If it's anything like the temple back home, that area might contain their offices."

"So while they were busy with that," Balthazar took up where the others left off, "I did sneak into the shrine."

Thea leaned forward in her seat, her interest piqued. "What did you see in there?"

Bal shrugged. "Probably what you would expect. It's a huge room with a large brazier in its very center. A roaring fire burned above that brazier and was constantly attended by the priests and priestesses."

Elladan frowned at the lieutenant. "There are priests? So far we've only seen priestesses outside the temple."

"Maybe they're shy," Ruka commented from where she lounged on the bed.

Thea snickered at the sly remark, then focused her attention back on Balthazar. "Was there anything else in there?"

Balthazar shook his head. "There were smaller braziers scattered around the room—though none were lit—and a stone altar at the other end with decorations of their bird god plastered all over it."

Thea leaned forward even further. "No stairs?"

"None," Balthazar replied.

Thea raised both eyebrows in clear surprise. The entrance to the vaults in Penwick were below the temple. She wondered where else on the grounds it could possibly be.

Elladan mirrored her thoughts. "So, there's no indication of where their vaults are?"

Pallas, Balthazar, and Cloud all exchanged a glance and shook their heads.

"Then we obviously need more intel," Donnie interjected. The slim elf tapped a finger to his chin. "Maybe I should go and hunt down Vitalis. I might be able to 'coax' the information out of her."

Ruka leapt off the bed and stomped over to the table. "Whoa, there, lover boy. What makes you think that'll work twice?"

Donnie met her intense gaze with a hurt stare. "I can be very charming."

"Yeah, snake charming," Ruka retorted, the corner of her mouth curving upward.

Thea silently agreed with Ruka. Sending Donnie after Vitalis again might just backfire on them—especially if she found out by now that he wasn't the real Donatello. She thought it over for a few moments until a sudden idea struck her.

She peered tentatively at Elladan. "You know, she seemed quite enchanted with you as well."

To his credit, Elladan's brow knit into a deep frown. "Just where are you going with this?"

Thea laughed at his reaction, though deep down inside it pleased her as well. She fixed him with a shrewd stare. "Don't bards have song spells to loosen lips?"

A look of relief spread across Elladan's face. "Oh, I get it. I can try, though if she's strong willed, there's no guarantee it will work."

Thea couldn't help smiling at his reluctance to chase down the beautiful and amorous priestess. Still feeling rather pleased, she reached across the table and placed her hand over his. "I have faith in you."

The temple complex turned out to be as huge as Pallas described. Much like the one in Penwick, a thirty-foot crenelated wall surrounded the area. Towers with battlements stood on either side of the main gate and at each corner of the outer wall. A raised portcullis hung over the gate with a pair of guards standing post, but neither impeded Elladan's entrance.

The security here seems tighter than most castles, Elladan noted wryly to himself. Considering the apparent wealth of the church and their proximity to the pirate coast, it was probably a necessity.

The path through the grounds led him directly to the terrace with the firebird statues. Those happened to be far larger and far more life-like than Elladan anticipated. After their near encounter with the real thing, it made him more than a bit nervous.

At least we have Cyclone and Ruka with us, Elladan reminded himself. Even so, he still missed Lloyd and Glo. This new group had yet to be tested together in battle and he wondered how'd they fare.

Beyond the terrace he spied the stairs leading up to the temple, but that was not his current destination. Instead, he took a side path that led off toward the rectory. Thea surmised that is where Vitalis would be when not on harbor duty.

The rectory was an ornate stone building with tall columns, numerous arched windows, and more of those firebird statues at regular spaced intervals along the edge of the roof. Elladan eyed the statues warily as he approached the front entrance. *Well, that's not creepy at all.*

The foyer of the rectory was equally ornate, decorated with more columns and a black and white marble floor. Paintings hung upon the walls of those firebirds from numerous angles. One in particular caught his eye. It depicted a giant firebird emerging from the caldera of the erupting volcano.

That must be Zharpita, Elladan thought with a shiver. *Definitely wouldn't want to meet him in a dark alley.*

Long halls stretched away on either side of the room. In the very center a lone priestess sat behind the front desk. Upon seeing Elladan, she looked him thoroughly up and down.

Elladan was used to attention, but not quite as blatant as this. "Ahem, excuse me miss, but the Priestess Vitalis told me to look her up if I came to the temple."

The priestess continued to eye him as she rose from her seat. "Lucky Vitalis. Wait here, I'll go and fetch her." She gave him a lurid smile as she passed and sauntered down one of the halls.

Just what kind of church is this? Elladan wondered to himself. To be honest, he was just a tad bit nervous. Thea had caught him by surprise with her suggestion that he approach Vitalis. Vitalis was a beautiful woman, but he had found it easy to ignore her charms with Thea right there beside him. Still, her charms might not be as easy to ignore once he was alone with the amorous priestess. He only hoped Thea's faith in him was warranted.

The front desk priestess returned shortly thereafter with Vitalis trailing behind. "Well, well, to what do I owe this handsome surprise?"

Elladan gave her one of his most charming half-smiles. "Sorry about before. I couldn't exactly take you up on your offer with my 'friend' standing right there."

"I see," Vitalis murmured softly. She moved closer and placed two fingers on his chest. "But she's not here now, is that it?" Vitalis said as she walked her fingers slowly downward.

"Something like that." Elladan replied, grabbing her hand before things became even more uncomfortable. He smoothly recovered by lifting it to his lips and kissing the back of her hand.

"Oh my, what a gentleman we have here," Vitalis crooned with a wink towards the other priestess.

"Definitely," the desk priestess responded, still eyeing Elladan up and down.

Vitalis moved to Elladan's side and laced her arm through his. "Very well. Why don't you escort me back to my quarters and we'll see if we can become 'friends' as well."

"Why don't we then?" Elladan responded with another charming half-smile.

Vitalis' room was rather gaudy, replete with red velvet décor. A plush red carpet covered the floor and red velvet drapes hung from the windows. Cherry wood furniture added to the motif including a large four-poster bed with sheer red curtains, a tall wardrobe, a wide vanity, and a trifold changing screen. There was also a cabinet and a small table in front of a luxurious love seat with red velvet cushions.

Elladan raised an eyebrow as she ushered him into the room. "Life in the church must be good," he noted dryly.

Vitalis followed his gaze and laughed. "It has its perks at times. Please make yourself at home," she added, sweeping her hand around the room. She ended not so subtly pointing toward the bed.

"Don't mind if I do." Elladan replied, purposely striding toward the couch.

A brief look of disappointment crossed her features, but was gone in an instant. Closing the door, she fixed him with a sultry smile as she sauntered over to the changing screen.

Elladan sat down on the sofa, sinking deep into the plush velvet cushions. "This is certainly comfy," he called out to her.

"Glad you like it," Vitalis called back as she flung her priestess robes across the top of the trifold screen. One undergarment, then another found itself flung over the red robes.

Elladan took a deep breath. Things were going a bit faster than he anticipated.

A few moments later, Vitalis came out from behind the screen. She now wore nothing but a bright ruby necklace and a short spaghetti strap piece of lingerie that hardly covered anything at all.

Elladan gulped. "Not that I'm complaining, but isn't that outfit just a bit tiny for a priestess of the cloth?"

Vitalis fixed him with a smoldering stare. "Zharpita is a god of fire. Thus, he welcomes any type of fire: fire of the soul and fire of the body."

Elladan felt the warmth rising in his own body. While he did his best to keep his cool, Vitalis sauntered over to the cabinet and pulled out a bottle of red wine and two glasses. "Drink?"

"Certainly," he replied with a smooth smile, though he felt far less certain of himself than he sounded. Needing a distraction, he summoned his lute and started to play a soft tune.

Vitalis glanced over her shoulder with a distinct look of pleasure. "My, oh my. I can't remember the last time anyone serenaded me."

The barely clad priestess sauntered over to the couch with two glasses of wine in her hand. She put down one on the table in front of Elladan and sat on the love seat right next to him.

Crossing her bare legs, she took a sip of the red liquid and purred to Elladan, "That's lovely."

Elladan could feel the heat of her body now so close to his. Between that and her near nakedness, he was really being put to the test. The bard closed his eyes and recalled to mind the image of a heart-shaped face with pale blue eyes framed in long, wavy black hair.

The visage helped him to focus, but he wasn't sure how much longer his will would last. He needed to try something before it waned much further.

"Thank you very much," Elladan responded in a soft voice. "Maybe you'll like this even more." The bard started to croon, tentatively weaving a bit of magic into his song.

The priestess' eyes widened ever so slightly. Elladan was almost certain she had caught him, but instead of chastising him, she put down her glass and purred, "You have such a lovely voice."

Vitalis sat back on the love seat, closed her eyes, and began to hum along with him. Emboldened, Elladan carefully enhanced the magic. It seemed to be working when she slid even closer, her head draping across his shoulder, and her hand gently caressing his knee.

Caught off guard, Elladan did his utmost to keep his song going. When her hand started tracing its way up his leg, however, he knew he had to do something or this would go a way he hadn't planned.

Thea had spent much of her teen years sneaking around the streets of Penwick for any number of reasons. Sometimes it was to avoid the attention her family garnered, other times it was in search of secrets such as the location of Eboneye's treasure. Thus, she was no stranger to moving about unnoticed when she wanted.

Wrapped in her dull gray cloak, she kept out of sight as she followed Elladan onto the temple grounds. The true trick though was remaining unseen once inside the rectory. Thankfully her skills included more than just shrouding herself in a simple cloak. To aid in her clandestine teen activities, she had picked up a thing or two from the spiritblade *School of Shadows*. Though no master like Pallas, her study of spirituality as a priestess only enhanced those long ago learned skills.

The woman at the front desk had been so fixated on Elladan, that she hardly noticed as Thea entered and slipped behind one of the tall columns. Stilling her mind, she went deep inside herself. In the core of her being she met the light and envisioned its power wrapping her in a cocoon of darkness. Warmth flooded through her body as any trace of her faded into the shadows.

Guess I really haven't lost my touch, Thea thought with a mixture of humor and relief. This could have gone quite poorly otherwise.

Thea moved as silently as possible from column to column sliding between the shadows. When Vitalis came to get Elladan, she followed the same way through the dark spots down the hall.

Luck proved on her side once again as Vitalis held the door to her room open. With Elladan's back turned and the priestess' attention fixed solely on him, Thea managed to slip through the doorway just before the priestess closed it. The darker red décor here aided her as she slid against the wall to a shaded corner of the room.

Thea cringed when Vitalis finally came out from behind the screen almost bare-naked. *Well, that escalated quickly. I hope we can get what we need before things go much further, or I may not be able to stop myself from gagging.*

She noted how flushed Elladan became as the priestess continued her crass advances. At the same time, to his credit, he had not succumbed as of yet.

When Vitalis began to run her hand up Elladan's leg though, Thea felt a pang of jealousy. She had to remind herself this was all her idea while repeating the sentiment *at least Elladan still has his clothes on.*

Thankfully, Vitalis stopped halfway up Elladan's leg. A dreamy look came over her face and her hand fell away as she slumped across the elf's shoulder.

Elladan continued to croon his song as he put the lute aside. Gently sitting the priestess back on the couch, he took up the lute again. He resumed the music, but his words were now framed into questions. "Vitalis, dearest, where are the scrolls they bought from the pirates?"

Roused from her stupor, Vitalis gave him a dreamy smile. "Why in the vault of course, lover."

"And where is the vault?" Elladan pressed her.

"In the aerie," she murmured dreamily.

Deep creases furrowed across Elladan's brow, mirroring Thea's own reaction. "The aerie?"

A soft laugh emanated from the priestess' throat. "Of course, lover boy. In the volcano, where the firebirds make their nests."

In the volcano? Thea mused. After a moment's reflection, she realized it did make sense. *After all, where else would firebirds roost?*

From the sour expression on his face, Elladan seemed none too pleased with her answer. Still, he pressed on. "And how does one get there, love?"

Vitalis blinked, and started to sit forward, looking as if she were coming awake. Thea thought for a moment she would need to step in, but Elladan started to sing again, amplifying the magic as he did so. After a few moments Vitalis settled back down into the cushions of the couch, that dreamy look returning to her face.

Elladan then tried once more. "Vitalis, love, if I want to see the beautiful firebirds, how would I get there?"

A sensuous smile spread across her face as she leaned forward and caressed his cheek. "Why through the entrance in the back of the temple." She sat up more and ran her hand down to his chest.

Elladan's spell appeared to be wearing off, but Vitalis had become so fixated on the handsome bard that she didn't appear to need further coaxing. "Do you want to go there now? I know a quiet place in the very back where we can make love while the birds watch."

Thea wanted to yak at the thought. *Eww, gross. I may owe Elladan for this one. I mean, each to their own, but damn that's oddly specific.*

Elladan didn't seem quite enthused either. "Won't I get burned?"

Vitalis laughed again and tugged at the amulet around her neck. "Not with this, silly. This protects us from the flames." She got up off the couch and went over to the cabinet right next to the corner where Thea was hiding.

"I have a spare one in here somewhere..." Vitalis murmured as she rummaged through the drawers.

At that point, Thea had heard enough. Allowing the spirit energy to fade from her body, she stepped out of the shadows beside the half-naked priestess. With a quick swipe, she conked the smutty priestess with the butt of her knife on the back of the head. Vitalis slumped to the ground without so much as a whimper.

Turning towards Elladan, she mimicked the priestess' voice. "Would you like to make love in the aerie with all the firebirds watching?"

She had thought to shock him, but instead he stared her straight in the eye and said, "With you, anywhere."

That response caught her completely off guard. Thea could feel the heat rising to her cheeks. Though she knew she was blushing furiously, she still managed to fire a comeback. "I bet you say that to all the girls."

Before he had the chance to reply, she pulled out some rope from her pack. "Come and help me tie up lover girl here before she wakes up."

Elladan got up and assisted her as she requested, but started to croon again as he did so. There was no magic in it this time, but his voice made her feel tingly all over, nonetheless.

17
IT TAKES A THIEF

The entire affair with hunting down the scrolls so far had Bal grinding his teeth. Her majesty certainly wouldn't be happy with them summoning Ruka. He could live with it for now since she promised to return with them when this was all over.

Bal certainly didn't find the church's use of extortion to be all that unexpected. Donatello's method of bartering, on the other hand, had been questionable. In spite of that, he supposed he couldn't argue with the results.

What Bal could argue with was dealing with the pirate clans. Other than gaining the information they needed, he wanted to completely steer clear of them. Things could have gone worse though. They now knew the Parthians would show up tomorrow and thus had no time to waste.

Though Thea's idea of interrogating the priestess had merit, Bal didn't want to bet everything on it. So, while she and Elladan pursued that avenue, he decided to go to the temple and have another look around. In the meantime, the others gathered inside the grounds and prepared to create a distraction if and when necessary.

Now cloaked in his light-bending astral armor, Bal explored the grounds outside the temple. He found a grove of trees, a garden, and a few gazebos. Other than the rectory and a barracks, no other structures existed in the complex.

Not finding anything unusual on the grounds, Bal returned to the temple. He noted that the building butted up against the back outer wall. The base of the volcano rose up behind it though, so he guessed it made some sort of sense.

That's when Bal spied an open window on the second floor of the temple. It was far enough in the back that it had to be in one of the guarded areas Pallas and Cloud had told them about.

It might be worth investigating, Bal mulled over in his mind. He would need to adjust his armor to climb up there. That meant he would be visible while doing so.

Bal swept his eyes around the area, but there was no one in sight. A tall row of bushes blocked the view from the terrace. Another row, this time of trees, were evenly spaced along the back of the temple.

Thank the gods for gardeners, Bal thought dryly.

Bal stole over to them and slipped behind a thick trunk. Focusing his mind, he dispelled the light-bending armor. Now visible, he used his aura to generate another form of astral armor. Whereas the previous armor reflected light, this armor had the unique property of being able to reflect gravity.

With one last look around the grounds for good measure, Bal stole up to the side of the building. Focusing on his new armor, he dropped himself to one tenth of his normal weight. Now in essence ten times stronger, Bal easily propelled himself up the wall hand over foot like a spider.

Stopping just below the window, Bal listened for any signs of movement. Hearing none, he carefully slid through the opening.

Bal found himself in what appeared to be an office. Quietly padding to the door, he put his ear to it, but heard nothing. Opening the door, he spied an empty corridor headed in both directions.

Bal had just begun to change back to his light-bending armor when a soft voice emanated from the broach on his chest. "Balthazar, are you there?" It was the piece of jewelry that Donnie had lent him, the one that allowed the companions to talk to each other.

Bal swiftly closed the door behind him. "Um, this is not exactly a good time," he whispered into the broach.

"Sorry, but you're going to want to hear this," the voice responded. It sounded like Elladan.

Bal let out a short sigh. "Very well. Go ahead."

"Not only did we find where the vault is, but we also have something you're really going to need," Elladan told him.

"Okay," Bal replied, frankly amazed that their plan succeeded. "I'll come to you. Wait for me outside the rectory."

"Will do," Elladan answered and then the broach went silent.

After a quick check outside the door to make sure that no one had heard them, Bal scaled back down the wall and headed off across the grounds.

While Balthazar, Elladan, and Thea pursued their respective missions, Donnie and the others entered the temple grounds in small groups. Pallas, Cloud, and Seishin stayed outside on the terrace while Donnie, Cyclone, and Ruka continued one at a time into the outer courtyard.

Once inside the courtyard, Donnie roamed around looking at the holy relics there on display. His eyes fell upon a red-robed priestess admiring an ancient looking urn. He drew up beside her, planted a hand on his chin, and stared intently at the relic.

A carving in the side depicted a large bird raining fire upon a group of fleeing villagers. Donnie found it rather odd—he thought the church had tamed all the firebirds or at least had some sort of understanding with them.

After a few moments went by, the priestess cast a sidelong glance at him. His eyes still fixed on the urn, Donnie flashed her a brilliant smile. "It is a rather fine piece, is it not?"

A thin smile graced her lips. "It's from the days of the first settlement, before the priestesses learned the secret of the firebirds."

Having gained her attention, Donnie turned toward her with the most charming smile he could muster. "Oh really, and just what is that secret?"

The priestess' face reddened under his gaze. She appeared quite young really, probably still in her late teens if he had to guess. "I can't tell you that"—she glanced around over either shoulder—"at least not here."

"I'd follow you to the ends of the earth to uncover your fair secrets." He gave her that same smoldering gaze he used on Vitalis.

The young priestess blushed profusely. After a moment's silence she managed to stammer, "O-okay. Follow me."

The priestess led him out a side entrance and into a small garden surrounded by tall bushes. The place was deserted except for the two of them. She led him to a tree in the back, then leaned against the trunk and turned to face him. "Well, this is one of my secrets. Only the priestesses are allowed in here."

"I'm flattered," Donnie murmured softly as he leaned in close and gently touched his lips to hers.

The young priestess slid her hands around him and up his back as she ardently returned his kiss. As things started to get heated, Donnie slipped the knife from his belt and firmly conked her on the back of the head.

"Sorry milady," he whispered as he gently caught her sagging form. Donnie sighed as he looked at her unconscious face. She was truly pretty.

"Perhaps another time," he said wistfully as he dragged her inert body behind the tree.

Seishin meditated on a bench in the midst of the terrace just outside the Temple of Zharpita. Much had been going through his mind after seeing Solais here in Kaniron. He had not seen Kortiama's sister since the beach incident she brought up at the tavern. Although neither of them were fond of each other, seeing her somehow made him feel closer to Korti.

Seishin found it especially interesting that Korti confided in Solais concerning him. The fact that he and Korti had been seeing each other was supposed to be a well-guarded secret. If someone like her Uncle Rikton were to find out, Korti could lose her position as head of the clan. Thankfully, Solais was loyal to her sister to a fault. It was the one thing she and Seishin could both agree upon.

After thinking it through, Seishin felt better. He needed a clear mind for the battle ahead. Just when he thought he could put the matter aside, however, a familiar voice sounded in his head.

Hey Shin Tauri, the Galocerd went to the temple to steal back the scrolls.

Seishin recognized that voice. It was Solais! Realizing she must be using a spell to contact him, he responded in kind. *We are there now. Be ready to set sail.* That ended their brief communication.

Seishin rose from his seat and went to seek out Pallas and Cloud. By the time he found them halfway across the terrace, a contingent of armed guards came marching out of the temple. Those guards ushered a mass of visitors from the temple and turned everyone else away as they continued to march down toward the terrace.

Pallas eyed the approaching line warily. "Something must have happened inside. Any chance they captured Balthazar?"

Cloud shook his head. "Not likely."

Seishin swiftly explained the message he got from Solais.

Pallas' expression darkened, his brow knitting into a deep frown. "That may be it, but either way I don't think we can turn back now."

"Not while Bal is still in there," Cloud concurred, drawing a nondescript grey bag from his belt. The gnome pulled out his skyrider board for the first time since they left Lanfor. The blue crystal in the center of the board flared to life as he leapt up onto it.

"Then we stand and fight," Seishin agreed with a grim nod.

All three of them drew their weapons and lined up side by side to face the oncoming guards. One of the temple guards spotted them and barked out an order across the intervening space between them. "This is temple property! Lay down your arms and prepare to be escorted from the premises."

None of them answered, all three holding steadfast where they stood. Seishin felt a surge of energy stem from Pallas. Out of the corner of his eye, he saw the warrior's blades come alight with bright red and yellow flames.

Seishin was duly impressed. These so called *spiritblades* did indeed know something about channeling the spirit.

Not to be outdone, Seishin took a deep breath and stilled his mind in the way of the Shin Tauri. His breathing slowed as he reached inside and connected with his spirit. The energy surged out from his abdomen, into his arms, and across his blades. The air around them seemed to catch fire. Yellow flames danced up and down the shafts of both weapons accompanied by the occasional arc of blue lightning.

Pallas cast him a side-long glance. "Nice touch."

The two warriors with flaming blades and the gnome on a sky-board with the jet-black short sword gave the guardsmen momentary pause. It didn't last long, however. After building up their nerve, the guards rushed the waiting warriors.

Seishin set himself for the inevitable clash, when out of nowhere, a thick bank of fog rose up between them and the charging guards.

At the same moment, a familiar voice called to them from the edge of the terrace. "What's going on?"

Elladan and Thea came charging down a side path, the latter's arms still raised from the release of a spell. Seishin was again impressed, this time with the priestess' cleverness. Spells like that could make all the difference in controlling the flow of battle.

After swiftly catching each other up, Thea snorted a close-mouthed laugh. "Well, I guess that solves the riddle of which clan was telling the truth."

Seishin had reached the same conclusion. While he still did not completely trust Solais, it gave him some peace of mind to know that she hadn't outright lied to them.

"Either way, Bal's going to need that distraction more than ever," Cloud pointed out.

"Heck, if I know Donnie, Cyclone, and Ruka, they're already creating a disturbance inside the temple," Elladan said with a grin.

"Well then, let's join them, shall we?" Pallas declared.

After rendezvousing with Elladan and Thea, Bal returned to the temple and stole through the halls of the upper floor. After a brief search, he discovered a doorway that opened to a path leading up the face of the volcano.

Bal followed the winding trail up the mountainside to a cave opening. The near-invisible lieutenant fingered the amulet around his neck as he stepped inside the cave. The hot blast of air that hit him as he did so, made him thank the gods that he had gone back for it.

Woah, Bal nearly drawled out loud as he glanced around the cavern. The place that stretched out before him was huge.

Bright pools of lava lit up most of the floor while light streamed in from tunnels in the mountainside above. Each wall of the cavern stood at least a hundred yards away, leaving enough room for the dozens of firebirds in here to comfortably roost along their faces. The rocky ground had a reddish tint as if it were near molten itself. The heat rose from it in waves visibly warping his vision.

Taking a moment for his eyes to adjust, Bal spied a long path leading to a tall pillar in the very center of the cavern. Four figures in red moved along the trail toward the structure. Bal stole along the path, arriving just in time to see the four red-robed figures step through a door that led inside.

Bal watched in amazement as the floor of the pillar rose upward taking the priestesses with it. *Well, I guess I'm not going that way,* he thought to himself wryly.

A quick inspection proved there to be no other way up or down for that matter. With no other recourse, Bal swiftly adjusted his armor and started the long climb upward along the outside of the pillar.

With the priestess' robes wrapped carefully around him, Donnie slipped through the outer courtyard and followed a short corridor to the inner one. As soon as he crossed the threshold, he was forced to sidestep to avoid being trampled.

All the visitors in the place appeared to be headed back the way he came. He soon saw why. A group of temple guards followed the mob, herding them along with cries of:

"Temple's closed for now!"

"Move along, everyone!"

Donnie inwardly cringed as one of the guards headed his way. He instinctively pulled the hood of his robe tighter around his face.

"Excuse us, revered one," the guard said, stopping a few feet from him. "We shall have this place cleared out post haste as ordered."

"Carry on," Donnie replied in a high falsetto, shooing the guard away. Beneath his robes he had pulled the knife from his belt just in case.

Thankfully, it didn't come to that. "Yes, at once!" the guard responded, giving him a curt bow and scurrying away after any straggling visitors.

Donnie had to wonder at the hold these priestesses had on these people. True they controlled the firebirds, but none of them he'd met so far seemed all that scary. In fact, they'd been rather pleasant to him—especially Vitalis and that young girl in the courtyard.

Getting a hold of himself, Donnie shook the wistful smile from his face. Something strange was going on here. Why had the guards been ordered to clear out the temple? Would they do that if they caught Balthazar?

Donnie wished he had his broach but he had lent it to Bal. Cyclone had one, but he was still in the outer courtyard with Ruka last time Donnie saw them.

The slight elf shrugged. Those two could take care of themselves even against a platoon of guards. The best thing he could do now is to find out more about what was going on here.

Shrugging his shoulders, Donnie sauntered across the courtyard to the entrance to the shrine. None of the guards there gave him a second look.

The slim elf in priestess robes passed through another short corridor and entered into the Shrine of Zharpita. It looked exactly as Bal had described except that it was now filled with over two dozen priestesses. All of them were gathered around the huge brazier in the center of the room, chanting in a language Donnie did not recognize.

Three people had been strung up on wooden poles in a triangular formation around the large brazier. Donnie swept his gaze across the trio hoping that none of them were Bal. Abruptly his eyes settled on a familiar figure with blue hair.

That's Illyria! The captain of the Galocerd ship must have done something truly awful to end up in this less than desirable predicament.

Donnie tried a clandestine wave to get her attention, but Illyria's eyes were transfixed on the flames above the huge brazier. All of a sudden, her face twisted into a mask of terror.

Donnie followed her gaze and felt a chill go up his spine in spite of the terrible heat in the room. A pair of huge red eyes were forming within the giant blaze above the brazier.

Well, that can't be good, Donnie thought to himself blithely. He needed to do something quick to disrupt this ritual, before more of whatever that thing was appeared in those flames.

Scurrying across to the altar on the other side of the room, Donnie climbed atop it and threw off his priestess robes. He called out in a loud voice, "Hello ladies. Anyone care to dance?"

The chanting in the room abruptly stopped as all eyes turned upon him. Donnie fixed the mass of women one of his best smoldering smiles. Some of the priestesses began to smile back, but one in particular seemed immune to his charms. A slightly older woman, her robes were decorated with a bit more splendor than the rest.

"Don't just stand there gawking," she chastised her fellow priestesses. "Get him!"

A moment later, two fiery spells were launched at Donnie from the midst of the crowd. The agile elf nimbly dodged both, but had the feeling things were about to get far more heated.

Rukastana Greymantle struggled with her conflicting emotions. First, Donnie had broken the bond between them. She had given him her dagger. *Her dagger!* The dagger made from her very own scales. That bond was supposed to last for a lifetime, but Donnie had thrown it away like yesterday's garbage.

When he returned the dagger, it had crushed Ruka. Just when she thought it couldn't hurt worse, however, Ves turned around and betrayed her as well. How dare she ask the Queen to tuck them away like little babies! Still, in the end Ves got what she deserved.

Hoisted on her own petard! Ruka thought with grim satisfaction.

Ruka had little desire to face the Queen after being so easily manipulated. The more she thought about it though, the more she realized she had to. Ves might deserve her fate, but poor Maya certainly didn't.

That Cyclone, of all people, would be on her side seemed ludicrous. He was a dragon hunter of all things. They hated each other at first, yet he had accepted her dagger and now treated her better than Donnie.

Ruka cast a sidelong glance at the hunter. She had to admit he was handsome in a rugged sort of way. He also made an adequate sparring partner. Still, she wasn't about to put her heart out again for anyone. Donnie had taught her that painful lesson.

Sudden shouting roused Ruka from her dark musings. The guards around them were barking orders and herding folks towards the exit.

"Temple's closed!"

"Move along, everyone!"

Luckily, she and Cyclone had been off to one side, trying to remain inconspicuous. Most of the guards had escorted the throng outside before they finally got to them. At that point only a few guards were left in the courtyard along with a couple of priestesses.

The guard stupid enough to confront Cyclone ended up with a fist to his jaw before he had a chance to react. He was out cold before his body hit the ground.

"We've got a troublemaker!" Another nearby guard shouted across the courtyard. He and a second guard prepared to charge the hunter, when a nearby priestess waved them off.

"I'll handle this one," she declared haughtily. Tracing a quick spell through the air, the priestess unleashed a stream of fire at the waiting hunter. The smirk on her face died, however, as Cyclone hardly flinched.

"Is that the best you've got?" The hunter sneered at her.

The priestess and the guards stared incredulously at him. Her shock turning to fear, she began to back away. In doing so, however, she put herself in direct line with both guardsmen from Ruka's point of view.

Unable to resist, Ruka drew her shortsword, Inazuma, and sent a lightning bolt careening from the blade directly through the unsuspecting trio. Thunder rolled across the courtyard as all three dropped senseless to the ground.

"Nice shot," Cyclone snorted with admiration.

A satisfied smirk crossed Ruka's lips. Before she had a chance to respond though, a column of fire came roaring down on them. The flames engulfed them both, then just as abruptly ended, leaving the two of them singed.

Six more red-robed priestesses had lined up in front of the entrance to the inner courtyard. The eldest looking one in the center had her hands raised from the spell she just cast.

Wisps of smoke rising from his clothes, Cyclone drew the halberd from its sheath on his back. "Looks like someone wants to play rough."

A barrage of fiery rays shot from the hands of the remaining priestesses, but with a huge leap, Cyclone bound over the beams while Ruka dodged out of the way.

Cyclone landed in the midst of the line and swung his long pole axe in a huge arc. Two priestesses immediately went down, cloven in two by the deadly sharp blade.

Ruka came out of her roll and in one swift movement let another bolt fly. Thunder echoed once again as the bolt swept through the remaining line of red-robed figures. A moment later, they all collapsed.

Inside the aerie, Balthazar climbed the tall pillar to the roof of the cavern far above. As he approached the ceiling, he saw that the tower continued upward through a shaft of volcanic rock. It was easy to see as the black rock glowed with veins of angry red and orange.

Bal gulped as he felt the heat emanating from that shaft. *And I thought it was warm in here,* he thought to himself dryly.

Bal resumed his upward climb until he reached the edge of the shaft. There was just enough room beyond for him to squeeze between the pillar and the rock wall. Thanking the gods for the amulet around his neck, Bal continued upward into the shaft.

Emerging from the shaft a short while later, Bal's eyes nearly bugged out of his head. This upper cavern stretched even deeper into the volcano, making it nearly three times the size of the one below. More firebirds flew around in here, flitting between nests in the walls and large cracks in the side of the volcano. What really drew his attention, however, was the strange setup at the top of the pillar directly above him.

A suspended catwalk led from the pillar toward a square structure also suspended from the ceiling. Thick cables held each in place, but the catwalk didn't quite reach the square. Instead, it ended a few yards away near what appeared to be a winch. As if all this weren't odd enough, the square hung suspended over a large pool of bubbling lava in the floor of the cavern maybe a hundred feet below.

Bal reached the top of the pillar and adjusted his armor so that he could climb beneath the catwalk. While he did so, he heard the priestesses talking amongst themselves.

"I still don't understand why we had to come all the way up here," the one priestess said.

"It's because of those damn pirates," another one answered.

"But didn't we already catch them?" Another priestess complained.

"Ladies," the fourth priestess spoke to the rest in an authoritative tone, "the High Priestess merely wants us to double check the vault, just in case those pirates were a distraction."

"Seriously?" the first priestess responded with clear exasperation. "We're missing their sacrifice because the High Priestess has a case of the jitters? Besides, if anyone else had made it up here, the revered ones would have burnt them to a crisp by now."

"Ours is not to question why," the lead priestess recited in an officious tone. "Now, go roll out the rest of the catwalk while I talk with one of the revered ones."

Bal found the entire conversation rather enlightening. He wondered which group of pirates had tried to infiltrate the grounds. Whichever they were, it didn't sound like they'd be around much longer. In that same regard, he hadn't taken the one priestess' warning lightly. One wrong move up here and he would quite literally be toast.

While the lead priestess called down one of the firebirds, the other priestess went to the winch and cranked the handle. In response another section of catwalk slid out from below the first until it reached the square structure. It stopped before a recessed area that Bal could now clearly see was a doorway.

That has to be the vault, Bal reasoned. It was the only thing that could explain the extreme paranoid measures taken to isolate the square structure.

Just when Bal thought he had seen it all, however, the firebird summoned by the lead priestess lifted away from her and moments later landed and perched itself atop the square vault. It spun its long beak around in all directions as if performing some sort of guard duty.

Bal silently shook his head. *Talk about paranoid…*

In the meantime, the lead priestess had strode past the others out onto the extended catwalk. She paused for a moment and ordered the rest of them to wait for her there.

While she did so, Bal contemplated what his next steps might be. If the scrolls were anywhere, they would definitely be in that vault. He felt reasonably comfortable that he could get past those priestesses, but that firebird was another matter entirely. If he wanted to get past that he would definitely need some sort of distraction.

Bal thought back to how he had distracted the rebels in order to kidnap their leader. That had worked well enough. *Maybe I can do the same thing here,* he reasoned.

Focusing his will Bal crafted an ethereal crossbow and accompanying bolts once again. With one eye on the firebird atop the vault, he peeked out over the edge of the catwalk and shot each of the waiting priestesses. Like before, the bolts embedded themselves into their targets with not so much as a scratch.

Across the catwalk, the lead priestess had reached the door. Bal scampered beneath the walkway closing the distance as fast as he could. At the same time, the priestess pulled out a key and unlocked the door.

Bal drew up beneath her just as she pushed the door open. Focusing his will, he turned all three ethereal bolts solid at the same time.

Loud screams erupted from the catwalk behind them as all three priestesses doubled over in pain. Bal waited for a count of three, then launched himself up and over the railing.

Distracted by the cries of pain, the lead priestess never saw him coming. Bal slammed into her feet first, knocking her down before she knew what happened. Loud squawking arose from above as he scurried atop the downed priestess and plucked the key from her clutched fingers.

Not wasting any time, Bal launched himself through the open doorway. As he went to shut it, however, blue bands of energy formed around him freezing him in place.

Out on the catwalk, the priestess lay propped up on one elbow, her outstretched hand reaching for him, her brow drawn into an intense frown. She had cast a holding spell on him!

If it had been anyone else, things might have been over, but Bal had other resources at his disposal. His mind not bound, he instead focused on his armor.

Bal poured more and more energy into that armor until it began to visibly glow. Pushing it to its limits and beyond, the armor suddenly erupted in a violent flash of psychic energy. The wave fanned out in all directions, knocking the priestess back down and breaking her concentration. It also backlashed on Bal sending him flying into the opposite wall of the vault.

Momentarily stunned, Bal could do nothing as a giant flaming head appeared over the catwalk. It nudged the priestess a few times with its long beak, but she had been knocked out cold.

Bal regained his senses as the bird's giant eye turned upon him. Aware of what was coming next, he bolted for the vault door. He reached it just as a cascade of fire erupted from the bird's beak.

Bal just barely slammed the door shut in time. He jammed the key into the lock and twisted it effectively sealing himself inside. Safe for the moment, he spun about and leaned against the door, his breath coming in short, ragged bursts.

Phew, that was way too close, he silently chastised himself. Perhaps the amulet might have saved him, but somehow he doubted even it would have survived a direct blast from one of those firebirds.

Either way, he was now stuck. His heart still racing, Bal touched the broach on his chest and proceeded to call for help.

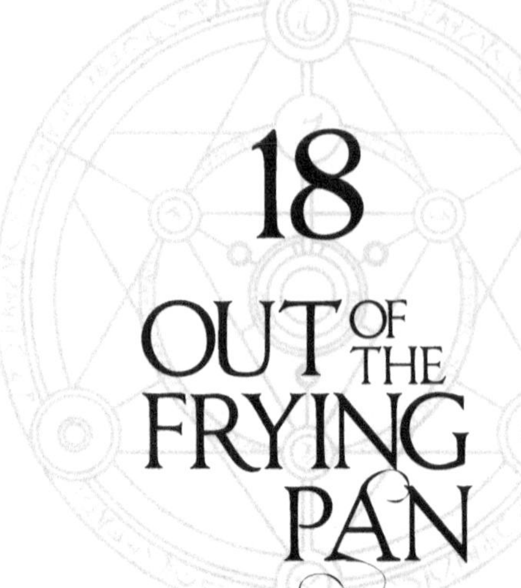

18
OUT OF THE FRYING PAN

"Blood and fire. Blood and fire. Zharpita. Zharpita."

Elladan stood back and watched with growing appreciation as the others waded into battle. Seishin reminded him very much of Lloyd, spinning and twisting with his two blades aflame. Pallas cut a swath through his opponents, his glowing katana flickering back and forth with crisp, precise movements. Thea's blue blade darted in and out finding her foes' weak spots with expert precision. As if that weren't enough, Cloud strafed over the guards, his black blade raining death from above.

The elven bard aided his friends as best he could. He played music to bolster their spirits and cast spells to hamper any flanking guards. Some went down in pools of grease, while others attacked each other in utter confusion. Still, more guards continued to pour into the terrace from all directions.

The others fanned out, forming a semicircle to meet these new threats. With their escape options fast dwindling though, Elladan thought they should call a retreat. Before he could say anything, however, a shout rang out from the broach on his cloak.

"Hello! I could use a little help here."

Elladan immediately recognized the voice as Balthazar. Keeping his eyes fixed on the battle, he answered the lieutenant's plea. "This is Elladan. Where are you?"

"I found the vault," came the immediate reply. "However, I'm trapped inside of it."

Well, that doesn't sound very encouraging, Elladan thought to himself. Still, he wasn't about to say that to Balthazar.

"How do we get to you?" he spoke instead into the broach.

Balthazar hesitated for the briefest of moments before replying. "I don't think you can directly—at least not without magic."

Elladan grimaced. This was sounding worse and worse. He could only think of one way to effectively escape this mess and reach Balthazar at the same time. To do so, however, might be extremely dangerous. Regardless, he had to try.

"Can you describe where you are to me?" Elladan spoke into the broach. If he could create an image in his mind of the lieutenant's location, Elladan could open a portal to him. The more detailed the better. Anything less and they'd run the risk of ending up somewhere else inside the volcano.

Balthazar hesitated once again before answering. "That might take a while to explain. Would a mental image do?"

Elladan raised both eyebrows. "You can do that?"

"Yes."

"That would do just perfect!" Elladan chortled with sudden glee.

"What's so funny?" Thea cried back over her shoulder as she fended off an advancing guard.

"Balthazar needs our help! He's stuck in the vault in the middle of the volcano," Elladan shouted back to her.

At that moment, Balthazar's mental image appeared in Elladan's mind. It was so vivid that he felt momentarily disoriented, as if he were both on the terrace and in the vault with him at the same time.

When his head cleared, he was too late to stop Cloud. The Lanfor captain had finished off a guard and then taken off into the sky toward the volcano at incredible speed.

Realizing it was too late to stop him, Elladan focused instead on opening the portal. With Balthazar's image firmly fixed in his mind, he traced the symbol through the air and invoked the spell.

"*Planum porta.*" As soon as the words tumbled from his lips, a blue, glowing, six foot oval appeared in the air before him.

Wanting to make certain it had worked, Elladan stuck his head through the blue oval. On the other side he spied a large room with a number of different sized boxes embedded into each wall. Pressed up against the only door stood Balthazar, still breathing heavy.

Elladan gave the lieutenant a half-smile. "Looks like it worked! I'll send the others through."

With that, the bard pulled his head back out and cried to the others, "It's open!"

"You go first!" Pallas cried to Thea.

Thea finished off the guard in front of her, then pulled back while Pallas and Seishin closed ranks to fill the gap. With a brief smile at Elladan, Thea leapt through the glowing blue oval.

"She's through!" Elladan announced to the others.

Pallas and Seishin each dispatched a guard in turn, then bolted for the portal. Elladan jumped through just before them with the two warriors following close behind.

As the last of them disappeared into the portal, the glowing blue oval whooshed shut.

Seishin had almost forgotten what it felt like to fight beside warriors of his own ilk. It had been some months now since he left the army behind, along with his fellow Shin Tauri soldiers. These spirit-blades, however, proved to be just as effective as his old platoon, if not better in some ways. Pallas handled his long katana almost as well as a Shin Tauri master while Thea proved to be deadly accurate with her thin pointed blade.

The battle on the terrace had been quite exhilarating up to the point where they needed to leave. However, it was probably just as well. The flow of new temple guards seemed to be never ending and their goal of distracting them had run its course anyway.

When Seishin stepped through the portal, he felt momentarily disoriented. He had never used one before meeting Elladan and the bard seemed to love to cast them. He had to admit they'd come in handy and Seishin was getting used to them.

The momentary feeling passed and Seishin found himself in a large square room. Balthazar, Thea, and Elladan were already there when he arrived and Pallas followed close behind. As soon as they were through, Elladan closed the portal with a wave of his hand. The shimmering blue oval collapsed in on itself with a distinct whoosh.

"Thanks for coming," Balthazar greeted them. "Not to be picky or anything, but where's Cloud?"

Elladan quickly explained to him how the skyrider took off on his own.

"Sounds just like him," Balthazar agreed with a pained expression.

It was at that point Seishin began to feel the heat in the room. He sheathed his swords and fanned himself as beads of sweat formed across his brow. "Phew, I guess we really are inside a volcano."

Thea fixed him with a sympathetic gaze. "I think I can help with that."

The priestess traced a symbol through the air ending with the words, *"Donec A Ignis."*

The magic released and a column of sparse red energy rose from the floor around Seishin. It rushed up to the top of his head, then disappeared leaving a reddish glow around his body. That, too, abruptly faded.

Thea then did the same for Elladan, but when she came to Pallas he merely held up his hand. "I've got this."

Seishin felt a surge of spirit energy from within the warrior. In answer, an aura of reddish flames enveloped his body. Moments later it faded away, leaving Pallas unaffected by the heat.

Again, Seishin found himself impressed. These spiritblades had taken the art in directions the Shin Tauri never thought of.

Pallas fixed Thea with a questioning stare. "What about you, sis?"

Thea reached up and touched the amulet that hung around her

neck. The gemstone fixed in its center shone a bright ruby red. "I'm fine with this. We gave the priestess' necklace to Balthazar, but I kept her spare."

Pallas chortled with amusement. "You always did have a thing for treasure."

Thea stuck her tongue out at her brother. "Not all of us can be *perfectly* Pallas."

Pallas visibly winced at her choice of words. Seishin supposed it was a personal dig at the elder Stealle's exacting nature.

Seishin half expected another round of insults to fly between the two, but thankfully Balthazar interrupted them at that point. "Speaking of treasure—now that you're all here, how about we find those scrolls?"

Turning his attention to the vault, Seishin noted numerous boxes of various sizes embedded into the walls. Nine square boxes made up the first wall. Two large rectangular boxes filled up the opposite wall. One large box comprised the entire final wall across from the door.

Balthazar gingerly rubbed his chin. "So, which one do we start with?"

Elladan held his hands out wide. "As my mom used to say, *go big or go home.*"

Balthazar shrugged. "The big one it is." He strode over to the box that took up an entire wall, then glanced back over his shoulder. "You all might want to stand back."

Everyone moved to the other side of the room as Balthazar turned the handle and pulled open the door. He was rewarded with an explosion of fire that engulfed his entire body.

Seishin shielded his eyes from the blast that nearly reached across the room. When he opened his eyes again, the flames were gone.

Balthazar stood in the same spot he had before looking completely unharmed from the blast. He glanced back over his shoulder and peered at the rest of them while fingering his ruby necklace. "I guess these amulets really do work."

"Look at that, would you!" Elladan drawled.

Inside the box Balthazar just opened stood a full suit of golden armor. It looked a bit heavier than what Isandorian warriors typically wore, but there was a style and grace to it that caught Seishin's eye.

"That's very nice armor," Pallas commented, "but not exactly what we came for."

While the others moved onto the smaller boxes, Seishin went for a closer look. The golden helmet sat on a shelf next to the rest of the suit. Seishin picked it up and held it aloft in his hands. While quite sturdy, the helmet felt much lighter than he expected.

Seishin noted runes carved into the sides of the helmet. While he did not recognize them, he supposed they could be magical in nature. Perhaps the lightness of the armor could be attributed to them.

Even more curious now than ever, Seishin lifted the helmet above his head and lowered it onto his shoulders. As he did so, a voice sounded within his mind.

Greetings warrior, I am Flandril.

Seishin's brow knit into a frown. *Flandril? Like the former King of Lanfor?*

I am his armor, the voice replied, *but I can help any who are true of heart.*

Seishin found himself more and more intrigued. *What exactly can you do?*

Many things, the voice responded. *Put me on and you shall see.*

Seishin pulled the helmet off and took a few moments to mull things over. He sensed a dull power within the armor, but nothing to indicate it as dark or light.

In the meantime, Balthazar had opened one of the other two larger boxes. That was accompanied by another explosion of flame. Once it dissipated, Seishin spied a greatsword sitting in that box.

At the same time across the room, the door to the vault had turned a dull red. Elladan must have noticed it as well as he tapped Balthazar on the shoulder and pointed it out to him.

"Were you expecting company?" The bard asked glibly.

Balthazar eyed the door warily. "That's probably the fire bird that they set to guard this place."

"Someone should tell it there's not enough room in here," Elladan quipped.

Realizing they were fast running out of time, Seishin picked up the helmet again. This time he cast his thoughts to it without putting it on. *Are you immune to fire?*

I can be with the right wearer, Flandril responded.

Though the answer had been cryptic, it was not a flat out no. Seishin asked the armor one more question. *How are you at locating items?*

I can if your will is strong enough, Flandril replied.

That answer had been a bit more direct. The door to the vault was growing brighter by the minute. They didn't have much time left.

Seishin finally reached a decision and started putting the armor on.

In the meantime, Balthazar had moved onto the smaller boxes. He opened four of them without finding the scrolls, but when he opened the fifth, the floor of the vault suddenly dropped out from under them.

Seishin had been half standing in the box with the armor at the time and was barely able to avoid falling. Balthazar also somehow managed to hang onto the wall. Elladan, Pallas, and Thea, however, all fell out of the vault.

Desperate to save them, Seishin pulled on the last piece of armor. As he did so, a surge of power abruptly coursed through it. With all the pieces connected together, it had far more power than he previously sensed.

Amazingly, he could see through the helmet almost as if it weren't there at all. A few yards below the vault, Elladan, Pallas, and Thea all floated on what appeared to be a magic carpet.

Thea seemed equally as shocked at its appearance as Seishin. She gave Elladan an incredulous stare. "Not that I'm complaining, but where did this come from?"

Elladan laughed. "It's a present from Balthazar—a souvenir from that rebel fortress."

Seishin laughed to himself as well. These folks were amazingly resourceful. With everyone safe at least for the moment, Seishin turned his attention back to their main objective.

Which box has the scrolls? he asked the armor.

A vision appeared before his eyes as if he could see through the walls. Inside the middle left box he spied multiple scroll cases. Seishin called out to Balthazar. "The scrolls are in the middle left box."

Balthazar eyed him dubiously. "How could you possibly know that?"

Seishin hesitated a moment before answering. "Well, this is going to sound crazy, but—the armor told me."

Balthazar arched an eyebrow at him, but before he could say anything further, Pallas interrupted them from below. "We've got company! You guys coming?"

Balthazar eyed Seishin for a moment longer, then called back down, "We think we found the scrolls. Can you buy us some more time?"

"We'll lead them off!" Elladan yelled back.

"Hang on!" Seishin heard the elf cry, and then they were gone.

Cyclone had been greatly disappointed by the opposition thus far. He had hoped for a better challenge, like one of those firebirds perhaps. Unfortunately, there were none here in the temple.

After handily dispatching the line of priestesses blocking the way, Cyclone and Ruka ran through a short corridor and entered into the inner courtyard.

The moment they emerged, the two of them were engulfed in a hemisphere of fire. It only lasted for a few seconds, and then the fire winked out. The ball of fire hadn't really damaged either of them, but smoke rose from Cyclone's tunic and it showed signs of blackening in spots.

These feeble attempts to ruin his clothes were starting to annoy the hunter. Brushing off her dark leathers, Ruka expressed the same sentiment. "I'm going to have to do some serious mending after this."

More guards and priestesses were gathered in the inner courtyard to block their way. At the very back, Cyclone spotted a group of six priestesses gathered in a circle. He could hear them chanting all the way from here. A line of about twenty guardsmen stood between them and the circle, lances raised and ready.

"Shall we disrupt their little party?" Ruka asked, the corner of her mouth raised ever so slightly.

"Yeah, let's," Cyclone agreed with a slight smirk of his own.

Ruka raised her sword and cast another bolt of lightning. Two stray priestesses fell in its wake. Meanwhile, Cyclone leapt forward and cleaved through a group of guards in the line.

As the last one fell, a ray of fire slammed into the center of his chest. Cyclone shrugged it off, but then dodged three others that were headed directly for him.

All of a sudden, a loud roar echoed across the courtyard. Ruka had shifted to her true form and let loose with a bolt of lightning breath.

More guards and priestesses fell. Those that hadn't been downed, turned and ran at the sight of the large dragon.

Unfortunately, they were too late. The priestesses had finished the ritual. A large red-hot flame rose up in the midst of their circle. Nearly the size of Ruka, it appeared to have vaguely humanoid features.

"Fire elemental," Cyclone breathed the words with a trace of excitement. Things were finally starting to get interesting.

The circle parted as the elemental strode forward to face them. At the same time, shouting broke out from the hallway behind the circle.

That has to be coming from the inner shrine, Cyclone realized. Looking around, he abruptly realized the slim elf was no longer with them.

Ruka mirrored his thoughts. "Donnie must have gone and gotten himself into trouble again."

Cyclone let out a grudging sigh. He really wanted to fight this elemental, but couldn't in good conscience let the elf face whatever was in the shrine alone.

"Go ahead, I got this," Ruka encouraged him.

Silently cursing the careless elf, Cyclone let the anger feed into his rage. As he did so, a set of bronze wings sprouted from his back. With a great flap he took off and flew past the fire creature slamming through what was left of the circle.

The creature must have started to come after him. Cyclone caught a flash of light out of the corner of his eye and heard the boom of thunder echo across the courtyard.

"Your fight is with me," he heard Ruka's voice growl as the thunder died down.

Cyclone breathed a derisive snort. Ruka had a temperament just like his. It was one of the things he liked about her. A wide smirk crossed the hunter's face as he hurtled toward the inner shrine.

Donnie was feeling a bit hard pressed. While he never expected to enchant all the priestesses in the shrine, he thought that at least a few of them might succumb to his charms. Yet that's not happened at all. The slight elf now dodged red-hot ray after red-hot ray, trying his best not to be barbequed.

Dropping behind the altar, Donnie cried out to them, "Ladies, can't we be reasonable?" His plea was rewarded with cries of outrage and another barrage of fiery rays.

Realizing he was a sitting duck back there, Donnie rolled from behind the altar and ran for the side of the chamber. Another barrage of red-hot rays followed closely behind the hapless elf.

That's when Donnie noticed the line of lit braziers along the wall. The slight elf leaped on top of one of them and tipped it over in an attempt to distract his pursuers. Hot flaming oil spread out onto the floor, virtually setting it on fire.

Unfortunately, instead of causing the chaos he anticipated, the priestesses seemed to like the idea. "Yes. Yes. More fire. More fire," the High Priestess chanted with the others swiftly joining in.

Though they had stopped trying to roast him, the High Priestess had them fan out and knock over more braziers. The contents spilled out across the shrine until the entire floor had been set on fire.

Donnie had never seen anything like it, and he'd seen quite a lot of crazy things in his time. With the floor itself grown dangerous, the slim elf decided to retreat up higher.

"*Aranea Repere.*" Donnie spoke the words to invoke his *Boots of the Spider.* He then leapt up to the wall sticking to it with his hands and feet.

Meanwhile, over in the center of the room, the priestesses themselves now stood in the fire. Though it did not appear to burn them, the flames wrapped themselves around their bodies. Those nearest Illyria and her cohorts reached up for them.

Quickly slipping a dagger from his belt, Donnie sent one sailing across the room at the nearest priestess. The dagger caught her in the back and sent her sinking to the floor. As she did so, her blood spilled out and mixed with the raging fire.

The priestesses all across the chamber stopped what they were doing and began to chant, "Blood and fire. Blood and fire. Zharpita. Zharpita." They continued that chant until a huge glowing ball of reddish yellow light appeared where the eyes had been over the huge brazier.

Despite the heat in the room, a shiver went up Donnie's spine. *Well, that can't be good,* he thought to himself.

At that same moment, Cyclone came hurtling into the shrine. The hunter stopped and hovered in mid-air, his eyes fixed on the great glowing ball of light. "What in the seven hells is going on in here?"

Not stopping to answer his cry, Donnie pulled on one of his special gloves that dispelled magic, then reached down and touched the floor. In response, the fire along the entire floor winked out.

A hush fell over the shrine, the priestess all gaping at him in amazement. Leaping from the wall, Donnie seized the moment and cried out in as an authoritative voice as he could muster. "I am Zharpita! Bring those prisoners here to me."

Still in shock, some of the priestesses climbed up and cut down Illyria and her crew. Just as Donnie thought it might work though, the High Priestess countermanded him again. "It's a trick! Stop them!"

With one eye on the ominous glowing ball in the center of the room, Donnie opened his mouth to attempt one last bluff. Cyclone, however, was not having any of it. The hunter dove straight down and clove the High Priestess in two.

19
THE GOLDEN WARRIOR

I will need to drain some of your life force.

Elladan didn't like to talk about his misspent youth. Born to a wealthy house in the elven city of Kai-Arborous, the young elf constantly rebelled against his family. He would take expensive things from the household to show off to his ne'er-do-well friends. One of his father's prized possessions just happened to be a magic carpet—a possession which Elladan absconded with on more than one occasion.

The young elf would give wild rides around the city on it, more often than not being chased by the elven guard. Thus, Elladan learned to do things with a flying carpet that seemed impossible. Little did he know that the gains of his ill-gotten youth would come in handy this day.

Making the carpet rise had been easy. It all relied on the choice of words which in that case happened to be, *"Fugere ortum."*

Commanding it to hover had been equally simple requiring the single word, *"Tabernus."*

With two more firebirds bearing down on them, things got a bit more complicated. It got worse when their loud squawking alerted the firebird trying to get into the vault.

Elladan could only think of one way to lead all three birds away from their friends. Unfortunately, it would be highly dangerous.

"Hang on!" Elladan cried over his shoulder to Thea and Pallas.

"Urinor celer," he commanded the carpet.

The flying rug shot forward, dipping at a steep angle toward the lava below. Elladan had to practically lean back into Thea's lap to avoid being thrown off.

"I hope you have a plan!" Thea screamed as the bubbling lava pit rose up fast to meet them.

"Of course I do," Elladan lamented, feeling hurt at her questioning his intent. He'd seen those firebirds in action and knew they couldn't outrun them. Nevertheless, he intended to use their speed against them.

As the lava approached, Elladan traced a familiar pattern through the air. This time, however, he made the symbol twice as large as normal.

"Planum porta." As the words tumbled from his lips, a blue, glowing, oval appeared in the air just above the pool of lava. This portal was double the usual size.

"They're right on our tail!" Pallas yelled from the back of the carpet.

Elladan chanced a quick glance over his shoulder. Sure enough, one firebird after another had lined up right behind them. The first bird's huge beak was only a few yards from Pallas' head.

Snapping his gaze back to the front, Elladan concentrated harder than ever before. He had to time this just right.

They'd nearly reached the portal.

Twenty feet…

Ten feet…

Five feet…

Elladan brought his hands together as they plunged through the open portal. The blue oval whooshed closed nearly on top of them, the edge of the carpet barely squeaking through in time.

Back in the cavern, the first bird hit the lava with a great splash. Unable to stop itself, the second bird followed.

The last bird pulled up just in time. It hovered there watching its friends splash about furiously in the molten pool. At first it seemed as if they might escape, but even their fiery hides finally succumbed to the unfathomable heat. The last bird was left alone as its companions sizzled and disappeared into the glowing depths.

Moments after the others disappeared, the vault floor swung closed again. Balthazar tested the floor with his foot. "Seems solid enough."

Climbing down, Balthazar then carefully opened the box Seishin previously pointed out to him. This time, thankfully, there was no explosion.

An incredulous expression spread across Balthazar's face. "Looks like you were right," he said, waving for Seishin to join him.

Seishin stepped out of the box. The entire armor felt much lighter than he imagined. In fact, it didn't feel much heavier than typical Isandorian armor. Peering over Balthazar's shoulder, he saw the same seven scroll cases the armor had shown him earlier.

Balthazar grabbed them one at a time and stuffed them into his pack. He had just finished with the last one when they heard an ominous rumbling. The entire vault began to shake, then abruptly tipped over.

Seishin went flying head over heels toward the vault door. He slammed into it, knocking the already partially melted door off its hinges. The door went flying out into the cavern, leaving Seishin hanging there.

Above him, Balthazar hung from the wall which had shifted now to become the ceiling. He peered down at Seishin, panic in his voice. "What was that? An eruption? One of those firebirds?"

Wedging himself with his hands and feet, Seishin chanced a look out the door. There were no firebirds near the vault, but the structure appeared to be hanging from two cables attached to the ceiling of the cavern. Looking down, Seishin saw two more cables hanging loosely from the vault. Below that, a section of what appeared to be a catwalk slowly sunk into a pit of lava.

Seishin shuddered at the sight. That could have just as easily been them. Taking a deep breath, he reported what he had seen back to Bal.

Bal grimaced when he heard the news. "Must have been a quake then. Well, I guess we're not getting out that way."

With no other choice, Seishin leapt from the doorway and onto the wall which was now where the floor should have been. At the same time, Bal dropped from the ceiling and landed next to him.

The rest of the boxes now on the ceiling had popped open, their contents fallen onto the floor. Gold coins, large jewels, and other expensive baubles lay in that pile, but one thing in particular caught Seishin's eye—a solid gold statue of a flaming bird with a pair of rubies for its eyes.

Bal bent down for a closer look. "That must be Zharpita."

The statue was not overly large, nor did it appear that much more expensive when compared to the other treasures. Perhaps it had some other significance.

Balthazar seemed to be thinking along the same lines. "Might as well take this with us. Maybe we can study it later—if we ever get out of here."

Bal's words had an ominous ring to them. This vault had become a death trap. One more quake like the last and they would also end up in the lava pit.

Seishin had just been about to suggest they contact Elladan again, when Cloud came surfing into the vault. The gnome sounded out of breath, his eyes wide with excitement. "It's crazy out there. The entire volcano was shaking and there are firebirds everywhere!"

"Your timing couldn't be better," Bal exclaimed with clear relief. "We just found the scrolls and need a way out of here."

"Who's your friend in the golden armor?" Cloud asked motioning toward Seishin.

Seishin pulled off the helmet. "It's only me."

A thin smile spread across the gnome's lips. "That's great and all, but I can only fit one of you with me—and that armor doesn't exactly look very light."

"You'd be surprised," Seishin responded, though he still doubted he'd fit on Cloud's board while wearing it.

A sudden idea struck him. Pulling the helmet back on, Seishin spoke to the armor. "Can you fly?"

"I can," Flandril immediately answered, *"but to do so I will need to drain some of your life force."*

That sounded quite ominous. "Permanently?" Seishin asked aloud.

"It is a temporary measure," Flandril responded, *"one that the master used to replenish with food and rest."*

That seemed far better than what Seishin originally thought. "You two go ahead," he told Cloud and Bal. "I'll be right behind you."

Bal eyed him skeptically for a few moments, then shrugged. "If you say so."

Bal's brow furrowed, deep creases forming across his forehead. Seishin noticed a distinct violet glow appear around his body. It disappeared a moment later, then Bal jumped on Cloud's board. The two of them then took off and flew out the vault door.

"Let's go," Seishin said to the armor.

An interesting sensation came over his body. It felt very much like when he invoked his spirit, but afterwards he felt weak in the knees.

As Seishin tried to shake off the feeling, the armor lifted up into the air. A moment later it shot out the door after the receding skyrider and his passenger.

The cavern out here was huge, going far back into the volcano. Cloud hadn't been exaggerating. There were firebirds everywhere in here, flitting all over the place.

The skyrider banked upward and headed toward multiple tunnels embedded into the wall of the volcano. Light could be seen streaming through them from the outside.

They had only gone a short distance when a firebird dove directly for them. At the very last minute, Cloud executed an amazing spin. He flew up and around the bird just passing over its head. As he did so, Bal jumped off and landed square on the firebird's back.

After Cyclone dealt with the priestess that accused them of being fakes, a hush fell over the shrine. Not the type to give up easily, Donnie tried to twist things back to their advantage. He swept a hand through the air, motioning theatrically toward Cyclone. "Behold my champion. Any who question the will of Zharpita must answer to him!"

The rest of the priestesses seemed awed and confused, their gaze shifting back and forth between Cyclone and the giant glowing ball hovering above the huge brazier. In the meantime, Illyria and her crewmates wove through them unhindered to Donnie.

They had just reached him when all of a sudden, the ground started to shake violently. Donnie's boots helped him to maintain his balance, but many folks in the room were not so lucky.

In the center of the shrine, the bright glowing ball suddenly expanded outward forming a huge shimmering portal. Donnie figured it had to be at least three dozen yards in diameter. To his horror, a giant bird head slowly rose out of the portal, its beak easily the size of a man.

Donnie felt a hand grasp his arm. He broke his gaze away from the emerging monstrosity to see Illyria rising up off the ground.

"What in the nine hells is going on?" Donnie asked the Galocerd captain.

"It's that damn volcano," Illyria swore. "The priestesses said it would erupt once they summoned their bird god."

Donnie had seen some crazy things in his time, but this beat all of them hands down. "Well, I vote we're not here when it does!"

"Sounds good to me!" Illyria agreed.

Motioning to her crew, they took off toward the shrine entrance. Donnie started to follow, but then realized Cyclone wasn't with him. Stopping and turning about, he saw the hunter still hovering in the air, his eyes firmly glued on the emerging bird god.

Donnie called out to him, "Aren't you coming?"

Cyclone glanced over his shoulder and shook his head. "You go ahead. I'm going to keep bird brain here busy."

Donnie let out a deep sigh, but knew there was no arguing with the hunter. "Alright, your funeral!" he called back. With that, Donnie spun on his heel and took off after the pirates.

Thea had been on some wild rides before, but never came that close to ending up in a pit of lava. She thought Elladan was completely nuts until they emerged unscathed in the courtyard of the temple.

She was about to give him a piece of her mind when a tremendous flash of lightning erupted across the yard. The bolt slammed into a large fire elemental disintegrating the creature on the spot.

As thunder echoed throughout the temple, Thea spied Ruka at the other end of that bolt. She could barely see the bronze of her scales beneath all the dark spots where she was singed.

A moment later, Ruka collapsed.

"Ruka!" Thea cried in dismay. She and the others leapt off the carpet and ran across the yard towards the downed dragon.

They had nearly reached her when all of a sudden, the ground around them began to shake. Thea and Pallas barely managed to maintain their balance, but poor Elladan ended up flat on his ass.

"Was that the volcano?" Elladan asked when the shaking finally stopped.

"That and worse!" A voice cried from the entrance to the shrine.

Three pirates came running out into the courtyard, all of them looking as if they'd seen a ghost. Moments later Donnie followed and swiftly explained what was going on inside.

Thea arched an eyebrow in disbelief. A bird god manifesting itself into their world? The last time the gods walked this earth they nearly shattered it to pieces. If this were truly a god coming through, they were in more trouble than even from a demon invasion.

Ruka's eyes fluttered open. Thea knelt down next to her and placed a gentle hand on her snout. "Ruka, can you shift? We need to get out of here."

"I—I think so," Ruka stammered, her voice laced with pain.

Thea stepped back as the teen dragon forced herself to rise. Still in obvious pain, she managed to shift to her human form. Thea gasped as she saw the burn marks all over Ruka's body.

Ruka managed a wan smile. "That hurt—more than I expected." She suddenly wobbled on her feet, but Donnie caught her.

Ruka glared at him, but did not push away. "I'm not a baby."

"Then stop acting like one," Donnie chided her.

Before she could retort the ground started shaking again, this time worse than before. When it was over, Thea helped Elladan to his feet again.

Elladan gingerly rubbed his butt where he had fallen twice. "I think it's time to get out of here."

"I think you're right," Donnie agreed.

Elladan traced a symbol through the air and opened yet another portal. "Everybody go!" He cried motioning them forward.

The three pirates went through first.

Ruka was about to follow, but then stopped and swept her eyes around the yard. "Wait. Where's Cyclone?"

Donnie gestured toward the shrine. "Back there, fighting a god."

A brilliant glow now emanated from the entrance and loud cries could be heard echoing down the corridor. Ruka took a step toward it. "Alone? Someone needs to…" Before she could finish her sentence, her knees gave out from underneath her.

Once again Donnie caught her, this time sweeping her up into his arms. "Sorry, hon, but this is for your own good."

"Let me go!" Ruka cried, beating him with her fists.

Donnie winced, but held on to her nonetheless, carrying her through the portal.

After watching them go, Thea glanced back toward the shrine. The glow had gotten brighter and the cries louder. She cast a leery glance at her brother. "Shouldn't we be trying to stop this thing?"

Pallas hesitated a moment, mixed emotions playing across his face. When he finally responded, it was through clenched teeth. "I hate to say this, sis, but stopping a god might be just a bit beyond us."

Thea couldn't believe her ears. This was her brother—the man who wanted to save everyone. How could he walk away from something like this with so many lives at stake?

"But…" she began.

Before she could get another word out, Pallas and Elladan each grabbed an arm and dragged her through the portal with them.

Seishin watched incredulously as Bal tried to ride a firebird. The bird weaved this way and that, trying to throw its rider off. All of a sudden, a red-hot ray lanced across the cavern and struck Bal in the back. Two more rays followed, but Bal somehow managed to avoid him. Still, between the rays and his bucking mount, he was hard pressed to hang on.

Back the way they came, Seishin spied six priestesses standing on the remaining portion of the catwalk. All of them were taking turns shooting fiery rays at Bal.

Even though he wore the heat resistant amulet, Seishin doubted Bal could take many more hits from those red-hot rays. He had to do something. Once again, he spoke to the armor. "Is there any way we can block those beams?"

"A few of them," Flandril responded, "but too many direct hits will begin to melt me."

Seishin thought that over for the briefest of seconds, then decided.

"Do it," he commanded the armor.

Flandril flew them into a position where they were directly between Bal and the priestesses. Seeing this new target in their way, they took aim at Seishin instead.

Seishin took two glancing blows, but then got pelted with two direct hits. Though he didn't feel a thing, the armor voiced its concern. "Sir, we seem to now be drawing their fire. May I begin evasive maneuvers?"

"I think that might be wise," Seishin agreed.

As Flandril began to weave back and forth, Seishin saw help was on the way. The priestesses had been so fixated on Bal and Seishin that they lost track of Cloud. The skyrider now plowed into them, sweeping across the catwalk with his board and knocking them all off one after another.

"Nice going!" Seishin cried, pumping a fist in the air at the skyrider.

Cloud looked his way and gave him a quick salute.

With the priestesses dealt with, Seishin turned his attention back to Bal. He found him still on the back of the firebird now just a few dozen yards away.

Something strange was happening though. Bal's arm was buried deep into the bird's back. The huge bird struggled beneath his grasp, then abruptly went limp. A moment later, Bal pulled his arm out and held in his hand a huge red gem.

At the same time, the limp bird began to fall. Seishin cried out to the armor, "Quick, we need to catch him."

"I'll need to drain more of your life force," Flandril warned.

"Do it!" Seishin commanded without a second thought.

Seishin felt another pull on his spirit accompanied by a second moment of dizziness. The armor then took off at an incredible rate swiftly catching up to the falling Bal. He grabbed him and lifted him off the bird's body as the firebird tumbled away into the lava pit below.

All of a sudden, the entire cavern began to shake around them. The lava pit bubbled and popped, then started to slowly rise.

Cloud came zipping across the cavern and skidded to a stop in front of them. "Climb on board!" he cried to Bal. "I think this thing is about to blow!"

Motioning for Seishin to follow, Cloud started to climb again towards the tunnels near the top of the cavern. They nearly made it to the entrances when another firebird tried to intercept them.

Bal looked tired from his prior exertions and Cloud could only do so much with a passenger on board. Drawing his curved blades, Seishin told them, "You two go ahead. I'll hold it off."

Bal gave him a grateful nod. "Go for the heart. That's its weak spot."

As the duo took off, Seishin turned to face the giant bird alone.

20

INTO THE FIRE

Between the emerging bird god and the erupting volcano,
the people of Kaniron didn't stand a chance.

Cloud had been in service to her majesty since the War of the Crystal Tower almost one hundred and forty years ago. He'd fought through two rebellions, a war with the Parthians, and even played a small part in the Giant Wars across the straits in Essek. Despite having lived through all of that, he'd never seen anything quite like this.

When Cloud first reached the volcano, he found the place swarming with firebirds. Thankfully he was small and fast enough not to be noticed. It also didn't hurt that the birds were pretty darn stupid. Much as it irked Ragnarök, Cloud continued to avoid them until he found a way inside. Even afterwards, he hung near the ceiling while he continued to search for the vault.

Though Cloud hadn't exactly been thrilled when the volcano started to shake, the chaos that ensued enabled him to rescue Bal. When the two of them finally shot back out into the open, Cloud breathed a sigh of relief. That didn't last long, however.

"We've got company!" Bal cried in warning. Grabbing Cloud by the shoulder he pointed up towards their two o'clock. One of those stupid firebirds must have spotted them and now dove in their direction.

Finally a battle! Ragnarök reveled with obvious glee.

I'm glad at least one of us is happy, Cloud thought back with far less enthusiasm.

The firebird closed on them fast, its beak opening and flames forming at the back of its throat. Cloud would have to time it perfectly if they wanted to come out of this unscathed. He waited until the very last second. The moment the fires sprang from its beak, he swept his board upward. He then leaned into a tight spiral to sweep beneath the unsuspecting bird.

As he did so, Ragnarök's blade iced over. The sentient sword had exhibited some amazing powers since Cloud acquired it from its deadly guardian nearly a century and a half ago.

A semi-transparent astral blade sword joined the black sword courtesy of Bal. Together they gutted the flaming bird nearly splitting it from head to tail. The hapless firebird fell from the sky and quickly dropped out of sight below.

Bal clasped Cloud on the shoulder. "Phew, that was some fancy flying."

Cloud responded with a terse, "Thanks." While he appreciated the sentiment, they weren't out of the woods just yet.

Without warning, the entire mountainside started to shake again. Above them, flaming rocks shot out of the top of the caldera and left fiery trails behind them as they crossed the darkening sky. Trails of glowing gold liquid appeared around the lip of the cone and began to flow down the mountainside.

Below in the temple grounds the wide dome above the shrine started to crack. Cloud watched in utter amazement as it shattered outward to reveal an enormous yellow-orange firebird head. Red flames danced over the creature's scalp as it let out an ear splitting "caw" that reverberated across the grounds and beyond.

Based on the size of the head alone, the rest of the thing would have to be three times the size of the other firebirds. That would make it nearly a hundred feet tall—bigger than Lisirianna, the Queen's ancient gold dragon.

"Now there's something you don't see every day," Cloud quipped to Bal. With all the tragedy he'd seen in his life, he'd learned to use humor to keep himself from plunging into insanity.

Unfortunately, Bal hadn't learned that lesson just quite yet. The blood had drained from his friend's face as he stared at the incredulous sight.

"What's in Arinthar is going on out here?" Seishin's voice sounded behind them.

Cloud turned to see the armor encased warrior flying out from the mountainside toward them. The sight of the golden armor had caught him by surprise. Cloud had seen it many times in paintings throughout the royal palace, but never thought he'd see King Flandril's armor in real life. He had to wonder how it ended up in the vaults here in Kaniron, but that was a story for another time.

"That." Bal merely pointed in answer to Seishin's question, his eyes transfixed on the gargantuan head sticking out of the temple roof.

"What is that thing?" Seishin asked, his voice filled with a mixture of awe and terror.

"I'm going to take a wild guess that's Zharpita," Cloud answered with more than a touch of irony. It was the only thing that made sense in this totally nonsensical situation.

As the three of them hovered there watching the unbelievable sight, a small figure leaped through the hole the creature had made in the temple roof. The figure planted itself firmly on the edge of the roof and swung at the enormous head with what appeared to be a long pole axe.

"Is that Cyclone?" Seishin asked with clear astonishment.

"Sure looks like it," Cloud replied wryly.

Just when he thought things couldn't get any crazier, of course the hunter would appear to challenge the gargantuan creature. Still, Cloud had to admit to being impressed. Though the hunter was obviously beyond crazy, no one could ever question his courage.

Seishin watched on incredulously as Cyclone faced off against the bird god, Zharpita. Though he admired the hunter's bravery, he knew there was no way he could defeat that thing alone. Even if he, Bal, and Cloud were all to join in with him, they would still not be a match for something that size.

Even so, something needed to be done. Chunks of flaming rocks now rained down upon the city. Fires sprang up wherever they touched and fanned out from there. A steady stream of molten lava now flowed down the mountainside. It wouldn't be long before it reached the temple and the city beyond.

Between the emerging bird god and the erupting volcano, the people of Kaniron didn't stand a chance. If they could just hold off Zharpita, however, many might still escape out to sea.

Realizing what needed to be done, Seishin again spoke to the armor. "Do you think we can help him hold that thing off?"

"Hmm," Flandril murmured at first.

Seishin thought perhaps he had asked too much of the armor. This might even be beyond its great powers.

"It might be possible," Flandril finally answered. "It really depends on the strength of your spirit."

Seishin again wished his uncle had come on this mission in his stead. A Shin Tauri master, his uncle's spirit was the strongest he'd ever seen. Unfortunately, Draigo was not here. The fate of Kaniron, and maybe the entire world, rested squarely on his shoulders.

Images flashed through Seishin's mind. He saw the faces of his father, his mother, and his little sister. He saw the Queen of Isandor who had sent him to find Draigo in the first place. Even the wizard Aldurin's visage flickered through his mind. Ultimately, his visions settled on the face of his one true love, Kortiama.

All these people either believed in him or depended on him. He couldn't let them down—wouldn't let them down. Taking a deep breath, Seishin responded to the armor. "I have to try."

"Very well," came Flandril's resolute response, "but be warned— I will need to drain a significant amount of your life force."

Seishin grimaced. The previous two times the armor had drained him, it had left him feeling weak. He couldn't imagine what this would do to him. Nevertheless, he had little choice.

"Do it," he gave the order.

Seishin felt that same strange tingling at first, but it swiftly grew into a feeling akin to daggers piercing every inch of his body. It was all he could do to keep himself from screaming.

Somewhere in the periphery of his awareness, he observed that the armor began to glow. The light grew brighter and brighter, almost as if to rival the sun.

He vaguely heard Cloud's voice, as if from somewhere far in the distance. "Is it supposed to do that?"

"Seishin? Seishin? What's going on?" He heard Bal cry, his distant voice filled with alarm.

All at once, the drain on him stopped. Seishin gasped at first for air, but somehow managed to find his voice. "You two—get out of here. Flandril and I—are going to try and help—Cyclone."

"Are you crazy?" Bal admonished, but his voice fell far behind as Seishin plummeted down toward the temple.

Cyclone felt a rush of excitement when the gargantuan head poked its way out of the portal. He had wanted a challenge, and what could be more challenging than facing a god? The size of the thing didn't deter him. He'd been raised from a very young age to fight creatures far larger than himself.

Still, fighting something this size in the confines of the shrine had been less than desirable. There were too many of those damn priestesses in the way and they didn't seem to take kindly to him attacking their god. The fanatical bird worshippers interposed themselves between him and his target while continuously pelting him with rays of fire.

This is starting to get annoying, Cyclone thought as he swept a few of the pesky priestesses out of the way.

Apparently, the bird god felt the same. It rose up and pecked its way through the dome above them without any concern for its followers. Though the glass itself shattered outward, sections of roof crumbled around it and fell on more than a few of the priestesses.

Deftly dodging the falling debris, Cyclone flew up through the hole and landed atop what was left of the flat section of roof. Now out in the open with room to work, the hunter hauled back and swung at the gargantuan creature with all his might.

Once, twice, three times in succession he rained down his heaviest blows against the creature. Huge gashes opened up in the bird god's yellow-orange hide, but the heat radiating from the thing quickly cauterized those wounds.

Panting heavily from exertion, Cyclone stepped back and growled up at the creature. "Why won't you die, you overgrown turkey!"

On top of everything else, the heat the bird god radiated grew with every passing moment. Cyclone began to think this might be the place where he dies, when a figure in glowing gold armor landed on the roof just a few yards away.

This day is just full of surprises, Cyclone thought with an ironic snort. *First a bird god and now a flying suit of armor? What's next, creatures from outer space?*

Still catching his breath, Cyclone watched warily as the armored figure drew a pair of thin curved swords, one slightly shorter than the other. Arcs of lightning crawled up each hilt until the blades were engulfed in an aura of crackling blue.

Without a word, the golden warrior rushed the gargantuan bird and swung two quick blows with deft precision. Both attacks sliced across its yellow-orange neck leaving deep gashes in their wake.

The bird god flinched, this time the wounds not healing quite as fast as before. A moment later, the gargantuan head tilted to look down upon them.

A wicked grin crossed Cyclone's face. *That got its attention.*

Closing his eyes and stilling his mind the hunter tapped into the rage constantly seething below the surface. The air around him began to stir and tiny arcs of electricity swept across his body. His hair rose of its own accord and his eyes snapped open, now a crimson red.

Hefting his axe, the hunter waded back into battle beside the golden warrior.

"Yup. He's going to die," Cloud said as Seishin sped off toward the temple below.

Even with Seishin's now glowing golden armor, Cloud was most likely right. Despite their bravery, both the warrior and hunter faced certain death against something as powerful as a god.

Bal wished there was something he could do, but what good would his gifts be against an all-powerful deity? All of a sudden, something struck him.

"Maybe. Maybe not," he responded to Cloud as he rummaged through his backpack.

Bal pulled out the replica of Zharpita they had found in the vault. Quieting his mind, he reached out with his aura to touch the statue. Something stirred within the idol.

Bal nearly gasped out loud. He sensed another mind linked to the replica—a huge mind in fact. The mind of a bird god!

Suddenly realizing what he was holding, Bal placed a hand on Cloud's shoulder. "Can you set me down on the temple roof?"

Cloud peered back at him over his shoulder, his brow knit into a deep frown. "Now you're nuts."

Bal intrinsically understood his friend's concern, but he didn't have time to explain right now. "Please, Cloud. Just do it?"

Cloud shut his eyes, a pained expression crossing his face. His eyes snapped open a moment later and he shrugged. "Fine. It's your funeral."

Bal watched with growing apprehension as Seishin landed and waded into battle. While he did get the god's attention, Bal was afraid he'd pissed it off more than hurt it.

As Cyclone joined back in with Seishin, Cloud landed them a short distance away, on the pinnacle of a pitched section of rooftop. Bal jumped off the board and proffered his backpack to the skeptical gnome. "If things go south, make sure you get this stuff to the others."

"Fine," Cloud murmured in response as he took the pack from Bal's hand.

Bal knew the skyrider thought he was nuts. *He's probably right,* Bal thought wryly, but if this idol is what he thinks it is, it might just be their only chance.

Bal grabbed the idol and once again reached out to it with his mind. Encircling it in the purple glow of his aura, he formed a psychic link to it. If he was right, he might be holding the very artifact meant to control the bird god.

Exerting his will, Bal thought at the idol. *Return from whence you came.*

The bird god abruptly halted its attack on the hunter and the warrior, and swung its head around to look directly at Bal.

Bal felt a cold shiver race up his spine. Without warning, the huge mind pushed back on his and severed the link. The resulting force sent Bal stumbling backwards.

"Bal!" he heard Cloud cry, as he fell and skidded down the side of the rooftop.

Cyclone and the golden warrior took turns attacking the gargantuan bird. It now felt every blow, but the heat it gave off was taking its toll. The figure next to him had to be feeling it too inside all that armor.

Cyclone lifted his axe for another swing when the colossal beak suddenly struck down at them. Warrior and hunter scrambled aside as the sharp beak slammed into what remained of the roof.

Chunks of stone went flying everywhere. Cyclone brushed most aside, but then cleaved a particularly large one that came straight for him.

The great head rose back up again, those huge eyes flashing an even deeper crimson. It appeared as if the creature's miss had only served to anger it further.

All of a sudden, the colossal bird went still. It only lasted for a few moments, then Cyclone heard a cry from behind him. He spun about just in time to see Balthazar go sprawling down the roof with Cloud on his board chasing after him.

"Watch out!" another voice cried.

Cyclone instinctively leaped out of the way as the giant beak came crashing down again, this time into the roof where he had just been standing. He landed a few yards back and looked up to see the giant head recoiling for another blow.

All of a sudden, a huge lightning bolt lanced across the sky and smacked directly into the side of the great head.

"Hey ugly, over here!" a familiar voice echoed across the sky along with the accompanying roll of thunder. They all looked up as a large bronze dragon strafed over the enormous bird's head.

It's Ruka! Cyclone thought with grim satisfaction. Another wicked grin crossed his lips. With the dragon now in the game, they might have half a chance against this stupid thing.

His glee was cut short, however, when the ground all around him started to shake again. This time the quake was so bad that it sent him sprawling across the roof.

Once it finally subsided, Cyclone clawed his way to his feet. The warrior in gold armor had ended up next to him and started talking as they both rose.

"The armor told me the volcano is about to explode. When it does, it's going to take most of the city with it."

Cyclone recognized the voice as Seishin's, but what he said sounded absolutely crazy. He looked at the warrior as if he was daft. "The armor said?"

Seishin grunted in response. "I know, I know, it sounds crazy, but this armor is sentient. It's been right so far, and those quakes are getting worse by the minute."

Above them, Ruka made another pass, hitting the bird god with another massive lightning bolt. The creature flinched back and sent a stream of flame after the dragon, but Ruka nimbly dodged out of the way.

That's when Cyclone realized they were running out of time. This thing was way too tough to beat before the volcano blew its top, but they also couldn't take the chance that it might get free. To be honest, he'd gladly sacrifice himself if it meant taking this thing down with him, but he couldn't ask that of anyone else.

A sudden idea struck him. *Maybe none of us have to.*

He narrowed his gaze at Seishin. "Can you keep this thing busy for a bit longer?"

"I can try," Seishin shrugged, armor and all. "What are you going to do?"

A thin smirk crossed Cyclone's lips. "Take a leap of faith."

21

LEAP OF FAITH

First one wing, then the other, broke through and spread out to an inconceivable span.

The resulting recoil from the severed mind link actually made Bal stumble backwards. Before he could regain his balance, Bal found himself skidding down from the pinnacle of the roof towards the outer edge. His mind still reeling from the force of the blow, he couldn't quite focus enough to form any kind of armor. It was all he could do to stop himself from completely losing his balance and tumbling down end over end.

Bal nearly reached the edge of the roof when Cloud finally caught up to him. Paralleling his slide, he swerved in closer and yelled to Bal, "Grab on!"

With almost no rooftop left beneath him, Bal lunged and caught the edge of the skyrider's board with his hand. That stopped Bal's descent, but left him hanging there at the very edge of the roof.

"Two hands might be better," Cloud chided him.

Bal peered down at his other hand. Somehow, by the grace of the gods, he had managed to hang on to the bird idol.

"Not an option," he told Cloud emphatically.

"Great time to take up collecting," Cloud retorted with the vaguest of smirks.

While Cloud maneuvered his board around so that he could climb on, Bal explained as simply as possible the significance of the statue.

When he was done, Cloud fixed him with a dubious stare. "That worked so well the first time. Sure you want to try again?"

Before Bal had a chance to respond, the huge quake hit.

Thick smoke now rose from the cone of the volcano, totally blocking out any trace of the sun. The flaming rocks shooting out of the caldera had grown larger and more frequent. The lava flows had also grown thicker and reached farther down the side of the mountain.

Across the temple rooftop, Seishin and Cyclone were recovering from that last shockwave. Thankfully, Ruka had entered the fray and managed to keep the bird god busy. Unfortunately, that was merely a delaying tactic. Their only real chance they had lay in the idol Bal held in his hands.

Cloud flew them up to the pinnacle of the roof and Bal jumped off to try again. He had just started to refocus his mind when Cyclone abruptly shot upward into the air. That left Seishin to face the bird god alone.

"I wonder what that's all about?" Cloud mirrored Bal's thoughts.

Bal watched uncertainly as the hunter intercepted Ruka in mid-air and nimbly landed on her back. The dragon let loose another massive lightning bolt at the bird god, then dodged out of the way again as it sent a stream of fire chasing after her.

Ruka swept down into a low arc just over the rooftop. She deposited Cyclone just a few yards away from them before pulling up and banking around to rejoin the battle.

Bal and Cloud exchanged a perplexed glance as Cyclone came running up to the two of them. Bal was nearly taken aback by the change in the hunter's eyes. They now glowed an intense shade of red as they fixed themselves upon Cloud. "I need you to get us as far away from here as fast as possible."

Cloud's brow knit together as he gazed at the hunter. "What about the others?"

"I have a plan," Cyclone said simply.

Cloud cast a hesitant glance at Bal.

Bal had no idea what the hunter had in mind, but he definitely wasn't the type to run from a fight. Whatever he was planning, it had to be extremely important. It might be the only way they'd get out of this alive.

Bal nodded to Cloud. "Go ahead."

Cloud peered back at him as if he were crazy, but then shrugged. "Okay—just don't go fall off any roofs without me."

Despite the desperateness of the situation, Bal breathed a closed-mouthed laugh. "I'll try not to."

Cyclone hopped on the board behind the skyrider. The two of them then shot away from the temple out across the city at incredible speed.

Seishin stood alone on the roof with the bird god towering over him. Perhaps he should've been frightened, but he had faced death before. Last time he had been completely helpless, buried up to his neck in the sand. This time was different, however. He had both his Shin Tauri training and the amazing golden armor.

Even so, Seishin had made little headway against the gargantuan god. Every wound he opened healed itself before he could do any serious damage. Even together with the dragon hunter, they'd been unable to truly hurt the creature. In addition to that, all this exertion and the extreme heat had already begun to sap his strength. So how in all Arinthar was he supposed to keep this thing busy?

Thankfully Ruka had entered the fray, but even her massive lightning bolts seemed unable to truly damage the god. No, something else was needed—something beyond extreme.

Seishin once again spoke to the armor. *Flandril, can you give me enough power to hurt this thing?*

The armor hesitated for the briefest of moments before replying. *I can, but to do so, I will need to drain much more of your life force.*

The weary warrior had expected as much. Many thoughts played through his mind, but as before it all came down to Korti. Seishin realized if he were to do this, he might never see her again. Yet what choice did he have? If the bird god were to get free, it would destroy Arinthar as surely as the demons.

Having made up his mind, Seishin braced himself as he spoke to the armor. *Very well, go ahead.*

This time instead of that tingling feeling, Seishin immediately felt those daggers. It dug deep into his skin with such intense pain that he actually screamed. The armor glowed even brighter than before, so bright that it lit up the surrounding sky.

When the drain finally stopped, Seishin fell to his knees. A wave of dizziness flooded over him and he thought he would pass out.

All of a sudden, a strength flowed into him unlike anything he'd ever experienced. He shot to his feet and quickly took in all that was happening around him.

Ruka had the bird god's entire attention, pelting it with bolt after bolt, then dodging away as it struck back. She could not keep that up indefinitely though.

On this last go round, the edge of the bird god's breath caught her with a glancing blow. The heat of that flame charred the scales along the one side of her body.

Faltering in mid-air, Ruka let out a horrifying scream.

Seeing the dragon in trouble, Seishin waded in and struck the bird god twice in rapid succession. Two huge gaping wounds opened along its torso. The bird god reeled back and let out a deafening scream of its own.

Thankfully, Ruka recovered and flew off.

Frustrated beyond belief, the enormous bird freed itself from the temple. First one wing, then the other, broke through and spread out to an inconceivable span.

Despite her wounds, Ruka banked around for another pass. Seishin knew it would not be enough though. Even if he were to repeat his previous attack, the damage would not stop the bird god from escaping.

Seishin could think of only one thing that might stop it—something he'd only seen his uncle do, but never tried before himself.

Sheathing both swords, the young Shin Tauri slowed his breath and gathered his spirit. The energy he called on was enormous, like nothing he'd ever felt before. It coursed through him, flowing to all his limbs at once.

Abruptly, the colossal bird went still again.

That was when Seishin struck. In a movement almost too fast to see, he shot through the air toward the creature's neck, drew his katana, and sliced through the bird god in a single devastating strike.

As soon as Cyclone and Cloud took off, Bal focused once again on the idol in his hands. He had just started to reach out with his mind when a loud cry broke his concentration.

Across the rooftop, the golden armor glowed brighter and brighter. It grew so bright, in fact, that Bal had to shield his eyes. Even through closed lids he could still sense the brilliant light.

When it finally faded, his eyes snapped open. Across the rooftop, Seishin had fallen to his knees.

Bal grimaced and shook his head. *What is he thinking? The last time he tried that, it left him gasping for air.*

Realizing their only chance of survival lay in the idol in his hands, Bal shut his eyes tight once more. Blocking out everything else, he focused solely on the replica of the bird god.

More screams erupted around him, but Bal forced himself to ignore them. Reaching out with his mind he reformed a psychic link to the idol.

Bal started to exert his will, but abruptly froze. This was it. This could mean life or death for them all—for the Queen—for their entire world. He had to put everything into this. There couldn't be any holding back.

Taking a deep breath, he called on all his years of training—of proving himself worthy of the trust Amaya and the Queen had placed in him. Digging deeper than ever before, Bal pushed with all the mental force he could muster.

Return whence you came!

The return push came almost immediately and with terrific force. Expecting it this time, Bal did not stumble. Even so, the pressure on him was excruciating.

Somehow, Bal managed to stay his ground against that titanic mind, but he knew he couldn't hold it forever. Even now, his mental strength had begun to wane.

Just as he felt himself slipping, a huge scream erupted from across the rooftop. At the same moment, the bird god's pressure on him abated.

This is my chance, Bal thought wildly. Marshalling what mental powers he had remaining, he gave it his all in one last desperate push.

Return from whence you came!

Bal felt the bird god trying to fight back, but it was too late. His assault broke through its mental barriers.

Bal opened his eyes to see the gigantic bird form fade and co-alesce into a great glowing ball. Strangely, the idol in his hand did the same. It grew so hot, in fact, that he found it hard to hold.

In one final act, Bal reformed the weightless armor around his torso. Using the augmented strength, he flung the idol over the roof across the intervening space between himself and the bird god.

Now completely spent, Bal fell to his knees. He watched with a detached sense of curiosity as the two glowing balls merged together and rose up high into the air above them.

Kneeling there and feeling numb, Bal noted out of the corner of his mind a bronze dragon sweeping down from the sky towards him. Strangely, the creature held a gold armored figure in one of its front claws. The dragon strafed along the roof at blinding speed, catching him in its other claw.

Bal grunted from the impact and then the world around him went dark.

Ruka flew as fast as her wings would carry her away from the giant glowing ball in the sky. She instinctively sensed the incredible power within it, and perhaps even more so, the danger it posed.

She only hoped she could put enough distance between them before catastrophe struck. Unfortunately, her one wing had been singed by that overgrown chicken and she could not fly at her top speed. If she could not, then Cyclone would be their last hope.

Now there's something I'd never thought I'd hear myself say, Ruka thought wryly.

The bravery of the hunter and the duo she carried in her claws absolutely amazed her. Though neither stirred, they had given their all in the titanic encounter with that overstuffed chicken.

Ruka half-laughed to herself. *Just when I thought humans had let me down, they go and do something like this. Perhaps there is hope for the human race after all.*

The city below flew swiftly past them. Fires burned everywhere, buildings smashed in from the flying debris, and streets choked with thick smoke. Thankfully, the place appeared to be deserted.

I guess you learn to move fast when you live below an active volcano, Ruka snorted ironically.

They had made it maybe three quarters of the way to the harbor when a loud *boom* suddenly sounded behind them. Ruka flinched as the force of that sound knocked her out of the sky.

Though sent spiraling out of control, Ruka refused to give up. She was a dragon by the gods, and she would not falter, not when these brave heroes depended on her.

Folding her wings in close, Ruka used the fall to recover her speed. She waited until the buildings were almost upon them, and then with a great flap shot forward once again.

Unfortunately, she now had a new worry. A rush of heat creeped up on her tail, swiftly growing hotter and hotter.

Come on wings! She urged her tortured body, trying to squeeze every bit of speed out of them.

Sadly, it was not going to be enough. The massive heat she felt behind her was quickly overtaking them. Pulling her two charges even closer, she tried for one last burst of speed.

The heat became unbearable as the very air around them turned white hot. Abruptly, the world faded from existence.

Cloud and Cyclone had reached the harbor faster than the hunter could've imagined. While he was hardly squeamish when it came to flying, the little gnome proved to be a maniac on that board. He zipped through and around obstacles as fast as any full grown dragon.

While in flight, Cyclone had contacted the rest of their party. Already aboard the *Black Cat* they waited for them halfway out in the harbor. Swiftly landing, Cyclone explained his plan to the others. The hardest part came next.

The hunter was used to being in the thick of battle. This waiting and watching from the sidelines was killing him.

How does anyone stand this? He thought while agitatedly twirling the dagger he held in his hands.

Up in the crow's nest, Donnie watched what was going on through a spy glass. The chatty elf shouted down a blow by blow description of the battle, making Cyclone wish more and more that he had not left it behind.

Maybe I was wrong, the hunter thought to himself. *Maybe I should have stayed and duked it out with that overgrown turkey.*

When the bird finally turned into a giant glowing ball, everyone could see it, even from here. A moment later, Donnie cried out from above, "She's got them!"

Cyclone immediately held up the dagger. It was Ruka's dagger—the one he had previously used to summon her. He had done that on his own, however, with no one else around and no sense of dire urgency.

Feeling the pressure, Cyclone's shoulders tensed as he did his best to concentrate.

Come to me, he thought at the dagger in his hands.

Nothing happened.

Maybe he was trying too hard. Cyclone shook out his arms and shoulders, then tried again.

Come to me, he thought at the dagger. He felt a familiar tingling this time, but again, nothing happened.

All of a sudden, a huge flash erupted over the city. The glowing ball exploded into a disc of white flames spreading out in all directions. The volcano was the first to go, practically disintegrating from the onslaught.

"I've lost track of them!" Donnie cried from above, his voice filled with sheer panic.

Stupid knife, Cyclone railed at dagger in his hands. *Why won't you listen to me?*

Feeling the anger well up inside, Cyclone used it to fuel his efforts. He held the dagger out in front of him as a red aura traveled up his arms and enveloped it. Cyclone let the rage burst from him and screamed his will at the dagger with all the force he could muster.

"Come to me!"

His voice reverberated across the deck and out into the surrounding harbor. At the same time, the city of Kaniron disappeared in a flash of white flames.

Still raging, Cyclone hauled back to hurl the stubborn dagger when something popped into existence overhead. A bronze dragon strafed over the topsails of the ship carrying two inert forms in its claws.

"Ruka!" Donnie shouted with glee.

Cyclone felt like shouting as well, but before he could a loud *boom* washed over them from the direction of the mainland. The force of the sound was so great, that it knocked everyone off their feet.

22
THE SEVEN SCROLLS

Each scroll had an extremely intricate rune carved upon it.

Pallas grasped onto the aft rail, his balance off as he rose from the deck. His ears still rang from the force of the *boom* that had knocked them all off their feet. It felt remarkably like the aftereffects of one of Alys' sonic screams, something he had personally experienced more times than he cared to remember.

His eyes went wide with horror as he caught his first glimpse of Kaniron. The white-hot blast that followed that *boom* had nearly decimated the entire city. Burnt out husks of what once had been tall buildings spread out as far back as the base of the volcano. Not a single tree or blade of grass could be seen anywhere in those charred remains. The top of the mountain itself had been blown off, though thick smoke and lava still spewed from its caldera.

Pallas fought a rising panic at the scene that so vividly matched his nightmares. A vision from the destruction of Penwick overlayed itself atop the burnt remains of Kaniron. For a few brief moments, Pallas could not distinguish between the two.

"We've got survivors!" Donnie's voice echoed down from the crow's nest above.

The encouraging announcement shook Pallas out of his waking nightmare. Thankfully the blast hadn't reached into the harbor. Ships filled with escapees dotted the waters, though many of those were merely lifeboats.

Captain Solais drew up beside Pallas at the aft rail. She briefly peered out over the waters, then barked out orders to her crew. "Bring us back in closer to the city! Prepare to take on refugees!"

A thin smile spread across Pallas' lips as he eyed the captain with mild surprise. "I thought pirates didn't have hearts?" he said to her half-jokingly.

Solais scoffed at his insinuation. "It's my damn sister. If she found out I left these folks to fend for themselves, I'd never hear the end of it." Though she tried her best to sound tough, he could see the compassion in her eyes.

Pallas had railed at first when Elladan portaled them to the docks by the *Black Cat*. In spite of his misgivings, Solais had honored her agreement to take them aboard without question. Pallas found it extremely uncomfortable being on a pirate vessel, but now he was starting to have second thoughts.

Maybe not all pirates are that bad, he reflected to himself solemnly.

After circling around, Ruka landed and deposited Seishin and Balthazar on the sterncastle where they all had gathered. Thea immediately moved in to check them out. She started with Balthazar while Pallas removed Seishin's helmet.

"He's alright. Just extremely exhausted," Thea pronounced after a quick once over. She then moved on to Seishin and declared the same of him shortly thereafter.

Solais stood next to Pallas with a curious expression on her face. "Where did lover boy get the fancy armor?"

"It was in the vault," Elladan told her. The bard swiftly explained what they had found in there.

Solais' raised both her eyebrows before letting out a soft chuckle. "So, he stole it? Maybe he does have the makings of a pirate."

In the meantime, Thea fixed Ruka with a deliberate stare. "Didn't I just heal you?"

Ruka, again in human form, had a few burn marks along the one side of her body. She folded her arms across her chest and met Thea's gaze evenly. "Yeah, well bird brain out there had other ideas."

"Tsk," Thea clicked her tongue at the dragon teen. "I'll deal with you later. Right now, these two need serious rest."

Elladan gave Solais one of those typical half-smiles of his. "Do you have anywhere on board we can take our friends?"

Solais seemed completely unaffected by the elf's charms, thus scoring further points with Pallas. She motioned to one of her nearby crew. "Show these folks to the quartermaster's cabin."

"There are two bunks in there they can use," she explained to Thea.

Cyclone went to pick up Seishin when Donnie finally joined them on deck. He stood over Ruka, eyeing her with obvious concern. "Ruka, you're hurt again!"

"So I've been told," Ruka answered, casting a cynical eye at Thea. Returning her gaze to the slim elf, she folded her arms across her chest. "Plus, what do you care, anyway?"

Donnie's face fell at her harsh admonishment. "But—I do care," he stammered.

Pallas felt kind of sorry for the elf. He had obviously done something to piss the teen off to the extreme. Despite his continued attempts to assuage her, she continued to snub him.

"Um, can we get going already?" Cyclone demanded impatiently, interrupting the awkward conversation. The hunter held Seishin in his arms, armor and all, as if he weighed next to nothing.

Pallas went to grab Balthazar, but Ruka held up her hand in front of him. "I've got him," she said. "Besides, apparently I need my boo-boos patched up."

Thea didn't bat an eye as she led Cyclone past the irritable teen. "Don't blame me if your scales end up permanently tarnished."

"Gee, maybe I'll turn copper…" Ruka retorted as she trailed after them.

Solais let out a closemouthed laugh as the group of them

descended from the sterncastle. She cast an eye up at Pallas. "Are those two always like that?"

"Have been since I've known them," he affirmed.

The Black Cat sailed forth and picked up refugees from the lifeboats. Before long a group of nearly two dozen folks had gathered on the main deck. Solais ordered they be taken down to the cargo hold and a watch posted over them.

Pallas raised an eyebrow at the harsh treatment. Perhaps he had been wrong after all about there being a few good pirates. "Isn't that a bit barbaric?" he admonished Solais.

The pirate captain fixed him with a dark look, but before she could speak, they were interrupted by a shout from above. "Incoming from the sky!"

Pallas snapped his gaze upward. A flock of firebirds had descended out of the clouds. They now dove down and strafed the ships that had stopped to pick up the refugees. As he watched in horror a few of the birds peeled off and headed their way.

Ruka and Cyclone had just returned from below. The dragon teen glanced at the hunter with an angry look. "I'm getting tired of these overgrown chickens."

"Me too," Cyclone agreed. "How about we go teach them a lesson?"

A wicked grin spread across the teen's lips. "I'm with you."

"Count me in," Cloud exclaimed, taking out his board again and leaping onto it.

Cyclone jumped onto the back of Cloud's board while Ruka shifted back to her dragon form. The three of them then took off into the skies to meet the approaching firebirds.

Between the dragon, the hunter, and the skyrider's black blade, they made short work of the oncoming firebirds. The threesome then sped on to help the other ships in the area.

Pallas had been engrossed in watching them when he felt a subtle jab in his arm. Elladan whispered in his ear. "Don't look now, but I think one of those refugees is wearing a fire amulet."

Pallas followed Elladan's gaze. He pointed out a young looking woman with long dark hair wearing brown robes.

Pallas noticed her robe opened slightly as she fingered something between her bosoms. It looked very much like the fire amulet both Thea and Balthazar now wore—the amulets they had confiscated from that priestess, Vitalis.

"You're right," Pallas whispered back to Elladan.

The two of them decided to warn Solais. As they approached her, Donnie joined in with them.

"What's going on?" the slim elf asked.

"Apparently we've got an unwelcome guest," Solais said with a nod towards the woman in question.

Donnie peered over her shoulder. "I'd say more than one. Look at the woman next to her—the one trying to hide her face. Isn't that Vitalis?"

Pallas followed the elf's gaze. Sure enough, he was right.

"Alright, let's go about this smart..." Solais began.

Unfortunately, Donnie had other ideas. The slim elf sauntered right up to the two women before anyone could stop him. He grabbed Vitalis by the hand and kissed it. "Vitalis, my dear. It's so good to see you again."

The woman tried to pull her hand away. "I'm sorry. I think you've mistaken me for someone else."

"Ah, but I never forget a face," Donnie exclaimed. In a blinding quick motion, the elf ripped the hood from her head, revealing her to indeed be the Kaniron priestess, Vitalis.

Vitalis' expression immediately hardened. "Ah, my dear Donatello, I really wish you hadn't done that."

She pointed a finger at him and let loose a ray of fire. Somehow the agile elf managed to dodge out of the way. The errant beam went flying straight for Solais.

Reacting out of pure instinct, Pallas stilled his mind and called on his spark of spirit. An aura of flame surrounded his body as he leapt in front of the unsuspecting captain. The fire beam struck Pallas directly in the chest, but merely bounced off not leaving a mark.

"You know you didn't have to do that," Solais chastised him as she drew her swords.

Pallas gave her a weak grin as he drew his own blade. "Sorry, force of habit."

"You better watch it or you'll get the reputation of a pirate friend," she teased as the two of them rushed forward together.

"I've been called worse things," Pallas retorted.

Any further banter died down as they waded into battle. As it turned out, more priestesses had snuck on board than just the two. All in all, they discovered a half dozen of them intermixed within the refugees.

They ended up slaying a few, but Donnie managed to knock out Vitalis. When it was all over, Solais ordered them to throw her in the brig along with one other captured priestess.

As Pallas sheathed his sword, Solais regarded him with a thoughtful stare. "Was that as strange for you as it was for me?"

Pallas snorted. "You mean fighting beside a pirate?"

"I meant fighting beside a Stealle," Solais countered, her eyes sparkling with amusement.

Pallas found himself laughing out loud. This woman was smart and funny to boot. She was not at all what he expected. He gingerly rubbed the back of his neck. "If anyone had told me about this a few weeks ago, I'd have said that they were stark raving mad."

"Agreed," Solais said, sheathing both of her swords. "How about we drink to that—to stark raving madness?"

Pallas thought it over for a moment or two, then nodded. "I like the sound of that."

Thea sat in the quartermaster's cabin silently contemplating what she could do to help Seishin. He and Balthazar now lay in bed, both men in the deepest state of sleep. She had examined each in turn and healed their physical wounds in a matter of minutes.

From what Thea could determine, Balthazar's state stemmed from a case of pure mental exhaustion. She was intimately familiar with the condition after years of dealing with her wizard mother. A couple of days of bed rest and Bal should be good as new.

It was Seishin's condition that truly worried her. Thea had seen spiritual exhaustion before. Both her brothers had developed a case of it from pushing themselves too hard to master the art of the spiritblade. In each circumstance, a few days of rest resolved their issues. Unfortunately, in the Isandorian's case, he seemed to be growing worse, not better.

To Thea's trained eye, his skin had further paled and his breathing had grown a bit too shallow. She placed a hand on his forehead. It was cool to the touch—too cool for her liking. *What could have caused this?*

She swept her eyes around the room, her eyes falling on the pieces of golden armor lying in the corner. Cyclone had piled them there before putting Seishin to bed.

Following her intuition, Thea strode over to the pile. She sensed a dull power emanating from the armor, but nothing major. She bent down and picked up the golden helmet. It felt surprisingly light in her hands. On pure instinct, she lifted the helmet over her head and lowered it onto her shoulders. As soon as she did so, a voice sounded in her mind.

Greetings warrior, I am Flandril.

Thea's brows knit together into a frown. *Wasn't that the name of the last King of Lanfor?*

It was indeed. I am his armor, the voice replied, *but I can help any who are true of heart.*

I see, Thea nodded to herself. *Tell me, Flandril, just how do you do that?*

The warrior's spirit fuels my powers, Flandril explained. *The stronger the spirit, the more I can do for him, or her.*

Both Thea's eyebrows raised at the same time. *Tell me, Flandril, is that what happened to your last wearer?*

Indeed, Flandril responded without the slightest hesitation. *He wished for the power to strike at a godling. I warned him of the risks involved, but he chose to proceed, nonetheless.*

So that's what happened to him, Thea mused with sudden comprehension.

It is, Flandril responded.

Thea hadn't meant the thought for the armor. Apparently, as long as she wore the helmet, it would continue to read her mind. Well, she might as well take advantage of the fact. *Flandril, did the king ever deplete his spirit near the point of death?*

Once, Flandril responded, its voice tinged for the first time with a touch of regret.

Thea found that quite surprising. Apparently, the sentient armor had been imbued with a sense of conscience.

What did he do in that case? She pressed on.

The Queen used the tower crystal to replenish his spirit, Flandril answered, *or at least enough for him to recover on his own.*

Thank you, Flandril, you've been most helpful, Thea told the sentient armor.

I do my best, Flandril replied with the vaguest trace of satisfaction. *Let me know if I can be of further assistance.*

Thea pulled the helmet off, her mind whirring now that she knew what she was dealing with. Unlike the Queen of Lanfor, she had no tower crystal at her disposal. Yet she had seen that crystal and knew it channeled spirit or soul energy.

Thea had spent the last four years learning to channel spiritual energy to heal bodies. She could even help heal minds to a degree, although that was an extremely delicate practice. Perhaps she could channel that same energy to reenergize Seishin?

Closing her eyes and clearing her mind, Thea prayed to her god.

Arenor, God of Life and Light, I need your guidance.

As it had been in the last four years, her prayer was immediately answered. *Yes, my dear child. What is it you wish to know?*

Thea swiftly explained Seishin's condition to the deity and what she had gleaned from the sentient armor. There was a moment's pause before Arenor answered.

This is doable, but the spell involved is of an order beyond your present abilities.

Thea balked at the god's response. *Seriously? A good man here might die and you're concerned with orders of spell difficulty?*

There is a reason for such things, Arenor replied, his tone calm as if talking to a petulant child.

"Dragon dung," Thea said aloud. "I've been your faithful servant for four years now. I left behind my former life to follow this path you put me on. I think you owe me more than just 'there's a reason for such things'."

Arenor actually sighed. *It is to protect your own mind and soul from harm, my child. If you attempt such a complex spell, you could permanently damage yourself.*

I accept the risk, Thea replied without hesitation.

The god of light did not immediately answer. When he did, his tone was one of extreme reluctance. *Very well. It is your choice to make, after all. Prepare yourself. I will fill your mind with the pattern to use. Just be aware that you may not be able to retain it.*

Watch me, Thea responded adamantly.

The auric priestess opened her mind and allowed her god's guidance to flow through her. A pattern spread out in the forefront of her mind, one more complex than she had ever seen before.

It was difficult to follow at first and she had to start over three times before getting through the first part—and still there was more. The entire process was grueling and Thea's head began to hurt after a while, but she refused to give in. Seishin's life depended on it.

Pushing herself to her very limits, Thea retraced the pattern over and over again. She finally almost had it, but the last part seemed to elude her.

"Damn it all!" She cried aloud in bitter frustration.

Arenor chuckled in her mind. *Is that any way to talk in front of your god?*

Sorry, Thea replied with chagrin, *but I am so close!*

You are, in fact, Arenor acknowledged with the faintest hint of surprise. *Why don't you try once more?*

The encouragement in her god's voice helped Thea to calm herself. Fixing her mind on the last part of the pattern, she traced through it one more time. Abruptly, she reached the end.

"Was that it? Did I finish it?" Thea gasped aloud.

You did, Arenor acknowledged with a hint of pride. *Now go ahead and heal that young man.*

Thank you! She replied in earnest as she rushed over to Seishin's side.

Thea now stood over the warrior and gathered her will. She then traced the complicated symbol through the air in one pass. It took her almost a minute to finish the entire thing. The divine energy that flowed into the pattern surpassed anything she had ever dealt with before. It was so potent that it made her hair stand on end.

Once the symbol had been completed, Thea spoke the words of invocation Arenor had implanted in her mind. *"Magna renovatio."*

The energy spewed forth from the symbol and swept around the body of the exhausted young man. A whitish-green light encircled him and slowly seeped into his inert form.

Thea watched with bated breath as the color returned to his skin and his breathing returned to normal. She touched his forehead. It felt warm again.

Thea breathed a sigh of relief. She had done it. A sudden wave of dizziness passed over her. Thankfully, it only lasted a moment. *Or perhaps overdone it,* she thought to herself wryly.

The auric priestess pulled up a chair and plopped herself down into it. Moments later she was fast asleep.

After dealing with priestesses hidden amongst the refugees, Elladan's thoughts turned to Thea. While the others were occupied settling in their new 'guests', he went to check on her. The quartermaster's cabin was below the sterncastle along the same corridor that led to the captain's quarters. Elladan softly rapped on the door, but received no answer. Now more worried than ever, he opened it a crack and peeked inside.

He found Thea fast asleep in a chair alongside the recuperating Bal and Seishin. Elladan quietly stole across the room and stood over the sleeping young woman. Her hair partially covering her face, soft snoring noises emanated from her barely opened mouth.

She looked positively adorable. Elladan's heart melted just a little bit more as he watched her. Deciding not to disturb her, he pulled a blanket from the foot of Seishin's bed and carefully laid it atop the sleeping priestess. Unable to resist, he bent over and kissed her gently on the forehead.

A tender smile crossed his lips as he left her sleeping there. He had nearly made it to the door when a soft voice rang out behind him. "Where are you going?"

Elladan turned about to see Thea staring at him from beneath the blanket. A half-smile crossed his lips as he whispered back, "I thought you were asleep."

Thea yawned and stretched. "I was and I might be again very soon since somebody gave me this nice warm blanket." She pulled the blanket closer around her and snuggled into it while grinning like a little kid.

A soft chuckle escaped Elladan's lips. "Well then, I won't stop you, but you're going to miss all the fun."

"What fun?" Thea purred sleepily, her eyelids growing heavy once more.

"Oh nothing," Elladan responded in a casual tone. "We're just going to take a look at the scrolls is all."

Thea immediately shot out of her seat. "Well why didn't you just say that in the first place?" she chided him as she straightened out her long skirt.

Elladan fought back another laugh. That had gotten her interest. He pointed to Bal and Seishin. "What about these two?"

Thea waved a nonchalant hand at the sleeping duo. "They'll be fine now. Nothing a day or so of rest won't fix."

Elladan fixed her with another half-smile and put out his arm for her to take. "Well, you're the doctor."

The captain's quarters on the *Black Cat* did not appear much different than that of a Penwick ship of the line. Bright light flooded in from the array of windows at the back of the room. A long mahogany table stood in front of those windows, surrounded by a mismatched set of ornate chairs. A globe sat on a circular stand in a corner next to a tall bookcase. A plush cupboard bed was set into the opposite wall beside an elaborate mahogany wardrobe.

Solais sat with her feet up at the table surrounded by Pallas, Donnie, and Cloud. A bottle of rum stood opened between them as they sipped from a set of wooden cups.

A wry smile crossed Thea's lips as she watched them all sharing a drink. *My brother, the pirate hater, cozying up to a pirate captain? The world really is coming to an end.*

Solais offered them both a cup as she and Elladan joined them at the table. Elladan gladly partook, but Thea declined, still feeling sleepy from the exertion of healing Seishin.

"Where are the others?" Thea asked as they all sat back down.

"Cyclone and Ruka are keeping an eye out for more of those stupid birds," Cloud informed her. "Plus, I don't think this is really their thing," he grunted as he lifted up Bal's backpack and dropped it on the table with a solid *thud*.

The others around the table winced. "You might want to be careful with that," Elladan cautioned the gnome.

Cloud chuckled. "Don't worry. Bal's got more padding in here than a swaddled baby."

What Cloud told them proved to be true. As he opened the pack, Thea got a glimpse of its thick quilted lining.

"I guess he's used to carrying around precious objects?" Donnie surmised.

Cloud shrugged. "You might say that."

The slim elf's droll smile spoke volumes. Given Bal's position and his talent for moving about unnoticed, they had all concluded that he was some sort of spy for the queen.

Everyone watched on eagerly as Cloud pulled out a group of gilded scroll cases from the pack. Thea counted seven in total.

Donnie bent in for a closer look at the designs on each case. "Those are definitely Isandorian markings," he affirmed with a nod.

Solais reached over and placed her hand on a specific symbol. "That glyph signifies the House of Tauriyama."

Pallas narrowed an eye at the pirate captain. "And just how do you know that?"

Solais snorted at the question. "I had a very good teacher. Plus, I'm interested in anything having to do with weapons—especially swords."

Pallas fixed the captain with a begrudging smile, but Thea could tell how impressed he was with the knowledge she just shared. The corner of Thea's mouth lifted ever so slightly. *These two are far more alike than either is willing to admit.*

Donnie motioned across the table toward Elladan. "You've got the most experience with this sort of thing. Maybe you should open the scrolls?"

"If you insist," Elladan concurred. He popped open one scroll case at a time and cautiously allowed the contents to slide out. Handling each parchment with extreme delicacy, Elladan gently unrolled them out onto the table.

Each scroll had an extremely intricate rune carved upon it. To Thea's eye they looked similar to the writing on the cases, but neither Donnie nor Solais could interpret the symbols.

While Elladan examined one closely, Donnie took out a sketchbook and began to draw a copy of each symbol in turn.

"Aha!" Elladan suddenly cried, his eyes lighting up with recognition. "I believe I know what language this is."

The bard reached for a nondescript bag at his belt and pulled the drawstring open. Thea had seen him use it enough now to realize that was his portal bag.

Elladan rummaged around practically down to his shoulder before pulling out a tome that read, *Secrets of the Laurentian Empire*. The bard rifled through the book until he found the section he'd been searching for. He placed the open tome on the table next to the unfurled scrolls.

"The Laurentian empire fell during the Age of Madness, an infection caused by the appearance of the Baleful Moon," Elladan explained. "Much of the surviving human kingdoms fled south and established the Kingdom of Isandor."

Thea bent over the book and examined the symbols written there upon the two pages. While they indeed looked similar to the writing on the scroll cases, she could see definitive matches between them and individual parts of the complex runes.

They all took part in pouring over the Laurentian symbols until they deciphered the meaning behind each rune. The list they came up with included: Warrior, Faith, Peace, Wisdom, Existence, Angel, and Protection.

When they were done, Solais puzzled over the list. "Does anyone have an idea what effect these runes might have on a blade?"

The folks gathered there appeared as puzzled as Solais. Thea swept her eyes around the group with a wan smile. "Maybe our expert smith might know something? She did study with the Tauriyama clan for a couple of years."

Pallas guffawed at her. "I can't imagine they'd share those secrets with Amada in that short a period of time. Regardless, I think we have bigger problems to worry about at the moment."

Thea folded her arms across her chest and fixed her brother with a withering stare. "Such as?"

Pallas smirked, knowing full well he had gotten under her skin. "Such as the Parthians. While I doubt we have to worry anymore about the Cult of Zharpita, I'm certain the Parthians will be looking for these scrolls."

"I could put them in my portal bag," Elladan offered.

Donnie placed a hand on the bard's shoulder. "Um, might I remind you of the time Anya stole it right from your belt."

Elladan cast a dark look at his friend. "What did I say about mentioning her name in front of me?"

"My apologies." Donnie pulled back from his fellow elf and raised his hands in mock surrender. His eyes, on the other hand, danced with amusement.

Solais peered around the group while tapping her chin. "I do happen to have a box which is impenetrable to scrying."

"How much?" Elladan asked, his eyes glinting with the thought of bargaining.

While the two of them bartered over the price of the box, Thea decided to contact Lloyd and let them know they had found the scrolls. Stepping away across the room, Thea cast a spell to allow her to communicate briefly with her other brother. She carefully thought out what to say as the spell had its limitations.

Lloyd, we found the scrolls. Seven in total. We'll return with them as soon as possible.

A minute or so passed before she received a response, the contents of which caught her by surprise. Elladan and Solais had just come to an agreement on the price of the box when Thea rejoined them.

"Um, folks, we have a slight problem," she said tentatively.

Knowing her as well as he did, Pallas immediately hushed everyone around the table. He then turned back to Thea. "Go on, sis."

Thea took a deep breath and blurted it all out at once. "I just talked to Lloyd and apparently there are fourteen scrolls in total."

The room went silent. Everyone stared at her dumbfounded until Elladan finally found his voice. "You've got to be kidding. Does he know this for a fact?"

Thea responded with a firm nod. "He asked Amada."

The bard threw up his hands in disgust. "Well, there goes that!"

Pallas addressed Solais. "Do you know of any more scrolls other than these?"

Solais slowly shook her head. "No, but I could contact my sister. She might have heard something more about them."

Donnie appeared lost in thought as he gingerly stroked his chin. "Perhaps the Galocerd know something." A sly smile crossed his face. "Illyria did say she owed me. Maybe it's time I collect."

Cloud, who had been silently watching everything up until now, finally chose to speak. "I could also message Commander Amaya. She might have some information on any more scrolls."

Donnie eyed him with a knowing stare. "You mean she's going to check with her spy network."

"Something like that," Cloud responded without batting an eye.

23
DEAD IN THE WATER

Well then, it looks like we've both been played.

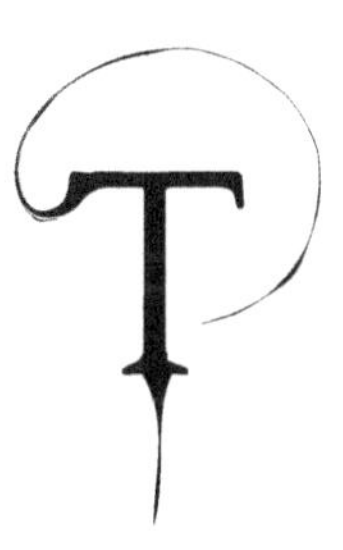he destruction that had befallen Kaniron left Donnie mortified. When the bird god exploded, it nearly wiped out the entire city. Only a very few buildings remained standing, those on the very edge of the once great seaport.

Things had gotten way out of hand this time. Donnie thought for certain spilling that urn would've put a crimp in the priestesses' plans. It caught him completely by surprise when it instead hastened things along. What frightened him the most, however, was that Ruka almost died as a result of his actions. Balthazar and Seishin nearly paid the price as well.

It's my curse! It has to be, Donnie chided himself. Only Cyclone's quick thinking had saved them in the end.

Who would have thought? he mused with clear irony. After all, the hunter wasn't exactly known for his brain power.

Regardless, Donnie needed to do something more to ensure Ruka's safety. Despite the fact that he pushed her away, he couldn't deny he still cared about her. Perhaps he could talk to the hunter—explain to him about the curse. Between the two of them, they should be able to keep Ruka safe.

Now was not the time, however. Ruka and Cyclone were still busy chasing down firebirds, and he needed to find out what happened to the other seven scrolls. The Galocerd ship sat anchored a short distance across the bay. Donnie commandeered a couple of Dasati sailors and took one of the *Black Cat's* rowboats over to it.

A three-masted galleon, the Galocerd vessel's great hull towered above them as they drew near. Donnie noted the ominous name etched across the bow of the ship—*The Annihilator.* Though obviously meant to strike dread into those who saw it, he found the designation more interesting than intimidating.

In his time with the clans, Donnie found that they strived to outdo each other in every conceivable way. That included coming up with menacing names for their ships. Some clans tended to be more dramatic than others. Apparently the Galocerd fell into that category.

Once they drew up alongside the vessel, Donnie hailed the crew. "Ahoy, there!"

A burly looking pirate stuck his head out over the rail and growled down at them. "What do you want?"

Donnie fixed the man with a charming smile. "Why, I'm here to see Captain Illyria of course."

The pirate responded with a harsh laugh. "And what makes you think she'd want to see you?"

"Well, first of all I'm the original Dodger and secondly I just saved her life." Donnie continued to smile as he ticked off each point on his fingers.

The pirate stopped laughing. "Oh, you're that elf," he grunted. "Wait here and I'll go ask her."

A few minutes later, the burly man reappeared at the rail. "Yeah, she'll see you," he called down. "Come aboard."

Not too long afterwards, the sailor ushered Donnie into the captain's quarters. It looked remarkably like Solais' cabin on the *Black Cat* except for the blue drapes, tablecloth, and bedcovers.

From her seat at the head of the table, Illyria motioned for the sailor to depart. "Close the door on your way out," she told him.

"Yes, Captain," the burly pirate responded with just a trace of fear in his voice.

Donnie didn't doubt for a second that his fear was warranted. One on one, Illyria could probably best any member of her crew. You didn't rise to the captaincy of a clan ship without earning it.

The Galocerd captain pointed to the empty chair beside her. "Come grab a seat."

Once Donnie sat down, she motioned to a bottle of rum on the table. "Drink?"

"Always," Donnie replied glibly.

Illyria filled a pair of mugs. Placing one in front of him, she took a drink from the other, then sat back in her chair and eyed him curiously. "I have to say, I didn't expect to see you so soon. To what do I owe the pleasure?"

Donnie took a swig from his mug, then set it down and flashed her one of his most charming smiles. "Does a gentleman need a reason to call on a beautiful lady?"

Illyria eyed him incredulously, then suddenly burst into fits of laughter. She laughed so hard that her face reddened and she nearly lost her breath.

His ego only slightly bruised, Donnie continued to sip his rum until she laughed herself out.

Fanning herself, Illyria managed to respond in between gasps. "Oh my…you are funny. Now I understand…why Morfind'l was… so fond of you."

Donnie gave her a toothy grin. "It's part of my charm."

Finally getting a hold of herself, Illyria leaned forward across the table and stared him directly in the eyes. "Now seriously, why are you here?"

Donnie leaned forward as well, his face coming within inches of hers. He noted that she smelled like lilacs, an unexpected yet welcome fragrance. "As I told you he would, my man managed to pilfer the scrolls from those bird loving church dwellers. Unfortunately, he only found half the scrolls in the vault."

A frown crossed Illyria's brow. "How do you divide seven in half?"

Donnie met her gaze evenly. He had dealt with charlatans and scoundrels all his life. He was certain he would know if she were lying, yet he saw no deceit within her eyes.

"He found seven," he responded after a moment's pause.

Illyria narrowed her gaze even further. "Are you saying there are even more than that?"

Donnie responded with a subtle nod. "According to my source who saw them while they were still in Isandor."

An ironic smile spread across Illyria's lips. "Well then, it looks like we've both been played. I was only given the seven to sell to the bird lovers."

Donnie inched just a bit closer to the exotic looking captain. "And who was it that gave them to you?"

"Lord Captain Hahe, the head of our clan," Illyria murmured, not pulling back in the slightest.

"It doesn't sound like he trusts you very much," Donnie said in a soft voice.

"He doesn't trust anyone," Illyria replied with the slightest of smirks.

A sudden twinkle appeared in her eye. Her voice dropped low and took on a throaty tone. "You know, I never really got to thank you properly for saving my life. Perhaps I could do so now?" She moved even closer, her head tilting slightly to one side.

Illyria was most certainly beautiful and the blue hair gave her an exotic appeal. Yet for some reason he couldn't quite fathom, Donnie felt something holding him back.

He stood and murmured apologetically, "I really shouldn't stay that long."

Illyria was obviously used to getting what she wanted. She also rose, then pressed up against him while wrapping her arms around his neck. "I'm sure you can stay long enough."

Tilting her head again, she pressed her mouth against his. The softness of those lips, the smell of her hair, and the warmth of her skin drove away all his previous inhibitions. Slipping his arms around her waist, Donnie gave in to the throes of passion.

Cloud stopped by to visit Bal before contacting Commander Amaya. There'd been no good time to do so up until now between that god-tier explosion, the firebirds, and checking the contents of the scrolls. He found his friend still fast asleep. According to the Penwick priestess, he would most likely continue to do so for the next day or so.

In all the time they'd spent together, Cloud had never seen Bal quite this bad. He let out a deep sigh. *I tried to warn him taking on that bird god was crazy. Although I suppose if he hadn't, the entire world would probably be in real trouble right about now.*

With Bal still out of commission, Cloud knew what he had to do. Rummaging through his friend's pack, he pulled out a palm-sized amber stone. He then went out on the main deck, hopped on his board, and took off into the air.

Once he was out of ear shot of the ship, Cloud pulled the stone from his pocket. At first it felt cool to the touch, but it swiftly warmed within his palm. As soon as it did, Cloud sensed another mind reaching out to his.

Amaya? Cloud thought at the stone.

Cloud, is that you? The commander answered almost immediately.

Yeah, Cloud answered.

Where's Balthazar? She thought back, sounding worried. It amazed him how much inflection he could sense via the stone.

Cloud hesitated a few moments before answering. *That's a long story. Let's just say he's fine now.*

Alright, Amaya sighed. Cloud could tell she was dying to know more, but they really didn't have the time for that right now.

So then, what can you tell me? Amaya pressed him.

Well, I have good news and bad news, Cloud responded.

What's the good news? Amaya asked after a moment's pause.

We found the seven scrolls, Cloud reported.

That's fantastic! Amaya commended him. *So, what's the bad news?*

There are actually fourteen of them. Cloud snorted aloud as he answered.

Oh. Not so fantastic then, Amaya responded, her previous enthusiasm suddenly dampened.

We were kind of hoping you might have information on the other seven, Cloud got to the point.

There was a brief pause before she responded. When she did, it wasn't exactly the answer he was hoping for.

I kind of have my hands full right now. We're still cleaning rebels out of the city, and the Queen is livid about Ruka's disappearance. I trust she's with you? She ended pointedly.

Guilty as charged. Cloud shrugged, though he knew Amaya couldn't see it.

I don't suppose there's any way you can send her back? Amaya asked tentatively.

Not sure I would if I could, Cloud told her definitively.

Why's that? Amaya asked.

Cloud didn't mince words. *Honestly, she's been a big help. I'm not sure Bal would have survived without her.*

What exactly happened out there? Amaya asked with growing alarm. *Wait, never mind,* she immediately contradicted herself. *I'm sure it will all be in your report.*

Don't you mean Bal's report? You know I don't do paperwork, Cloud reminded her.

Fine, she responded, knowing better after all these years than to argue with him on that point. *So then, what are you going to do with the dragon girl?*

In truth, were it up to Cloud, he'd let Ruka go her own way when this was all over. He hadn't been overly fond of the way the Queen treated her and her sisters. Nevertheless, Bal had made a deal with the girl to return with them, so that's what he reported to the commander.

Cloud could actually hear Amaya sigh with relief. *Thank the gods. I haven't seen the Queen this mad since Anya took off with the royal family yacht.* She paused a moment before going on. *Anyway, I'll check with the network and see if anyone knows anything about the rest of those scrolls.*

That would be most appreciated, Cloud responded.

Slipping the stone back in his pocket, Cloud let out a long sigh. *Well, that was no help.*

Perhaps Donnie might find out something from the other pirates, but somehow Cloud doubted it. Until they had more to go on, they might as well be dead in the water.

The sun sat low over the western horizon when the *Black Cat* finally put out to sea. Most ships had already left the burning remains of Kaniron behind, but surprisingly Solais waited until the waters were clear of refugees. Even the Galocerd had left before them, lifting anchor not long after Donnie returned from his rendezvous with their captain.

Unfortunately, neither Donnie nor Cloud had gleaned any additional information on the whereabouts of the missing scrolls. With Bal and Seishin still recovering and not knowing their next destination, it made sense to stick with the Dasati's for the time being. Solais knew a number of small towns along the coast where they could drop off the refugees. Thus, they set sail for one of those ports.

The next morning they pulled up to the docks at the small town of Lupanga. Not far north of Kaniron, the townsfolk there had felt the earth tremble when the volcano erupted. Even now, the sky to the south remained dark with ash-filled clouds and the glow from the volcano could be seen at night. Thus, understanding their plight, the people of Lupanga welcomed the refugees with open arms.

Pallas found it interesting that these townsfolk showed no fear of the pirates. In fact, they seemed rather cordial, welcoming them ashore as well and inviting them to restock their supplies. His curiosity piqued, he brought up the topic with Solais.

Watching from the quarterdeck as the refugees disembarked, Solais fixed him with a withering stare. "We're not all bloodthirsty curs, you know. Albeit there are a few," she added, her face momentarily clouding over. "Even so, those of us who abide by the mandates only take from those who trespass across our waters."

"Tsk," Pallas clicked his tongue contemptuously. "Tell that to the people of Penwick."

Solais' face darkened even more so. He could clearly see a mixture of pain and anger in her eyes. Her voice took on a hard tone.

"That was a mistake. To this day, most of us have no idea why Eboneye led us there."

"Most of us?" Pallas repeated skeptically.

Solais shrugged and shook her head. "There might be a few who do—Rikton for one."

"Rikton?" Pallas repeated the name.

"Eboneye's younger brother and a total bastard," a voice sounded behind him.

Pallas glanced over his shoulder to see that Seishin had joined them on deck. Both he and Bal had woken earlier that morning, ravenous, yet seemingly recovered.

Pallas narrowed an eye at the Isandorian. Though his choice of words had been harsh, his expression remained neutral. "You've met this Rikton, I take it?"

A trace of anger swept over Seishin's normally stoic features. "He was one of the pirates standing over me while I was buried up to my neck in sand"—he cast a critical glance at Solais—"among others."

Solais grunted back at him. "Hey, you brought that on yourself."

Seishin dipped his head to one side and shrugged. "True. At least you didn't gloat over me like Rikton did."

Pallas' mouth twisted to one side. "This Rikton character sounds like a real gem."

"You don't know the half of it," Solais murmured under her breath.

"From what Korti told me, if her Uncle Rikton had his way, he would lead the Dasati down a bloodthirsty path just like his brother did twenty years ago," Seishin elaborated.

The thought sent a chill down Pallas' spine. A momentary flash of his recurring nightmare flashed before his eyes. It abruptly faded, however, when something in Seishin's words struck him. "Wait— you said her Uncle Rikton. If he's her uncle and he's also Eboneye's brother..."

"...she's Eboneye's daughter," Seishin finished for him.

Pallas' jaw dropped at the sudden revelation. Eboneye, the scoundrel that led the destruction of Penwick all those years ago, had a daughter who now led the Dasati. Yet, from everything he'd seen and heard, his daughter was nothing like him.

Something else suddenly dawned on Pallas. He peered warily at Solais. "You're Korti's sister…"

"Adopted sister," Solais immediately corrected him. "Eboneye is not my father, if that's what you're implying."

For some reason, the revelation filled Pallas with relief. He was about to ask more about this Rikton fellow when another voice interrupted them.

"We just heard back from the commander." This time Cloud had joined them on the quarterdeck.

Solais gave the gnome a curt nod. "Very good. Let's take this conversation down to my quarters."

Seishin felt amazed to be alive. He had poured almost every last ounce of his spirit into that fight with the bird god. He didn't think there would be any coming back from that. According to Thea he nearly didn't. Somehow, she managed to revive his spirit, but cautioned him to never push things that far again.

With so much still left to do, Seishin humbly accepted her advice. Apparently, they had only procured half of the actual existing scrolls back in Kaniron. He needed to help these folks find the rest. After that, he would continue his search for the Shin Tauri blade. Beyond that the real challenge began—fighting back the demon hordes.

Realizing he was getting far too ahead of himself, Seishin abruptly reined himself in. Everyone had gathered in Solais' quarters to hear what Commander Amaya had found about the missing scrolls.

At the moment, Bal was speaking. "According to Amaya, the rest of the scrolls are not in Parthos."

"Well, that's a relief," Elladan sighed.

Donnie leaned forward in his chair. "Did she have any idea where they might be?"

Bal shook his head. "Nothing concrete, but there are rumors that the Parthians have a secret base somewhere in the south seas."

"And she thinks they might be there?" Elladan prompted.

Bal shrugged in response. "Unless you have a better idea."

"It sounds like as good a guess as any," Cloud agreed with his fellow officer.

"More like searching for a needle in a haystack," Ruka said with a disparaging smirk.

Seishin had to agree with her. The south seas were vast and they had no idea even where to begin.

"Maybe, maybe not," Pallas murmured. He peered quizzically at Solais. "We know where at least one Parthian ship is supposed to be in the next couple of days."

Solais gave him a begrudging smile. "So, you're suggesting we go back to Kaniron and waylay it."

Pallas fixed her with a wicked grin. "And why not?"

Thea smacked her brother on the arm. "Why, Pallas, how very mercenary of you."

"I think he's got the makings of a pirate after all," Donnie winked.

Seishin had to admit, it was a decent plan. That was assuming of course that they could take over a Parthian ship. From what he'd seen of them, it might not be all that easy.

"There wasn't much left of Kaniron," Elladan pointed out. "There's no guarantee that they'll even be there."

"You don't know the Parthians then," Bal interjected. "If they fail their God-Emperor, their lives will more than likely be forfeit."

"Sounds like a real swell guy," Elladan said with a raised eyebrow.

Pallas stared at Solais intently. "So, what say you then? Are you willing to take us back to Kaniron?"

Solais sat back in her chair and kicked her feet up on the table. "That all depends. What do I get out of it?"

Seishin was taken aback by her sudden mercenary attitude. He immediately admonished himself for being surprised. Solais had been just a bit too helpful these last few days. This seemed more like the pirate he had come to know.

Apparently, he was not the only one caught unawares. Everyone else at the table appeared equally shocked. Thea in particular was highly incensed. The priestess rose from her seat and fixed Solais with a heated glare. "I guess it's not enough to save the world from a militant nation and hordes of demons?"

Solais sat up again and locked eyes with the priestess. Both women radiated power. Seishin could feel the heat rise in the room as the two of them glowered at each other.

All of a sudden, Solais burst into raucous laughter. She rose from her seat, doubled over, and slapped her hand against her thigh. "You should see…the looks…on your faces," she managed in between fits.

Seishin stared at the pirate captain in utter confusion. Had she gone stark raving mad?

Solais finally got a hold of herself. "No, seriously, I'm just messing with you. I already checked with Korti. She wants us to make sure the Parthians don't get any of those scrolls."

The pirate captain swept her eyes around the table, the corner of her mouth curved slightly upward. "So, I guess I'm stuck with the lot of you a bit longer."

A flood of relief washed over Seishin. He should've trusted more in Korti. Solais would never do anything against her sister's wishes.

With the tension broken, Donnic stepped forward and flashed the pirate captain a toothy grin. "Admit it, we're growing on you."

Solais eyed him back dubiously. "Don't press your luck."

24
THE IRON SHIP

"You don't like what I serve, then no bacon for you!"

Cloud soared low over the coastline as he neared the remains of Kaniron. Though not quite sundown, the ash-filled sky obscured the light, helping to hide his clandestine approach. Thick smoke rose from what was left of the volcano, even as thin streams of lava flowed down its sides. Half the city had disappeared, buried beneath hardened magma. The burnt-out skeletons of what once had been buildings made up the rest.

The sight made Cloud sick to his stomach. All this carnage seemed utterly insane to him. Yet, that had always been his experience with zealots. Folks like that were impossible to reason with, their belief systems lacking any basis in logic.

Cloud let out a heavy sigh. *There's just no fixing stupid,* he silently reminded himself.

Not long afterwards, Cloud drew within sight of the harbor. At first glance it appeared empty, but then he spotted a single ship.

Anchored a slight distance from the shore, something looked off about the vessel. He couldn't spot a single sail. What's more, instead of masts along the deck, there appeared to be a set of flaming smoke stacks.

That's an iron ship! The realization abruptly dawned on Cloud. He'd heard rumors of the Parthians building them, but had never actually seen one before.

Dropping down below the tree line, Cloud followed the curve of the harbor for a closer look. A dark grey, the hull definitely had to be made of iron. Also, much of the ship appeared to be underwater—all except for the smoke stacks, some hatches, and a central tower.

The tower in particular drew his attention. Inset within it sat a number of large glass windows. Over and above those a flat platform spread out across the top. Cloud observed a single figure marching back and forth along that platform.

That cinched it. They would need a carefully crafted plan if they were going to get the information they needed from this ship.

Bal wished they'd had more time to prepare as they sped through the water toward the iron ship. He supposed he should be thankful though. Without the bronze dragon, they wouldn't have even gotten this far. The speed and distance she could travel underwater made this hasty plan even remotely feasible.

The young lieutenant bent low against the dragon's back, holding tight as the water rushed past. Lined up just behind him, Donnie and Cyclone flattened themselves against the dragon's scales.

For this critical mission, they had chosen a three-pronged approach. The three of them had gone with the dragon based on their abilities to breathe underwater. Bal crafted a sealed astral armor with a large pocket of air along the back. Donnie wore a ring of underwater breathing. Cyclone shifted to his winged form which gave him water breathing abilities akin to the bronze dragon.

While the four of them raced toward the front of the ship, the others approached from the opposite direction. Cloud made up the last prong, keeping a watch from the ashen sky above.

Ruka came up from a healthy depth to stop just below the prow of the iron ship. This was where things got interesting.

Bal left the others behind as he swam to the hull. He followed upward and broke the surface. Placing both hands on the smooth iron hull, he focused on each gauntlet in turn.

Bal reformed the first one into a heat gauntlet like the one he used at the rebel keep. For the second one, he created an astral armor he'd never tried outside of training. As soon as the gauntlet formed on his hand, it adhered to the iron hull with a soft metallic *clunk*.

It worked! Bal thought with keen satisfaction. Unlike his other armors which bent light or gravity, this new armor radiated a magnetic field.

Pulling himself up out of the water, Bal reformed both his sabatons into magnetic armor as well. With both feet now firmly planted against the ship, he melted a tiny hole through the hull.

Giving it a few moments for the hole to cool, Bal put an eye up to it. Inside he spied what appeared to be a sink. A figure in white abruptly blocked his view.

Shifting about, Bal observed that the person wore a white hat. A moment later he spied a ladle in the person's hand.

Bal let out a soft sigh. By some stroke of luck, they had found the kitchen.

Behind him, Donnie, Cyclone, and Ruka, now in human form, surfaced. Bal signaled for them to wait as a plan formed in his mind.

Once again using his heat gauntlet, Bal made the hole slightly larger. He now had a clear view of the kitchen. Three cooks moved about a series of large pots hanging in a huge hearth.

A voice abruptly shouted through the kitchen door. "Is lunch ready yet?"

One of the cooks grumbled to the others, then shouted back, "Hold your horses. It'll be ready when it's ready!"

With the cooks all preoccupied, none of them noticed the hole in the hull. That played perfectly into Bal's plans.

Focusing his mind, he formed an ethereal crossbow and three accompanying bolts. Balancing the weapon between his magnetic arm and chest, Bal loaded it with his free hand. Carefully taking aim, he shot the bolts through the hole.

The first two hit their marks with nary a sound and disappeared. The last one, however, proved more difficult. The one cook moved about so frantically, that Bal had a hard time targeting him. Finally, after reconjuring two extra bolts, Bal managed to tag his mark.

With all the bolts embedded, Bal now began to widen the hole. He nearly had it big enough to fit through when one of the cooks finally noticed him.

"What the…" the cook cried. He never got to finish his sentence.

Bal pushed with his mind at all the bolts simultaneously. As one, they turned solid, causing all three cooks to double over in pain.

"Help!" Bal hissed over his shoulder as he leapt through the hole and into the ship. Cyclone flew in almost immediately after him, followed shortly thereafter by Ruka and Donnie.

In a matter of seconds, it was all over. They stowed the bodies in an adjoining meat locker, then Donnie, Cyclone, and Ruka all dressed up as cooks.

As Bal switched to his light-bending armor, footsteps suddenly sounded outside the door. A voice cried through it, "Come on already, what's taking so long?"

Not missing a beat, Donnie yelled back in a gruff voice, "Stop your complaining. I told you, it'll be ready when it's ready!"

Thea held more than a few reservations as their group hurtled toward the iron ship. The plan in and of itself didn't worry her. Their three-pronged approach definitely held strategic merit. In addition, each group had taken appropriate steps to camouflage themselves.

Cloud flew above the ash-filled sky. Ruka took the second group underwater. Thea and the rest of them approached on the flying carpet, surrounded by an illusion that made them appear to be a flock of seagulls. Even so, there were too many unknowns.

First, they had no idea of the crew size aboard that ship. Second, what kind of weaponry did they carry? Third, Bal and Seishin had only just recovered. Seishin in particular nearly died. Though she'd stressed to him how foolish he'd been, she was just as certain it hadn't sunk in.

A sharp elbow in her side roused her from those troubling thoughts. "Wake up, sis. We're nearly in range," Pallas hissed in her ear.

Thea instinctively elbowed him back. "I wasn't asleep, you dolt."

"Could have fooled me," Pallas retorted, his eyes dancing with amusement.

Elladan's illusion could only get them so close. The nearer they drew, the more likely the sentry atop the tower would notice it was fake. Thus, it fell upon her to distract the guard.

Pulling in her will, Thea traced a swift symbol through the air. Mana poured into the pattern, filling it as she went. Once the symbol had been completed, she invoked the spell with a single word.

"Nebula."

A swirl of mist rose from nowhere atop the tower. It quickly billowed into a thick bank of fog, effectively shrouding the sentry within.

"Nicely done!" Elladan complemented her.

Feeling rather pleased with herself, Thea beamed back at him.

"Sure, until he alerts the others," Pallas drawled like the voice of doom.

"Maybe not," Seishin chimed in, pointing up into the sky.

Thea followed his gaze to see a figure on a flying board swooping down at an incredible rate. A black blade firmly gripped in both hands, the figure zoomed into the bank and whooshed out the other side a few moments later. Banking around, the skyrider gave them a quick salute, then shot back up toward the ash-filled sky.

Elladan glanced over his shoulder, that familiar half-smile adorning his lips. "Problem solved."

"For now," Pallas begrudgingly agreed.

While Thea understood her brother's concerns, his grim attitude wasn't helping matters. Still, Pallas was Pallas, and there was no changing him—unless your name was Alys, of course.

Skirting over the back of the ship, Elladan brought the carpet up even with the top of the tower. Taking them to the edge of the fog, he stopped them there and hovered.

Thea rose to her feet and with a sweeping motion dispelled the thick bank. As the cloud dissipated, she involuntarily blanched. Cloud had neatly severed the sentry in two. Though not the first dead body she'd seen, Thea disdained death in all its forms.

It is a necessary part of the wheel, she reminded herself. Life to death and death to life in a never-ending cycle of creation.

Landing atop the tower, the four of them disembarked. A round hatch protruded from the top of the tower. A small-spoked wheel sat atop the hatch.

Following their predetermined plan, Elladan magically masked himself in the guise of a Parthian officer. Now garbed all in red, his outfit vaguely resembled a Penwick uniform, though far gaudier.

While Elladan disguised himself, Pallas drew forth his spirit and faded into the shadows. When they were both done, Seishin spun the wheel on the hatch until they heard a soft click. The gold armored warrior then lifted the lid and stepped back out of the way.

Light filtered upward from inside the ship. Thea took a peek within. A tall ladder led down to the floor below. Two men stood before a long console that stretched the full length of the wide windows.

All of a sudden, one of the men pointed out the window. "Look, there's a ship!"

Lifting her gaze, Thea saw a three-masted ship with wide white sails entering the harbor. Though hard to tell from this distance, it had to be the *Black Cat.*

Thea inwardly cringed. The *Black Cat* was supposed to pick them up once they took over the iron ship. Unfortunately, they had timed their arrival just a bit too soon.

They needed to do something fast, before those sailors alerted the rest of the ship. With its tough iron hull, Thea doubted that even the swift *Black Cat* could win in a one on one fight with the Parthian vessel.

Elladan abruptly drew up next to her. "Play prisoner," he whispered in her ear.

With immediate understanding, Thea drew her blade, handed it to Elladan, then climbed down the ladder.

Parthian officer Elladan followed right after her, calling down into the tower, "Look at what I caught skulking about outside!"

Both sailors spun about, their eyes widening as they fell upon her. Thea stopped at the bottom of the ladder and looked herself over. *Is there something wrong with my outfit?*

She then noticed both men's eyes straying towards places where they shouldn't. *Oh,* it dawned on her. *They like my outfit just a bit too much.*

Feeling embarrassed, Thea's first instinct was to cover herself. Yet with so much at stake, she couldn't afford to let this opportunity go to waste. Steeling herself, she lifted her arms and feigned a vacuous voice. "Fine, you caught me fair and square. Now whatever are you going to do with me?"

Appearing thoroughly enamored, both sailors came forth and surrounded her on either side. "Wherever did you find this one?" One of them asked Elladan.

"She's probably from that ship," the other one answered, still staring hard at her.

Though she had been playing along, the sailor's proximity made Thea feel very uncomfortable. She regretted at that point handing her sword over to Elladan.

Luckily, Elladan recognized her discomfort. He barked at the men in an authoritative tone, "Stop ogling the prisoner and alert the captain already!"

"Yes, Sir!" Both men snapped to attention, saluted him, then spun about.

Thea felt a mixture of relief and confusion at the same time. Though she appreciated that those sailors were no longer on top of her, weren't they trying to avoid alerting the rest of the ship?

At that moment, a figure appeared out of the shadows and cut down one of the sailors before he knew what hit him. At the same time Elladan threw Thea her sword. Instinctively catching it, she lunged forward and in one smooth motion skewered the second sailor before he could utter a cry. With both men down, the tower was now clear.

Thea breathed a sigh of relief. "Well, that was cutting it just a bit too close."

Pallas sheathed his sword and fixed her with a mocking stare.

"Now whatever are you going to do with me?" he repeated her words in a falsetto voice.

Thea folded her arms across her chest and glowered at him. "Hey, if you think you can do better, next time you play the damsel."

Seishin reached the bottom of the ladder and nodded toward the downed sailors. "It seemed effective to me."

Thea gave him a grateful smile. "Thank you, Seishin."

She then turned her gaze upon Elladan. "What, no comments from you?"

The elf, however, seemed fixated on the downed men. Without looking at her, he held up two fingers about an inch apart. "I was this close to gouging their eyes out."

Taken by surprise, his words sent a feeling of warmth flooding throughout Thea's body. "Good answer," she said emphatically, her gaze softening as she peered at him with renewed interest.

As the door swung open, Donnie grabbed the first thing in sight—a serving tray filled with bacon and a frying pan. A man in a gaudy red uniform stood there in the doorway gaping at him. "Who in the hell are you?"

No stranger to awkward situations, Donnie instinctively acted indignant. "You don't like what I serve, then no bacon for you!"

His outrageous claim caught the Parthian sailor off guard. Before he could recover, Donnie lashed out with the frying pan and conked him in the head. The sailor dropped like a sack of potatoes, out cold before he hit the floor.

Donnie stared appreciatively at the pan in his hand. "This thing comes in pretty handy."

Behind them, water had started to splash in from cresting waves within the harbor. The more water that poured in, the more the ship tilted toward the prow.

Ruka stared pointedly at the fast growing pool beneath the hole. "That doesn't look too good."

Ruka was right. Before long, the entire kitchen would be flooded. Bal had disappeared from sight, but Donnie assumed he hadn't left the kitchen without them. He directed his words toward the empty space next to Ruka. "Maybe you should have cut the hole a bit higher?"

"Next time one of you can do the honors," Bal's disembodied voice answered from the opposite side of Cyclone.

Donnie swung his gaze toward the voice and shrugged. "Fair point."

"Can we get out of here already?" Cyclone asked impatiently as the water started to pour through in earnest.

The three of them each grabbed a tray and briskly strode out through the door. They entered a large room with four long tables. The two nearest were occupied by over a dozen soldiers, eagerly awaiting their next meal. All heads turned towards them as they walked out of the kitchen, but a number of the men focused their gaze on Ruka.

Donnie found the attention she drew quite disconcerting. *You would think these fellows had never seen a girl before.* He would never admit that somewhere deep inside it had sparked just a tinge of jealousy.

Things from there only got worse. As Ruka walked by, a few of the sailors whistled. One called out as she bent and set the tray down on the table. "Hey, good looking, you new around here?"

In typical fashion, Ruka's response was heavily laced with sarcasm. "Been here the entire trip. Maybe you should get your eyes checked."

A round of laughter sprang up around the table at the ill-mannered sailor's expense. Had it ended there, things might have been fine. Unfortunately, at that moment, the sailor next to Ruka took it upon himself to reach over and pinch her butt.

Caught completely by surprise, Ruka jumped up and yelped.

An unabiding anger swept over Donnie. He started for the sailor, but didn't quite reach him in time.

Ruka's eyes suddenly flashed a bright yellow. A moment later, a sphere of electricity burst from her body in all directions. Nearly every sailor at both tables shuddered violently, then fell to the floor.

Donnie just barely dodged out of the way in time. Rising back to his feet, he saw that only two officers had survived Ruka's onslaught.

Cyclone swiftly silenced the first. As the second drew his sword, Donnie took the pan still in his hand and threw it at him. It caught the officer in the side of the skull causing him to collapse in a heap.

Donnie stared at the pan admiringly. "That thing really is useful."

Suddenly remembering Ruka's outburst, Donnie ran over toward her. Cyclone intercepted him though, holding up his hand in warning. "You might not want to do that."

Donnie stopped and took a closer look at the teen. Ruka stood frozen in place, arcs of electricity still playing across her body. Much as he yearned to comfort her, had he touched Ruka, he would have been fried.

Cyclone turned to face the teen, his voice smooth and calm. "Take deep breaths. Remember, you're in control."

Ruka turned her head just enough to look at the hunter. Her brow furrowed into deep creases as she concentrated and repeated his words. "I'm in control. I'm in control."

Each time she spoke, the arcs around her body lessened until they completely subsided. Once they were gone, the rigidness in her body faded. She swept her eyes around the room, a sheepish grin spread upon her face. "Guess I did all that?"

"They had it coming," Cyclone assured her.

Donnie felt utter amazement at the way the hunter handled Ruka's outburst. He appeared to be a better partner for her than Donnie had ever been. If that were so though, then why did he still feel so miserable about rejecting her?

Bal's disembodied voice interrupted his glum reflections. "Um, guys, we might want to get moving."

Back behind them, water had started to flow into the dining hall from the entrance to the kitchen. Donnie also observed that the ship had started to list noticeably towards the prow.

At the same time, voices wafted in through the doorway at the other end of the dining hall. "What's going on? Why are we sinking?"

Elladan considered himself quite worldly. He'd seen more than his share of the seedier side of life throughout his travels up and down central Thac. Thus, he was no stranger to men leering at a good-looking woman.

Yet this time felt different. When the two Parthians surrounded Thea gawking at her obvious attributes, an anger swelled up inside Elladan that he never knew existed. He literally wanted to grab both men and ring them by their throats.

Luckily, he had sense enough to let Pallas and Thea handle things themselves. Much as he would like to have defended her honor, deep down inside he knew she was far more capable of doing so than he.

With the two sailors out of the way, they'd bought the *Black Cat* some time. Nonetheless, to find what they came for they needed to progress further into the ship.

Another hatch like the one above stood in the floor of this tower. "Let me open it," Elladan suggested, motioning at his outfit. "I'm kind of dressed the part."

"Good idea," Pallas agreed. "I'll get ready, just in case." A moment later, he faded back into the shadows.

Elladan positioned himself over the hatch as Seishin unsealed it and pulled it open. As the lid rose, it revealed another ladder leading down to a room similar to this one. A trio of sailors came into view, all of whom looked upward at the sound of the opening hatch.

An experienced performer, Elladan instantly fell into character. His hands folded behind his back, he glared down at the sailors and barked at them, "Attention!"

The trio of Parthians snapped to attention without question.

"Who's in charge of this ship?" Elladan bellowed, continuing to play his role.

A hint of bewilderment crossed all three sailors' faces. Before any of them could answer, however, Pallas slipped from the shadows and cleaved one straight through.

The other sailors fell back in horror, crying out as they went for their swords. "Intruders!"

Elladan watched in amazement as Thea leapt through the hatch and landed in a crouch beside her brother. Almost as agile, Seishin scurried down after her, leaping off to one side as soon as he cleared the hatch. Two more sailors joined the fight against the twin spiritblades and the Shin Tauri warrior, but one fell almost immediately to Thea's blade.

As the battle moved away from the ladder, Elladan started down after them. That was when he first noticed the ship listing a bit toward the prow.

Must be taking on water, he reasoned. *Probably Balthazar's handiwork.*

Their original plan had been to capture the ship, but Elladan figured the others must have a good reason for wanting to sink it. The harbor here was probably shallow enough to salvage what they needed from the sea floor.

Spying the ship's wheel in the front of this room an idea began to form in Elladan's mind. Another sailor fell as he reached the base of the ladder. Seeing things were well in hand, he darted over and grabbed the wheel.

A console with multiple tubes and switches stood next to him. Elladan tentatively pushed the center switch. The ship started to move as it glided forward.

Behind him, the last sailor fell. With the ship picking up speed and the others in no imminent danger, Elladan called a warning over his shoulder, "Hang on!"

"What are you…" Pallas started to yell back. He never got the chance to finish.

Elladan swung the wheel hard to port. The ship responded far faster than he expected, tilting wildly as it made the hard turn. He hung on desperately as the others grabbed whatever they could to avoid being thrown into the walls.

"What in Thac was that for?" Pallas screamed as the ship righted itself.

Before Elladan had a chance to answer, shouts erupted from the tubes next to him. "What's going on up there? Why are we moving?"

Elladan exchanged a guilty glance with Pallas as he cried back into the tubes. "We're taking on water! Abandon ship!"

The voices from the tubes almost immediately echoed his panic. "Abandon ship! Abandon ship!"

Thea gave Elladan a begrudging smile, then elbowed Pallas in the side. "Pretty smart, wouldn't you say brother?"

Pallas responded with a noncommittal shrug. "Sure, if you want to sink this thing."

Elladan turned from the wheel and gave Pallas one of his patented half-smiles. "I thought that was the idea?"

Before Pallas could answer, three more soldiers burst through a metal door at the back of the room. As the three warriors lined up to meet them, a commanding voice boomed through one of the tubes. "Wheel room, why are we moving? Put on Lieutenant Storag!"

Improvising on the spot, Elladan cried back, "Sorry, sir, he abandoned his post."

Immediately wincing at his lame response, Elladan waited to be chewed out by the voice on the other side. The expected shout never came though.

A few moments later, the ship shuddered and started to rise upward. The sudden rise was accompanied by a loud clunking sound from somewhere far below.

25
FIRE IN THE HOLE

Behind him a column of flame shot out of the hatch up into the sky.

Cloud circled high in the ash-filled sky watching for any signs of trouble. The sky itself was strangely devoid of the fire-birds that had frequented this place only a day or so ago. Many had probably been killed in the epic blast that leveled the city and the volcano. With their home all but destroyed perhaps the remaining birds had migrated somewhere else. Where that could be though, he had no clue.

Cloud had caught sight of the *Black Cat* as it entered the harbor a few minutes ago. Other than that, all seemed quiet. The Parthian ship appeared to be ignoring the approach of the pirate vessel.

All of a sudden, the iron ship began to move. It picked up speed and then turned hard to port. As it did so, water poured profusely through the hole Bal had made in the prow. In response, the front of the ship sank lower into the bay.

Just as suddenly, the ship rose sharply out of the water. It was as if it had lost a ton of weight in an instant. Moments later, two deck hatches popped open. A pair of iron golems climbed out and parked themselves squarely on the metallic deck.

Both golems were fierce looking creatures. Nearly twice as tall as a human, their broad shoulders were almost half as wide as their height. A great iron head sat squarely upon each torso, inset with two eerily glowing eyes. The massive shoulders supported thick, grey arms that hung to their knees, ending in hands the size of boulders.

One golem was bad enough, but two along with an entire ship's crew might be more than his companions could handle. A sudden idea popped into Cloud's mind. Pulling Ragnarök from the sheath on his back, he addressed the sword with his mind.

Is there any way you ice the deck?

After a short pause, the sword responded. *Fly down there and point me at it.*

Following the sword's request, Cloud banked and dove down towards the iron ship. At first the golems didn't seem to notice him. When he drew within a few dozen yards or so, however, their eerie glowing eyes turned his way.

Cloud felt a moment's trepidation as those empty eyes locked upon him, but he immediately brushed it aside. Strafing just out of reach of those long arms, Cloud pointed Ragnarök at the deck.

A stream of ice sprayed from the tip of the sword, coating the deck beneath the golems with a gleaming sheet of ice. As Cloud pulled up, both golems lost their footing and fell to the deck, then slipped off the ship into the waters below.

Nicely done, Cloud praised the sword.

I do my best, Ragnarök responded, its thoughts tinged with a light touch of pride.

Ruka felt pissed—more so at herself than at the idiot that placed a hand on her posterior. He had gotten what he deserved. The fact that she had lost control again is what really bothered her. It had taken all her will to stop the electricity from lashing out yet a second time.

Ruka supposed she should be thankful for being able to stop at all. Her training with Ves and Cyclone had paid off in that regard. As an added benefit she got to see the concern in Donnie's eyes. Troll that he was for returning her blade, at least he still seemed to care about her somewhat.

A sudden thrumming in the floor beneath them interrupted her ill-tempered musings. Donnie stopped at the door to the hall and turned back to face them. "Is it me, or is the ship moving?"

Unable to resist herself, Ruka responded with a smart remark. "Yes, to both."

Donnie gave her a sour look, but any reply he might have had died on his lips as the ship made a hard turn. They all grabbed onto something as the floor tilted at a crazy angle.

"What in the heck is going on up there?" Donnie cried as he wedged himself into the door frame.

Ruka had started to wonder the same thing. The plan had been for the rest of them to commandeer the ship's wheel. Could something have happened to the others?

She instantly rejected the thought. *No way. Not between Thea, her brother, and that new guy who went toe to toe with a fire god.*

As the floor righted itself, a panicky voice blared from a tube embedded into the wall. "We're sinking! Abandon ship!"

Another group of equally frightened voices sounded off just moments later. "Abandon ship! Abandon ship!"

Donnie's eyes went wide as they met Ruka's. "That first one sounded just like Elladan."

"And that surprises you?" Ruka grunted. The elven bard had a knack for causing chaos wherever he went.

Donnie let out a soft sigh. "No, I suppose not."

Out in the hallway, they could hear more shouts. Sailors filed out of doorways and side passages, all headed further down the corridor. Donnie motioned for the others to follow as he fell in behind them.

All of a sudden, the floor moved again—this time rising up and nearly knocking them off their feet. At the same time, a loud *clunk* echoed through the ship from somewhere below.

"Well, that doesn't sound good," Donnie remarked as he struggled to maintain his balance.

"It could be worse," Ruka countered as she too fought to stay on her feet. "We could be headed in the opposite direction."

"Point taken," the elf replied with a begrudging smile.

Those ahead of them who had fallen scrambled to their feet and plowed ahead with renewed urgency. A short distance further down the corridor they came to the frame of a thick steel door. Beyond that doorway, a mass of sailors clambered around the base of a metal spiral staircase leading upward

"Hurry up! Abandon ship!" Folks cried as they struggled with each other to get to the stairs. Unfortunately, only a trickle made it through as the rest continued to jostle each other.

Ruka quickly lost patience. "This is ridiculous."

"I could clear us a path," Cyclone offered, reaching for the long pole axe strapped to his back.

Much as she had come to like the hunter, his answer to everything tended to be a bloody one. This situation required a more elegant solution. She held up a staying hand. "Nah, I've got a better idea."

Drawing her short sword, she leveled it at the crowd and fired off a charge of lightning. The bolt cascaded through the close-packed throng, catching over a dozen sailors at once. The unsuspecting Parthians shuddered and dropped to the floor, still spasming from the shock.

The few still left standing turned to stare at her incredulously. Outraged cries sprang from the lips of the foremost as they drew weapons.

"Who the hell are you?"

"What do you think you're doing?"

"You'll pay for that!"

Donnie and Cyclone drew weapons as well and the three of them moved forth to engage in battle.

An eerie feeling came over Bal as the floor of the ship rose up to meet them. His senses screamed at the accompanying *clunk* that echoed up from below the vessel.

Having learned long ago to trust his instincts, Bal turned back the way they came. He felt a momentary pang of guilt for leaving the others behind, but summarily dismissed it. Donnie, Cyclone, and Ruka had all proven they could handle themselves.

Bal found the floor drenched when he reached the dining hall. Two feet or more of water filled the kitchen beyond, but since the ship had risen the bay stopped pouring through the hole.

Wading across the waterlogged kitchen, Bal reached the hole and poked his head outside. Down below the waterline a dark shadow moved slowly from beneath the ship.

Something about the shape made Bal cringe. Again trusting his inner senses, he quickly shifted to underwater armor and dove out into the bay below.

After breaching the surface, Bal got a better look at the dark shadow. It appeared to be a smaller version of the ship he had just left behind. This iron vessel, however, appeared to be able to travel beneath the water.

As Bal drew closer, lights flared on at various points around the ship. It also appeared to be picking up speed.

His body tingling with a sense of urgency, Bal swam as fast as he could to catch up. Still, it was pulling away too fast. He knew he'd never reach it in time.

Taking a chance, Bal shifted the outer pieces of his armor to be weightless. With the added strength he shot forward coming within arm's length of the receding ship.

Nevertheless, it was still not enough. As the vessel inched beyond his reach, Bal refocused his will one more time. Changing his gauntlets to magnetic armor, he prayed that the attraction would make up the last few needed feet.

By the luck of the gods, it worked! Bal felt himself yanked forward even as the ship beneath him pulled away. Moments later his gauntlets struck the vessel's hull with a muffled *thump*.

Bal let out a heavy sigh. He had caught hold of the underwater ship. The question was where were they taking him?

Cloud watched with growing curiosity as the iron ship bobbed up out of the water. Moments ago, it had been clearly sinking. He wondered what sort of magic it would take to counteract the weight of the water the ship had already taken on. His musings were cut short, however, as a large group of Parthians climbed out of the hatches up and onto the deck.

Many of those sailors slipped on the icy patches he had sprayed across the top of the ship. Still others managed to hang on.

Cloud considered strafing the stragglers when two more large hatches popped open farther down the deck. Another pair of iron golems climbed out of them beyond the area he had iced.

Ready for another round? Cloud asked Ragnarök.

Always, the black sword responded eagerly.

Once again plunging down from the skies, Cloud swept the entire ship starting at the end with the sailors. Ice sprayed from the tip of his blade adding to the sheet already there. His efforts were rewarded as more Parthians slipped and fell into the waiting waters below.

When he reached the end with the golems, however, something strange happened. As the creatures began to slip, bright sparks appeared beneath their feet. With an audible *thunk* both golems adhered to the deck.

Pulling up and banking around Cloud resolutely addressed the black blade. *Guess we'll have to do this the hard way.*

Isn't that just too bad? Ragnarök responded, not sounding disappointed in the slightest.

Back beneath the ship's tower, the wheel in Elladan's hands suddenly became unresponsive. Furthermore, the ship itself began to slow down.

Pallas leaned over his shoulder and whispered in Elladan's ear, "I think they're on to you," with perhaps a bit more glee than the situation warranted.

"Well, you don't have to sound so happy about it," Elladan murmured back at him.

A harsh voice through one of the tubes drowned out Pallas' subsequent snicker. "Stay where you are infidels. You'll burn in hell for what you've done."

"Now what?" Seishin muttered anxiously under his breath.

Elladan placed a hand over the tube and winked at the dour warrior. "Don't give up just yet." Swiftly adopting an officious persona, he uncovered the tube and spoke into it. "This is Lieutenant Storag. The intruders have left the wheel room."

There was a momentary pause before the harsh voice responded. "You're not Storag. Surrender now."

Thea met his gaze with an arched eyebrow. "Guess we're done here."

"Guess so," Elladan responded with one of his half-smiles.

Elladan led the way as they went through the door leading further into the ship. They followed it down a short corridor where it opened into a wide chamber.

A spiral staircase stood in the center of that room. Elladan held a staying hand out in front of the other as he spied a group of Parthian sailors clambering up from down below. Most of them ignored him and his friends, climbing to an upper hatch and exiting through it into the open air beyond.

One sailor in particular caught sight of Elladan and halted. "Watch out! There are intruders down below." The sailor's eyes abruptly went wide as they fell on Elladan's comrades.

"More intruders!" the sailor wailed, causing others on the stairs to stop and stare at them.

"Here we go again," Thea observed wryly as she, Pallas, and Seishin waded into battle.

While Ruka and Cyclone took on officers with large swords, Donnie faced a guy with a double-bladed axe. Under normal circumstances, he would just outmaneuver his opponent until he could find an opening. Unfortunately, there was not a lot of room to move around in this chamber, especially with Cyclone and Ruka fighting on either side of him.

To top it off, this guy seemed very proficient with that axe. He spun it around deftly to either side, blocking all Donnie's attempts to get past his guard. It was all he could do to avoid the counters the sailor threw at him. Only his nimbleness and longer blade kept Donnie from being sliced a number of times.

The sailor launched a particularly nasty offensive at him when all of a sudden, a puddle of black liquid appeared beneath his feet. Unable to maintain his balance, the sailor fell unceremoniously onto his rump.

Seeing his chance, Donnie slid in and skewered the sailor with his blade. When it was over, he cast a glance up the spiral staircase.

Elladan stared back down at him, an all too familiar half-smile on the elf's lips. Donnie gave his friend a quick salute, then returned his attention to the other two battles still going on.

The officer facing Cyclone wielded a great flaming sword for all the good it did him. Thinking to intimidate the hunter, he tried to shove the flames in Cyclone's face. That was his last mistake.

With total disregard for his own safety, Cyclone ducked just beneath the blade, singing himself as he did so. In one swift motion, he brought his long-poled axe around and cleaved the officer straight in two.

The officer facing Ruka fared little better. He struck her multiple times with his great sword, but the dragon teen shrugged off each blow as if it meant nothing. Completely frustrated, the officer hauled back and tried to bring the blade down upon her head.

Ruka caught the blade with a single hand and ripped it from the officer's grasp. She then stepped forward and grabbed the guy by the collar. Lifting him up off the deck, he dangled there his face a mask of terror.

"Don't kill that one!" Cyclone cried out to her.

Ruka met his gaze, then shrugged. Sparks formed around her body and traveled up her arm to the man she held aloft. His entire body shuddered until he went limp.

She dropped him to the deck like a sack of potatoes and stared at Cyclone with a thin smirk. "Satisfied?"

Cyclone merely grunted, then turned to growl at a group of Parthians lined up down the hall. "Everybody drop your weapons or this will happen to you."

Donnie looked closely at the line of sailors. None appeared to be soldiers. Most were dressed like craftsmen and carried wrenches. One of them appeared to be a janitor with a mop. Their faces filled with sheer terror, they all dropped whatever they were holding to the floor.

Hearing footsteps on the stairs above them, Donnie looked up to see Pallas. The Penwick sailor called down to the cowering crew, "Where's the engine room?"

One of the crew slowly raised his hand and pointed back the way they came. Reaching the bottom of the spiral staircase, Pallas strode up to the man. "Can you show us?"

Before the sailor had a chance to answer, a voice echoed from a tube in the wall. "60…59…58…57…"

A chill went up Donnie's spine. That sounded like a countdown. In his experience, such things never indicated anything good.

His gut feeling was immediately justified by the crew's reaction. As one they started to panic and tried to run past Cyclone and Pallas towards the stairs. The officer and the hunter blocked their way.

"What's going on?" Pallas demanded.

The craftsman he had been talking to stammered, "The—the ship is about to be flooded with flames! We need to get out of here."

Pallas exchanged a brief glance with Cyclone then stepped out of the way. He waved to the crew and bellowed, "Everybody out!"

As the line of crewmen barreled up the stairs, Ruka shifted into a tiny hummingbird and flew up past them. As the last of the crew raced up the stairs, Donnie, Pallas, and Cyclone fell in behind.

"25…24…23…22…"

Elladan, Thea, and Seishin waited for them on the next floor. Elladan grabbed Donnie by the shoulder. "What in Thac is going on?"

"We've got to get out of here or we'll all be toast!" Donnie cried.

They raced up the stairs as the last crew member made it through the hatch. All of a sudden, a figure holding a shield blocked the entrance.

Before anyone else could react, Ruka shot the sailor with a lightning bolt. The Parthian shuddered from the blast and fell back out of the way.

"15…14…13…12…"

Donnie's heart skipped a bit. There was hardly any time left for them to escape.

Behind them Pallas shouted up the stairs. "You guys go ahead! I'll be fine."

"Same here!" Seishin yelled from the very rear.

"You guys are crazy!" Ruka shouted back at them.

"Get out of here!" Cyclone insisted from just behind Donnie.

Ahead of them all, Thea paused a moment and pulled the amulet from around her neck. She tossed it to Cyclone then scrambled up the hatch with Elladan right behind.

Muttering under her breath about "stupid barbarians," Ruka shifted to humming bird form again and flew up past them.

"3…2…1…"

Scrambling up last, Donnie just made it to the hatch when he heard the roar of flames from below. Feeling the intense heat, he dove through the hatch and up onto the deck. Behind him a column of flame shot out of the hatch up into the sky.

"5…"

As the others scrambled up the staircase, Seishin spoke to the armor. *Can you make me immune to fire?*

"4…3…"

To a degree, Flandril answered.

"2…"

Do it! Seishin commanded having no time to waste.

Above him Cyclone threw the amulet over his neck and Pallas drew upon his spirit.

"1…"

Seishin felt only slightly lightheaded as the armor drained his own spirit. It was none too soon though as flames shot up from the staircase below. The fire filled the entire chamber, burning so bright that Seishin had to shield his eyes.

A few seconds passed when Seishin started to feel the heat. Worried, he again spoke to the armor. *How are we doing?*

Surprisingly, well, Flandril answered. *Though I'm not sure how much more of this I can take.*

Seishin prayed that it would be enough. The young warrior began to sweat when the flames finally subsided. Above him Pallas and Cyclone still stood. Smoke rose from both their clothes and the tips of the hair appeared slightly singed, but otherwise they appeared to be okay.

Brushing himself off, Pallas looked up and down at the both of them. "We need to get to the engine room. If we cut the power, they can't pull something like that again."

Cyclone assented. "Good idea. Just one problem."

"What is that?" Seishin asked. From his understanding, Pallas was a ship's captain back home. What could the hunter possibly know that Pallas would not?

"Where's Balthazar?" Cyclone asked simply.

Pallas stopped, deep creases forming along his brow. "That's a damn good question. Last time I saw him was when we first entered the ship."

Seishin decided to ask the armor. *Can you locate Balthazar?*

After a slight pause, Flandril answered. *The entity of which you speak is not anywhere on this vessel.*

That answer caught Seishin by surprise. He relayed it to the others.

"Then where in the hell could he be?" Cyclone swore.

Seishin was surprised to see the hunter show concern about someone else. Then again, he had gone out of his way to save their lives when the bird god exploded.

"What if you go and find him?" Seishin suggested. "I'll help Pallas with the engines."

"Fine," Cyclone agreed.

The three of them charged down the stairs to the next level below. There they split up. Cyclone went back the way they entered the ship, while Seishin and Pallas headed in the direction the craftsman had pointed.

They passed a number of doors and side passages until they reached a thick steel door. Unfortunately, the door was locked.

Pallas tried it, but it wouldn't budge. Frustration clouded his face as he peered at Seishin. "You wouldn't have a can opener in there by any chance?"

"I can ask," Seishin responded.

Before he even asked, Flandril answered. *I can give you the strength to open the door.*

Surprised at the armor's proactive reply, Seishin graciously answered, *That would be most appreciated.*

After another drain on his spirit, Seishin felt a surge of strength through his limbs. Grabbing a hold of the door, he gave it a firm yank.

The groan of metal echoed down the hallway as he pulled on the door. Screeching in protest, the heavy steel door finally gave way, coming off at the hinges.

Carefully placing it off to one side, Seishin ushered Pallas forward. "After you."

Pallas arched an eyebrow at him. "That's what I call a serious can opener." The Penwick captain then charged through the open doorway with Seishin following close behind.

26

I AIN'T SAYING IT WAS ALIENS

*Bal found himself face-to-face with creatures he thought
only existed in nightmares.*

Thea wasn't worried about her brother. Pallas could handle a little fire. She imagined Seishin would be fine as well, although she prayed he didn't overdo it again using that golden armor. Her main concern revolved around Cyclone. She knew the hunter had some unique abilities, but wasn't quite sure whether he was immune to fire. That's why she tossed him her amulet before scrambling up atop the deck.

Unfortunately, in doing so they had jumped from the "frying pan" into the proverbial fire. Dozens of Parthian sailors now surrounded them atop the iron ship. Worse than that, two iron golems stood only a few dozen yards away. At the moment Cloud appeared to be keeping them occupied, but Thea had to wonder how long the skyrider could hold out against the pair of powerful creatures.

Spotting his plight, Ruka uttered a low growl. "Hold out here," she called to Thea. "I'm going to help Cloud."

The teen's body began to glow. It turned bright white as it expanded outward, a long neck and tail extended from the front and back. Large bat-like wings sprouted atop the bright glowing form. The ship's crew quickly back-pedaled away, watching in terror as the light faded and a bronze dragon now stood in their midst.

Ruka roared at the sailors, frightening them even further. She then lifted off with a great flap of her wings and swept just over their heads causing most of them to dive for the deck.

Ruka's intimidating tactics bought Thea some much needed time. They were surrounded by too many sailors to fight their way out of this. What they needed here was a more subtle approach.

Grabbing Donnie and Elladan by the arm, she murmured to them both. "I'm going to try something. Watch my back."

As she moved forward, Elladan grabbed her arm in turn. She half-turned and saw the profound concern within his eyes.

"What are you going to do?" he whispered.

Deeply touched, Thea placed a hand on his cheek, her lips twisting into a wry smile. "Why take a page from your book."

Elladan watched with utter bewilderment as she pulled away and took a few steps forward. In order for this to work, she needed to be as close to the center of the crowd as possible. Luckily, that wouldn't be a problem. With the dragon gone, the crew's fear dissipated and they closed in again around the trio.

Closing her mind to the impending threat, Thea pulled in her will. Focusing intently, she traced a pattern through the air, letting it fill with as much mana as possible.

"Incantare."

As the single word left her lips, the mana spread out from where she stood. It grew in an ever-widening circle, each person it touched stopping in their tracks. Thea waited until the mana reached the outmost sailors, and then she began to sing.

She was no Elladan, nor Alys for that matter, but she could carry a tune if need be. Plus, the spell made the quality of her voice irrelevant. The moment the melody left her lips, those in the circle became riveted to her song.

Well, almost all of them. A pair of sailors with gold epaulettes on their coats didn't quite succumb to her "charms."

The first one drew his sword and approached her, but Elladan stepped between them. The bard cast a quick spell bringing his hands together in a thunderous clap. The resulting soundwave knocked the officer off the ship and into the harbor waters below.

Donnie interposed himself between Thea and the second officer. Though a bit singed, the agile elf used the open deck to his advantage. The officer became so frustrated trying to keep up with him, that he eventually lunged just a bit too far and sent himself over the side.

Elladan clasped his friend on the shoulder, the two of them having a good laugh at the officer's expense. The bard then exchanged a glance with both her and Donnie.

I think we've worn out our welcome, he mouthed the words.

Reaching into his portal bag, Elladan pulled out the magic carpet. Briskly unfurling it, the rug rolled out and hovered there about a foot above the ship's deck.

Elladan climbed aboard and motioned for her and Donnie to join him. Still singing, Thea slowly strode over and stepped up next to the two elves. Elladan then invoked the carpet's magic and they rose high into the air. Once they were out of reach, Thea ended her song.

The crowd below shook their heads as if waking from a dream. Realization dawning upon them, they shook their fists and jeered at the hovering priestess.

A wide smile crossed Thea's face as she took a slight bow. "Thank you, thank you," she called to the irate sailors, throwing a kiss here and there to rub salt in the wound.

As they flew away, Elladan let out a raucous laugh. "Now that's what I call a captive audience."

Deep below the waterline, Bal clung on tight to the underwater vessel. Had he a moment to think, he would've marveled at the craftsmanship that went into building such a thing. He would also have worried about its potential as a threat to Lanfor. Sadly, he did not have the time for either.

Bal's primary concern at the moment was how long his magnetic armor would hold. The ship he clung to was picking up speed and he had never tested it under such strenuous conditions.

He was just debating whether to try and cut through the hull when a bright light flared out from the vessel right above him. Bal could see the shadow of a hatch as the light swung down toward where he crouched. Moving like a crab, he retreated away from the light towards the bottom of the ship.

Moments later, the light passed over where he had just been. The light flashed back and forth a few more times, then abruptly disappeared, the hatch closing behind it.

Bal breathed a sigh of relief. *Phew, that was close.*

He had been lucky indeed, but it irked him that whoever held that lamp knew just where to look. Bal could spy no windows in the side of the vessel, so how had they spotted him?

All of a sudden, the ship slowed down and rose up out of the water. Bal climbed back towards the top until he broke the surface.

A few hundred yards away he spied the *Black Cat*. He also observed that this ship was turning to face it. It was then that Bal noticed the huge cannon mounted to the tower atop this vessel. That cannon was now being trained on the *Black Cat*.

Bal couldn't even begin to imagine the destructive force behind something that huge. He needed to do something about it and quick, or the *Black Cat* would be soon sitting at the bottom of the bay.

With time of the essence, Bal climbed up to the hatch he had seen before. Spinning the wheel embedded into it, he heard a metallic *click*. Pulling the door open, Bal cautiously peered inside. A short wide corridor opened up before him. It was empty.

Stepping inside, Bal took a moment to shift to his light-bending armor. He then padded down to the end of the corridor. There he spied a steel door to his left and another hall on his right leading to a set of stairs. Wanting to get to the tower as fast as possible, Bal chose the stairs.

At the top he found another empty hall that curved around out of sight. Strange noises wafted down that corridor, sounding like a mixture of voices and beeps. A number of doors lined this hall, but none of them appeared to have a visible handle.

Bal went up to examine the closest one when the next door over abruptly swished open. A man in overalls walked out of the room fingering a pendant at his throat. He then turned and headed further down the hall. Listening to his intuition, Bal formed a crossbow and bolt as he fell in behind him.

The man in overalls stopped at the next door over and swiped the pendent over a buttoned panel next to it. In answer, the door swished open.

Well, that's interesting, Bal thought with growing wonder. The Parthians were not known for their innovation. He couldn't imagine that they were responsible for building this ship. Yet that left the question of who had?

Bal followed the man inside and took him down with the ethereal bolt. He then swiped the pendant and used it on the door. It swished back open as he suspected.

The whole ship around him now felt as if it were thrumming. Feeling a renewed sense of urgency, Bal followed the corridor in the direction of the strange noises.

The noises seemed to be emanating from a door just before the corridor curved back again. Using the pendant, Bal slid the door open.

Before him stood a huge viewport centered on the *Black Cat.* Below the viewport sat a long console with numerous buttons and lights across its length. Three large chairs sat in front of that console.

Bal could see the back of a Parthian officer sitting in the middle chair. The occupants of the other two chairs, however, caused him to freeze in place.

As the chairs spun about, Bal found himself face-to-face with creatures he thought only existed in nightmares. Two greyish humanoids peered back at him, each with a pair of large black eyes inset into their bulbous heads.

Zeta Reticulum? The word sent chills up Bal's spine.

Zeta Reticulum were supposed to be a myth—creatures from outer space that elders used to scare little children. Yet here were two of them staring Bal right in the face.

This is getting really annoying, Cloud griped to himself as banked around for another pass at the pair of golems. Despite their huge lumbering frames, those giant fists turned out to be incredibly fast. He'd almost gotten pummeled a number of times now. If one of those fists were to connect, he'd be toast.

Only the speed and agility of his board had saved him up until now. That and the fact that he'd chosen to go low at one of the golem's legs. Even so, it was taking far too long.

Ragnarök had done some serious damage, biting deep into the creature's thick leg joint, but it was taking too many passes. One careless move on Cloud's part, and he was sure to end up dead.

Out of nowhere, a huge bolt of lightning shot across the sky and slammed into the golem he'd been targeting. Arcs of electricity danced across its iron torso as thunder rolled through the salty air.

Cloud had been so focused on his singular target that he hadn't seen Ruka's approach. Luckily, the dragon was on his side. Even better, her electrical attack had messed with the golem's innards.

Taking full advantage of the fact, Cloud dove straight for the golem's bad leg and loosed Ragnarök upon it. With one great swipe, the black blade sliced straight through what was left of the golem's joint.

Balancing precariously on one leg, the golem teetered there for the briefest of moments. Despite being magnetized to the hull, the single leg was not enough. The golem fell over and clattering against the hull before sliding off into the harbor waters with a huge splash.

Now that's more like it, Cloud thought to himself, feeling a keen sense of satisfaction after all the trouble the golem had given him. His revelry was cut short, however, when he spied another ship breaking the water's surface a short distance away.

Cloud squinted at the new ship. It looked like a smaller version of this one except for the rather large cannon sticking out from its central tower. As disturbing as that might be, it became even more alarming when the ship turned to train that gun on the *Black Cat*.

I'm no expert, but if I had to guess, I'd bet one shot from that gun would probably put a hole clear through a wooden ship, Cloud reckoned to himself.

Then we should probably do something about that, Ragnarök answered him unsolicited.

Probably, Cloud agreed.

Spinning his board about he called out to Ruka. "Looks like the Black Cat might be in trouble."

"Go ahead," she cried back. "I've got this last one."

With a firm nod, Cloud banked around again and leaned forward as he headed at top speed toward the gunship.

Cyclone moved quickly through the ship following the trail back to the kitchen. As the golden armor had warned them, there was no sign of Balthazar along the way.

From a strategic standpoint, the Lanfor lieutenant was an extremely useful ally. They would never have gotten into that vault without him. Further, it was Bal who forced the bird god back to its home plane.

Cyclone also appreciated that he hadn't made a big stink about summoning Ruka. Aside from his respect for the lieutenant, he'd actually come to like him.

Slogging through the two feet of water that still flooded the kitchen, the hunter stuck his head through the hole they'd originally made in the hull. Again, there was no sign of Bal, but he did hear fighting from the deck above.

Across the harbor, Cyclone saw a ship that looked like the *Black Cat.* Between here and there floated another ship that looked similar to this one, except for the huge cannon sticking out from its top tower.

Climbing up into the hole, Cyclone braced himself and peered upward. He was just in time to see Cloud sail overhead, the gnome speeding across the skies towards the strange looking gunship. At the same time, Cyclone heard a roar from above.

He knew that roar. *That was Ruka.*

The dragon hunter launched himself upward and sailed through the air to land on the top deck. He instantly spied the bronze dragon bearing down on one of those iron golems.

He watched as a bolt of lightning leapt from the dragon's mouth. It caught the creature in the chest, cascading into smaller arcs all around its metal torso.

Very smart, Cyclone silently acknowledged. The electricity would slow the golem's movements and make it easier prey.

The deck here was slippery with ice, but Cyclone had a cure for that. Tapping into the rage within, he sprouted a set of bronze wings from his back. The hunter then hefted his halberd and took off towards the partially paralyzed creature.

Targeting its leg, Cyclone took a huge swing at the golem's knee. The axe swept through it from behind, partially severing the joint.

As the golem slowly turned towards its new adversary, Cyclone wound up and let loose with a devastating return swing. The second slice cut clean through the rest of the joint, severing the golem from its leg at the kneecap.

The hunter flitted out of the way as the golem teetered over and slammed into the deck with a metallic *clunk*. From there it slipped on the ice and slid into the waters around the iron ship.

"Good timing," Ruka greeted him.

Cyclone looked up to see the dragon hovering just overhead. He pointed off towards the weird looking gunship. "Any idea what's up with that thing?"

The dragon snorted. "Got me. Let's go find out."

Pallas was determined to get to the engine room. He'd studied the plans for the airships Penwick recently purchased. If this ship worked anything like those, then shutting down the engines would cut the power to the rest of the ship. That would stop them from flooding the ship with fire again or any other nasty traps of that sort.

The ship itself positively amazed him. The iron hull alone could probably withstand more damage than a magically protected wooden hull. The internal workings also seemed fascinating. The wheel console alone might take weeks to study.

Pallas imagined capturing the ship and bringing it home to Penwick. With his mother's ingenuity and the resources they had at hand, he was certain they could figure out this thing's secrets and even build some of their own. With it, Penwick would have no rivals anywhere along the coast of Thac.

His imaginings of grandeur came to an end when they reached the entrance to the engine room.

"Woah," Pallas gasped upon entering. A huge chamber, it easily spanned the width of the ship and stretched back an equal distance to the aft. A great circular central chamber dominated the room reaching all the way up to the ceiling. As Pallas surmised, it looked quite similar to the containment unit on an airship.

Those units housed the great wind elemental that generated the flight ring which propelled an airship. The major difference here, however, was the viewports in this unit shown a bright reddish orange. All things considered, Pallas bet that this unit contained a great fire elemental instead.

"You can say that again," Seishin agreed, sounding as awed as Pallas.

A half dozen people stood around the room. Most were in overalls, but two wore uniforms and were armed. One of the craftsmen stood at a console next to the circular chamber. He appeared to be talking into a pendant clasped around his neck.

As Pallas and Seishin stepped into the room, the soldiers drew their swords and advanced. They proved no match, however, for spiritblade and Shin Tauri training.

After the last soldier fell, the man holding the pendant turned his attention to them. He made a quick sign through the air and pointed a finger at Seishin.

Pallas instantly recognized it as a holding spell. Two crossed bands of blue light formed around Seishin. He froze in place for a brief moment, but just as suddenly the two bands shattered.

Pallas should have known a spell like that wouldn't work on a Shin Tauri. They typically only worked on weak-willed individuals, and one needed a strong will to harness the power of the spirit.

Seishin strode toward the craftsman who had tried to paralyze him. He looked quite intimidating in that golden armor.

"Stand down," he told the man with a dangerous edge to his voice, "or I will be forced to put you down."

The craftsman took a step or two backwards, then abruptly fell on a large lever on the side of the containment unit. His voice took on a fanatical tone as he screamed at Seishin, "Join me with Parthos in the flames!"

Seishin calmly walked up to the craftsman, hauled back, and decked him with a single blow. The man fell to the ground out cold.

Inside the containment unit, the flames appeared to be growing stronger. Sweeping past Seishin, Pallas pushed the large lever in the opposite direction. Sadly, it had no effect. The flames inside the unit continued to build.

Pallas spun about and barked at the rest of the craftsmen. "How do I stop this thing?"

One of the men pointed at the man Seishin had knocked out. "O—only the main engineer can stop it."

"Damn," Pallas swore. He'd hoped to capture this ship, but now they'd be lucky to get out of here alive.

The craftsman who answered him looked positively terrified. They all did, in fact.

Pallas addressed them in a sympathetic voice. "How much time do we have?"

The same man gulped, but forced himself to answer. "With—the containment field gone—the elementals will break free—within a matter of minutes."

"Elementals?" Pallas repeated incredulously. "As in more than one?" his voice rising an octave.

"Y-yes," the man stammered.

That cinched it. They were all doomed if they didn't get out of here before that happened.

Seishin must have reached the same realization as Pallas. "Is there a quick way out of here?" he asked the craftsmen.

One of the men pointed toward a panel at the opposite end of the room. "The emergency hatch is over there, but with the water rushing in we won't make it out in time."

"Don't worry," Seishin assured him. "I'll take care of that."

Pallas peered at the warrior quizzically. "You can do that?"

"Apparently," Seishin answered.

Pallas eyed the warrior uncertainly. That sounded like a glib answer, but seemed rather un-Seishin like. Perhaps the rest of their mercurial group was rubbing off on him.

As Seishin led the others across the room, Pallas took a moment to grab a rope from his pack and bind the head engineer. He then hefted the man over his shoulder and went to join the others.

"Do you have any more of that rope?" Seishin asked as he joined them. Pallas nodded and pulled out another length, this one far longer.

"Tie it around me," Seishin instructed him. "The rest of you grab on tight," he told the others.

Once everyone was ready, Seishin popped the hatch. Water immediately burst into the room flooding the floor in mere moments.

The golden armor lifted up into the air and rocketed forward dragging the rest of them with it. Moments later they were outside the ship and headed up towards the surface. They broke the surface shortly thereafter where the armor came to a stop.

"I suggest you swim to the shore," Seishin suggested to the craftsmen in a calm tone.

"Thank you for saving us," one of the men muttered incredulously. A round of thank yous followed from the others.

As the men swam off, Seishin grabbed Pallas in one arm and the head engineer in the other. The armor then took off again, flying them up into the sky.

Pallas spied what appeared to be a flying carpet rising from the deck of the ship. The figures astride it looked a lot like his sister, Elladan, and Donatello.

Pallas pointed them out to Seishin. The armor flew over to them, catching up out over the water.

Thea arched an eyebrow when she saw them. "What happened to you two?"

The corner of Pallas' mouth lifted ever so slightly. "It's a long story."

Seishin dropped the head engineer upon the carpet as Pallas related the abbreviated version of their encounter in the engine room. As if on cue, three huge fire elementals burst out from the back of the iron ship. Flames shot up all around them, the back of the ship melting from the intense heat.

The crew gathered on the top deck dove off into the waters to try and save themselves. Not all of them made it in time.

Pallas winced at the gruesome sight. Not even the Parthians deserved to die that way.

"I think that's our cue to leave," Elladan commented in a hushed voice.

For once Pallas agreed with the bard.

27
MIND OVER MATTER

You amuse me, brother. You have such a delicious mind.

Cyclone and Ruka had been so preoccupied with the golems that they hadn't noticed the huge cannon trained on the *Black Cat*. The hunter now clung to the dragon's back as they raced at top speed to reach the gunship.

Luckily, Cloud was far ahead of them. In a daring move, the skyrider reached the ship and parked himself right in front of the cannon's mouth. Cyclone watched with growing respect as the rider sent a flaming sphere hurtling down the barrel of the great cannon.

Cloud got out of there not a moment too soon. As the rider sped away, the huge cannon fired. A moment later, an explosion rocked the great gun and the entire ship attached to it. The shot ejected from the cannon landed far short of its intended target, the resulting blast sending a spray of water cascading a hundred feet into the air.

"Woah," Ruka gasped. "If that thing hit…"

"…there'd be nothing left of the Black Cat," Cyclone finished for her. He'd never seen a blast that powerful before. Whoever built these ships and weapons knew far more than the Parthians or any other race for that matter.

As Cloud continued to circle the ship, a group of sailors emptied out of the top hatches. Each launched a carefully aimed harpoon at the skyrider. Cloud managed to weave around the first two, but the last one caught the rider in the side.

"Cloud!" the two of them cried in horror as the skyrider faltered in mid-air.

Amazingly, he managed to pluck the harpoon from his side. The sailors weren't finished with him though as all three readied a second harpoon.

"Oh no you don't," Ruka growled menacingly.

The dragon drew in a deep breath and sent a fierce bolt of lightning racing across the intervening distance. The bolt caught two of the sailors frying them where they stood.

The flashy display momentarily blinded the third sailor. Taking advantage of his misfortune, Cyclone launched himself off the dragon's back. He landed atop the gunship, his halberd cleaving the sailor in two.

Ruka and Cloud both circled around and came to a stop in the air just above him. Cyclone noticed the gnome still holding his side.

"You okay there?" he asked him apprehensively.

Cloud waved him off with his free hand. "I'll be fine. It's just a flesh wound." He hesitated a moment, his eyes flickering behind Cyclone. "Plus, I think we've got bigger problems."

The hunter glanced over his shoulder and had to duck. The giant gun had begun to swivel around the side of the tower. They all watched with mounting confusion as it turned to train itself on the other iron ship.

The back of that ship had apparently exploded, but there were still many sailors on its deck and in the waters around it. Cyclone could now hear a steady hum coming from the gun as it prepared to fire.

"The bastards are going to kill their own people," Ruka growled.

"Not if I can help it," Cyclone declared. He'd had more than enough of these treacherous Parthians or whoever was actually running these ships. They'd already tried to fry them with no regard for their own people. Now they intended to blow up their own ship—crew and all.

The sailors had closed the hatch behind them. Cyclone tried spinning the wheel handle, but it wouldn't budge. His rage mounting, he grabbed the lip of the door itself and began to pull. A metallic groan echoed across the waters as it slowly began to give.

Unfortunately, it was too late. The great gun fired, its payload sailing across the sky towards the wounded ship and its helpless crew.

Bal slowly backed out the door, his mind still in shock at seeing creatures straight from his nightmares. One of the Zetas rose and followed him as he backed out into the hallway.

Other than the bulbous grey head and the large black eyes, the creature looked basically humanoid. It had two arms and hands that ended in long, slender fingers. He could not see if it had legs, however, as it wore floor-length robes.

An alien voice sounded in Bal's mind. *Who are you brother?*

Back in the room, the Parthian officer had not budged an inch. All of a sudden, everything made sense to him. There was no way the Parthians had the know how to build either of these ships. For once, they were not the aggressors. They'd been enslaved by the Zeta Reticulum, creatures who could control the mind.

A wave of empathy passed over the Lanfor lieutenant. He called out to the Parthian officer, "I am here to help, friend. I will save you from your persecutors."

An unearthly laugh echoed through Bal's brain. *You amuse me, brother. You have such a delicious mind.*

The creature motioned to Parthian officer. He rose and came out into the hallway. Bal noticed the sword hanging at his side and decided to retreat just in case. Briefly concentrating, he switched to his magnetic armor and climbed up onto the ceiling.

My oh my, what unique talents you have, the Zeta practically cooed. *Still, I wonder if can you handle this?*

As the words echoed through Bal's mind, a blast of pure mental energy leapt at him from the center of the creature's forehead. Bal threw up a mental shield just in time. The attack bounced harmlessly off of it, the rebounding force rippling through the air around him.

Very interesting, the creature murmured. *What is your name, brother?*

I am called Bal, he answered cautiously, careful not to give it his true name. In his studies he'd learned that knowing a thing's true name could give you power over it.

Welcome, Bal, the creature practically purred. *You would not be able to pronounce my real name, but you can call me—Fred.*

Bal noted how it cleverly circumvented giving him its true name in turn. It was then that he noticed the humming of the ship had stopped. A blast abruptly reverberated throughout the vessel. It was almost immediately followed by a loud explosion which resulted in the entire ship rocking around them.

Thankfully Bal's magnetic greaves and gauntlets held, but he still felt a bit shaken, nonetheless. 'Fred' nearly fell over, but his Parthian 'slave' caught him. Once the rocking subsided, Fred stood back up. Though its expression was unreadable, Bal could sense the creature's discomfort.

Fred peered back up at him. *So, Bal, what business brings you out here? And who are your friends? They seem rather—creative.*

Bal smiled despite himself. This creature didn't know the half of it. He decided to push a bit to see if he could get a reaction out of it. *They are. Perhaps more than you can handle.*

Fred stared back at him, its expression still unreadable. After a long pause, it calmly slid down the corridor beneath him to one of the doors he had passed on his way here. It motioned to him as it entered the doorway. *Come, Bal, let's talk.*

Bal hesitated for the briefest of moments, but then thought better of it. That attack before was merely a test. It definitely wanted something more from him or both creatures would have come at him at once. Curious to see where this was going, he decided to play along.

Bal climbed back down the wall and went to the open doorway. Inside, he found the Zeta seated in a comfortable looking chair behind a small table. He noted that its right hand was hidden beneath that table.

When the creature did not immediately speak, Bal decided to ask a question of his own. *Tell me, Fred, what business do you have with the Parthians? They obviously did not build this ship.*

Fred shrugged. It was the first humanoid reaction that Bal had seen the creature display. *They are a convenience—for the moment. They've supplied the manpower and resources we need to create this ship—and others.*

Bal suppressed any surface reaction to the Zeta's words, but his insides screamed at the thought of more ships like this. If the Parthians had a fleet of these things, they'd decimate the Lanfor navy.

Still, they are only so useful, Fred continued. *Someone like yourself, with a mind akin to ours, would be a much better suited ally.*

Bal narrowed his gaze at the Zeta. Now they were getting to the crux of what they wanted. *What would such an alliance entail?*

Fred's expression did not change, but there was a glint of excitement in its dark black eyes. *There would have to be allowances on both our parts. We would provide you with access to the same technology that went into building this ship. It would make your country the most powerful on the planet.*

And what would you want in return? Bal thought back at the creature.

Fred hesitated the briefest of moments before answering. *An audience with your Queen is all we ask. Once we explain our goals to her, I'm sure she'd become a—pliable ally.*

There it was. They meant to use their mind controlling abilities to take over the Queen. Even the power of the Amber Crystal might not hold up against such an attack.

Bal railed at the thought. *That's never going to happen.*

Seeing the truth behind his intent, Fred made no further efforts to convince him. Instead, it waved whatever it held beneath the table.

Bal found himself suddenly paralyzed. Unable to move a muscle, he almost panicked as the Zeta rose from its seat. Finding a shred of calm at the very core of his being, Bal latched onto it and focused solely on his armor. Just like he had done in the Kaniron vault, he poured more and more energy into it until it began to visibly glow.

Fred halted in its approach, sounding suddenly quite concerned. *Whatever are you doing?*

Pushing the armor to its limits and beyond, it suddenly erupted in a violent flash of pure psychic energy. The wave fanned out in all directions, sending Fred flying against the wall.

The backlash knocked Bal to the floor as well, but afterwards he found he could move again. Rising up onto both elbows, he spied the Zeta at the base of the wall lying there unmoving.

The more time Elladan spent with Thea, the more smitten he'd become. He'd been truly impressed with the way she captivated those sailors. Aside from being a clever idea, her voice wasn't half bad either. With a few lessons, she'd have the makings of an entertainer.

Elladan's pleasant thoughts had been shattered when those huge elementals burst from the back of the iron ship. The resulting death and destruction nearly turned his stomach. He thought he'd seen the worst of it until the new ship fired upon the *Black Cat*. The resulting massive explosion would have sent the pirates, ship and all, to an early grave. Just when he thought things couldn't get any worse, the great gun swiveled around to point in their direction.

Donnie gulped. "Are they pointing at us?"

Pallas placed a hand over his brow and squinted at the giant cannon. "No, the arc's too high," he said after a moment's pause. "If I didn't know any better, I'd say they're targeting their own ship."

As if on cue, the great gun let loose another volley. A giant cannonball sailed over their heads directly for the floundering ship they had left behind.

"What are they doing?" Thea cried. "They're still dozens of sailors in and on that ship!"

Without thinking, Elladan grabbed her by the shoulders and pulled her head into his chest. Closing his own eyes, he laid his head upon hers a moment before the projectile struck.

Boom!

The sound from the explosion rattled their ears and the waves of air rocked the carpet. When Elladan reopened his eyes, the iron ship had been shattered into more than a dozen pieces—all which sank into the water before his very eyes. There was no sign of any survivors.

Thea stood up, her fists clenched into a tight ball. "What in the hell is wrong with these people?" she screamed at the top of her lungs. Tears streamed down her reddened face, her eyes burning with unbridled fury.

Pallas lay a hand on her shoulder and tried to console her. "Take it easy, sis…"

She shook his hand off and glared hotly at him. "Don't you dare tell me to take it easy," she spat back at him through gritted teeth. "Those were their own people and they slaughtered them like cattle."

"I say we make them pay for it," Donnie said, his face uncharacteristically hard, his voice ominous.

"I agree," Seishin said firmly.

Thea looked from one to the other, then wiped her sleeve across her eyes and gave them a grim nod. "Yes, let's."

Elladan exchanged a worried glance with Pallas. This was a side of Thea he'd never seen before. He could see his own concern mirrored in her brother's eyes, but Pallas warned him off with a slight shake of his head.

Taking that to mean there was no reasoning with her when she was like this, Elladan instead urged the carpet on faster. It turned out just as well that he did. After the gunship fired, it started to accelerate away.

As it stood, they barely caught up to it in time. Everyone disembarked just as the gunship swept past the *Black Cat* toward the mouth of the harbor. Elladan saw the Dasati vessel come about to follow, but it had already fallen far behind.

In the meantime, Cyclone had ripped open the tower hatch. A short wide corridor opened up before them. In its very center stood a weird looking metal golem with a sword attached to the end of each arm.

"Well, that doesn't look very friendly," Donnie quipped as he lunged forward through the hatch. Mid-leap the agile elf let loose a knife at the metal creature. The dagger sailed through the air striking the golem on its hard torso. Just as Elladan expected, the knife merely bounced off.

"Can't blame a guy for trying!" Donnie remarked as he rolled to his feet.

"Coming through!"

Elladan ducked as Cloud skimmed over their heads and through the hatch. The skyrider went straight for the metal golem, corkscrewing around it at the very last minute. He was so fast, the golem couldn't keep up with him, its sword arms flailing at the thin air he left in his trail.

Cyclone took advantage of the situation and charged through the hatch at the creature. His huge swing connecting with a satisfying crunch, but in the end left a less than satisfactory dent in the golem's hard body.

"What's this thing made of?" the hunter burst out with obvious irritation.

Thea and Pallas both exchanged a knowing glance, then stepped inside the corridor. Each raised a sword and pointed it at the weird golem.

"You might want to back away," Pallas warned the hunter.

Cyclone begrudging took a few steps back as the two spiritblades each launched a fist-sized ball of flame at the metallic creature. The small fireballs raced across the corridor and slammed into the golem, each expanding into a person sized hemisphere of flame upon impact.

Elladan could feel the heat from the fire all the way back from where he stood. When the flames winked out, however, the golem was still standing, its metallic hide only slightly singed.

"What in the world is that thing made out of?" Pallas reiterated Cyclone's earlier frustration.

"Let me try," Seishin said, stepping through the doorway and unsheathing his long curved sword.

Elladan followed Seishin inside. The moment he passed through the doorway, however, the hatch suddenly slammed shut behind him. Spinning about, he realized they'd all made it inside except for, "Ruka!"

Elladan grabbed the inside handle and tried to turn the wheel. It wouldn't budge. A red light began to flash on a panel next to the door.

"Try this," Donnie called out to him.

Elladan spun about just as the slight elf threw something at him.

He caught the object and turned it over in his hands. It was a golden pendant.

Elladan narrowed an eye at the slim elf. "Where did you get this?"

"I might have swiped it off that head engineer guy," Donnie said with a sly wink.

"It might work," Pallas agreed. "We saw him using it on a panel in the engine room."

Elladan shrugged. "I'll give it a try." He swiped it over the panel next to the door.

Not a moment later, a voice came out of one of those tubes next to it. "Who's there?"

"Lieutenant Storag," Elladan responded without missing a beat.

"Very well. Follow the green line," the voice answered.

Behind him, a green line appeared on the floor leading down the hall. The golem stepped back out of the way to let them pass.

"What about Ruka?" Thea hissed at Elladan.

Before he could answer, they felt the ship around them lurch. It was followed by a sinking feeling in the pit of Elladan's stomach.

"Are we sinking?" Seishin asked, mirroring Elladan's concerns.

"I don't think so," Pallas said slowly. "For one, we're still moving. For two, the way these ships are built," he waved his hand at the tightly sealed door and the porthole next to it, "I wouldn't be surprised if they can travel underwater."

As if on cue, there came a knock at the porthole. Elladan peered out and nearly jumped. Ruka's face was pressed up right against it. Getting over his initial start, he observed her mouthing words at him.

...fine. Go ahead without me.

"Is that Ruka?" Thea peered over his shoulder. "What's she saying?"

Elladan swiftly relayed Ruka's message to all those gathered there. Seishin seemed taken aback. "Is she serious? I could force the door open."

"She's a bronze dragon. They could live underwater if they wanted," Cyclone explained smugly.

"Plus opening the door while we're underwater might not be the best idea," Pallas added.

"Okay, so what next then?" Donnie asked, eying the strange looking golem warily.

Elladan peered around the group and shrugged. "I guess we follow the green line."

Prior to this encounter, Seishin had limited interaction with the Parthians. There had been some at court before he left Isandor, but Seishin had been called to the Queen in secret. Even so, he would never have trusted anyone associated with the power-hungry high priest.

The wanton destruction of their vessel and its unfortunate crew only served to prove Seishin's point. These Parthians had no honor. Even now, they refused to face them directly in battle, instead of hiding behind this metallic construct. He did not trust for a moment that it had stepped aside. Thus, he kept a wary eye out as the thing followed them down to the end of the corridor.

The line brought them to a t-intersection, then turned left towards an open door. Beyond the doorway lay a room with multiple chairs and a large mirror on the wall. A short corridor stretched in the opposite direction, ending at a staircase leading upward.

Donnie peered into the room, then turned about wearing a puzzled expression. "Did anyone see where Cloud went?"

Elladan threw his hands in the air. "Don't look at me. I lost track of him after he buzzed that glorified can-opener's head."

Cyclone pointed a thumb at the stairs. "He must have gone this way."

The hunter started in that direction, but the golem immediately moved to block his path. This time, however, Cyclone was ready for it. He rushed the creature, but instead of attacking used his halberd to vault over the creature's head.

The golem flailed as he sailed by, but could not connect. As Cyclone landed though, the creature sprouted a third arm which sprayed him with a trio of magical projectiles. All three connected, but the tough hunter merely shrugged them off.

"Is that the best you've got?" Cyclone needled the golem.

Seishin didn't quite understand the hunter's reasoning in this situation. While such taunts might work against a live opponent, his words were wasted on the metal construct.

A moment later, he understood what was going on. While Cyclone kept the golem's attention, Elladan conjured a pool of grease underneath the creature.

It was actually quite a clever bit of teamwork. Unfortunately, it came to naught as the golem did not fall in the grease. Despite the setback, Donnie managed to take advantage of it.

"Coming through!" The elf cried, rushing the creature and sliding beneath it, his maneuver aided by the slippery liquid.

Seeing the slim elf get past its defenses, the golem once again pointed that third arm at him. Yet again, while Donnie kept its attention, this time Thea cast a spell on it. A black field appeared around the metal construct, completely enveloping it in darkness.

Seishin fell into a fighting stance, waiting for the creature to emerge from the darkness. A few seconds went by, but strangely it did not.

A boisterous laugh suddenly rang out down the corridor. "I think it's stuck in the grease!" Elladan cried with glee.

There was just enough room at the edge of the dark field to skirt by. Seishin waved to Pallas, Thea, and Elladan. "You all go ahead. I'll keep an eye on this thing."

Seishin waited until the others went through, then followed the rest of them around the blackness. Red flashing lights filled the stairwell as they all rushed up the stairs.

They had just reached the top, when Seishin felt a concussive blow hit him in the back. It was followed by another and a third. Thankfully, his armor absorbed the impact.

Seishin spun about to see the golem standing at the bottom of the stairs. He cried a warning over his shoulder to the others, "Watch out! That thing's free."

A long corridor stretched out before them, curving around out of sight. There were a number of doors along the hall. The others checked them while Seishin kept an eye on the golem.

It had stopped firing and instead started to climb the stairs. It did not seem well equipped for it though, and appeared to need all its concentration to perform the task.

Seishin breathed a quick sigh. At least that had bought them some time.

Meanwhile, the others had checked the first door and found an empty room. At the second door, however, they found, "Balthazar!"

Seeing the golem struggling with the stairs, Seishin decided to back up and join the others. They had found both Bal and Cloud along with something else.

As Seishin drew even with the door, he saw some sort of strange creature lying on the floor. It looked humanoid, but had grey skin, a bulbous head, and two large completely black eyes.

"That's a Zeta Reticulum," Elladan explained. "They're boogie men used to scare little children—or at least so I thought until now."

"Same here," Bal agreed.

"Where did it come from?" Thea asked in a hushed voice.

"Legend has it they're from the baleful moon," Elladan continued, "and might have been responsible for the plague of madness."

Seishin never heard of these space creatures, but had heard of the plague of madness. It started when the baleful moon first appeared in the sky and plunged the world into a thousand year long dark age. The madness came to an end with the fall of the baleful moon, but the resulting collision broke the world and sent Seishin's ancestors southward to form the nation of Isandor.

Back at the stairwell, Seishin could now see the top of the golem's head. "That golem is going to be up here any moment," he warned the others.

Bal motioned to the others. "Follow me. I'll take you to the control room."

Seishin nudged his head down the corridor. "You all go ahead. I'll hold this thing off."

"Be careful," Thea warned him. "Remember, you're not invincible in that armor."

"I'll try," Seishin responded gratefully. Her concern truly touched him. Despite their quirks, these folks were very brave and extremely honorable to their companions.

The thought bolstered Seishin's resolve as the others retreated down the hall. With a group like this, they just might be able to achieve the impossible. They would have to if they were going to save their world.

A few more seconds went by until the golem reached the top of the stairs. It retracted some sort of lower limbs, then set its sights on Seishin and charged.

Seishin fell into a defense stance. No matter what, this thing was not getting by him.

28
BRAIN DEAD

A strange voice filtered its way into her waking mind.
You cannot resist us.

al felt lucky to be alive. It was not every day that one faced their nightmares and lived to tell about it. Despite having done so, he still couldn't believe that Zeta Reticulum were real—even with the proof lying there at his feet. Thankfully, Cloud and the others saw it too.

Bal could just imagine the reaction Amaya would have to the report he'd have to eventually file. She'd probably suggest it was time he retire. He wasn't too sure he'd disagree with her either. Yet any such thoughts would have to wait.

They still had a job to do. They had boarded the other ship in search of the other seven scrolls, and still had no lead as to their whereabouts.

Bal guessed their best bet lay in this ship's control room. As they rounded the curve in the corridor, however, a pair of Parthians jumped out in front of them.

The sailors wore perhaps the strangest garb Bal had seen on any of them yet. Each was dressed in a black bodysuit which ended in a wide ring around the neck. A black helmet with a clear faceplate sat snugly atop the ring.

"Watch out!" Thea cried.

Both Parthians pointed a short stave at Bal. Before he could react though, something slammed into his side.

Bal found himself on the ground as two yellow beams flashed overhead. Instantly rising to a crouch, he spied Donnie kneeling next to him.

The elf probably just saved his life, but there was no time to thank him right now. Bal summoned an astral sword and prepared to leap at their attackers, yet before he could move a muscle, Pallas somehow teleported behind them.

The spiritblade executed a swift slice with his long curved sword, felling the Parthian in a single blow. At the same moment, Cyclone sailed across the hall, landing in front of the second sailor.

The surprised Parthian tried to shoot him, but Cyclone knocked the stave from his hand sending a yellow beam careening into the ceiling. The hunter then slammed the flat of his axe into the man's face knocking him out cold.

Donnie breathed a sigh as the two of them rose, "Phew, that was close."

"You're not kidding," Bal agreed. "By the way, thanks for the assist."

Donnie grinned and gave him a two fingered salute.

The door to the command room was now closed and locked. Donnie cried to Elladan, "Pass me back that pendant!"

Elladan tossed a golden object across the hall to Donnie. It looked exactly like the one Bal had taken from a sailor earlier.

As Donnie went to open the door, another cry rang out from down the corridor behind them. "Look out!"

Bal spun about just in time to see a slew of purple projectiles bearing down on them. Seishin lay flat on the floor with the golem on top pinning him there.

Realizing there was no time to duck out of the way, Bal threw himself in front of the others. Pallas must have come to the same realization. He also leapt in front of the others, the two of them taking the brunt of the attack. Each grunted and shuddered as a missile hit them and exploded with concussive force.

The wind momentarily knocked out of him, Bal wondered how Cyclone just shrugged these things off. His eyes went wide, his aches all but forgotten though as the sound of straining metal reverberated down the hall.

Seishin had broken the golem's hold and lifted it off of him. In a feat of amazing strength, the Shin Tauri warrior threw the metallic creature over onto its side. The golem sat there flailing about, looking very much like a turtle that had been placed on its back.

"That was amazing!" Elladan drawled as Seishin rushed over to join them.

Thea, on the other hand, seemed less than enthused by his performance. She eyed the warrior with an arched brow. "I just hope you're not overtaxing yourself again."

Seishin held up a golden gauntlet. "I know better than to incur your wrath, good priestess."

"Good," Thea exclaimed, her lips twisting into a satisfied smirk.

She then turned a critical eye on her brother and Bal. "As for the two of you,"—she held their stare for a moment, then placed a hand inches from each of their torsos— "hold still."

White light poured from the priestess' hands swiftly engulfing each of their bodies. The aches Bal had previously felt subsided within a few seconds.

"There." She nodded when she was done. "Now maybe think twice before doing anything that stupid again," she scolded them with an arched eyebrow.

A wry grin spread across Pallas' lips. "Why sis, you do care."

"In case anyone cares, I've got the door open," Donnie announced before Thea could retort.

Bal peered over his shoulder and saw the elf standing next to the open command door, his pendant hovering over the panel next to it.

"And none too soon," Elladan added, pointing back the way they had come.

The golem had shifted its body around to leverage its arms underneath it. Bal watched half in amazement and half in horror as the thing teetered back onto its feet with a resounding *thud.*

"Everyone inside!" He motioned toward the command room.

They all raced into the doorway, Donnie being the last to follow. As soon as the elf made it inside, he swiped the pendant over an inside panel and the door *swished* closed.

"Phew," Donnie sighed. "Again, too close."

The control looked the same as the last time Bal had been in here except for the fact that there were no Zetas. Instead, three Parthians stood in the room, all wearing those same strange black bodysuits sans the helmets. Even stranger, none of them had moved a muscle since they burst into the room.

Bal went over for a better look at them. Their eyes appeared glazed, their pupils dilated. He waved Thea over. "Can you take a look at this?"

Thea strode over to join him. Deep creases formed across her brow as she examined the Parthians. "They appear to be in some form of rigid sleep." She paused a moment, her nose crinkling as she sniffed the air. "Does anyone else smell something funny?"

"Noticed it the moment we walked into the room," Cyclone affirmed for her.

"And you're just telling us now…" Elladan stopped midway through berating the hunter, a huge yawn escaping his lips. A moment later, the elf froze in place.

Donnie stood over by the wide console. Engrossed in examining the controls, he seemed oblivious to their plight. "I think I might be able to pilot this…" Just like Elladan, the elf yawned and then stopped moving.

A second later, Pallas froze in place.

"What's wrong with them?" Seishin exclaimed.

"It's some sort of sleeping gas…" Thea trailed off, also yawning and going rigid.

Cloud swiftly followed.

Bal realized he had to do something fast or they'd all be incapacitated. Spying a tube in the console next to him, he pulled out the golden pendant and swiped it.

The tube responded with a loud whistle followed almost immediately by a disciplined voice. "Yes, sir?"

"Turn off the gas in the control room," Bal ordered in as commanding a voice as he could muster.

There was a brief pause before the voice responded, its tone apologetic. "I'm sorry, sir. I'm under strict orders to gas the whole ship except for here in the engine room."

Bal began to feel lightheaded. Focusing his will while he still could, he conjured himself his underwater armor. After a few breaths of clear air, he began to feel much better.

Bal peered around the room. Everyone now looked frozen except for Cyclone. He squinted curiously at the hunter. "How are you still okay?"

Cyclone snorted. "I'm sort of like a bronze dragon in this form. It would take a lot to knock me out."

Seishin abruptly spoke up, surprising them both. "I was starting to feel woozy as well, but apparently this armor can filter the air I breathe."

Cyclone swept his eyes from Seishin to Bal. "Well, this is great for the three of us, but what do we do about the others?"

"Apparently the key lies in filtering out the gas," Bal murmured, his attention drawn to the strange outfits the Parthian's wore.

On closer inspection, Bal noticed a square black box attached to the back of the suit. Two black hoses hung from the box, their other ends attached to nothing. Sweeping his eyes across the room, he spied the accompanying helmets on a counter near the door.

Bal called out to Cyclone, "Can you toss me one of those helmets?"

Without a word the hunter picked up a helmet and threw it to him. Bal caught it and flipped it around in his hands. As he suspected, the back of the helmet had two hose-sized sockets. Grabbing one of the hoses, he attempted to fit it into one of the sockets. It clicked neatly into place.

This is just like my underwater armor, Bal realized. He waved Cyclone and Seishin over. "Help me get the suits off of these three."

"What are we going to do with them?" Seishin asked hesitantly.

Bal started divesting the sailor in front of them. "With any luck, use them to wake up our friends."

"It's worth a shot," Cyclone agreed, removing the black outfit from another sailor.

"I guess it can't hurt," Seishin capitulated, going to undress the last sailor.

A short while later, they had outfitted Donnie, Elladan, and Pallas in the strange outfits. They had chosen the three of them since the black suits seemed a bit big for Thea and most definitely would not fit Cloud. The helmets fitted neatly in place, rotating into the ring with a solid *click*. As soon as they connected the hoses to the helmets, a soft *hum* emanated from each black box.

Once they were done, Seishin asked his armor to check them over. "Flandril says their vitals are improving. They should wake up in a few minutes."

Bal let out a relieved sigh. "That's great. Now we need to get those two suits out in the hall for Cloud and Thea."

"Or we go down to the engine room and turn the gas off altogether," Cyclone suggested.

"Or we do both," Bal countered.

"You two go," Seishin said quietly. "I'll keep the golem busy."

Bal gave the warrior a grateful nod. He'd always heard Shin Tauri were brave, but this Seishin had proved it time and again.

"Just make sure it doesn't get in this room," he warned as he picked up Cloud.

"It won't," Seishin said with firm conviction. Taking Donnie's pendant, he lined up in front of the door.

Cyclone picked up Thea while Bal converted his gauntlets and sabatons to magnetic armor. Bal then climbed up to the ceiling and gave Seishin a nod.

The second the warrior opened the door, the golem tried to push its way inside. Yet Seishin was ready for it. He charged the thing and grabbed onto it, catching it before it could get through the doorway.

At the same moment, Cyclone launched himself into the air and flew out over the golem's head. The golem tried to shoot him with its third arm, but the distraction cost it. With a hard push, Seishin forced the creature back out into the hall.

In the meantime, Bal climbed as fast as he could while still holding Cloud in one hand. Thankfully the gnome was rather light.

As soon as he made it out into the corridor, Bal heard that strained metal sound once more. Chancing a look, he saw Seishin once again push the golem over onto its side.

"Good luck!" Seishin cried after them. He then backed into the control room and *swished* the door closed behind him.

Ahead of him Cyclone had grabbed one of the downed Parthians and continued to fly down the hall. Leaping to the floor, Bal grabbed the second one and dragged him down the corridor behind him.

Thea tried to open her eyes, but her lids felt so heavy. In fact, her entire body felt lethargic, as if she'd been asleep for days. Yet something nagged at the back of her mind—she had to wake up. There was something she needed to do, although at the moment she couldn't remember exactly what.

Out of seemingly nowhere, a strange voice filtered its way into her waking mind. *You cannot resist us.*

The eerie words sent a chill up her spine. *Am I still dreaming? Is this a nightmare?* She thought wildly.

A familiar voice then broke through her rising panic. "Yeah? Watch me." The defiant statement was followed by the sound of breaking glass.

Thea's eyes snapped open. She found herself in a round chamber sitting opposite a wall-length window. Her eyes focused on a bronze dragon swimming through the water on the opposite side of the glass. The emerald eye facing her briefly sparkled yellow and then the dragon winked.

"Ruka?" Thea murmured to herself, her throat feeling thick and dry.

"They're awake," a familiar voice announced.

"It's about time," another answered, its tone thick with cynicism. Cyclone stood across the room in front of a smashed mirror affixed to the wall.

Thea attempted to shake the cobwebs out of her head when a

hand suddenly appeared in front of her. She looked up to see Baltha-zar standing there.

Thea grabbed his hand, clearing her throat as she rose. "Ahem, where are we?"

"Still in the ship," Bal answered softly.

Thea tried to process his answer, but got distracted by the stiffness of her body. *Wait, that's not me,* it abruptly dawned on her. Feeling around she found her head encased in some kind of helmet. In fact, her entire body was garbed in a full-length black suit.

She stared incredulously at the outfit. *What in Thac am I wearing?*

All at once, it came rushing back to her. This was that Parthian ship and these were those strange clothes the crew had worn. The question remained, why was she now wearing them?

Thea swept her eyes around the round room and spied Cloud sitting next to her. At least she thought it was Cloud. All she could see of the gnome was his head inside a helmet, the rest of his body lost in a black suit similar to hers.

Once again, she fought down a rising panic. "Where is my brother—and everyone else?"

Bal swiftly explained to her all that had transpired since they had been knocked out. As he finished, Cloud started flailing around, his voice rife with exasperation. "That's great and all, but how am I supposed to move in this thing?"

Thea gazed at the gnome with keen sympathy. "I can fix that." She swiftly traced a pattern in the air, releasing the spell once it filled with mana.

"Reformidant Objectum."

As the words left her lips, the mana flowed around Cloud weaving itself through the black fabric. The outfit shrank before their eyes until it fit snugly on the gnome.

No longer impeded, Cloud rose to his feet and moved his arms and legs about. "That's better," he announced with a grateful nod to Thea.

Pleased she could help, she then noticed her own suit. It hung just a bit large on her and was not flattering in the slightest. Once again, she cast the *shrink* spell directing the mana at her own body this time. When it was done, she looked herself over. The black suit had shrunk to fit her in all the right places. "There. Much better."

Across the room, Cyclone let out an exasperated sigh. "That's wonderful and all, but can we get going already?"

Thea cast a disparaging look at the hunter, but Bal answered before she could retort. "Sure."

Bal took out a gold pendant and swiped it across a small panel next to the door. Two buttons lit up on that panel, the bottom one engraved with the number "one" and top with the number "two."

Bal pressed the bottom button. Thea braced herself against the wall as the entire room began to sink. The motion continued for almost half a minute and then it abruptly stopped.

The single door in the room *swished* open. Before them lay a long chamber illuminated its entire length by red glowing lights. Along one wall stretched a group of horizontal pillars, all glowing a bright blue.

A console sat at the far end of the chamber below another mirror. Three chairs sat in front of it. The middle chair swiveled about revealing another one of those gray skinned creatures.

In her mind, Thea heard the same eerie voice that haunted her waking dream. *I've been waiting for you.*

The creature lifted a long slender finger and pointed it directly at Cyclone. *You are now my puppet.*

Thea felt a strange energy permeate the air. A moment later, the hunter grabbed his temples.

"Get…out…of…my…head!" he grimaced through gritted teeth.

Looking beyond the veil, Thea saw purple tendrils extending across the room from the Zeta, their ends wrapped around Cyclone's head. The strong-willed hunter fought back valiantly, but the Zeta's coils plied at him relentlessly.

"Hang in there!" Thea cried as she gathered her own will. Calling forth the power of the auric priestess, she sent white light fanning out in all directions. The brilliant light expanding until it encompassed the entire party.

As her aura encountered tendrils, they flinched away. Forced back, they reluctantly let go their grip on the struggling hunter.

Released from the psychic attack, Cyclone let go of his temples and cast a grateful glance toward Thea. "Thanks. That was starting to get really annoying."

In the meantime, Bal had conjured an astral creature that looked remarkably like a transparent lion. The lion now bounded across the chamber and launched itself at the sitting Zeta.

The gray-skinned creature did not even flinch, however. It watched with seemingly little interest as the lion pounced.

A little less than a dozen feet from the creature, the lion slammed into an invisible wall. A moment later, it vanished into nothingness.

Did you really think it would be that easy? The eerie voice rang through her mind.

Looking beyond the veil once more, Thea examined the invisible wall protecting the Zeta. It definitely appeared to be a psychic construct, but other energy coursed through it as well, augmenting its structure.

On a hunch, Thea turned her attention to the blue horizontal pillars. Her eyes went wide with what she observed. She immediately pointed it out to the others. "Those blue pillars are augmenting the Zeta's barrier."

Bal arched an eyebrow, then rolled up his sleeves and started across the chamber. "You three take care of that. I'll keep our manipulative friend busy."

As Bal charged across the room, Cyclone and Cloud drew their weapons. The three of them advanced on the blue pillars, Thea following to make sure they stayed in her aura. Both the halberd and Ragnarök slammed into the pillars causing sparks to fly everywhere.

Stay away from those! The eerie voice rang in her head, though Thea thought she detected a note of panic in it this time.

Across the chamber, Bal had reached the same point where the lion had previously disappeared. His brow furrowed with concentration as he reached out and pushed against the invisible wall.

Beyond the veil, Thea saw the wall flicker ever so slightly. Bal's hands sank into the wall as he slowly began to push himself through it.

No, stay back! The creature wailed, his superior attitude now completely shattered.

"Keep going! It's working," Thea shouted to Cyclone and Cloud.

Wicked grins crossed both their faces as they each took another swing at the blue pillars. Once again sparks flew and the blue glow dimmed a bit more.

All of a sudden, numerous holes opened along the length of the wall. A group of small metallic creatures skittered out of them and gathered around the cracks in the pillars. It appeared as if they were trying to repair them.

Meanwhile, others leaped out at Cyclone and Cloud. Cloud maneuvered his board out of the way, but the skittering things attached themselves to Cyclone.

"Get off me you creepy things," the hunter protested as he swept them from his body. The more he swiped away, however, the more poured from the walls.

"This is getting ridiculous!" the hunter complained, now completely covered with the skittering things.

More leapt at Cloud. The skyrider continued to dodge until holes also opened in the ceiling. Those creatures fell from above inundating the poor skyrider.

The creatures then came after Thea. If she didn't do something fast, they'd all be buried in a huge pile of these things. The trouble was what could she do? These were constructs, not psychic phenomena, nor undead.

Constructs, the word repeated in her mind. *Metallic constructs. Of course!*

A wild idea crystallized in her mind as she drew her blade and dagger. Stilling her mind, Thea attempted something she'd never done before—that no one had ever done before.

The world around her slowed as she reached inside and bonded with her spark of spirit. As always, the energy responded, rushing forth into her arms and out into her blades. This time, however, she made a minor adjustment to that power—something she'd seen both Seishin and Solais do. The blades ignited, yet this time instead of blue flames, they crackled with blue sparks.

Yes! Thea exulted with the momentary surge of triumph, but she quickly quelled it.

Now comes the hard part, she reminded herself.

The metallic creatures had reached her feet and began to crawl up her legs. If this didn't work, there would be no second chances.

Arenor, give me strength, Thea prayed as she executed her daring plan.

Concentrating like never before, she pushed the energy from both blades out into her aura. At first it would not budge, but then her spirit seemed to swell inside. It burst forth with incredible power causing the arcs to leap from her blades.

Electricity interweaved itself throughout the white light, sparking wherever it touched a metallic creature. Every creature it came into contact with sputtered and went inert. Within mere moments, every skittering thing within her aura stopped moving.

Thea let out a sharp gasp, her breath coming in short ragged bursts. She had done it, but almost completely drained herself in doing so.

A moment later, Cyclone erupted from beneath a pile of the inert creatures. "Well, that was fun," he grumbled, brushing off the remains of the skittering things from his body. His gaze then fixed upon Thea, his lips twisting ever so slightly. "Nice move there, by the way."

"Yeah, lucky I'm wearing this body suit or I'd be fried along with them," Cloud admonished her, now also free from the skittering creatures.

Thea responded with a weak smile. She'd been so intent on stopping the creepy crawlers that she hadn't thought about that.

Cyclone strode up to her and placed a hand on her shoulder. "Don't sweat it. We've still got bigger problems to worry about."

Thea followed the hunter's gaze across the room. In all the excitement, she'd almost forgotten about Bal.

With its augmented power gone, Bal had passed through the wall and now stood locked in a mental struggle with the Zeta. Tired as she was, she could feel from here the huge amounts of psychic energy that flowed between the two.

They appeared to be evenly matched when Bal suddenly manifested a blade of pure purple light. Lashing out with it, he caught the unprepared Zeta across the chest.

The Zeta reeled backwards, falling against the ship's console. Laying there breathing heavily, it railed against them with its mind.

My miscalculation. You are stronger than I thought. It paused briefly, a hand touching its wounded chest. All of a sudden, its demeanor changed.

Still, you have not won. Now we all will die together. Before Bal could move, the Zeta turned and slammed its hand on a big red button.

Bal pounced on the creature just a second too late. His final blow caused the Zeta to go limp and sink to the floor in a heap.

Unfortunately, the damage had already been done. Red lights now flashed around the chamber and a strange voice began counting down. 270, 269, 268…

Fear spurring her, Thea raced after Cyclone and Cloud as the duo rushed across the chamber. "What just happened?" She cried ahead of them.

"I'm not sure, but countdowns are never good," Cloud noted, his expression grim.

Bal swiped his pendant over the console and mirrored Thea's question. "What's going on?"

The same strange voice responded over the countdown. "Protocol seven has been initiated. Brain death will occur in 263 seconds."

"What happens…after that…" Thea asked, gasping for breath after using up the last of her energy.

"The ship will self-destruct," the voice answered coldly.

A warm breeze blew through the lush meadow, the vibrant yellow and orange wildflowers dancing in the wind. Tall verdant trees dotted the colorful field, their boughs reaching upward to the cloudless blue sky above.

Donnie sat cross-legged on a blanket in that meadow across from the woman who had been his first real love. The sandy-haired blonde demurely held the skirt of her blue and white dress in place as the wind blew through and ruffled its edges. A pair of emerald green eyes stared out at him from beneath those sandy locks, the corners of them brimming with moisture. "I'm truly sorry about your lady knight friend."

Donnie felt a sharp pang in his chest as he thought about Alana. He had let her into his heart and in the end, she paid the ultimate price.

A small hand reached across the blanket and laid itself softly upon his. Those emerald green eyes peered up at him. "It was not your fault. She was a knight and knew the risks."

Though her words were meant to soothe him, instead they only made him feel that much worse. "But—she didn't know about my curse," Donnie explained guiltily.

A look of keen sympathy filled Miranda's eyes. She reached out and touched his cheek. "Even so, you did right by the dragon girl. It must not have been easy for you to push her away."

The wind kicked up in the meadow. Though there was not a cloud in the sky, the sound of thunder rolled somewhere off in the distance.

Donnie grasped Miranda's hands and held them loosely in his own. "I had no choice. She would only die like the others"—he paused a moment and gulped— "like you…"

Miranda moved closer and leaned in next to him, her forehead pressed up against his. He could feel her warmth, smell the scent of her perfume—it was both heavenly and the worst torture at the same time. "But Donnie, I'm not dead."

Donnie's heart leaped in his chest. He shot up and grabbed her by the shoulders, looking her straight in the eye. "What do you mean? Wraithbone took you years ago. Where have you been this entire time?"

An expression of bewilderment crossed Miranda's face. At the same time the wind blew harder and dark clouds swept across the sky.

"I—I don't know," Miranda stammered. "It's as if I'm here, but also not here." She peered up at him, tears welling in the corners of her eyes. "Does that make any sense?"

Abruptly she began to cry in earnest. Donnie pulled her close as the wind turned into a fierce gale. It became difficult to stand his ground.

Donnie cried over the howl of the wind, "If you are still alive, I swear I'll find you."

Miranda stopped crying and pulled back, her eyes filled with puzzlement. "But how?"

A violent gust blew through the meadow and ripped her from his grasp. Donnie tried desperately to reach for her, but his efforts were in vain. The more he struggled, the further they were blown apart.

"I promise—if you're still alive I'll find you!" Donnie cried, but his voice was drowned out by the gale force winds.

As darkness overtook him, he heard her voice calling out, "Donnie, Donnie, please find me…"

Donnie woke with a violent start. The wind was gone along with the meadow and…

"Donnie!"

The slim elf looked up to see a golden helmet staring down at him. "Where am I?" he murmured, his throat feeling thick and dry.

"You're in the Parthian ship. You were gassed," the helmet answered.

Donnie sat up and looked around, the dream and the meadow swiftly fading as it all came back to him. The figure in the golden armor was Seishin and they were in the control room of the Parthian ship. He spied Elladan in the seat next to him and Pallas one seat over. Both were garbed in those strange black outfits the crew had been wearing.

Abruptly, Donnie realized he was also wearing one of those suits. He stared questioningly at Seishin. "So, why am I dressed like this?"

Seishin quickly explained what had happened since they all passed out. Just as he finished, the lights in the room flickered and went out.

"I guess they took out the power," Seishin's voice echoed in the dark.

"On the bright side, we no longer have to worry about that gas," Donnie said glibly.

A set of four globular lights suddenly appeared in the air above them. The lights spun and danced around as they shed their glow across the room. Elladan sat up in the next seat over. "I figured we could use a bit of light."

Donnie rose and stretched the stiffness out of his body, the dream now all forgotten except for Miranda's parting words. *Donnie, Donnie, please find me…*

The slim elf suppressed a shiver and strode over to the nearby console. "If I remember right, I think I figured out how to pilot this thing. All we need now is a bit of power."

As if on cue, the lights in the control room came back on, albeit a bit dimmer than before. At the same time, a voice sounded through the tube on the console.

"270, 269, 268…"

"Another countdown? Well, that's never good," Elladan drawled.

Intrinsically agreeing with his friend, Donnie slipped into the middle seat and grabbed a hold of the ship's controls. He fiddled with a lever and the vessel began to slow down. He tried another one and the craft began to surface.

Cyclone's voice suddenly sounded through the broach on his cloak. "Take us up and don't stop! This ship's going to self-destruct!"

"I'm going as fast as I can!" Donnie yelled back to the hunter.

"222, 221, 220…"

Elladan exchanged a worried look with Donnie. "I told you countdowns were never good."

The ship continued to slowly rise. Donnie played with a few more levers, finally turning the view port back on. The screen clearly showed a bronze dragon circling in the waters around the ship.

Alarmed at her close proximity, Donnie cast an anxious glance around the room. "Someone needs to warn Ruka."

"And how do you propose we do that?" Pallas asked pointedly.

Donnie opened his mouth to refute him, but realized he had no idea how to do so. The door to the control room chose that moment to *swish* open. Cloud, Thea, Cyclone, and Bal all came rushing in to join them.

"108, 107, 106…"

Gasping for air, Bal took a deep breath and excitedly pointed up at the ceiling. "I managed to access…the ship's records. There's a hatch…in the top…of this room…"

Donnie followed his gaze upward. The ceiling above them rose into a dome. About twenty feet above them, in the top center of the dome sat a hatch as Bal described.

"I think we're almost at the surface," Pallas announced, pointing at the view port.

Sure enough, the water outside had visibly brightened. Ruka swam by, then suddenly launched herself up and out of the water.

"57, 56, 55…"

The ship abruptly broke the surface and rocked back and forth before settling down. Donnie screamed at Cyclone, "Quick, get the hatch!"

The hunter flew up to the top of the dome and swiftly undid the handle. He pushed the hatch open and bright daylight flooded into the room.

"44, 43, 42…"

"Everyone out!" Bal cried as he jumped onto the back of Cloud's board.

Seishin grabbed Pallas and Thea, then rocketed upward. Cyclone dove back down and grabbed onto him and Elladan.

"29, 28, 27…"

Donnie heard the last of the chilling countdown as they flew out of the doomed craft. Out of nowhere, a bronze blur swooped down and grabbed onto them.

Ruka sped over the waters as fast as she could while holding both Cyclone and Seishin. The duo in turn still held onto Pallas, Thea, Donnie, and Elladan. Cloud and Bal paralleled them, the skyrider's board amazingly keeping up with the bronze dragon.

They had made it maybe about half a mile from the Parthian ship when Bal cried out, "It's happening!"

Ruka drew to a swift halt and turned about so they all could watch. Against the inky backdrop of the night sky, a strange light appeared around the Parthian ship. The vessel and the waters around it appeared almost to fold in upon themselves. The weird phenomena continued until the entire ship completely vanished leaving a hole in the sea. The waters swiftly flooded back in to fill the void.

Donnie couldn't help but comment. "Well, I know we were squeezed for time, but did we get what we came for?"

Nearly everyone groaned. Elladan reached over and smacked him on the arm. "That wasn't funny."

Bal next answered his question. "Actually, yes and no. The Parthians do have the other scrolls. They're keeping them somewhere called Iron Island."

"Iron Island?" Pallas murmured. "Never heard of it."

Bal nodded, his expression grim. "That's what I thought."

Donnie's brow knit into a frown. "They didn't happen to have coordinates for it?"

Bal peered at him and grimaced. "Not directly, no. There were a few sets though in the ship's logs."

"We'll need a map then," Pallas stated firmly.

"I'm sure Solais has one," Thea interjected pointing off toward the eastern horizon.

Donnie squinted and saw the white sails of a tall ship headed in their direction. It was hard to tell from this distance, but it had to be the *Black Cat*.

29
MIST

Down below, in the middle of the ring, sat a solitary island.

Stars twinkled brightly in the dark firmament as they flew over the open sea to rendezvous with the *Black Cat*. Between those nightmarish aliens and the wanton destruction, Pallas had been lucky to not have one of his flashbacks. Though thankful for that, he still remained uneasy.

Surface ships would be sitting ducks to vessels that could travel underwater. Pallas would have to warn his parents about this alarming new development as soon as possible. His mother and the other brilliant minds at the School of Magic would need to work out some sort of countermeasures—perhaps a way to detect those underwater ships and sink them before they could surface.

Pallas' dark broodings were cut short as they landed on the deck of the *Black Cat*. Solais came over to greet them though she seemed to be missing her usual swagger. "What was that ship? I'd never seen anything like it, the way it rose up from the depths. And that cannon—biggest damn thing I've ever seen."

Their encounter with the iron ship had obviously left the pirate captain rattled. Pallas couldn't say he blamed her. Her concerns mirrored his own.

Elladan tried to allay her fears in typical glib fashion. "Well, you don't have to worry about it now. It'll never see the light of day again," he told her with a laugh.

Solais gazed intently at the elf. "Are you saying you sank it?"

Elladan grimaced as he tried to explain, "Well, not exactly…"

Donnie stepped in front of his friend and spread out his hands in a shrug. "More like it exploded."

Solais placed a hand on her hip and fixed the elf with an incredulous stare. "It exploded?"

"I think the actual term would be imploded," Thea corrected him.

Pallas had to stifle a laugh. Their mother's academic nature had definitely rubbed off on his sister.

Solais mulled over their words for a few moments, then also laughed, her normal bravado momentarily returning. "Guess I owe you for saving my ship. That makes us even"—her brow then immediately furrowed again—"though that still doesn't explain how the Parthians built something like that in the first place."

"Um, I think we should talk about it further in private," Bal said before anyone else could speak.

Solais eyed him for a moment, then responded with a grim nod. "As you say. Follow me." She motioned for them to fall in behind her as she led the way toward her quarters.

Once they had all settled in around the captain's table, Pallas tried to ease into the topic of the aliens. "Though there were definitely Parthians aboard those ships, they weren't exactly the ones in charge."

Solais turned her chair to face him, her brows knit into a single line. "Who in the world could possibly boss around the Parthians?"

"No one of this world," Bal interjected quietly.

Solais sat forward in her seat, her eyes glued to Bal as he explained their discovery of the Zetas. When he was done she sat there in silence, her expression neutral. Abruptly, she burst into raucous laughter.

"Ha, that's a good one!" Solais screamed, doubling over, and slapping her knee. She continued to laugh until finally noticing that no one had joined in with her. The mirth died on her lips as her jaw fell open. "Oh, wait—you're serious."

"Unfortunately," Bal answered with a slight frown.

Solais sat back in her seat and tapped her chin, her expression thoughtful. "Maybe I shouldn't be so surprised at that."

Her sudden turn about caught Pallas off guard. "What do you mean?"

Solais breathed a short sigh. "Much as I hate to admit it, our tutor made Korti and I read a lot during our training. At the time I thought it less than useless, but maybe the old coot wasn't all that nuts after all."

"Ahem," Seishin cleared his throat. "You do realize that's my uncle you're talking about."

Solais turned her gaze upon him, a single eyebrow raised. "Right," she drawled. The corner of her mouth upturned slightly. "I guess it's true what they say—the apple doesn't fall far from the tree."

A trace of anger crossed the normally stoic young man's face. He started to rise, but Pallas placed a staying hand on his shoulder. As Seishin turned to meet his gaze, Pallas subtly shook his head.

The warrior hesitated for a moment, but then a look of calm came over his face. He gave Pallas the briefest of nods and resumed his seat.

Picking up on the whole thing, Thea artfully redirected the conversation. "You were saying about your reading?"

The hint of a smirk formed at the corner of Solais' mouth as she kicked up her feet and continued. "Well, according to Saricordi lore, there were sightings of little grey creatures after the fall of the Baleful Moon. Everyone dismissed those folks as crazy, but now I'm thinking maybe they weren't."

"How is that part of Saricordi lore?" Elladan asked.

"When the Baleful Moon fell, it sunk what had been the lands of the Saricordi," Donnie answered for Solais.

Pallas let out a soft whistle. "That was well over a thousand years ago. Is it possible the Zetas have been here the entire time?"

No one at the table had an answer. Pallas was left to mull over his own suspicions. The fact that those ships existed and the Zetas were in charge had far reaching implications. They must have infiltrated the Parthian government. They might even have control over the emperor. Either way, the danger Parthos posed to the rest of the world just grew immensely.

"Anyway, did you find what you were looking for?" Solais had risen and stood looking out the large windows in back of her quarters.

"Yes, and no," Bal answered her query. He swiftly related all he had gleaned from the gunship logs about Iron Island.

Solais went to her desk and drew out a large rolled parchment. She came back to join them, spreading it out wide across the table. The parchment turned out to be a map detailing the area around the Pirate Coast from Lanfor all the way south to Isandor and out to the west beyond Thac.

Bal recited the sets of coordinates from the logs of the gunship to them one at a time. The first set fell directly over Kaniron. The second set definitely pointed north beyond the edge of the map.

"That has to be Parthos," Elladan decided.

The third set fell somewhere west of their current position, out in the middle of the Camerian Sea. The map showed no islands in that area, but Solais confirmed it to be in the middle of what once was Saricordi lands.

Pallas exchanged a knowing glance with the pirate captain. "That can't be a coincidence."

Solais gave him a firm nod. "Okay, then we'll set sail out there."

The morning of the following day the *Black Cat* had nearly reached the designated coordinates. Though the skies were sunny, a heavy bank of fog appeared out of nowhere to block their path. Solais brought the ship to a stop while Cloud and Ruka both went ahead.

His board nearly as fast as the dragon, Cloud kept pace with her for the first few miles or so. After a couple of days aboard ship, it felt exhilarating to be airborne once again. It was made even more exciting by racing the dragon.

Ruka was far more fun than the Queen's stuffy gold dragon back home. Unfortunately, as the mists thickened, he had to climb above them. That effectively ended their race.

Cloud gave Ruka one last salute as he banked upward into the sky. She responded by spinning onto her back and shooting a stream of water up at him from her snout. The dragon then spun about once more and dove down into the waters.

Still laughing at the dragon's antics, Cloud ascended through the thickening mists. Now engulfed in a sea of white, he continued to climb farther and farther.

As the minutes passed, he started to worry. *Gods, how far up does this thing go?*

Cloud had almost given up hope when he burst through the mists into the brilliant blue skies above. He had never been so happy to see the sun as he was now. Below him, the mists stretched away as far as the eye could see. With no frame of reference it was hard to tell, but he guessed he had to be nearly half a mile above sea level.

Cloud had never flown this high before and found himself feeling somewhat lightheaded. Even so, he forced himself to continue on. After a few more miles, his perseverance paid off.

The mists started to thin out, and Cloud found himself in the midst of a wide ring of fog. Down below, in the middle of the ring, sat a solitary island. Thick white plumes of smoke rose from the prominent mountain in the isle's center. That smoke appeared to rise up and merge with the mists encircling the island.

Well, that's not strange at all, Cloud thought wryly. Now more intrigued than ever, the Lanfor skyrider banked down for a closer look at the suspicious isle.

Once the mists had grown too thick, Ruka bid goodbye to Cloud and dove down beneath the surface. With the mists blocking the sun the waters appeared black as night. Luckily, she could see very well in the dark.

Ruka continued on for a few more miles underwater. Having grown up in and around the waters of Thunderspire Isle, she was very familiar with the depths of the sea. As such, she knew to search for changes in the underwater currents or any sudden rise in the landscape. Either might indicate land nearby.

Strangely, the sea floor here was not as deep as Ruka expected. This far out in the middle of the Camerian Sea she should have had to travel a mile or more down to find the bottom. The floor here, however, was no farther down than a couple hundred feet.

Maybe it had been, Ruka contemplated silently. Maybe what she saw now was the remains of the Baleful Moon.

The other thing she noted was a distinct lessening of sea life in this area. These waters should have been teaming with life, but the number of fish continued to dwindle the more she swam on.

Ruka started to wonder if she'd ever find this island until she spied a school of dolphins ahead. Not wanting to spook them, she pulled up and called out to them in their own tongue of *clicks* and *whistles.* "Excuse the intrusion, but is there land nearby?"

The dolphins appeared wary at first, but grew curious at hearing their own tongue. A pair broke off from the rest and gingerly approached swimming in a wide circle around her.

"There is, but we don't go there," one of the dolphins finally responded.

"If you get too close, you never come back," the other one added.

That sounds rather ominous, Ruka thought wryly.

"Why is that?" she asked the two circling dolphins.

"The water is bad," the first replied.

"You get sick and die," the second one interjected.

Bad water? Ruka had never heard of such a thing.

"Can you show me?" she asked the pair.

The dolphins began to chatter back and forth, the clicks and whistles too fast for Ruka to follow. When they finally stopped the first dolphin answered her. "Alright, but not too close."

"Otherwise you die," the second dolphin affirmed.

Something in the dolphin's words made Ruka involuntarily flinch. The memory still lay fresh in her mind of being poisoned at the Darkwoods monolith. Thankfully she hadn't been alone at the time. Aksel stayed the poison and Donnie shared his life force with her— courtesy of Elistra of course.

The thought made Ruka momentarily choke up. Donnie had been so kind to her back then. Why did he have to be such an unmitigated ass now? They both loved Alana and suffered at her loss. If he would only let her, they could shoulder the burden together.

Realizing she was just torturing herself, Ruka forced her anguish back down. "I'll be fine," she barked at the pair of dolphins.

"Alright," they both responded in unison.

"But don't say we didn't warn you," the pessimistic one called back as the pair headed off along the sea bed.

That one's just as bad as Ves, Ruka thought wryly as she took off after them.

Cloud and Ruka returned a short while ago from their scouting missions beyond the mists. Donnie experienced a keen sense of déjà vu as each described what they'd found. The mists appeared to be coming from an island hidden in their very center.

The parallels to the City of Tears were too much for Donnie to ignore. In that case, the Empress had used a tower crystal to envelope the city and the surrounding marshes in a thick bank of fog. In this case, the mists came from a building with tall pillars on the opposite side of the isle. Despite the differences, the end result was the same. Both were there to dissuade anyone from finding what lay beyond.

The island itself seemed equally bizarre. Twenty miles wide in all directions, the large mountain stood in its very center. A fortress sat on the north side of the mountain, replete with a huge cannon like the one on the Parthian gunship. An inlet opened on the south side of the isle with a huge underwater gate barring the entrance.

They had just begun to discuss how they were going to get onto the island when one of Solais' crew knocked on her cabin door. "Captain, we spotted a ship on the horizon. From her colors it's a Galocerd."

Donnie arched an eyebrow at Solais. This location was far out of the shipping lanes—not a typical place at all to find a clan ship.

Solais appeared equally as surprised as Donnie. "What's its heading?" she asked the crewman.

"Directly towards us," the man answered.

"Well, that can't be a coincidence," Elladan drawled.

All of them now curious, they adjourned the meeting for the time being. Everyone went out on deck to observe the Galocerd vessel. Standing at the aft rail, Solais raised a spyglass toward the approaching ship. After a few moments, she lowered the glass, a thinly veiled smirk upon her lips.

"I believe it's your girlfriend," she said to Donnie, proffering the spyglass to him.

Donnie's brows knit into a single line as he took it from her hands. He raised the glass slowly to his eye and twisted the sections until the ship came in focus. There written across the bow, he spied two familiar words. *The Annihilator.*

Illyria's ship. What in Thac is she doing all the way out here? The answer was obvious, even if Donnie didn't want to admit it to himself.

With a deep sigh he lowered the glass and said to Solais, "Ready a longboat. I'm going to get to the bottom of this."

Less than an hour later, Donnie found himself once again alone with Illyria in her cabin. The blue haired pirate regarded him curiously as she rose from behind her desk.

"Fancy meeting you all the way out here," her tone amorous as she sauntered up and wrapped her arms around his neck.

Donnie gently removed them, though he held onto her hands, nonetheless. "I was going to say the same to you."

A guilty expression crossed the pirate captain's face, her eyes turning away from him. "That's a long story."

Donnie placed a hand beneath her chin and flashed her one of his best toothy smiles. "I'm not going anywhere."

Illyria sighed as she pulled away from him. She seemed torn as she slowly strode toward the bunk. Spinning about, she plopped down onto it, then bade him to sit next to her. Once he had, she explained just a bit further. "After the explosion in Kaniron, Hahe contacted me. He wanted to know what became of the scrolls."

Donnie felt his heart skip a beat. The last thing they needed was the head of a clan on their tail. "What did you tell him?" he asked her hesitantly.

Illyria placed a hand on his. "Don't worry. I told him they went up in the explosion."

Donnie breathed a sigh of relief. "Thank you," he told her in earnest. "Still, you haven't answered my original question."

"I was getting to that," Illyria replied, playfully smacking him across the arm.

"I'm all ears," Donnie quipped, motioning with his eyes towards the tips sticking out of his sandy hair.

Illyria laughed, his corny joke breaking the tension. "Thinking the scrolls gone, Hahe sent us on another one of his little missions."

From the look on her face and her tone of voice, Donnie could tell that she was less than thrilled with the head of the Galocerd. He fixed her with a wry smile. "Let me guess. He wanted you to come out to the island and pick up the rest of the scrolls."

Illyria's eyes widened with surprise. "So you figured it out?"

Donnie responded with a nonchalant shrug. "It wasn't that hard exactly. Well, except for that Parthian ship we had to sink on the way."

Illyria eyed him sharply. "That's no mean feat. Color me impressed."

Donnie moved in just a bit closer. "So, what did he want you to do with the rest of the scrolls then?"

Their faces now mere inches apart, the charming pirate captain's focus strayed back and forth between his eyes and his lips. "He wanted me to hold onto them—said he was making his way out here."

Donnie found that highly interesting. "Clearly, he's got some sort of deal going on with the Parthians."

"It would seem so," Illyria murmured, reaching up and running her fingers over his lips.

Donnie took her hand and kissed her fingertips. "If you ask me, it sounds like he's playing you again."

She looked up to meet his gaze. "I can't say I'm exactly fond of it," she admitted softly.

"How'd you like…to turn the tables…on him?" Donnie said, kissing her fingers in between words.

The blue-haired captain pulled back and scoffed. "Hahe is a

dangerous man—not one to cross lightly."

Donnie could see the fear in her eyes. He fixed her with another one of his best smiles. "We can be dangerous too if you haven't already noticed. After all, we did defeat a god."

Illyria laughed again, the fear in her eyes swiftly dissipating. "True. I wouldn't mind taking him down a peg or two, either. It might leave a nice vacancy in the Head Captain's position."

Donnie grinned as he moved in closer. "Sounds like a win-win for the both of us."

"It does, indeed," Illyria agreed, wrapping her arms around his neck again.

Upon Donnie's return he related the deal he had worked out with the captain of *The Annihilator*. While it sounded plausible on the surface, Bal held quite a few reservations. Foremost of those was his lack of trust of any pirate.

While Solais had been surprisingly honorable, Bal considered their current arrangement tentative at best. Though he had to admit she had been helpful, that might only be because their interests currently aligned. Once they no longer did, they could easily find themselves at odds over the fate of the scrolls.

As for this Illyria, Bal trusted her even less. Perhaps she did feel beholden to Donnie. Her desire to depose the head of her clan didn't seem out of character either. Yet could they trust her to stick to her word or would she turn on them the first chance she got?

Strangely enough, Solais seemed to share his reservations. She swept her eyes around the captain's table, her tone mocking. "Are you sure you want to trust a pirate captain?"

Donnie fixed her with an ironic stare. "Aren't you being just a tiny bit hypocritical?" he asked, holding his thumb and pointer finger less than an inch apart.

Solais snorted as she rose to her feet. "Maybe"—she strode over to the window and peered out at *The Annihilator* just a few hundred yards away—"but if I were you, I wouldn't even trust me—at least not fully."

Bal found it quite interesting to hear his own thoughts mirrored in her words. Instead of voicing his agreement, however, he gave the others a chance to speak their minds.

Pallas pushed back his chair and joined Solais at the window. As Bal had come to expect, the Penwick captain shared his pragmatic point of view. "We harbor no illusions about who and what you are. Still, you have been an honorable ally while our interests align."

Solais turned her head towards him, the corner of her mouth curved upward. "I knew there was a reason I liked you."

Donnie sat back in his seat, crossed his arms, and began to sulk. "Well, if anyone has a better idea, I'm all ears."

As one might expect, his friend Elladan tried to assuage him. The bard placed a hand on the slight elf's shoulder. "Now don't get your drawers all in a bunch, Donnie. Your plan might still be our best option."

Thea had been listening attentively this entire time. The priestess finally chose now to voice her opinion. "Much as I understand the risks involved, I'm afraid I have to agree with Elladan."

Not surprisingly, Cyclone had grown impatient with all the discussion. The hunter planted his hands on the table and stood with a sigh. "Can we just agree on something already?"

"I say we go with Donnie's plan," Ruka interjected from the other end of the table.

That caught everyone by surprise. It was no secret the dragon teen held some sort of grudge against the sandy-haired elf.

"With a couple of caveats," she added, glaring at Donnie as if daring him to contradict her.

Donnie immediately stopped sulking and sat forward in his seat. "By all means," he responded to Ruka, flashing her one of his sparkling smiles.

Ruka's face reddened for the briefest of moments, but then caught herself and got down to business. Everyone sat and listened attentively as she laid out her addendums to Donnie's plan. In the end, they all agreed to her proposal.

As they rose to leave, Solais left them with some ominous parting words. "I'll wait for you here for the next twenty-four hours. Anything more and I'll assume you're all dead."

She wasn't wrong, but Bal found her choice of wording questionable at best. He thought about calling her out on it, but Pallas beat him to it.

"Spoken like a true pirate captain," Pallas said with a wicked grin.

"Touché," Solais replied, smirking back at his pointed response.

Once they transferred over to *The Annihilator*, the ship set sail into the mists. Bal stood with Cloud at the rail above the navigator's box trying to keep an eye out ahead. Their efforts turned out to be futile as the mists were so thick they couldn't see much past the bow.

Despite Illyria's assurances that they wouldn't run aground, Bal's real solace lay in the fact that Ruka paralleled them underwater. Even so, Bal let out a sigh of relief when the mists finally parted.

There before them lay the solitary island looking exactly as the Cloud had described. The central mountain reached up nearly as high as the surrounding wall of swirling mist. Steam rose from behind the mountain joining with the mists just as Cloud had said.

All of their group except Bal, Cloud, and Cyclone now wore the bodysuits they'd acquired on the Parthian gunship. With the isle in sight, the others slipped over the side to join Ruka. In the meantime, Illyria signaled ahead of their approach.

"This is *The Annihilator*. Here to pick up the package for High Captain Gidemoya," she spoke aloud, using a spell scroll to send the message. The reply came back almost immediately signaling that they'd been expected.

Illyria set course for the inlet at the southern end of the island. Within the hour they sailed into the harbor unharmed. A large cave appeared amongst the rocks at the other end of the harbor. Bal, Cloud, and Cyclone sequestered themselves behind a tall stack of crates as *The Annihilator* sailed into its mouth.

The cavern turned out to be huge, at least a half a mile long and equally as wide. A pair of docks jutted into the waters about halfway along the east side of the cave. A couple of buildings stood back from the dock. The larger one appeared to be a warehouse while the other appeared to be a guard station. About a dozen Parthian soldiers filed out of it as they approached and lined up at the end of the wharf.

As they pulled up to one of the docks, the soldiers helped the pirates moor *The Annihilator*. In the meantime, Illyria met with their lead officer. After a brief discussion, the officer ordered the soldiers to help the pirates unload some cargo. He then spun about and marched back up towards the guard house.

Bal reasoned that if anyone here knew where the scrolls were being kept, it most likely was that officer. Cloud apparently reached the same conclusion.

"I'd say we found our target," the skyrider whispered.

Bal exchanged a brief glance with his two compatriots. "Shall we then?"

While Cloud drew out his board, Cyclone shifted forms and sprouted a pair of wings. At the same time, Bal focused his will and encircled himself in his light-bending astral armor.

Cloud then turned his attention to Cyclone. "Hold still." He traced a symbol through the air and mumbled a couple of words at the hunter. A moment later, Cyclone completely faded from view.

Satisfied, Cloud whispered to Bal, "You might want to step on board before I do this."

Bal gingerly hopped on behind the skyrider before he cast the same spell on himself. A few moments later, Bal could no longer see the gnome nor the board he rode on. Thankfully, he could still feel his hands on Cloud's shoulders and the skyboard beneath his feet.

"Let's go," Bal whispered to the others.

They lifted off and sailed out over the docks. Below them, soldiers and pirates wheeled crates off the ship and over to the warehouse. Cloud veered away from the workers and landed by the guard station.

"Wait here," Bal whispered to the others.

Multiple windows stretched across the front and sides of the building. A set of glass double doors stood in their very center. Bal stole up to the glass and peered inside.

A large single room spread out before him taking up the entire width of the building. It appeared to be some kind of common room where the soldiers spent their time when not on duty. At the moment the room stood empty.

Bal whispered to the others, "Follow me." He cautiously opened the door and stole inside waiting there until one of the others grabbed it from his hand.

A closed wooden door stood at the back of the large room. Bal padded over to it and pressed his ear up against it. He heard the sound of muffled voices.

"He's in here"—he whispered to the others—"and he's not alone."

Bal cracked the door open, but the voice continued on as if they had not noticed. He pushed it in a bit further and peeked around the edge.

Another room, not quite as big as the first, spread across the width of the building. A console sat at the other end similar to the ones in those Parthian ships. Two figures sat at the console along with the officer. The one in the middle wore a strange metal helmet with wires coming out of it that attached to the console. The third person was garbed in robes.

Bal had a bad feeling about this, but at this point they had little choice. Unlike his armor, Cloud's invisibility spells would only last for so long. With no other recourse, Bal pushed the door further open and stepped into the room. Unfortunately, the robed figure spotted it almost immediately.

"Intruders!" he cried pointing at the open doorway. A flash of violet light leapt from his fingertips and shot across the room directly for them.

Bal instinctively raised a psychic shield just before it hit. The energy wave broke against it, but unfortunately the blast caught Cyclone. Suddenly visible, the hunter was momentarily stunned by mental assault.

The man in the helmet did not move, but the officer leapt for a great sword hanging on the nearby wall. Before anyone else could move though, Cloud appeared overhead.

A stream of ice sprayed from the tip of his black sword causing the robed figure to freeze over. The attack was so brutally cold that the frozen figure shattered into a dozen pieces. Bal had little time to dwell on it though as the officer came at him brandishing that great sword.

Focusing his will, Bal formed a psychic sword in his hand barely in time to block the officer's swing. Bal reeled from the force of that blow. Another one would most likely break through his guard.

Raising his free palm, Bal directed a psychic blast straight at the officer's torso. The resulting force knocked the officer to the floor and sent the great sword spinning out of his hands. The man laid there on the ground stunned.

At the same time, Cyclone regained his senses. The hunter bounded across the room toward the Parthian wearing the strange helmet. Unfortunately, he was a second too slow.

As the hunter brought his halberd around, the soldier reached out and slammed his hand on a bright red button sticking out from the console. It was the last thing he ever did.

As the last Parthian slumped to the ground, a red crystal on the console started to flash. Cloud cast a dubious glance at Bal and Cyclone. "Well, that's not disconcerting at all."

"Let's be quick then," Bal responded. "You two search the officer. I'll check out the console."

Cyclone bound the officer while Cloud searched him. In the meantime, Bal examined the console. The red crystal appeared to be flashing faster. His concern growing, Bal put on the helmet.

At first, he heard a multitude of strange voices, but Bal didn't quite recognize the language. After a few moments concentration, he was able to distinguish a singular voice, its cadence sounding very much like a countdown. Bal swiftly informed the others.

Cloud gave him an exasperated look. "Not again."

Throwing down the helmet, Bal went over to the tied-up officer. "What did you find on him?"

"Just these." Cloud held out a pair of pendants similar to the one's they'd found in the Parthian ships. The colors of these differed, however, these two being orange and light blue.

Back at the console, the crystal now flashed even faster. Realizing they only had seconds left, Bal focused his will on the stunned officer.

Touching his mind, he asked him a single pointed question. *Where are the scrolls?*

The officer hesitated, but his will was no match for Bal's. *They're—down below. The general has them—but you'll never get there,* he added finally breaking Bal's compulsion.

Bal felt a tap on his shoulder.

"Um, I think we should go now."

He turned to see Cloud eying the red crystal warily. It was blinking like mad now.

Cyclone hefted the officer over his shoulder, then took off into the air through the open doorway. Bal leapt onto the back of Cloud's board and held on tight as they sped after him.

They raced across the common room and out into the cavern beyond. They'd only made it about a dozen yards when the building behind them erupted in a fiery explosion.

30
INTO THE MINES

The track ended rather abruptly over a dark abyss.

Seishin felt on edge the entire trip through the harbor and into the cave beyond. Despite using both the water and *The Annihilator* as cover, he couldn't help thinking that something was bound to go wrong. As it stood, he barely trusted Solais. Despite Donnie's assurances to the contrary, he expected at any minute for this Illyria to give them up. Thus, it came as a pleasant surprise when she did not.

Between fighting pirates along the Isandor coast and his previous run in with the Dasati, Seishin had an ill impression of the clans. To date, Korti was the only exception to that rule. Now, however, he was starting to rethink his opinion of the pirates in general. Both Solais and Illyria had kept to their word when it might have benefitted them to do otherwise. Perhaps just like every other people, there were both good pirates and bad ones.

With Ruka's aid, the six of them passed the docks where *The*

Annihilator moored and swam toward the back of the cave. The dragon shifted to human form as the lot of them surfaced by the water's edge. Though lights had been set up all around the vast cavern, long shadows clung to the walls and filled the spaces in between. A hundred yards farther back, the dim lights revealed another building. From here it appeared deserted adding to the eeriness of the cavern.

Pallas used his shadow abilities to clandestinely scope it out. "It appears to be some sort of mining facility," he reported upon his return. "There are a few carts and a set of tracks that disappear off into a tunnel below."

Pallas had barely finished speaking when one of the buildings by the docks suddenly exploded. A huge ball of flame flared up around it knocking everyone nearby to the ground.

"Holy crap!" Elladan exclaimed.

"I hope the boys weren't in there," Thea added fervently.

"They weren't," Ruka responded assuredly. "Look!" she said pointed above the still burning blaze.

A set of dark outlines stood out against the fiery backdrop. One definitely had wings while the other two stood upon an airborne board.

They all let out a collective sigh at the sight. A moment later, a voice sounded through both Donnie's and Elladan's broaches. It was Cyclone. "The scrolls are somewhere down below with somebody called the 'General.' You all go on ahead—we'll take care of things up here."

"Sounds like those carts are our only way down," Seishin pointed out hesitantly. Much as the scrolls were their top priority, he didn't like the idea of leaving his comrades behind.

Thankfully, Ruka solved the problem for them. "Go ahead without me. I'm going to give them a hand."

Before anyone could say a word, she took off at a run along the water's edge. A few strides away she shifted back into a dragon and moments later was airborne.

With Ruka joining the fray, Seishin felt much better about going ahead. Pallas led the way across the cavern floor to the deserted building. Just as he had told them, a set of rail tracks receded from the side of the building down a steep slope behind it. Another fifty yards or so, the tracks disappeared into a dark tunnel.

Three mine carts sat along the rails all lined up against a bumper.

Donnie and Thea leapt into the first cart, the latter crying, "Someone give us a push!"

Seishin exchanged a quick glance with Pallas. "I'll take the first cart if you get the second."

A distasteful expression crossed Pallas' face as he reluctantly eyed Elladan. "I guess," he agreed, not sounding very enthused.

Seishin had noticed for a while now that the Penwick captain seemed less than thrilled with the elven bard. Having a little sister of his own, he could understand how Pallas felt.

Seishin pushed the cart down the track until they reached the top of the hill. As soon as it started to pick up speed he leapt inside behind Donnie and Thea. The cart sped down the slope and disappeared into the dark tunnel.

Back up top, the explosion flattened any nearby soldiers. As they started to rise Cyclone strafed them, bowling them over again with the officer he carried. Banking around he launched into them just as Bal leapt into their midst. Between the two of them and Cloud they could easily handle this lot, but more soldiers now rushed their way from the direction of the warehouse.

Cyclone prepared to do something drastic when Ruka came barreling in at breakneck speed. The dragon landed right between them and let out a terrifying roar.

The soldiers abruptly stopped in their tracks, their faces turning all shades of gray. Almost as one they dropped their weapons, then turned about and ran in the opposite direction.

Cyclone felt just a twinge of annoyance as the dragon turned her head around towards him. "You know I could have handled that myself."

Ruka let out a delightful chuckle. "Yeah, but this way was more fun."

Meanwhile, over on *The Annihilator*, the pirates started throwing the rest of the Parthians overboard. One look at the dragon on the shore and the soldiers all swam in the opposite direction. With the last of the Parthians taken care of they caught up with Illyria on the docks.

Cyclone fixed the pirate captain with an ironic stare. "I thought you didn't want to get caught helping us?"

Illyria placed a hand on her hip and cocked her head to one side. "A girl's allowed to change her mind. Besides, if you're going to start blowing things up, I'd rather be out in the open seas."

Cyclone snorted. She had a point. Considering their track record, this could turn out to be another Kaniron.

"I'm sure we can arrange that," Ruka answered her from the edge of the dock, the teen still in her dragon form.

Illyria looked past them and gave the dragon a grateful nod. "That would be much appreciated."

Something in the pirate captain's words left Cyclone with an uneasy feeling. They had run into a lot of strange things in those Parthian ships. This place could be loaded with more of the same.

Feeling the sudden urge to catch up with the others, he pulled Bal aside. "Can you guys handle that? I'm going to go give the others a hand."

Bal gave him a grim nod. "Go ahead. We'll join you as soon as we're done here."

Donnie stood at the front of the cart barely able to rein in his excitement as the cart careened down the tracks. He reminded himself this was serious business—that the entire world was at stake. He had taken great pains to convince Illyria and the others to work together—well, perhaps 'pains' was not the appropriate word. Even so, the thrill of speeding down the rails was undeniably fun.

"Someone should make a festival ride out of this!" he yelled over the wind whipping through his hair.

"It is quite exhilarating!" Thea cried back.

Seishin, on the other hand, remained predictably silent. Donnie tried to cajole the stoic Isandorian to see his point of view when the tunnel abruptly ended.

Another dimly lit cavern stretched before them, its sloped floor further speeding their descent. A building stood alongside the tracks about halfway down the length of the cavern.

Donnie squinted as a solitary soldier rushed from the building and pulled on a lever next to the rails. It was then that he spotted a secondary track leading off from the first. The track ended rather abruptly over a dark abyss.

Seishin immediately spurred into action. Climbing up next to Donnie he paused a moment to address the elf. "I'll try and slow us down. You take care of that switch."

In an incredible feat of agility, the warrior jumped in front of the cart, an armored foot landing on either rail. He then placed his back up against the cart grunting as he pushed.

The cart groaned back in response, its wheels screeching against the rails. Amazingly their descent slowed.

Even so, the switch was coming up fast. Donnie leapt from the cart and took off at a dead run for the lever. The soldier tried to block his path, but Donnie tumbled beneath his blade.

The agile elf then used his momentum to leap up at the switch. Grabbing ahold he managed to flip it moments before the cart reached the split. The tracks shifted barely in time averting a very nasty plumet.

Still, despite Seishin's best efforts, the cart moved quickly along the rails. Donnie immediately took off after it, his legs pumping as fast as they could.

Thea now stood at the back of the cart, precariously balanced there with both hands outstretched. "Come on, Donnie!" she urged him.

With one last burst of speed, Donnie closed the final gap and managed to grasp Thea's hands. Her grip proved surprisingly strong. With a mighty heave, she yanked him off the tracks.

The two of them tumbled back into the cart, Donnie landing right on top of the comely priestess. Still breathing heavily from exertion, he managed to grin down at her. "Thanks, milady! That was…a most…cushy landing."

Thea snorted up at him, but was interrupted before she could fire off a proper retort.

"Out of the way!" Seishin's voice rang out from the front of the cart.

Donnie pulled Thea to the back with him as Seishin barreled over the front edge. The warrior unceremoniously landed in a heap where they both had just laid.

Thea knelt down next to him. "Are you alright?"

"I'll be fine," Seishin responded. "What about the others?"

A thin smirk crossed Thea's face. "They're right behind us. The guard was so intent on Donnie that he didn't see Pallas coming until it was too late."

Things calmed down briefly as the cart entered another tunnel. A few minutes later they exited the other side into a well-lit cavern. The floor of this one leveled out, the rails stopping at another buffer next to a tall metal-framed tower. Donnie's eyes focused on a strange arrangement of ropes and pulleys that hung within the frame.

"Looks like we've got company," Thea pointed out.

Following her gaze, Donnie went cold inside. Nearly a half dozen Parthian soldiers stood on a narrow ledge a short way up the tower. Each carried a bow in their hands. As soon as their cart rolled into range, those soldiers started taking pot shots at them.

"Well, that's just not fair," Donnie decried, ducking as an arrow flew over his head.

"I'll try and hold them off," Seishin declared.

The warrior again climbed up onto the edge of the cart, using his body to shield the rest of them. The arrows bounced off his golden armor giving them a brief respite. Yet he couldn't stay like that forever.

Donnie observed the dings in the armor left by the sharp arrowheads. He needed to do something soon or Seishin would end up looking like a pin cushion.

Squinting at the tower ahead, Donnie spotted a stray rope hanging off the side. As soon as they drew within reach, he leapt for that rope. Between his own momentum and the momentum of the cart, the nimble elf was able to swing himself up and land next to the archers.

Drawing his blade, Donnie skewered one of the unsuspecting

archers. Unable to help himself, he quipped as he pushed the soldier off the tower. "You know why you guys are going to lose this battle? Because you have fallen archers!"

The next soldier over tried to shoot him, but Donnie ducked behind the frame of the tower. When he peeked back out, Pallas suddenly appeared behind the last archer. Pallas stabbed the man with his blade and pushed him off as well.

"I think he got the point!" Donnie quipped yet again.

The archer nearest Donnie dropped his bow and drew a sword coming after him. Timing it perfectly, the agile elf ducked beneath the blade and tripped the man sending him over the edge.

At the same time, Pallas parried another soldier's blade and expertly disarmed him. Having lost his balance, the soldier flailed wildly before also falling off the tower.

Now surrounded on both sides, the last archer threw down his bow and ducked into the framework of the tower.

Donnie peered at Pallas and winked. "I guess he got the point."

Pallas stared back at him and groaned.

Thea hadn't been part of a group since the tragedy on Thorn Isle. Afterwards she lost her childhood friends, all either moved or sent away. It felt oddly strange to again be part of a team, each playing to their strengths while covering each other's weaknesses. Thea hadn't quite realized until now just how much she missed it.

While her brother and Donnie kept the archers busy, the cart she traveled in came to a stop. No longer being rained on with arrows, Seishin leapt out to see if he could help them.

Confident they could handle the remaining soldiers, Thea began to look around. That was when she spotted another lever next to the tracks. Reaching over the side of the cart, Thea yanked on it. As she did so, the buffer they'd stopped at suddenly swung open. Still on a slight slope, the cart rolled forward into the tower.

Thea found herself on some kind of platform that took up half the inside of the tower. Looking up the shaft she saw a number of sturdy- looking ropes traveling upward from the platform to a set of large pulleys.

The ropes traveled over the pulleys and back down again past her on the other side of the shaft. Peering down over the edge she saw the ropes and shaft continue on downward as far as the eye could see.

"It looks like some sort of giant dumbwaiter," Elladan said as he jumped into the cart with her.

The corner of Thea's mouth lifted ever so slightly. "If there's a giant butler at the bottom of this thing we might be in serious trouble."

Elladan started to laugh, but abruptly stopped, his brow furrowing. "I certainly hope not."

Thea swept her eyes all around the shaft. "Well, some kind of mechanism must make this go then."

Her eyes and Elladan's converged on a panel attached to the tower frame with another lever on it. Elladan frowned. "Perhaps this?"

Before she could stop him, the elf pulled on the lever. As soon as he did so, the platform began to sink, the pulleys rotating as the ropes fed through them.

Thea cupped her hands to her mouth and shouted as loud as she could, "Pallas, Donnie, Seishin, we're going down! Hurry!"

Seishin appeared a few seconds later and leapt down into the cart next to them. Shortly thereafter, her brother and Donnie peeked their heads into the tower. By then, however, the platform had descended too far for either of them to make it safely.

Abruptly, Donnie pointed down the shaft. "Look out below!"

Thea again peered over the edge and saw another cart on a platform rising up the opposite side of the tower. Unfortunately, that cart happened to be filled with more Parthian soldiers and another one of those metal golems.

Elladan leaned over next to her and outlined a quick spell in the air. He released the magic with a single word. *"Disorientatio."*

Down below the Parthians started fighting with each other. Elladan let out a hearty laugh. "That ought to keep them busy."

The Parthians continued to fight amongst themselves as the two carts drew next to each other. Nevertheless, the golem had not been affected, so Thea and the others ducked as it went by.

As the second platform continued to rise, a Parthian soldier leaned out of the cart and cut one of the anchoring ropes. That side abruptly tilted downward, throwing its passengers into further disarray.

Unfortunately, it also caused one of the ropes holding their own platform to go slack. The cart they were in pitched forward as well, forcing them all to grab onto the sides.

Thea cried out in dismay. "Are they crazy? Won't that drop both carts?"

"If they're confused, they may not care," Seishin answered, his voice sounding equally distressed.

"Maybe that wasn't such a good idea after all," Elladan agreed, hanging his head. It only lasted a moment though before the bard's face lit up once again. "Still, I can fix it."

The elf reached into his portal bag and pulled out the flying carpet. Unfurling it in the air before him, he ushered Thea aboard with a flourish of his free hand. "Ladies first."

Thea gave him a sour look, but climbed aboard the carpet anyway. Elladan went to grab her hand when a second rope suddenly went slack. The entire cart tipped over and Seishin fell out plummeting down the shaft.

"Seishin!" Thea screamed, still hanging onto Elladan by one hand.

Two soldiers fell past them as Thea did her best to hang onto the elf. She just managed to grasp him with her other hand, when a golden armored figure rose up the shaft and grabbed the elf by the waist.

A few moments later, Seishin landed on the carpet with Elladan in hand. He unceremoniously dropped the elf onto the rug, then flopped down next to him.

Thea fixed Elladan with a scathing stare. "You were saying?"

The elf scratched his head, a wan smile forming on his lips. "Guess that could have gone better."

A snapping sound from above interrupted her retort. "Watch out!" she heard her brother's cry.

The platform above them, cart and all, had broken loose and now tumbled down straight for them. Thea grabbed Elladan and prepared to leap from the carpet when Seishin suddenly took off like a shot.

The golden armored warrior rose up to meet the platform. Thea held her breath as he collided with it, but by some miracle he managed to catch it.

"Way to go, Seishin!" Elladan cheered him on.

Still, something didn't quite seem right. Seishin appeared to be struggling to hold up the platform. Frozen in place, Thea watched on in horror as the golden warrior started to lose ground.

All of a sudden, the platform stopped moving. Thea spied the tip of a bronze wing flapping over the edge. A moment later, she heard Cyclone's voice. "Give me a hand with this thing."

Thea breathed a sigh of relief as together the duo lifted the platform. Cart and all, they brought it upward and dumped it safely outside the shaft. They had just finished doing so when a pair of projectiles came whizzing at them from above.

Boom! Boom!

A single missile hit each of them causing them both to momentarily flinch. Hanging onto the framework above them, Thea spied the metal golem along with two more Parthian soldiers. They must have jumped out of their cart just before it fell.

Swiftly recovering, Cyclone shot up the shaft and grabbed a hold of the metal golem. Yanking the creature from the tower, he fell into a head first dive down the shaft while still holding onto it.

"Are you crazy?" Thea screamed after him as the duo plummeted past.

"You don't know by now?" Cyclone's voice echoed back up the shaft.

Seishin once again spurred into action. Lifting off the carpet, he hovered there for a moment and addressed Thea. "You get the others. I'll go after him."

Thea gave him a firm nod, then the golden warrior plummeted out of sight after the reckless hunter.

Cloud kept a cautious eye on the harbor as *The Annihilator* sailed towards its mouth. Between that gunship, those metal golems, and the gray aliens they'd run into these last few days, he'd come to expect just about anything.

In the meantime, Ruka and Bal had gone ahead underwater to take care of the gate barring the ship's way. With Bal's unique abilities and the dragon's strength, Cloud was fairly confident they could open the gate and let the ship out to sea.

Things appeared to be going fairly smooth when something came flying across the sky from the direction of the mountain. Whatever it was definitely had wings, but they seemed to be fixed in one position. It also appeared to be moving quite fast.

As Cloud moved to intercept it, the thing let loose a barrage of missiles that sailed through the sky straight for *The Annihilator*.

Unsheathing *Ragnarök,* Cloud shot a stream of ice at the strange flying golem. The thing banked out of the way though far quicker than he anticipated.

Nevertheless, he had drawn its attention away from the ship. The flying golem banked around and fired another barrage of missiles, this time aimed at Cloud.

The projectiles came for him faster than he expected. Cloud had to execute a corkscrew aerial maneuver to circumvent the multiple missiles. Even so, one caught the edge of his board, exploding and nearly knocking him off of it.

Cursing in about five different languages, Cloud let loose another stream of ice at the flying golem. The creature dove down toward the water to avoid his attack, but that ended up being its undoing.

As it tried to pull out of its dive, Ruka burst out of the water and caught the golem with a terrific bolt of lightning. The golem faltered in mid-flight, allowing Bal to leap from the dragon's shoulders onto its back.

A psychic sword formed in Bal's hand. He stabbed it into the golem's back. The golem started flailing about trying to dump Bal off of it.

Seeing his chance, Cloud zoomed in and slashed across the creature's metallic torso with *Ragnarök*. Smoke rose from the gash he left behind and the golem began to lose altitude.

Cloud banked around and drew close enough to allow Bal to leapt onto his board. The two of them then watched together as the weird flying golem spiraled into the sea.

"Well, that was fun," Cloud commented as the thing hit the water.

Bal responded with a closemouthed laugh. "My friend, you've got a strange definition of fun."

Ruka rejoined them as *The Annihilator* left the harbor and headed out to the open sea. "We should probably go find the others before someone does something stupid."

Cloud fixed the dragon with an ironic stare. "And by someone you mean Donnie."

The dragon grinned which turned out to be a rather menacing sight. "Or Elladan," she added with a snort.

"Can't argue with that," Cloud conceded as he banked his board around.

The three of them headed back towards the cave as fast as their wings and board would carry them.

Still holding onto the golem, Cyclone plummeted down the shaft. The hunter was sure he'd been in stranger predicaments, but at the moment couldn't quite think of any. Nonetheless, this seemed like the best way to keep the golem from hurting the others.

Even now the mindless creature continued to shoot him with those missiles. Though he could shrug off one or two, the constant barrage was starting to get to him.

Now annoyed, Cyclone hauled off and began punching the thing's metallic hide. Though not sure if he was actually hurting it, it certainly made him feel better.

The ground below finally came into view. This had been his plan along—to let the force of gravity take care of the mindless thing.

The shaft opened up into a large cavern when Cyclone finally let the creature go. Unfortunately, the single-minded thing did not want to let go of him. It reached out and grabbed him by the ankle as he tried to halt his descent.

"Let go you idiot!" Cyclone cried as he pulled out his halberd. In one swing he lopped off its arm letting it fall the rest of the way to its demise.

The golem slammed into the ground with a satisfying *crunch*.

Pieces of the creature flew in all directions proving once and for all that these things weren't indestructible.

Unfortunately, Cyclone could not pull up in time himself. The hunter hit the ground hard, rolling across the dirt floor of the cave. Finally coming to a stop, he lay there catching his breath for a few seconds.

The hunter now ached all over, but that wasn't his biggest problem. Rising to his feet, he found himself surrounded by three dozen or more Parthian soldiers.

"Tsk," Cyclone clicked his tongue. "This just keeps getting better and better."

Falling into a deceptively relaxed stance, Cyclone motioned towards the surrounding soldiers. "Well, which of you is going first?"

The soldiers in front of him stepped aside as a Parthian with gold epaulettes pushed his way through the crowd. The rest of the soldiers formed a circle around them as the officer drew a long-poled axe from his back and set himself into a fighting stance.

Cyclone eyed the officer for a moment then smirked as he let out a derisive snort. "What kind of douche bag uses a halberd?"

Seishin had come to respect Cyclone. Though the hunter appeared to be reckless on the surface, much of that had to do with how much punishment his body could take. It had also become obvious to Seishin that a lot of what the hunter did was to draw attention away from the others.

This case in particular was a prime example. The metal golem he had grappled was exceedingly tough. They had yet to defeat even one of these creatures. To date they'd only been able to distract or stall them.

The pair were still locked in combat as Seishin soared down after them. Though he slowly closed the gap, the ground below rose up fast to meet them.

Seishin breached the roof of the cavern just as the golem smashed into the ground. He had to admit it was rather satisfying to see one of these things finally destroyed. Unfortunately, they were far from out of the woods.

Cyclone crash landed in the midst of a large group of Parthian soldiers. Interestingly enough they did not attack him all at once. Instead, the soldiers waited for their leader to come to the forefront.

As Cyclone prepared for a battle he could not win, Seishin thought of a tactic to dissuade their adversaries and buy them a bit of time.

Can you give me a boost to my strength? He asked the armor.

Certainly, Flandril answered. *To what end may I ask?*

Seishin had noticed the armor becoming more and more proactive lately. It was almost as if it were learning from its interactions with him.

Let's just say we're going to intimidate these Parthians a bit, Seishin responded.

I think I'd like that very much, Flandril said with a hint of approval.

Raising an eyebrow at the unexpected reaction, Seishin paused a moment before taking off for the ground. Soaring downward at a fast rate, the warrior aimed himself for the ground in the middle of the ring of soldiers.

Seishin slammed into the ground fist first, ending in a crouch a few yards behind Cyclone. The powerful landing cracked the floor of the cavern and caused the ground to shake for about a dozen yards around him. He could see the fear on the Parthians' faces as they flinched away from this new foe.

Standing up to his full height, Seishin called over to Cyclone in as tough a voice as he could manage. "You got this?"

Not looking behind him, Cyclone responded with a curt nod. "Yeah."

Thea couldn't believe the recklessness of Cyclone. She had just begun to feel they were a team when he went and pulled a bone-headed stunt like this. Was he really that confident or did he perhaps have a deep-seeded death wish? Either way, she was not about to let him die on her watch.

All these grim thoughts raced through Thea's mind as they descended the shaft after the hunter. When they finally breached the cavern roof, they spied both Cyclone and Seishin surrounded by a mass of Parthian soldiers.

Thea's heart leapt into her throat at the sight. Frightened for the duo, she grabbed Elladan by the shoulder and shook him. "We've got to get down there fast!"

"Hold up a minute," Pallas countermanded her. "Look closely, sis. They don't seem to be ganging up on either of them."

Thea paused and took a calming breath. Pallas was right. The only two who appeared to be facing off were Cyclone and a Parthian officer holding a halberd. Even at that, those two seemed to be feeling each other out instead of attacking in earnest.

Even so, Thea was not about to leave their comrades alone in the midst of that ring of foes. "Land next to Seishin," she instructed Elladan.

Elladan stared back at her wide-eyed. "Land where?"

Thea gave him a hard look. "You heard me."

"Alright, alright," Elladan agreed with a sigh, though he didn't look quite happy about it.

The moment they landed, Thea leapt off the carpet and drew up next to Seishin. "What's going on?" she whispered to him.

"It's a duel of honor," Seishin whispered back. "We can't interfere."

Thea eyed the golden clad warrior dubiously. "Well, that's just plain crazy."

Feeling a hand on her shoulder, she turned to see Pallas standing beside her. "No, I understand it. He wants to prove he's the best with his chosen weapon. It's actually quite an honorable goal."

Thea narrowed an eye at her brother and let out a derisive snort. "Men," she exhaled in as derogatory a tone as she could muster.

Out in the center of the ring, Cyclone continued to trade tentative blows with the officer. From what Thea could tell, they seemed evenly matched, at least in skill. The hunter, however, looked like he had taken a beating from his fight with the golem.

All of a sudden, Cyclone threw his weapon at the officer. The Parthian easily swept it aside, but left himself momentarily open in doing so. Moving impossibly fast, the hunter grappled the officer around the waist rendering his long reach weapon virtually ineffective.

His wings fanning out on either side, Cyclone took off with a huge flap soaring up straight for the cavern roof. Not stopping, he pile drove the Parthian officer head first into the rocky ceiling. He then flew the man back down and slammed him into the cavern floor for good measure.

The officer now lay in a heap completely out cold. All the soldiers who had been standing around began to slowly back away. A few moments later, then all turned and took off.

Thea cast a scathing look at both Seishin and Pallas. "Battle of honor, huh?"

Pallas wore a sheepish grin while Seishin merely shrugged. Still staring them down, Thea walked past the duo and strode over next to the hunter. From what she could see of his aura, it was amazing that he could still stand.

"I trust you'd like to be healed?" She asked with more than just a touch of sarcasm.

Cyclone winced, his lips curved slightly to one side. "Yeah, that'd be nice."

As Thea began to pour white light into the hunter's wounded body, Pallas interrupted them. "Wait, where's your boyfriend?"

Thea stared at him with daggers in her eyes. "He's not my"—she paused and swept her eyes around the cavern—"wait where did he go?"

"And where's Donnie?" Seishin added.

*A long tube stuck out of that shield, the angry red glowing end
pointed directly at him.*

Elladan still felt foolish about what happened in the shaft. He never expected his confusion spell to backfire so dramatically. It could've gotten them all killed. What hurt the most, however, was the look of disappointment on Thea's face.

In truth Elladan was feeling pressured. It had taken them nearly an entire week to find the first set of scrolls. Another three days passed tracking down this hidden island. For all they knew, the demons could be marching forth this very moment from their tower in Thac.

With little doubt that Cyclone would win this battle, Elladan swept his eyes around the cavern beyond. He quickly spied a corridor leading from the cavern off to one side.

As soon as Cyclone grappled his opponent, another officer separated from the crowd and ran toward the exit. Elladan elbowed

Donnie in the shoulder and nudged his head at the receding officer. "I wonder where he's going?"

"Maybe to get some popcorn?" Donnie responded in his typical glib fashion.

"Very funny," Elladan drawled. "Still, I think we should follow him."

"Right behind you…" Donnie's words were drowned out by the crowd's jeers as Cyclone flew up and smashed the officer into the ceiling.

Still disguised as a Parthian, Elladan ignored them and pushed his way through the crowd. Unlike the caves they had already traversed, this one was constructed of smooth stone. Glowing tiles lit the way along the entire corridor similar to the ones they had seen in the iron ships.

The well-lit corridor ended at a metal door about fifty feet from the cavern entrance. Just like in the Parthian ships, the officer swiped his necklace across a panel next to it. In response, the door slid back into the wall.

As the officer entered, Elladan whispered over his shoulder, "Quick, before it closes!"

The elven bard then took off at a run without looking behind him. He reached the open doorway and slid through before it could shut.

Elladan found himself in a second corridor similar to the first. Already halfway down the hall, the Parthian officer suddenly stopped, turned about and drew his sword.

His eyes narrowed as they met Elladan's, a deadly edge to his tone as he spoke. "Prepare to meet your maker."

Elladan ushered Donnie forward. "I think this is more your area of…"

The elven bard abruptly choked on his words. The door behind him had slid closed once again and Donnie was nowhere to be seen. Panic set in as Elladan realized he was all alone with the Parthian officer.

The officer's eyes burned with fire as he purposely advanced on the bard. Elladan had to do something quick or this would be the end of the road for him. He briefly thought of casting confusion, but that hadn't gone so well the last time.

With the officer nearly on top of him, the bard tried a desperate ploy. Kneeling down, he swiftly traced a pattern on the ground.

"Ah, prepared to meet your maker then?" the Parthian decried in triumph.

"Not exactly," Elladan murmured.

As the officer stopped and raised his sword for a killing blow, the bard slammed his hand into the ground and released the mana with two words. *"Tonantis Fluctus."*

A sound like thunder erupted from the symbol sending out ripples in the ground ahead. The undulating earth swept beneath the officer knocking his feet out from under him.

Having bought himself some time, Elladan screamed at the closed door, "I could use a little help in here!"

Slowly rising, the officer's voice was filled with malicious glee. "Your friends can't save you now."

With no other recourse, Elladan repeated the *Thundering Wave* spell. Knocking the Parthian prone once again, he pleaded toward the door, "Donnie, where are you!"

The officer rose more slowly this time, rubbing his backside where he had fallen. His face now reddened with anger, he glared at Elladan. "Just for that, I'm going to make this slow and painful."

Elladan tried to trace the spell one more time, but had to pull his hand away as the Parthian stabbed at the ground with his blade. The man locked eyes with him and waved a finger back and forth. "Ah, ah. That will be enough of that."

Elladan backed away from the man until his back hit the wall right next to the door. Turning his head, Elladan yelled one last plea. "Donnie, you're cutting it way too close!"

A wicked smile crossed the Parthian's lips as he drew his blade back for the killing blow. Just as he was about to strike, the door slid open. A lithe figure came tumbling through knocking the officer down once again.

Donnie rolled to his feet, blade in hand, and called back over his shoulder to Elladan. "Are you okay?"

Elladan huffed at his fellow elf. "Well it's about damn time you showed up!"

Donnie shrugged as the officer rose again. "Give a fellow a break. Do you know how hard it is to pick these stupid locks?"

Elladan fixed his friend with a disparaging look. "Don't you have one of those pendants?"

A sheepish grin spread across Donnie's face. "Well, yeah."

Their banter stopped as the Parthian officer engaged with Donnie in a test of swordsmanship. It was a test he proved lacking in compared to the elf and quickly fell prey to Donnie's blade.

With the officer dealt with, Elladan let out a sigh of relief, then clasped Donnie on the shoulder. "Thanks—even if you were a bit late."

Before Donnie could say a word, the others rushed through the door led by Thea. Her eyes flickered over the body of the Parthian officer before smacking Elladan on the arm. "Why'd you run off like that?"

This time Elladan wore a sheepish grin. "I thought Donnie was with me."

Donnie drew up beside Elladan and hung his head. "It's actually my fault. I didn't realize he was gone until it was almost too late."

Thea's eyes smoldered with anger as they swept between the pair. Both elves fixed her with chagrined smiles until she finally relented. "Oh, very well. As long as you're both safe." She paused and wagged a finger at them. "But from now on we stick together."

"Deal." Both elves nodded fervently.

Thea was worried. The further they went down into the island, the more dangerous it became. Instead of proceeding with caution, however, her companions acted more and more reckless. She supposed she could understand to an extent. She too felt the pressure to find the rest of the scrolls, yet she couldn't abide any of their company dying in order to do so.

Thea lost nearly everyone back on Thorn Isle. Though her memory of it still seemed hazy, they'd run afoul of something far worse than pirates and paid the ultimate price. Had it not been for her brother and Ruka they'd all still be dead.

Determined not to allow a repeat performance of that tragedy, Thea felt hyperaware as they proceeded down to the end of the corridor. There they found another door with one of those panels next to it. Donnie swept his pendant over the panel and the door *swished* open.

"Now there's something you don't see every day," the slight elf noted glibly.

Beyond the entryway stood a wide circular shaft. Like the corridors they had just traversed, the walls were made of smooth stone with glowing tiles at regular intervals. Embedded in the ceiling just above sat a circular opening that resembled the iris of an eye.

The shaft disappeared into the depths below, the bottom not visible from the entryway. There were no ladders or indentations in the walls indicating a way down. Still, Thea noted something peculiar about the shaft. The very air within it seemed laced with a strange power.

Elladan peered down the shaft, his expression one of awe. "It reminds me of the shaft in the Golem Master's monolith, but that one had a disc to ride on."

Donnie gently tapped his chin. "I have a theory…"

The elf stuck his foot out into the shaft and poked the air ahead with his toe. After a few attempts, his face abruptly fell. "That's weird. I would have bet a gold coin there'd be an invisible floor here."

Elladan jabbed him in the side. "Too bad. I would have taken that bet."

Donnie half-smiled at his friend when his face suddenly lit up as if an idea had struck him. "What if…"

Before anyone could stop him, Donnie stepped out into the shaft. Thea gasped, but much to her relief the thin elf just floated there wearing a triumphant smile.

Elladan gawked at his impetuous friend. "Do you have a death wish or something?"

Still floating in midair, Donnie flashed him a toothy grin. "Nah, I knew it all along."

Thea moved up next to Elladan and nudged him in the arm. As he turned his head towards her, she met his gaze with a knowing look. "I wouldn't worry about it too much. I probably could have patched him up"—she paused and turned her eyes towards Donnie— "the only thing I can't fix is stupid."

A hurt expression crossed Donnie's face. He placed his hands over his heart as if holding onto an arrow embedded there. "Ow, cut me to the quick!" he exclaimed.

All of a sudden, Donnie began to flail about. Both Seishin and Cyclone rushed to the edge, but stopped as the slim elf recovered.

Now slowly floating downward, a boyish grin crossed his face as he motioned for them all to join him. "Looks like our ride is here. people!"

Seishin, Cyclone, and Elladan joined him, but Pallas and Thea both poised on the edge peering down. Grasping her hand, a wry smile crossed her brother's face. "Shall we?"

Thea met his gaze for a moment, then shrugged. "Oh, what the hell."

They stepped out into the shaft together and floated down after the others.

Pallas had been leery at first about trusting another pirate, but Illyria had been true to her word. She helped them sneak onto Iron Island without giving away their presence. Unfortunately, their covert approach ended when the guard house exploded. It had been a wild ride since then, but by the grace of the gods they'd managed to further infiltrate the island.

Even so, Pallas prayed they were close to finding this "General" with the scrolls. This mad dash through the bowels of the island could only get them so far before their luck ran out.

Even now, Pallas braced himself as they floated down the mysterious shaft. Maybe fifty yards down they came across three doors around the shaft equidistant from each other. Pallas tensed as their descent abruptly halted in front of them.

All three doors had one of those panels embedded in the walls beside them. Donnie pointed to each in turn while reciting, "Enie, meanie, minie, mo." Not surprisingly, he ended up back at the first door.

Elladan gave his friend a sour look. "Were you expecting a different outcome?"

"Not particularly," Donnie responded with a sly smile.

Expecting the worst, Pallas drew his sword as the slight elf swiped his pendant across the panel. Thankfully the doorway opened to a small empty room.

With a shrug, Donnie floated over to the next door. Pallas positioned himself to one side as the elf swiped the accompanying panel.

The door swished open to reveal another tiny room. This one, however, contained a smaller version of those metal golems they'd run into.

Before anyone could react, a tentacle snaked out from the creature straight for Donnie. Though floating in midair, the agile elf somehow managed to flip himself out of the way. The metal tentacle continued past him and wrapped itself around Elladan's waist.

"Woah, there!" Elladan exclaimed. "At least buy me dinner first."

Pallas raised his weapon to strike, but Seishin beat him to it. In a lightning quick move, the Shin Tauri warrior drew his weapon and sliced the tentacle in two.

Another tentacle snaked out from the golem and tried to grab Seishin. Readied for it, Pallas stepped in and sliced the end off before it could reach its target.

In the meantime, Donnie had made it back to the door panel. Swiping his pendant over it, he shut the door before another tentacle snaked out into the shaft.

Elladan let out a sigh of relief. "Maybe we should rethink opening these things."

For once, Pallas didn't disagree with him. Unfortunately, they had little choice. Before opening the last door, however, Seishin, Pallas, and Cyclone all lined up with weapons readied.

As the last door swished open, Pallas barely stopped himself from leaping inside. This small room contained another small golem. This golem, however, remained stationary. Its eyes closed, it appeared to be connected by a thin cord to a socket in the wall.

Closing the door, they all gathered back in the center of the shaft. As soon as they did so, they began to descend once more.

From his life as a young thief on the streets to his days along the pirate coast, Donnie thought he'd seen it all. Nonetheless, these last few months with Elladan and friends proved him wrong over and over.

This latest adventure was no exception. Donnie marveled at the strange magic which allowed them to float down this long shaft. Unlike any spell or even Lloyd's flying cloak, it seemed to work without the gathering of mana or command words to invoke the magic.

Either way, Donnie found it all positively intriguing. His enthusiasm remained undiminished despite those two doors farther down that wouldn't open. The stubborn last door at the bottom of the shaft though finally succeeded in dampening his spirit.

"Why won't you open?" he complained to the panel as he swiped over it again and again with his golden pendant. Each time the panel beeped at him and displayed an orange colored light.

Completely exasperated, Donnie spun about and threw up his hands. "Well, we're not getting in that way."

Cyclone motioned for him to step aside. "Guess we'll just have to do this the hard way."

The hunter pressed up against the door and began to push. The muscles on his broad arms strained as he exerted them, but the stubborn door still would not budge.

"Perhaps if I help?" Seishin offered politely.

Cyclone shrugged. "It couldn't hurt."

The warrior and the hunter lined up side-by-side and pushed against the obstinate door. At first nothing happened, but then the sound of straining metal echoed through the surrounding shaft.

Slowly, but inexorably, the metal door began to give. It buckled just a bit at first, but then the one side bent inward. The duo continued to push until they'd twisted the door enough for each of them to fit through one at a time.

A strange hum now emanated through the opening they'd created. Donnie peered through the gap and observed a dim reddish glow.

Donnie whispered to the pair, "That's probably good enough. I'll go first."

"I'll be right behind you," Pallas stated firmly.

Donnie gave him a curt nod. The spiritblade's uncanny knack of slipping in and out of shadows might come in hand in the dim area beyond.

"One more thing," Thea hissed just as they were about to slip through.

Donnie stopped and peered at her quizzically over his shoulder.

Thea met his gaze evenly, but he could see the concern in her eyes. "Ruka and the others are on their way down. I told them where to find us."

Donnie gave her his best reassuring smile. "Don't worry, we'll be careful until then."

The priestess arched a doubtful eyebrow at him. Donnie supposed he couldn't blame her. No matter how hard he tried, trouble always seemed to find him.

Taking a deep breath, Donnie carefully slipped through the crack in the door. He found himself in a large dimly lit chamber. His eyes immediately focused on the source of the red glow.

Nearly a half dozen figures stood behind a large metal shield midway across the room. A long tube stuck out of that shield, the angry red glowing end pointed directly at him. The hum Donnie had heard changed to a high pitched whine as the light grew increasingly brighter.

"Donnie, duck!" He heard Pallas cry from somewhere nearby.

Not having to be told twice, Donnie launched himself toward the floor. Tucking his body into a ball, he rolled across the stone floor just in time.

A beam of blinding red light lanced from the tip of the tube across the room to where Donnie had just been standing. Coming up into a crouch, he shielded his eyes with his arm until the light disappeared.

Lowering his arm, Donnie peered at the wall behind them where the beam had struck. The wall there had been blackened and sizzled.

Donnie's jaw went slack. *That's worse than Glo's and Andrella's fire rays combined.*

Spinning his gaze toward the deadly tube, Donnie now spotted a single Parthian soldier peering above the metal shield. The soldier's eyes were focused on him as the strange cannon turned in his direction.

Donnie gulped when all of a sudden Pallas appeared behind the glaring Parthian. His curved blade came down upon the soldier and dispatched him in a single swipe.

Donnie's relief was short lived as the rest of the figures converged upon Pallas. Launching himself across the room, he rushed to the aid of his valiant companion.

Elladan grew more and more on edge the further they descended into the island. Not only had he messed up in the giant "dumbwaiter" shaft, but had nearly gotten himself killed chasing after a Parthian officer. On top of that, that strange metal golem had gotten rather "handsy" with him—or perhaps "tentaclely" was more accurate.

Either way, Elladan felt like he was standing on pins and needles as Donnie and Pallas disappeared through the crack in the door. The duo had only been gone for a few seconds when the humming sound changed to a high-pitched whine. A moment later a brilliant flash went off inside the room.

"Donnie!" Elladan cried, his heart leaping into his throat.

The others immediately spurred into action. Cyclone leapt through the crack followed by Seishin and then Thea. Elladan squeezed his way through right after them his elven eyes swiftly adjusting to the dim light inside.

Across the room, Pallas stood behind some sort of strange looking cannon. The Penwick officer was doing his best to fend off a quartet of Parthians that surrounded him.

Racing across the room Donnie had nearly reached the battle while Seishin, Cyclone, and Thea were already halfway there. Yet that wasn't the worst of their problems.

Marching forth from the side of the large chamber, Elladan spotted five of those metal golems they faced in the gunship and more recently in the "dumbwaiter" shaft. Though Cyclone had found a way to destroy the last, he doubted even the hunter could survive pile driving a quintet of them into the ground.

Fearing this a battle they could not win, Elladan did what he did best. He summoned his lute and played like mad. His fingers danced up and down the strings, sending waves of inspirational magic coursing through the air towards his comrades.

Moments later, Donnie swept into the mix, pulling one of the soldiers away from Pallas. Seishin and Thea soon followed turning it into a fair fight all around. That left Pallas with just one opponent—an older Parthian wearing gold epaulettes and a slew of medals on his chest.

Could that be the "General" we've been looking for, Elladan wondered?

Meanwhile, the golems were closing in fast. Cyclone must have noticed them as well. With all the Parthians engaged, he went straight for the strange looking cannon.

Elladan watched in amazement as the air around the hunter stirred. Tiny arcs of electricity swept across his body and his hair rose of its own accord. Lastly, a set of bronze wings sprouted from his back.

With his swift transformation complete, Cyclone grabbed the large cannon and lifted it into the air. Swinging it about to point at the advancing golems, he then leapt up behind it and fired the cannon.

An intense ray of red energy lanced across the room. Elladan momentarily blinked, but when he looked back, the top half of a golem had completely disappeared. What was left of the metal creature collapsed to the ground in a heap.

"Alright!" Elladan cheered, but his enthusiasm was short lived.

One of the golems had reached Pallas and inserted itself between him and the General. The General immediately disengaged and ran towards the back of the room.

That was when Elladan first spied the force field along the back wall. A chill went up his spine when he saw what stood behind it. A grey skinned bulbous-headed Zeta stared out from behind the barrier impassively watching the ensuing battle.

Though greatly concerned about the Zeta, Elladan could not

worry about it now. The rest of the golems must have deemed Cyclone as their greatest threat. Almost as one, they fired off a barrage of missiles at the hunter.

Cyclone barely had time to duck as the purple projectiles zeroed in on him. Multiple explosions went off around the cannon making it impossible to see if they'd done in their target.

32
BUT IT WAS ALIENS

Its bulbous, black-eyed head looked like a weird octopus sans the tentacles.

Donnie had little time to think as he engaged one of the soldiers. All caution had been thrown to the wind when the Parthians tried to fry them with their hot "ray" cannon. Pallas had saved them by taking out the gunner, but four on one might have been too much even for the expert spiritblade to handle. Thankfully, Seishin and Thea rushed in behind Donnie, turning it into a fair fight.

Feeling out his opponent with some short thrusts and a feint, Donnie found his swordsmanship to be sorely lacking. Opening up his guard slightly, he lured the soldier to attack. Sure enough he took the bait.

Catching the man's blade on his own, Donnie counter parried, then lunged and ran him straight through. The soldier doubled over in pain then fell to his knees, the lifeblood swiftly draining out of him.

With a short sigh at the waste of a life, Donnie withdrew his blade and swept his gaze across the battlefield. The entire fight had taken less than a minute, but a lot had happened in that short time.

Seishin and Thea seemed to have things well in hand, but the approaching line of metal golems made Donnie gulp. One alone proved to be almost indestructible and now there were five of them.

The nearest golem had already inserted itself between Pallas and the Parthian General, when Cyclone turned the ray cannon on the rest. With a blinding flash, the hunter blew the top clean off the next golem in line.

Overcome with joy, Donnie grinned and gave the hunter a swift salute. "Guess they're not so indestructible after all!"

Donnie's glee proved short lived, however, as the rest of the golems retaliated. Cyclone barely managed to duck behind the cannon's shield as a barrage of golem missiles homed in on him.

The projectiles exploded in a cacophony of bursts engulfing the hunter in a thick cloud of smoke. It expanded so quickly it overtook Donnie, burning his nose and making his eyes water.

Wiping the tears away, Donnie tried to peer through the smoke to see what happened to Cyclone when a loud wrenching sound drew away his attention. Back by the entrance, the door to the chamber suddenly burst inward along with a good portion of the wall.

Ruka came barreling through the opening with Cloud and Bal trailing behind her. Quickly assessing the situation, the dragon sent a lightning bolt careening across the chamber directly at the golem attacking Pallas.

The bolt slammed into the golem's side, cascading into smaller arcs all around its metallic torso. The creature's movements visibly slowed, in fact almost coming to a complete standstill.

Donnie smacked his forehead at the sudden realization. *Of course—these things have the same weakness as an iron golem!*

That discovery changed the entire complexion of the battle. Moving quickly in and out, Pallas began to hack away at the golem without any effective reprisals. Having finished his foe, Seishin joined in and the two warriors cleaved wide swaths in the golem's metal carcass.

Donnie was sorely tempted to join in, but knew his rapier would be ineffective against the creature's tough hide. So instead, he returned his attention to Cyclone.

The smoke had cleared enough to reveal that the hunter had survived the golems' onslaught. Thea was now at his side, her white aura already healing his wounds.

Seeing he wasn't needed here, Donnie decided to go after the Parthian General. He found him at the back of the room pounding frantically at the transparent barrier.

"Let me in, master. Please let me in," the Parthian officer pleaded.

A grey-skinned Zeta stood on the other side of the barrier, coldly regarded the hapless Parthian. The sight made Donnie cringe—its bulbous, black-eyed head looked like a weird octopus sans the tentacles.

Almost feeling sorry for the man, Donnie called out to him, "Surrender the scrolls and I'll let you live."

Donnie could see the fear in the General's eyes as he turned about. Holding his stare, Donnie added in a solemn tone, "You have my word."

The older Parthian stared at him incredulously. "You would truly just let me walk away?"

Donnie opened his mouth to assure him when all of a sudden, the man's face went blank. Without a word he drew his sword and lunged at Donnie.

The general had enough skill that Donnie had to take him seriously. With little choice, he fought in earnest and in the end ran him through.

When it was over, Donnie turned his attention to the Zeta. The creature hadn't moved an inch, but now regarded him with the thinnest of smiles. It was the first sign of emotion Donnie had seen from one of these creatures.

Anger welled up inside of Donnie at how the Zeta had used the General. Unable to contain himself, he railed at the callous creature. "Is this how you treat your comrades?"

In response he heard a cold chuckle in his mind. *Comrades? More like fleas to us.*

As Donnie held the creature's stare he felt a sudden pressure around his head. As the pain worsened, a brilliant flash suddenly erupted from his body and the pressure disappeared.

The flash had originated from the black ring on Donnie's finger—a gift he had received from the Thul Dunin, Karathralla. The slim elf made a mental note to thank the fallen angel, that is if he ever saw her again.

The Zeta regarded him with renewed interest. *You are not quite like the others. Your mind is not so easily swayed.*

Donnie shrugged, the corner of his mouth twisting upward. "What can I say? I'm just thick headed."

The Zeta seemed none too pleased with his answer. *Thick headed is it? We shall see.*

Once again, the creature's stare intensified. This time the pressure grew so great that it made Donnie wince. Just as he thought he would lose his mind, the black ring flashed once more rebuking the Zeta's attempt to control him.

Gingerly rubbing his temples, Donnie couldn't help taunting the Zeta. "Guess—you must—be losing—your touch."

The look of anger that crossed the creature's face made him immediately regret his words. The bulbous-headed grey creature drew closer, its eyes practically boring into his skull.

Cursing himself for his quick witted tongue, Donnie prepared for the worst when Cloud suddenly appeared overhead. The skyrider swooped down dropping Bal off before speeding away again to rejoin the ongoing battle.

A transparent crossbow in his one hand, Bal waded into the barrier. For a moment it appeared as if the transparent field would hold, but then Bal slipped right through.

Before the Zeta could react, Bal raised his crossbow and fired a bolt straight at its chest. The translucent bolt hit its mark embedding itself soundlessly into the creature. The Zeta doubled over, its expression a mixture of pain and disbelief.

Donnie whooped in exultation. "Fleas, huh? More like hornets that sting!"

Despite Donnie's promise to the contrary, Thea knew they were headed for trouble. With the racket they'd made wrenching that door open, she was surprised the entire island hadn't been waiting for them inside. If they'd only waited for Ruka like she wanted, they might have had the element of surprise on their side.

Still, there was no use belaboring the point. Cyclone had been hit with nearly a dozen projectiles. She doubted even the hunter could just shrug that off.

Expertly felling her opponent, Thea rushed through the smoke in search of the hunter. Murmuring a soft prayer along the way, the white aura flared up around her just as she reached his side.

Curled up into a ball, Cyclone sat unmoving behind the cannon's shield. Fearing the worst, Thea leaned down and placed a hand upon his shoulder. The hunter immediately shot up to his full height, his eyes burning a crimson red as he drew back a brawny fist to strike at Thea.

Standing her ground, Thea refused to flinch. "Whoa there big guy! I'm just trying to heal you."

Recognition abruptly dawned upon the hunter's face. Dropping his arm, his expression turned apologetic. "Sorry about that. Guess I'm just a bit jumpy."

"Can't imagine why," Thea snorted back at him. "Still, I think Ruka could use our help."

The dragon teen had crashed through the door and already stunned one of the golems. In doing so, however, she became the target of all the rest.

Though now one less in number, the remaining golems sent a barrage of missiles careening towards the hovering dragon. Amazingly she managed to dodge a few, but the rest slammed into her with concussive force.

Seeing Ruka in danger, Cyclone grabbed the cannon and wrenched it around toward the next golem in line. He then leapt up to the controls and began to mash on a big red button. Unfortunately, nothing happened.

Slamming down on the button a second time, the hunter berated the cannon. "Why won't you fire you stupid thing!"

Though Thea had never seen a "ray" cannon before, she'd seen her fair share of strange projects in her mother's lab. Looking beyond sight, she quickly discerned that the innards of the cannon ran on electrical current. There appeared to be a break in the flow between the button and the firing mechanism. That sparked an idea in her mind.

Placing both hands on Cyclone's upper arm, she gently pushed on him. "Let me have a look."

The hunter glared at her for a brief moment, then stepped aside and ushered her forward. "Be my guest."

Placing her hand over the button, Thea reached inside and bonded with her spark of spirit. As always, the energy responded, rushing forth into her hands. Pushing it outward, she sent a tiny bit of electricity coursing through the line where she saw the break. As she hoped, the spark jumped the gap.

A second later a red-hot beam shot from the tip of the cannon. In the blink of an eye, it lanced across the chamber obliterating the top of half of the golem in its sights.

Thea turned to peer at the hunter, feeling rather pleased with herself. "See, it just needed a little coaxing."

Not batting an eye, Cyclone merely nodded. "Good. You keep firing then and I'll go do some slashing."

Without another word, the hunter leapt into the air and flew across the chamber to join Ruka.

"Wait, but you're not fully…healed…" The last word trailed off Thea's tongue as she realized her concerns had fallen on deaf ears.

Things had not gone quite the way Pallas planned. After the noise they made ripping that door open, he'd expected some sort of welcoming committee. Even so, he thought he might retain the element of surprise by sticking to the shadows. Any such thoughts went out the window, however, when he witnessed the destructive force of that cannon.

Pallas had been left with little choice but to reveal himself and take out that gunner. Luckily the rest of the Parthians were not all that adept with the blade. The General turned out to be their best swordsman and he'd been a tentative opponent at best. His back to the cannon, Pallas kept the four of them at bay until reinforcements arrived. From there he could've easily bested the General if that golem hadn't gotten between them.

Pallas was being badly beaten until Ruka's timely entrance. Her electrical attack made all the difference, allowing him to get past the golem's defenses and savage the creature's tough metal hide. Once Seishin joined in, together they finished it off.

Pallas let out a heavy sigh after all that exertion. "Phew, I thought that thing would never go down."

Seishin responded with a curt nod. "Agreed, but I don't think we can breathe easy just yet."

Across the chamber Ruka had just shrugged off a barrage of missiles. The dragon retaliated by swooping in and clamping down on the nearest golem. The moment she did, her body lit up with electrical current sending arcs coursing through her held opponent.

Gods she's clever, Pallas thought with keen approval.

At nearly the same moment, his sister fired off another round from the cannon. The sizzling beam lanced across the room disintegrating the top of yet another golem.

Pallas' lips curled to one side. *Way to go, sis.* His enthusiasm, however, proved short lived.

Cyclone leapt from Thea's side to join Ruka. Unfortunately, that left one more golem unchecked. Now seeing Thea as the biggest threat, the metal creature fired off a round of missiles directly for her.

Acting out of pure instinct, Pallas reached inward to the very core of his being. Swiftly connecting with his spark of spirit, he pulled the energy forth and swirled it around himself, opening a portal to the astral plane.

A split second later, Pallas stood in front of his sister. He had no time to brace himself as the pair of missiles slammed into his torso.

Thud! Thud! Each projectile connected with enough concussive force to rattle his teeth.

Reeling backwards, Pallas fell to the ground, his chest smarting from where the missiles had hit. A moment later his sister was at his side, her glowing aura already bathing him in its healing light.

Thea fixed him with a scathing stare. "You do know I can take care of myself?"

Feeling a bit like their younger brother, Pallas stared back at her with a stupid grin. "Old habits die hard, sis."

Across the chamber, Ruka managed to stun the golem that shot Pallas. Between her, Cyclone, Seishin, and Cloud the two last golems fell in record time.

Donnie felt a mixture of relief and elation after Bal shot the Zeta in the chest. Considering all the pain it had caused others he felt it more than well deserved. That elation died on his lips when the Zeta pressed a button on its belt.

Two doors swished open in the wall behind the grey skinned alien allowing another pair of metal golems to emerge. The golems immediately placed themselves between Bal and his target, allowing the Zeta to stagger away and disappear through another door behind it.

"Oh come on now, that's not fair!" Donnie lamented. He quickly got over it though when it dawned on him Bal was alone with the golems.

Pressing his face up against the field, Donnie yelled to Bal, "Can you drop the barrier?"

Bal cast a quick look in his direction. "Maybe, but not with these two golems on my tail."

The astral knight's brow momentarily furrowed before he faded from sight. That didn't stop the golems from searching for him though. They lumbered around behind the barrier swinging their arms about in hopes of finding their invisible quarry.

Uncertain what to do, Donnie turned to the rest of the party for help. He was just in time to see Thea obliterate the top half of a golem with a single shot from the cannon.

That gave Donnie an idea. Rushing across the room, he reached the cannon just as the last two golems fell. Pointing back the way he came, he cried out for everyone to hear, "Give me a hand turning this thing around! Bal needs our help."

Cyclone, Seishin, and Ruka all pitched in pointing the cannon towards the barrier. Donnie took the controls from Thea as she used her aura to heal those who'd been hurt.

From what he could see, most of them looked pretty banged up from their fight with the golems on this side of the barrier. He didn't want to think what would happen to Bal if those other two caught him.

Once everyone lined up, Donnie fired the cannon. The blast lanced across the room and struck the barrier dead on. Unexpectedly, the beam just bounced off of it. They all had to duck as it came flying back their way.

Still covering his head with his hands, Elladan glowered at Donnie. "Are you trying to get us killed?"

Equally agitated, Donnie threw up his hands and shrugged. "How was I supposed to know it would just bounce off?"

"Aim for the ceiling above it," Thea interrupted before either of them could say another word.

"Say what?" Elladan peered at her skeptically.

"I can see the power flowing to the barrier through the ceiling," the priestess explained.

Seeing the certainty in her eyes, Donnie motioned to those nearest the cannon. "You heard the lady, help me aim this thing at the ceiling!"

"You might want to hurry." Cloud's voice sounded strained as he hovered nearby on his board.

Behind the barrier, the golems now stood at opposite ends of the chamber. Donnie watched with growing concern as they both headed towards each other flailing their multiple arms as they went. Unless Bal could somehow fly, they were sure to catch him.

Swiftly adjusting the cannon's aim, everyone lined up back in place. Once they were out of the way, Donnie got ready to fire.

"Here goes nothing," Donnie murmured as he pressed the button.

The red-hot beam shot from the cannon and struck the ceiling just above the barrier. A good chunk of the ceiling evaporated on impact. The barrier itself suddenly began to flicker and a moment or so later completely disappeared.

Cheers went up amongst the group as they rushed forward. Turning to face these new foes, the golems fired on the approaching line.

Seishin took two direct hits and faltered in his tracks. Pallas faded into the shadows, the two missiles passing through the space where he had just been.

All of a sudden, lightning flashed across the room. Ruka had angled herself off to one side and caught both golems with the same bolt. Arcs of electricity danced across their metal frames as both golems virtually froze in place.

Bal abruptly appeared behind one of the golems and sliced at it with a psychic sword. Pallas leapt from the shadows and joined him. At the same time, Cloud and Cyclone plowed into the other golem.

Having recovered, Seishin joined them. Shifting to her human form, Ruka joined in as well. Less than a minute later both golems were piles of scrap.

Bal wore a grateful expression as he swept his eyes around the group. "Thanks everyone."

"So know what?" Donnie asked, peering warily at the door where the Zeta disappeared.

"Now I say we filet some little grey men," Elladan answered glibly.

Bal sincerely hoped they had reached the heart of the island. Based on the powerful defenses they'd found down here, one would certainly think so. It reminded him of the fortifications in place at the palace in Palt. The heaviest of those centered about the throne room and the Queen's chambers.

That being the case, the scrolls had to be somewhere down here as well. The General who supposedly had them was dead, but at least one Zeta remained behind the next door. From their experience with the gunship, the Zetas were probably in charge here anyway.

The panel next to this door turned out to be black in color. Bal had obtained a black colored pendant from the officer they'd searched up in the guardhouse. Fairly certain he could open the door, they took a few minutes to discuss what tact to take. Once it had been decided, everyone lined up appropriately.

"Get ready," Bal announced over his shoulder. He counted to three in his head and then swiped the pendant across the panel. As anticipated, the door *swished* open.

Behind the door they found a well-lit room strikingly similar to the command room in the gunship. A large viewport took up the entire back wall. At the moment it showed nothing but a cloudy image. Below it sat another long console once again filled with numerous lights and buttons. In place of command chairs, one long table stretched parallel to the viewport with five Zetas gathered around it.

All the aliens wore body suits except for one garbed in an orange. That Zeta had the symbol of a skewed rectangle on its chest decorated with seven stars. One of the Zetas appeared to be wounded. It must've been the one Bal had shot.

According to plan, those who could not be easily mind controlled rushed in first. Cloud zipped into the room, his link with Ragnarök protecting his mind. The gnome strafed overhead, but all the Zeta's ducked out of the way.

Donnie rushed the table with Bal, a quip spouting from his lips as he skewered the wounded Zeta. "I'll turn you into calamari!"

Bal pounced on another one, but it blocked his psychic sword with one of its own.

Cyclone, Seishin, and Pallas came in along with Thea and El-ladan. The priestess extended her holy aura to help protect them from the Zeta's powerful minds.

Cyclone faced off with the Zeta wearing the orange body suit. The surprisingly spry creature ducked under his axe and retaliated with multiple sharp blows to the hunter's chest.

The Zeta's responded with a flurry of mental attacks. Bal sensed them all unfold in rapid succession.

The Zeta locked in combat with Bal tried to freeze him in place, but he easily ignored the mental suggestion. Another tried to take Cyclone's breath away, but the hunter shrugged it off between Thea's help and his own strong constitution. The last Zeta tried to take over Cloud's mind, but Ragnarök responded by hitting it in return with a sharp mental slap.

Taking advantage of Ragnarök's rebuke, Donnie launched

himself over the table and skewered the Zeta with another snappy quip. "I'll send you back to squid row!"

Meanwhile, Cloud strafed the Zeta fencing with Bal. Caught from either side, the Zeta quickly fell to their combined attacks.

At the same time, Cyclone continued to battle the head Zeta. The agile alien dodged one blow, but got caught with a quick back swing. Falling back, the Zeta resorted to a mental attack.

Bal heard clearly in his mind the Zeta commanding Cyclone to *die*. The hunter froze for a brief moment, then met the Zeta's stare and said, "You first."

The Zeta's huge black eyes widened even further as Cyclone lashed out with his long pole axe. Bal could feel utter fear radiating from the creature as the hunter clove it clean in two.

The last Zeta ran for the console. Reaching it, it slammed its grey hand down on a big red button. In response, the lights in the room flickered off, but then came back dimmed. A split second too late, Pallas appeared out of the shadows and cut the Zeta down.

Everything went eerily quiet. Cloud was the first to break the silence. "Well at least there isn't another countdown."

Though Bal agreed, he still wondered what that red button actually did. Making his way over to the console, he examined the area around the button.

Bal spotted a small plaque with strange writing a short distance below the button. Elladan came up beside him and ran his fingers over the plaque. "This looks like Ignan, the language from the plane of fire."

"Go figure," Donnie commented with a wry smile. "I'm sure the Zetas didn't build this place and we all know how much the Parthian's love fire."

"So what does it say exactly," Bal prodded the two elves.

"Oh." Elladan refocused on the plaque. "It says, *Press here to cut main power.*"

"I think we already knew that," Cloud chided.

Elladan fixed the skyrider with a half-smile. "There's more."

Bending forward he continued to read. "*Warning, the center of the isle will sink.*"

"Now that's concerning," Cloud admitted.

"I think we need to find those scrolls as quickly as possible," Pallas interjected. "I imagine the Zetas would have kept them close by."

"Probably in here." Donnie stood in front of an open door that Bal hadn't noticed before. Peering beyond the elf, he spied a number of boxes embedded in the wall—just like the vault back in Kaniron.

"I'd swear that door wasn't there before," Elladan mirrored Bal's thoughts.

A sly smile crossed Donnie's lips. "It was hidden, but I noticed a faint scrape across the floor in front of it."

Bal strode over next to Donnie. "Can you check those boxes?"

"Will do," Donnie said with a nod.

Bal turned back to Elladan. "In the meantime, can you decipher any more of those controls?"

The bard shrugged. "I can try." He peered questioningly at Thea. "You seem to have a knack with these electrical devices. Want to give me a hand?"

"Sure, why not," she said with a twinkle in her eye.

Bal watched on as Donnie examined the vault. The elf's keen eye spotted and disarmed a nasty trip wire that would have set off a conflagration. The entire inside of the vault would have been destroyed along with everything in it.

Meanwhile, Elladan and Thea managed to bring up an image of the outside on the viewport. The image confirmed they were under the sea and sinking.

"Eureka!" Donnie cried from inside the vault. The elf stood over an open box holding a pair of gilded scroll cases in his hands.

Bal went to stand over him and saw five similar cases within the box. Seishin confirmed the markings on the cases were Isandorian and they carried the glyph of the House of Tauriyama.

Cheers erupted amongst the group, but they were quickly overshadowed by harsh squeaking sounds. Bal stuck his head out of the vault and saw a grey bulbous head staring back at him from the viewport.

"Turn that thing off!" he shouted across the room at Elladan.

Thea reached past the elf and touched a couple of dials on the console. A moment later the image disappeared.

"Well that wasn't disturbing at all," Cloud noted wryly.

"Yeah, I was sort of hoping we'd seen the last of those Zetas," Bal agreed.

Thea found herself extremely grateful that everyone survived the battle with the Zetas. With a silent prayer of thanks to Arenor, she pumped healing energy into her aura to abrogate any outstanding wounds.

The subsequent discovery of the rest of the scrolls almost made this entire crazy journey worth it. Even so, she couldn't help worrying they weren't quite out of the woods just yet. The fact that more Zetas still existed somewhere out there made her feel rather uneasy. Furthermore, they were far underwater and still sinking.

Once all the scrolls had been safely tucked away, Thea broached the subject with the others. "So just how do we get out of here?"

"If we can get outside, I can swim us to the surface," Ruka answered.

Thea exchanged a knowing glance with her brother. "It did say just the center portion of the isle would sink…"

"…so depending on how large that is, we might be able to portal out of here," Pallas finished her thought.

Elladan pressed his lips together and nodded. "That might just work. I could open a portal. If water starts pouring in, we know we've got our way out."

The bard pulled out the stored helmets to go along with the body suits from his portal bag. In turn he put the rest of the scrolls in the bag with the others for safekeeping.

As everyone pulled on their helmets, Donnie fixed Elladan with a dubious stare. "The last time we stored something important in your bag, you nearly lost it."

Elladan glared at his fellow elf. "That's not fair. Anya's thief stole it from my belt."

A sly grin crossed Donnie's lips as he threw up his hands in a warding gesture. "I'm just saying."

Elladan raised a finger at his friend, but seemed to think better of it. Stopping himself he spun about and held the portal bag out to Cyclone. "Here, you take this."

The hunter's brow furrowed for a moment, but then he shrugged. "Alright, if you insist."

Elladan turned back to Donnie with a triumphant nod. "There! I'd like to see anyone stupid enough to try and take it from him."

Donnie flashed his friend a toothy smile. "Can't argue with that."

With that settled, everyone prepared for travel underwater. Though space in the control center was limited, Ruka transformed back into a dragon.

Donnie climbed atop the dragon's back followed by Cyclone. Seishin grabbed onto Pallas who begrudgingly held onto Elladan. Bal wrapped his arms around Thea's waist and she in turn grabbed tightly onto Cloud. Ruka then grasped both Seishin and Bal in her front claws.

Everyone collectively held their breath as Elladan opened up a huge portal. Thea let out a heavy sigh as water gushed in through the great shimmering oval.

"Hang on tight!" Ruka cried before launching herself forth.

One minute they were in the control center and the next somewhere deep underwater. It was so dark down here, Thea couldn't tell which way was up.

Luckily, Ruka had the uncanny senses of a dragon. She unerringly took off swimming at a speed faster than the fastest horse. Though Thea could breathe in her body suit, she held her breath, nonetheless. After what seemed like an eternity, the water above them slowly became brighter.

A few minutes later they breached the surface. It must have been late in the day as the sun sat low on the horizon.

"Just how long were we down there?" Elladan drawled.

Pallas placed his hand over his eyes as he stared at the horizon. "Based on the position of the sun, I'd say almost the entire day."

Elladan eyed her brother disdainfully. "I know that. I was expecting a smart remark from Donnie."

Thea peered up at Ruka, but saw no sign of the elf on her back. For that matter, she couldn't see anyone there.

"Donnie? Where's Donnie?" Elladan's voice rose an octave.

"Better question. Where's Donnie and Cyclone?" Thea added sweeping her eyes around in a circle. All she could see in the nearby vicinity was empty water.

Ruka swore profusely in about three different languages before finally catching herself. "Alright, you all stay here. I'll go and look for them." Before anyone could stop her, the dragon dove into the water, her wake crashing over their heads.

With Ruka gone, Cloud drew out his board and he and Bal climbed up on it. Elladan surprised them all at that point by taking out his portal bag and pulling the flying carpet from it.

Thea narrowed an eye at the bard as he unfurled the rug and climbed up on it. "I thought you gave your bag to Cyclone?"

Elladan firmly shook his head. "No, that was my spare bag. I bought two of them after what happened back at the Greystone Vault."

Thea had a momentary flashback to the incident at the vault. She would have laughed if Cyclone and Donnie weren't missing. Elladan was nothing if unpredictable, yet perhaps in a good way.

With everyone now out of the water, the six of them sat there and waited in silence. Thea wondered what was taking Ruka so long.

What had happened to Donnie and Cyclone? Losing their friends was bad enough, but the latter carried the portal bag with all fourteen scrolls in it.

After everything we just went through, how could we possibly lose them now? Further, what would that mean for the fate of the world?

These dark questions continued to plague Thea as the setting sun sank below the western horizon.

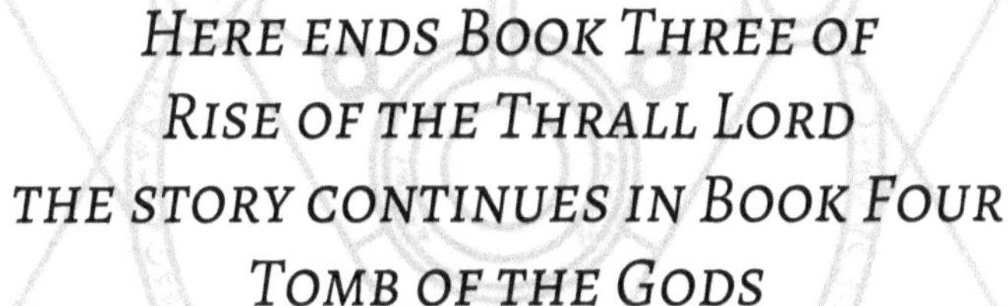

HERE ENDS BOOK THREE OF
RISE OF THE THRALL LORD
THE STORY CONTINUES IN BOOK FOUR
TOMB OF THE GODS

ABOUT THE AUTHOR

F.P. Spirit writes high fantasy fiction inspired by the likes of Tolkien, Eddings, Brooks, and Piers Anthony. An avid science fiction fan, he became hooked on fantasy the moment he cracked open the Lord of the Rings in high school. When he is not writing, F.P. is either spending time with his wife and sons, gaming, doing yoga, Tai Chi, or walking their dog.

A long-time lover of fantasy and the surreal, he hopes you enjoy his fun contributions to the world of fantasy and magic.

You can learn more about F.P. Spirit by visiting his website at:
Fpspirit.com